If You Say Yes

by H.M. Shander

Jennifer
who do you choose?
#teamNate
#teamLucas
♡HMShander
Oct-2020

If You Say Yes
Published by H.M. Shander at CreateSpace

Cover Design: Ashley Michel of AM Creations
Editing by: PWA & IDIM Editorial
Shander, H.M., 1975—If You Say Yes
ISBN: 978-0-9938834-8-4
First Edition

Thank you for believing in me,

and for wanting there to be more.

HMS

Table of Contents

♥Chapter One ... 1
♥Chapter Two ... 11
♥Chapter Three ... 19
♥Chapter Four ... 28
♥Chapter Five ... 47
♥Chapter Six ... 53
♥Chapter Seven ... 58
♥Chapter Eight ... 74
♥Chapter Nine ... 81
♥Chapter Ten ... 86
♥Chapter Eleven ... 93
♥Chapter Twelve ... 102
♥Chapter Thirteen ... 111
♥Chapter Fourteen ... 125
♥Chapter Fifteen ... 135
♥Chapter Sixteen ... 139
♥Chapter Seventeen ... 145
♥Chapter Eighteen ... 152
♥Chapter Nineteen ... 160
♥Chapter Twenty ... 165
♥Chapter Twenty-One ... 175
♥Chapter Twenty-Two ... 184
♥Chapter Twenty-Three ... 193
♥Chapter Twenty-Four ... 206
♥Chapter Twenty-Five ... 218
♥Chapter Twenty-Six ... 232
♥Chapter Twenty-Seven ... 242
♥Chapter Twenty-Eight ... 254
♥Chapter Twenty-Nine ... 262
♥Chapter Thirty ... 270
♥Chapter Thirty-One ... 278
♥Chapter Thirty-Two ... 287
♥Chapter Thirty-Three ... 301
♥Epilogue ... 310
Dear Reader ... 320
Other Books by H.M. Shander ... 321
Acknowledgements ... 322
About the Author ... 323

Chapter One

Aurora linked her fingers behind Nate's damp neck and pulled him closer. A quick lick of her lips was all she got before his lips brushed across hers, tender and purposeful. She'd waited—and practised—for this moment for days. For weeks. For what felt like a lifetime. His kiss was everything she desired, and everything she needed, all in one sweet package. She'd got her man, he'd got his girl, and all was perfect with the world again.

He tucked a wisp of hair behind her ear, his focus only on her. She inhaled every scented molecule of race fuel and rubber coming from him. No place on Earth could be as satisfying. Except maybe at home, in her bed, naked in his arms. A perfect ending to the day.

"So, tell me, how do I get you home?" he asked. "Last time I tried this, it didn't work out so well."

"Many stops." She sighed, searching the pit of racers and crew for his little brother, Lucas. He'd know exactly what to do.

Cars were everywhere the eye could see. The grandstand she'd stood in only minutes ago, was desolate, the majority of the spectators already gone. But some, the die-hard fans, mingled in the pit after the race, surrounded by officials, racers, and crew members.

Twenty minutes ago, she'd stopped him from announcing his retirement, something that would harm him in the end. She'd saved him. Standing so close to him, it was hard to believe she'd succeeded in her goal of getting to the track. However, the best part of the day still lay ahead. If only she could find Lucas and they could all get the hell out of there.

"Lucas has the outline for you somewhere. He printed it out before picking me up."

"There's an outline?" His laugh was infectious. "What were you two up to that warrants an outline?"

"I'll tell you all about it someday. First, I want to get you home and peel this race suit off you."

"Oh, it'll come off."

"Can I watch?"

"Anytime you want." He bent down and kissed her again, the urgency and carnal desire pushing against her.

It warmed her core, igniting embers of lust deep within. They parted, and she took a deep breath, trying to calm her racing heart.

Where is Lucas?

In the sea of people, Lucas was invisible, lost in amongst the hundreds of people.

Racing season was officially over until the spring, and celebrations were in full swing. Music blasted from a portable radio, sitting high on a stack of race tires. Laughter and cheers floated in from all around, and racers paraded around their trophies from the evening's wins. Although Nate finished first in the final race, Aurora was sure he hadn't placed top three for the season. He had a rough season in the second half which had been completely her fault, even if Lucas tried to convince her otherwise.

Nate smirked, his dimple deep. "I still can't believe you're really here." His eyes showed his disbelief as they took her in, making her feel naked but desired.

She wanted to assure him that if he blinked she would not

vanish, but…in a minute. It had been too long since those eyes were hers. "Well it wasn't without its challenges, that's for sure."

The warmth she'd missed from him she made up for as her arm slipped into the unzipped portion of his race suit and wrapped around his waist. She hadn't let go of him since he'd parked his race car in his designated spot. Lucas—her best friend—had disappeared quickly, taking the car with him. How sweet of him to load the race car onto the trailer while she and Nate held and kissed each other. Too much time had passed since they'd touched. Too long. The summer of pushing herself to hell and back had paid off. She'd succeeded in stopping his retirement announcement. Perhaps now, she'd finally get her happily ever after.

She rested her head against his sweaty cotton shirt, not caring in the least if it had a bit of a needs-shower-badly smell. She'd almost given up on them, and would take whatever she could get, scents and all. It cemented to her this was no fantasy. This was real. Even in her brightest visions, the smells were vacant, the infectious laughter missing, and the warmth now flooding across her cheeks completely absent. It was only him. At least she wasn't dreaming. He really stood beside her, his fingers linked in hers, his thumb rubbing the tips of her knuckles.

His free hand rubbed her back, and she melted into him as the gentle pressure along her spine calmed the rush within. His fingers traced back up and danced across the nape of her neck as though they'd done it a million times before. A large inhale of air filled her lungs, and she opened her eyes.

Nate stood there, a huge smile across his face, his eyes reflecting the overhead lights. "You like that?"

"I do," she said, her voice a whisper. Touch had become her new drug, and she craved it. Getting it from Nate was like getting the purest form of the best drug—euphoric as a little went a long way.

"Lucas," Nate said, his chest rattling as he spoke. His body shook as he waved.

"There you guys are." Lucas had his game face on—no smile,

all seriousness. His eyes weathered as he glanced from her up to his big brother. "She's all loaded up." He produced his keys and dangled them in front of Nate. "Drive my car home, she's used to that right now. There's a bag packed in the trunk for you, with a few overnight things."

It was hard to miss Nate's blush. He grabbed the car keys and pocketed them.

Lucas laughed. "Aw, c'mon, man. Anyone with half a brain would know you wouldn't be going home tonight."

Nate squeezed her, and she couldn't wait to get him back to her apartment, rip his clothes off and make up for lost time. The thought of waking up in his arms thrilled her.

"Whenever you're ready," Lucas said, "I'll follow behind with the truck and trailer."

Nate brushed the hair off her face. "When would you like to go?"

Now, ideally. But... It was still a big step. Excited to be at home with Nate, there was still the problem of *getting* home. He'd drove her three times previously, each with the aid of a mysterious pill that blocked her mind from remembering anything. Her last trip home from the track, with Kaitlyn, she'd be under the influence of a bad combo of prescription drugs. Tonight, she'd be going home un-drugged. "Um... whenever, I guess. I just need to mentally prep myself."

Nate turned to Lucas. "How long did it take you to come down?"

He rubbed his ear. "Seventy? Seventy-five minutes?" Lucas shifted his focus to her and spoke in her direction. "We stopped twice. Each time was about twenty minutes or so?"

"Something like that."

Nate's gaze darted between the two. "Well, it's almost eleven. At that rate, we won't be home until twelve thirty."

She swallowed, loud enough for both brothers to hear.

Lucas rubbed her shoulder. "You'll do fine."

She didn't miss the questioning exchange between the boys. Nate's brow furrowed in curiosity.

Lucas wore pride like a badge. "I'll be right behind you."

"My goal was getting here. I didn't think about how to get back home."

Lucas snickered briefly and stepped closer. "I promise, you'll be fine. Nate can pull over if it gets to be too much. But honestly, you'll do great."

He was her security blanket and knew how to interpret her signals. What if Nate didn't? What if he mistook one, and instead of stopping, he kept going? It was important he understood the outline, so there would be no screw-ups, and no opportunities for the darkness to descend upon her. Sourness pooled in her stomach and involuntary shudders rippled throughout her body.

"Are you really that nervous? Nate can handle this, and *you* can do this. You've trained for this."

"I don't know… You know…" Her gaze flickered from Lucas to Nate and back again.

"She's right, Bro. I think my first trip, I'd better sit in the backseat and observe. I can see how she's doing, and what you do. I don't want to undo everything you've accomplished by doing something foolish." His calloused squeeze held her hand tight. "Is that okay? I think you'd be more comfortable with him too."

She nodded. "Thank you."

"Go see if Mom can take the truck and trailer home. Shouldn't be too much of a problem since Bill brought her down."

"They came together?" Lucas' voice held shock.

"Yeah." Nate craned his head as if trying to see above the crowds. "They were going to spend the night in the trailer and close it down for the season tomorrow."

Aurora smiled and leaned into Nate. *Whoever thought spring was for lovers never hung around the race track at the end of the season. There is love everywhere tonight.*

Lucas walked away, head bobbing as he searched left and right. The fans thinned out as the grandstand lights flickered off throwing it into a muted darkness. The only remaining people in the pit were the drivers and crews and the staff members cleaning up after what was arguably the most exciting race all season, complete with the electric winner's speech, thanks in part to Aurora's arrival.

"I still can't believe you're really here."

"I'm really here." She looped her hands around his neck and pulled him closer. Her bottled-up-for-weeks wanton desire threatened to explode from her. Her pulse rose as fast as a screaming engine and her breathing shuddered. Tingly sensations radiated out from her core to the tips of her fingers and she felt as light as a feather.

His tongue pushed his way past her lips, and she groaned as the heat flared. She reciprocated as her hands tangled up in his soft, brown hair. His hand shifted lower, resting firmly on her lower back. He pulled her close and her breasts squished into his chest.

Gasping for air, she broke off the kiss.

"It's been a while."

She couldn't stop staring at him. He was real, and standing in front of her. "Too long."

"Tonight's going to be magical."

"A fireworks show I suspect. I've missed you." She tenderly brushed her lips against the crook of his neck, a low throaty growl rumbling beneath.

"There he is," Nate said, his voice gaining strength.

Lucas approached. "Kay, mom's good with hauling the beast home sometime tomorrow. I'll drive the first leg. You take mental notes and follow the outline." To Aurora he said, "You'll do what you've been doing all along; relaxing as best you can and taking it moment by moment."

"I can do this," she whispered.

"I know you can." He nodded to the back of the pit. "Shall we go? See if we can outrun the storm?"

"There's a storm?" The breeze drifted around her and suddenly, she was frozen.

"It's far away. It won't stand a chance. Just like the storm a few weeks ago, which you managed beautifully."

"I also wasn't trapped in a car."

"No, you were stuck with me and that damn combat game." Lucas laughed.

Nate stayed silent, wrapping his arm across her shoulders.

Lucas led the way to the rear parking lot where the drivers parked their street legal vehicles. "How serious are Mom and Bill?"

"They're having fun. For now."

"Does it bother you?" Aurora asked. The hurt in Lucas' voice resounded with her. She couldn't imagine her daddy dating either.

"Meh."

He tried acting tough pretending it didn't bother him, but she saw the slight change in his demeanour. His narrow shoulders rolled inward just enough and his face tightened.

"I understand." She patted him on the shoulder. "But think of the bright side. Tonight, you'll get the whole house to yourself."

"Goody."

A glimmer of sadness darkened the otherwise joyful mood she bathed in. Lucas wouldn't be staying in her apartment tonight, Nate would be. Lucas would be moving back home essentially, but at least his first night home he wouldn't have to deal with his mom and the endless battles they engaged in.

She wished she had thought through to the end of the night. Her whole summer goal had been to get to the track and see Nate. Nothing beyond that existed. Never once did she think what would happen after, or more specifically, what would happen to Lucas' accommodations.

The assumption was for things to continue the path they were on, although as she thought about it now, the sleeping situation would be super awkward. Her best friend and her boyfriend—could she call him that now?—were brothers. How weird would it be to have Nate in her bed, and Lucas down the hall? Probably super uncomfortable for everyone. Especially the first night, or the first weekend.

She sighed, and both the men froze in their tracks. "Sorry," she said, glancing between them, "mentally planning for the ride home."

"You'll be fine." Lucas gave her a gentle bump. They stopped behind Lucas' car. "Pop the trunk," he said to Nate.

The lid of the trunk lifted with the press of a button, and Lucas added in the poster she made, laying it overtop Nate's overnight bag.

"See you later, Lucas," a soft, girlish voice called out from behind them.

"Who's that?" Aurora asked, eyeing the female who sauntered by and jumped into a big truck.

"Amaya. She races the baby grands. We're meeting for coffee after I drop you off."

"At twelve thirty?" Her stomach hardened.

"Why not?"

"Kind of late, isn't it?"

"Nah."

Nate covered up a grin and faced away from Lucas. "Shall we go?"

Nervousness built up, and a chill rattled through her bones. As she paced around the car, Lucas explained the basics to Nate, what the hand signals meant, and where the first stop *should* be. He went over the outline, step by step.

"I'm not gonna explain on the drive, as I'll need to concentrate on the road *and* her. She'll hum or tap against her lap, which is totally normal. It's her safety bubble, so don't do anything to pop it. Trouble starts when she stops."

"And then what?"

"It's a good thing I think fast on my feet." He checked out the sky. "Read the list. We gotta stay ahead of the storm."

She glanced over to Lucas and exhaled. No matter how hard she shook out her arms, the nervousness refused to leave. Pacing hadn't reduced the energy. Her whole body remembered what lay ahead, and it terrified her.

Lucas beckoned her over with the curl of his finger.

Five quick steps and she stood in front of him, focused on him, and drew from his strength as hers faded quickly.

"You can do this." He placed his hands on her shoulders and

tapped out a familiar count of three.

She inhaled a deep breath and nodded, but she didn't feel confident. Fear was too dominant.

"Trust me. I'll be right beside you." His hands ran down her arms and firmly gripped her hands, pulling them together.

Aurora looked past the brothers standing side by side and shivered. A quick peek to Nate who studied her face as intensely as Lucas. "But there's…"

"Breathe."

Shaking off another wave of nerves, she leaned in toward Lucas and whispered, "But we… never practised during a storm before."

Lucas wrenched his head, searching across the sky. A cloud in the distance lit up. "The storm's south of us. We'll be driving away from it. It shouldn't be a problem." His sigh betrayed his confidence.

Nate pulled her hands out of Lucas' and rubbed his dry thumb over her knuckles.

"This'll be a first for both of you." Lucas shrugged, but kept his focus on her. "But, Aurora, you can do this. I believe in you." Stepping back, he opened his passenger door. "Whenever you're good to go." Lucas glanced at Nate. "Get ready, Bro."

Nate walked over to the driver's side and leaned against the roof of the car.

Huffing and puffing, Aurora took another pace and stopped beside her seat.

Lucas gave her a reassuring shoulder squeeze. "You've got this. Promise." To Nate he said, "Roll down her window."

Nate twisted the key in the ignition enough to activate the onboard systems, but not enough to start it. The window rolled down smoothly.

She peered over at Nate, hoping for a confident smile. Instead his expression was a mixture of confusion, tinged with nervousness. She shook her head, uneasiness settling over her, and stole a peek at Lucas. Like an animal in a zoo, the weight of their stares burned into her. She'd have to fight extra hard tonight and prove herself to Nate. This was, essentially, their first un-drugged trip together, and she wished it wasn't fraught with uncomfortableness and trepidation.

Nodding to Lucas, she took another deep breath. The sweat built up in her pits. Focused only on Lucas, she lowered herself into the passenger seat. Deep breath in, large exhale out. Another nod. Reaching behind her, she grabbed the seatbelt and clicked herself in. Thankful to be sitting as the feeling washed out of her legs. She gave the thumbs up signal to Lucas.

"In you go," he said to Nate as he made his way around the vehicle. Once Nate had wedged himself into the confines of the backseat, Lucas slipped behind the wheel. "Ready?"

She gave another thumbs up.

"Let's go watch the airplanes."

The door closed. As the track disappeared behind them, Aurora instinctively called out Lucas' name.

♥Chapter Two♥

Nate

Geezus, she's really here.

He twisted uncomfortably in the tight confines in the joke of a backseat. Cameros weren't known for a lot of leg room and a cramp formed in the back of his thigh. *Oh well. If she can handle this, I can handle a little ache.*

He desperately wanted to touch her, especially when her hand sailed through the air. It would be uncomfortable for both if he produced his own hand, not to mention how unsafe it would be for him to be unbelted so she wouldn't have to reach so far. Another day. Another time.

Lucas was right. She did hum, but he couldn't figure out what song she attempted to sing. Her right hand tapped against her lap, and she kept her eyes firmly sealed. As her left hand hunted for purchase, Lucas reached it first, holding it tight. Immediately her pitch lowered and her hum changed to a more upbeat rhythm.

Must remember. She likes to have her hand held. She likes to hum.

The gravel road leading away from the track was arguably the worst road ever, but it was fun to fish-tail on and gain valuable handling skills. When he was alone. Lucas loved that too, but tonight he drove like a ninety-year-old lady. It still bounced them around, a cloud of dust kicking up behind them, glowing an eerie shade of orange. His focus darted between Lucas, who sported a grin and Aurora, who was shrinking into the passenger seat, but was breathing calmly.

Never in a million years did he truly believe she'd be a passenger in a car, without drugs. Had she completely given them up? He'd wondered as it was unlikely based on the past. Not long after they broke up, he saw her in the library and she was hella-angry, like she'd gone clean, but after spotting her and Matthew kissing in the staff room, he wondered if she were high again. Anyone in their right mind would need a tonne of drugs to spend anytime with that no-talent ass clown. What a douche.

The highway rolled smooth beneath them, a pleasant change from the gravel road. Aurora's breath hitched.

"Everything okay?" he whispered to Lucas.

"Just the change in vibration."

Sitting back, he glanced over to Aurora. He'd seen her nervous many times, but the way she looked now was different. A tight little ball of fist rested on her lap. Her chest rose and fell in short little spurts. Head back against the head rest, her eyes were closed shut. The glow from the dashboard gave her face an eerie ghostly glow.

Maybe he should've asked Lucas if she was prone to tossing her cookies. He hoped not as he wasn't good with puke.

Aurora mumbled, but he missed it.

"Say again." Lucas' voice was calm but firm.

Another item he'd need to remember. Be firm but gentle. He was so glad to be witnessing this in the flesh than trying to recall it off a sheet of paper. He was more of a hands-on type of guy.

"I'm okay." Her words were there but the confidence truly lacked in her voice.

No further reaction from her, or Lucas for that matter, so he tried to settle himself back. The car ride was uncomfortably quiet, but he was unsure if he should carry on a conversation with Lucas, or if the silence was what Aurora needed most. He held up the outline and scanned it.

No mention of it. *Damn.*

"She's doing really well. This is all normal for her." His voice was quiet.

"I'm glad you're here." He patted his brother's shoulder. "Thank you."

"We'll stop at VIC and stretch the legs and unwind. I think you're more tightly wound than she is."

"I doubt it." But he relaxed his shoulders and a dull ache surfaced. He *had* been hunched and tightly wound as Lucas put it.

He still couldn't believe it. Aurora was riding with him in a car; drug free. He was taking her home, sort of. And, damn, she seemed to be doing so well. The last time they tried this, she used a questionable drug, and she'd *still* passed out. A quick peek to his right. Her lips moved, and she was still conscious. Her hand while still in a tight fist, bounced in a weird pattern. Two quick thrusts down, one longer drop, two quick. Whatever she tapped out, it worked. He'd take it over the drugs any day of the week.

"Time for music?" Lucas asked.

"Opera," she breathed out.

"Sure." Lucas beamed. His finger hovered over the CD button and pressed.

Instantly the vocal stylings of familiar music filled the cabin space, *Rigoletto. How interesting he chose this CD to play in his car.* It was his favourite song. A smile he couldn't stop spread across his face and he stole a glance at the dark-haired beauty beside him. Had Lucas played his favourite music to her during training sessions? Little bugger. There were so many questions to ask. So much he wanted to know. For starters, how long had they practised this? And why the hell didn't he say anything? There wasn't a hint he'd been anywhere other than work.

"Good... song," she breathed out in bits and closed her eyes again.

Yeah, it was a great song. Simple, yet beautiful. It always managed to put him at ease, so he let it. He needed it too because he was still in shock she was riding shotgun. A dream come true. The only thing was he wished he knew how she did it, what methods worked, what happened when they failed. His imagination ran away as he envisioned the moments where she'd crashed. How had Lucas picked her up? Had therapy been involved? Geez, if it had, his whole family had kept it from him. Was Marissa somehow involved? Had she played a role, being a distraction to keep him from seeing what was going on right under his nose? Damn.

So many questions, all of which he had zero answers for. But there would be time. After tonight. First, they needed to get to her apartment and make up for lost time. Then he'd ask about her summer.

He stole another glance at her. So beautiful and finally starting to relax. Her face, still an eerie shade, was no longer scrunched up. As he watched, her mouth twitched a little, enough for him to know she was still conscious, or at least not trapped in her mind.

Twenty heart pounding minutes later, he sighed with relief as they pulled into the visitor information centre. That short drive was more exhausting mentally to him than any race he'd competed in. In the beast, he could focus on himself and the task at hand. This was a whole different race track. Now, he needed to be completely aware of her emotions, something he wasn't yet accustomed to, but was willing to learn.

"We're here," Lucas said as the engine settled. The music silenced in the cabin as he opened his door and popped the driver seat forward.

Her eyes opened wide. "We're here?"

He tried to unlatch her seatbelt for her as she kept wiggling in trying to get out and hadn't successfully freed herself. "There you go," he said as the seatbelt flew from his hand, glad Lucas already had her door open, otherwise it could've broken the window with the amount of force she applied.

"Yes, I did it," she said as she jumped out and paced away to the nearby park bench leaving them both standing there. One more helpless than the other.

Nate shot a questioning glimpse at Lucas.

"Sorry. As soon as the car shuts off, the door needs to opened ASAP, otherwise she feels trapped. I should've mentioned it before."

He stood there, torn between wanting to be mad at Lucas and wanting to comfort Aurora. He really needed to have a long chat with his little brother, to get all the info the outline didn't provide so he wouldn't have to guess at what she needed. But first, he needed to make sure she was okay. That he'd been good at once. He walked over to her. "How was the drive?"

Lucas piped up as he approached from behind. "You did great. Didn't she do great, Nate?"

"Of course, she did." *Sure as hell better than the last time.*

Aurora leaned against the picnic table, her fingers curling and relaxing. The cool wind blew strands of hair into her face, but she made no move to brush them away.

Nate stepped closer and rubbed her bare arms. "Geezus, you're freezing."

"It's not that bad." Her blue eyes fixed on his as he removed his jacket and wrapped it over her shoulders. Gently, he pulled her hair out from under the coat, allowing the breeze to sweep it off.

"So, you like opera, eh?"

"Mmm-hmm." Her voice soft.

Her eyes closed as she took in a deep breath. "Tired?"

"A little. And there's still a long way to go."

"You'll be just fine, Aurora," Lucas said. "That was the longest leg, remember?"

He watched as Lucas sat down on the bench beside her and patted her leg.

Nate studied his little brother, making more mental notes. She walked away from the car, but he followed her. Was it to provide comfort? Make sure she didn't toss her cookies? Is it a mental thing to physical distance yourself from the thing that scares you? Sheesh, maybe he needed an appointment with his sister to get it all figured out. He didn't have the knack for reading people like Lucas and Chris did.

"I know," she whispered, leaning her head on Lucas' shoulders.

Nate reached for her hand, relishing in its softness. "So how long do we wait?" Nate asked Lucas after tipping his head toward the south.

A streak of lightning twisted across the horizon.

Lucas twisted his body to him. "She calls the shots. When she's ready, we go."

With that sentiment, Aurora rose and walked around the bench, stretching with each step. "Just like you need to get into the zone, so do I." A wink in his direction, which melted his heart. As she paced, her fingers shook beside her, as though she was trying to throw her energy into the ground. It wasn't working based on the amount of time she kept doing it.

"I think you should try this leg." Lucas gave him the keys.

"I don't know."

"You'll be fine, and I'll be in the back seat. It'll be a great transition for her. You both need this."

Nate sighed and inched up to Lucas, whispering when he said, "What can I do to help her? What's a good thing to say?"

"Keep an eye out for her, but stay safe. And drive like Grandma if you must. Lord knows what would happen if you were in an accident with her."

Nate shuddered violently. Her reaction to his tiny accident on the track had been to walk away from them. If he was in an accident with her in the car, well, it would be murder-suicide. "Fair enough. So, what's next on the agenda?"

"Stop inside the city limits. There's a Timmy's on the right-hand side."

Yes, he was familiar with that stop. It was a common one to stop at on the way home from the track to grab a bagel and a coffee. Racer fuel. Eyes back to Aurora as she covered her mouth in a huge yawn. "Has she ever been this tired before?"

Lucas laughed. "Ah, yeah. But watch it. It's been an emotional day for her, in addition to having to fight her demons, she could go off."

"And I'd notice how?"

"She froths at the mouth."

Nate's eyes bugged out of his head.

"Oh my god, I'm kidding." Lucas placed his hands on his knees as he laughed. Catching his breath, he said, "Seriously... she'll probably zone out. But she's really good at telling me."

This is what I need to know. "How?"

"She tells me. She says she feels the darkness creeping in."

Nate sighed and watched how Aurora paced about, mumbling to herself. If she had worked so hard to overcome this, maybe it wasn't the best idea for *him* to drive her. He needed to be an observer on a few more trips. His heart did a dip and his voice lowered. "You should drive her all the way home. You know what you're doing and I don't want to cause a setback."

"You'll learn what works, you need to." Lucas clapped him on the back. "She wants to be with you. She's trying unbelievably hard to get over this, to be a part of your world." His voice turned firm. "Don't you dare turn your back on everything she's worked hard for."

Nate's jaw dropped. Lucas had never spoken to him like that. "I wouldn't. I just don't know what I'm doing."

"It's common sense, man. She'll warn you, and you then get her talking about anything other than her momma or sister, those are the main people popping in from the darkness. Talk to her about opera music, or her new job or the classes she's taking. But make her talk at that point. Don't let her mind swallow her alive."

Nate nodded. "Is she in university?"

"Not me, her. You two have some catching up to do."

Apparently.

Nate leaned on the car, to block the breeze which dropped the temperature quite low. Looking south, he scanned the skies. No flashes announced an impending arrival, hopefully the storm fizzled out. However, he wished he'd brought another coat as a shudder moved him, although he adored seeing Aurora wrapped in his. Another lap around the small picnic area, and she stopped in front of him.

"Okay. Let's carry on."

He stroked her face, trailing his fingertips down her cheeks. A quick tilt of her head, and he leaned in for a kiss. Oh, how he'd missed her soft, cherry-tasting lips, and the way she'd press into him.

She broke it off by pulling back and sucking off his bottom lip. "Kiss me like that again, and I'll want to stay here all night. Let's go before I change my mind."

"Is that a possibility?" He couldn't take his eyes off hers. They stared up at him with such wanton lust.

"It's debatable." The irises in her eyes sparkled as she spoke. "However, my need for getting home is only slightly stronger than my desire to rip your clothes off and make a man out of you."

"Let's get you home, because I like the sound of that."

♥Chapter Three♥

Lucas' bright, metallic blue car emblazoned with the number sixty-seven zoomed past her in the inside lane as Nate, in the sparkling white stock car, sat on his tail. The air sucked out of her lungs at each pass as the two brothers raced by, hitting speeds in excess of a hundred miles an hour.

Pushing her bangs off her face as five other stock cars thundered past, she followed and locked on her men—her best friend and her boyfriend—as they raced for top spot. It would be a close finish. The roar of the engines made her heart accelerate to cardio speeds although she did nothing more taxing than turn in her spot. Each pass was one lap closer to finish, and then her heart would be able to rest.

Normally, she had the best vantage point in the pit, high up in the spotter's cage, where she saw the half-mile long track with ease. This time, she leaned against the inside wall near the finish line. She needed to see the finish up close. A bet between the brothers hinged on who placed first. It was more than bragging rights. It was far more personal.

Her men zoomed past, catching up on the lead cars as they closed the gap. They floored it on the straightaway between corner two and three, engines screaming at the push.

A flicker of movement from her left, and she turned her head to figure out what it was. Most likely sunlight as it reflected off the tower.

But it was different enough to catch her eye.

The third in the lead, the number twelve, fishtailed out of corner two. The back end swung left and right as the driver attempted to regain control of the red car. Nate, forced up high into the corner as he and Lucas went two-wide, slammed on the brakes to avoid the erratic fish-tailing from the number twelve, causing his own to weave throughout the corner. The red car, twisting and turning, drove its nose straight into Lucas' back end as Nate sailed above.

Lucas' blue car spun hard right, by-passing the number twelve as it motored toward the inside wall, and connected head-on with the car behind him.

Nate! Lucas!

She screamed as the crunching of metal and the smell of rubber permeated her senses. Smoke twisted in the air as the other cars drove past the wreckage. Running as fast as her legs could move her, she dashed through the pit, leaping over car-markers and extra tires.

No one emerged from either vehicle, and safety personnel in tow trucks and ambulances lit up the immediate area with their blazing sirens. Her focus, however, remained on the two fused cars, unsure of where the blue car ended and the white began.

Why is no one moving?

"Lucas! Nate!" Her heart pounded hard enough to be heard over her scream and she crossed the threshold between pit and track.

Neither man had dropped their window nets. No gloved hands raised to signal to the others they were okay.

"Nate! Lucas!"

Someone pushed her out of the way as he sprinted over to the white car.

A crackle. A pop. Instinctively, she stepped back.

She cried out once again for either man to respond.

She blinked, her eyes fluttering as rapidly as her heart beat. A soft greenish glow emitted from the clock on her bedside table flashing a time she'd rather not see. Unable to hear over the blood pounding in her veins, she rolled her head to the left.

Nate.

He was alive.

It had all been a wicked, horrible nightmare. But it had felt real. Too real.

Her breaths came in spurts, and she inhaled as quietly as she could to try and get them under control. Quick breath in, hold, breathe out for three.

The heat in the bedroom became unbearable. She lifted the mountains of sheets and welcomed the cool blast of air across her sweaty body. Beads and bands of sweat lay across her forehead, along her spine and in a host of other less attractive places. Without verifying, she knew her hair was plastered to her head in an ugly heap.

Over the *bam-bam-bam* of her heart, Nate snored deeply beside her, unaware she was awake. Unaware of the adrenaline coursing through her as if the veins were a super speedway track and their goal was first place. Unaware of the sheer terror she'd witnessed in her mind.

Unable to stay in bed, or if she was being honest with herself, not *wanting* to be there any more, she moved as slowly as possible with a body fighting to sprint around in excitement.

A few purposeful, methodical movements which contrasted with the go-go-go attitude consuming her, and she stood silently beside the bed, staring at Nate. Perfection in fine form. His brown hair stuck to his head. His face relaxed in deep sleep. The corner of his mouth twitched. His hairless chest rose and lowered, the edge of the rib cage visible with each inhalation. He was truly alive. Fearing the sound of her hammering heart would wake him, she tiptoed like a mouse down the hall to the kitchen.

To calm her racing heart, she paced around the living room, shaking her arms, and breathing slowly. Every five steps she breathed in nice and deep, exhaling on the fifth step. It took a while, a long while, to feel like her body was settling down. That had been a helluva nightmare. Why does her mind constantly show her shit she doesn't want to see? There's a reason she avoided thinking about such things. They were scary as hell.

She walked into the kitchen and poured herself a glass of milk, the light of the fridge brightening up the tiny galley space. Surely the milk would help ease the acidic burn in the pit of her stomach? A cool gulp slipped down her throat. She set the glass on the counter and grabbed for the dishtowel, wiping her face and neck down.

Anxiety is terrible enough when it comes on full steam during the day. It's absolute hell to wake up in the middle of a full-blown attack. Her thoughts turned to her purse. Hidden deep inside were a couple of Xanax. Nate was sleeping—he'd never know, right? She could sneak one and make it back into bed before he knew anything had happened. The tried-and-true method of calming down wasn't working as fast, or as well, as she hoped.

A peek toward the bedroom, and her ears stretched out hard. Sounded like he was still sleeping as a soft snore floated through the air. She crossed the hall in two quick steps and searched for her purse. It was on the floor last time she remembered. Dammit, where did she put it?

Another peek back to the bedroom as she walked into the living room. A thick cloud cover over the city cast an orange glow in the apartment, lighting up the room enough to see easily enough. But she still didn't find her purse.

She searched the coffee table. Nope. Patted around under the end tables. Not there either. With her foot, she kicked beside the sofa, as she remembered she had attempted to study earlier and dropped her stuff there. Nothing.

Fuck.

Tiptoeing over to the kitchen table, she narrowed her eyes as she checked out the top. No purse. What the fuck?

Back into the kitchen she went as she needed another gulp of milk. The glass slid from her hand as a muscle spasm ran through her arm, and she released it. Thankfully she caught it before it crashed although some spilled onto the floor. Throwing a towel over it, she mopped it up with her foot, and kicked it off to the side. The anxiety started its retreat, however, she wasn't stable enough to be able to go back to sleep. The adrenaline had yet to exit her body. She'd need to burn it off, because as much as the sweat was trying, it failed.

Music! Yes, music would help her relax especially since she couldn't find her purse. With the Xanax. Tomorrow when she found it, she'd be putting those pills some place that didn't change location all the time.

Tiptoeing back into the living room, she knelt in front of the radio, and lowered the volume the instant she turned it on.

Ah, something soft. A love ballad. The two-part harmonies sang in tune about needing the other.

She stood and waltzed across the room, twirling and spinning as she danced in perfect synchronisation with the beat. Light as air, she moved effortlessly, releasing her nervousness into the room. Each step, each tap of the toe, each movement of the arm calmed her as the words danced in her heart.

Every inhale soothed her, and every exhale released the anxiety. She danced, and moved, and spun, and even as the song ended, it didn't slow her down.

"I could watch you all night."

His warm and husky voice startled her, and she froze on the spot. He leaned against the wall. The only piece of clothing he wore—his pajama bottoms—hung loosely around his hips. In the low glow, he radiated sex appeal. "Oh, don't stop."

He crossed the room in a few steps and wrapped her up in his strong arms.

Another slow song whispered from the radio.

"May I?" he asked, his voice low as to not to disturb the soothing mood. With a subtle nod, he extended her right hand in his, and smoothly twirled her, dancing around the room. "How come you're up?"

A small laugh escaped her as his whisper tickled her ear. "I couldn't sleep."

He pulled her close and kissed her forehead before twirling her out to the end of his arms. Catching her hand, he squeezed it, reigning her in and holding her tight. "Nightmare?" Tenderly, he cupped her lower back with one hand and held her with another as he proceeded to dip her.

"Anxiety attack after the nightmare, or during it, I don't know. But I woke from the nightmare in the middle of it." A shudder interrupted her smooth motions.

"Are you okay?"

Her body pressed in closer to him. "Better now." His musky scent comforted her as much as his strength.

"Well, if that's the case, we'll keep on dancing," he said as the distance between them all but disappeared as their bodies merged.

Moving as one unit, they danced in the low orange glow, mirroring the other's movements in time to the romantic ballads.

Neither spoke until Nate interrupted the interlude. "My favourite song," he breathed into her ear as his hand inched against her lower back.

A familiar song. A song about falling in love in mysterious ways. She placed her head against his muscular chest, the drumming of his heart threatening to drown the melody. Each beat, each word resonated inside of her. It never ceased to amaze her how wonderful he was, and how she nearly threw it all away.

The pounding in her veins had vanished, and her breathing returned to a normal rate. The fear and anxiety she awoke to was long gone. But she didn't let go of him. Needed to hold him close. To breathe him into the depths of her soul.

Coming down from the anxiety attack was almost as bad as going through it. Although the physical sensations had ceased, the emotional part held her captive longer. And the buildup approached. It pushed and pushed relentlessly, begging for escape. Unable to fight it anymore, the tears broke the threshold.

"Aurora?" His hold on her slackened.

Her body shook as the buildup peaked its crescendo. "Don't let go."

A tender kiss on her forehead. "I'm right here."

His safety and security wrapped around her like a blanket, and she melted into his arms, allowing wave after wave of emotional instability wash over her. It was better to let it happen than it was to fight it anymore. She'd learned that lesson the hard way. The more the tears fell, the more drained she became until there was nothing more for her to do except completely depend upon him to hold her up.

He moved her to the couch where she curled up beside him. The silence punctuated by the sound of music and the occasional sniff. Her post-attack cry was always the strong, silent, body-shaking variety. Likely as painful to watch as to endure.

***

The next morning the aroma from a strong cup of coffee, and the scent of melted peanut butter rose her out of a deep sleep.

"I brought you this," Nate said, setting a large paper cup of hot, fresh coffee on the bedside table. "I figured you should eat something."

She sat up and rested herself against the headboard. "Thank you," she said, unwrapping the waxy paper.

"Hope you like it. It's a PB&J bagel."

"Mmm, smells wonderful. Thank you."

Nate sat at the foot of the bed, dressed in a long-sleeve tee and jeans.

"What about you?"

He produced his own paper-wrapped bagel.

"When did you sneak out? And how? You don't have a key to the building?"

"I borrowed yours. You left them on the table."

"Oh." The scent of melted peanut butter ticked her nose.

"How'd you sleep?"

"Much better after–" She cast her gaze away, not needing to see pity in his eyes.

"I'd like to talk about that."

"There's nothing to say."

"But I'm curious. Where did it all come from? You haven't given any indication you were stressed over anything."

The first bite of the bagel was delicious. Who knew it was what she wanted? As she chewed, she searched his face. Those beautiful eyes held so much concern, so much worry and so much love for her. "I don't have to be stressed to have an anxiety attack. That's sort of a myth." A quick rinse of her mouth with a sip of the coffee, chased away the peanut butter breath. "I had a nightmare, and the attack started at some point within it." *Because of what I saw.* She shuddered.

"What was it about?" Her gave her covered leg a gentle rub.

"I don't want to tell you." A flash of the mangled cars. A whiff of burnt rubber. Her heart skipped a beat at the recall. Even without looking at him, the weight of his stare pressed on her.

"Would it help if I told you it was just a dream?"

"Not really." She shifted in bed and pulled the blanket closer to cover her chest. "It was pretty real to me."

Nate shifted and tore off a bite of bagel. "Has it happened before?"

"What do you mean?"

"Have you had an attack in the middle of a dream and woke–"

"Up to it? Yeah. Several times." A blanket of shame wrapped around her. It wasn't like she had any control over when the attacks happened. They happened when they happened. And the panic didn't give two shits about who was or wasn't around.

"When was the last?"

A large lump formed in her throat. "The night before I came to the track to stop you from retiring."

Two weeks ago.

"I see." A catch in his throat, and he coughed. "And how'd you deal with it?" He scratched his whiskery chin and ran his fingers through his hair. "Did Lucas ever witness?"

"More than I'd like to admit." She sighed, climbing out of bed and adjusted her nightshirt. "There were more moments of me wanting to give up, you should be surprised I even made it to the track."

"So, Lucas witnessed?"

She laughed. "Witnessed? He was part of my anxiety, sometimes. He was in such an icky spot. Needing to be secretive and keep this all from you, and yet, he needed to be there for me in all the ugly ways. Trying to find a way to deal with the middle of the night anxiety was hell. He used to camp out on the sofa, so at least when I fell, I had a buddy to come with me." She searched his face, hoping to see a twinge of amusement on it, but it was devoid of joy. If anything, it was full of concern and sadness. "Lucas suggested movement, so that's what I did. I danced and moved around, trying to rid my body of the fears. And I'd cry, just like I did last night."

Nate swallowed. "And after?"

"He held me when I cried. I think it was as much for him as it was for me. My attacks can be emotionally draining on everyone involved."

He patted the bed, and she sat back down, curling up to him. "I'm so sorry you need to deal with it like that."

"I'm not."

His face crinkled. "What do you mean?"

"It was the only way to learn *how* to cope. Before it was easier to take a Xanax and let the chemicals do their thing. But Lucas, he… I don't know how to explain it. He gave me another way to cope, a drug free way. The movement and the dancing, they soothe me. Being touched, soothes me. He figured out a way to incorporate it all into healing from the anxiety."

Nate hung his head.

"Hey," she said, her voice soft. "Last night with you bordered on sexy and had I not been in the state I was…" She raised an eyebrow.

Long fingers stroked her cheek. "You thought I was sexy?"

"Thought you were? Or think you *are*? Because I'm going with the here and now." She traced the waist of his jeans, freeing his tee-shirt from its hold.

♥ Chapter Four ♥

"That's a lotta food." Kaitlyn laughed and dropped a heavy bag on the floor.

"Thanks again for picking me at the supermarket."

"As if you'd be able to walk home with all of this. I saw you dragging your tired ass around the store." Kaitlyn stared at the kitchen table laden with half the store.

"That's why I asked if you'd come help me earlier than planned. I was exhausted from a horrible sleep." In a mock expression, she placed the back of her hand against her forehead.

"And now? Still tired?" Kaitlyn was all serious, not even a hint of a smile.

"I have a second wind coming on."

"Well good. You're going to need it making all this food for everyone. There's what? Eight, nine of us?" She looked around again.

Aurora did a quick double count. "No, there's seven coming for Thanksgiving." She rifled through a few bags. "Are you sure I bought enough food?"

"Totally because I'm going to be peeling potatoes all afternoon." She hoisted up a ten-pound bag and as an afterthought asked, "Seven? Shouldn't there be more?"

"Umm, you, Brenda, Nate, Lucas, Chris, Max and me." Each

name a quick tap on her fingers. "Seven."

"Aw. Cole isn't coming?"

"Because he lets his staff take the day off, he needs to be there."

"Well that's too bad." Kaitlyn sulked.

Aurora's father was the only man Kaitlyn ever showed interest in. If he were twenty-five years younger and not her dad… Aurora shuddered.

"Oh well, more turkey for everyone else." She checked on the large bird thawing in a sink of chilly water.

Aurora double checked. "Yep, feels about right." She started mumbling as she unwrapped the twenty-five-pound bird. "Do you think there's going to be enough turkey? I don't know if this is big enough."

"Seriously, between the bird, the potatoes, the thirty-pack of buns, the two different salads and the veggies, you could feed half the building."

"I don't know about that."

"You're nervous, aren't you?" Kaitlyn said as she started peeling potatoes.

"Nervous, me? Nah." But a giggle escaped.

Kaitlyn gave her the side eye. "Yeah, you are, but why? It's not like anyone's a stranger."

"I know, it's just… I'm trying to impress them. Well, Brenda I guess."

"Why? She's given Lucas nothing but grief." A piece of potato skin flew into Aurora's side of the sink. She scooped it out, avoiding the raw turkey.

"Yeah, but I'm with Nate." She sighed. "Forget it. It's complicated."

"Try me."

Aurora had her arm, nearly elbow deep, into the cavity of the turkey and laughed at the grossed-out expression on Kaitlyn's face.

A half-second later, Kaitlyn gagged.

"Really, Kait?"

Her best friend spun around. "Seriously, that's like the most disgusting thing. The poor bird, being all violated like that."

"It's dead. It's not feeling any of this." She laughed out loud when another gagging sound came from her left. "It's not that big a deal."

Kaitlyn wiped her hands on a nearby towel and stepped around the wall of the kitchen. "Tell me when you're done."

She couldn't stop laughing. It wasn't *that* disgusting. "Have you never put together a turkey dinner?"

"No, and I know you haven't either. That's why I'm here helping you."

"True, but I've helped clean a turkey before. Momma used to get me to help every Easter, Christmas, or Thanksgiving."

"Can't you buy them pre-cleaned?"

"Not where I shop."

"I'll need to marry rich, because I ain't ever cleaning out a dead bird."

"Is Tatiana rich?"

"Not that I'm aware of."

Aurora beamed. "Then I guess all your major holidays will be spent at my house. I don't mind doing it." She retrieved a white bag full of innards and set it on the counter. "Got the good stuff out."

"Do I even want to know what the good stuff is?"

She rubbed her chin on her shoulder to scratch it. "Probably not. I'm not going to make use of them anyways."

"Almost done in there? I still have 9.8 pounds of potatoes to peel." Kaitlyn's voice had an edge, this impromptu wait was probably killing her. "You know, you never answered my question."

"About?"

"Brenda. Why is it so important for you to be on her good side? Aren't all mother in laws supposed to be distrustful of their daughter in laws no matter how wonderful they are?"

Distrustful. What a loaded word. She rested her arms on the edge of the sink, but she shook it off, hoping Kait didn't truly think about its meaning. "We just got back to together and you're already calling her my mother-in-law?"

"You're dodging my question."

She placed the cleaned bird on to the roasting pan and tossed the bag of innards into the trash. "All clear."

Kaitlyn entered the tiny space and resumed her peeling. "But seriously, why such a big deal? You should be putting on this dinner because you want to, not because you're trying to impress her."

"I'm not trying to impress her. My last Thanksgiving dinner was three years ago. With Momma, Carmen, and Daddy, boyfriends and a neighbouring family. We were happy, and dinner was perfect." Her eyes glazed over as she floated back in time. "It was such an amazing Thanksgiving. We had so much to be thankful for. Who knew it would all change within six months?"

Indeed. Everyone was healthy and happy and living life to the fullest. It seemed like yesterday, everyone was gathered around the MacIntyre family table, laughing, and sharing jokes. Carmen had come home from university and surprised everyone by bringing along her boyfriend. Not that it mattered as Momma always made too much food and insisted the family up the street come join them as well. To her it wasn't extra plates to set, it was more fed bellies and memories.

"I want to recreate those moments."

"You want a family."

"Exactly." She rubbed her homemade turkey seasoning all over the turkey, pushing it deep into the skin. "I worry that because of me sort of getting in between Lucas and her, she dislikes me, and the whole thing with the drugs and Nate before that, didn't help."

"She likes you. If she didn't, she wouldn't be coming over tonight."

"What if she's doing it because she thinks she should and not because she really wants to?"

"That's her problem. Don't make it yours."

"I want her to see Nate and I truly belong together."

"Anyone who sees you together would know you're both madly in love with each other. It's almost repulsive the way he looks at you with those googly eyes of his." A plop as a potato fell into a pot of water. "I've been meaning to ask you, what's going on with you and Lucas?"

"What do you mean?" She stepped to the side to allow Kaitlyn to put the pot on the stove.

"Well, before you got back with Nate, he used to be over here. Like all the time. And now he's not."

"Yeah, that's extremely complicated."

"You and everything being so complicated. Try me." Kaitlyn stood with her hands on her hips.

"It's just… I don't know. Lucas agreed with me how weird it'd be for him to stay here, like a roommate type of thing, when I'm dating his brother, so he's back at the house, but he's not happy there. He studies here until late and goes home. But he says it's uncomfortable there. When he and Brenda are alone, it's tension filled, and when others are around, she basically ignores him."

"All because of the switch in careers?"

"Mostly, but there's more to it. He's not saying, no matter how I ask." She sighed. As close as they were, there were going to be things Lucas didn't share. "However, I've been contemplating having him move into one of the spare bedrooms. With the issues between him and Brenda, this is a safe place for him, right?" Kaitlyn nodded in agreement. "But there's the issue of Nate. How can I have my best friend move in, and not also extend that offer to his brother—my boyfriend?"

"Yeah, that does complicate things."

"Having Nate move in is a different expectation than Lucas. I'd be sharing more than my apartment with Nate, I be sharing my bed and bathroom. At least Lucas would have his own private space. I'd lose all of mine with Nate." She slumped. "See what I mean? Complicated."

"So just like that, Lucas is staying home?"

"On occasion. He's there during the week, but stays over at friends on the weekend."

"At a friend's or at a *friend's*?" Kaitlyn's eyebrows wiggled up and down.

"Yeah, a different *friend* every weekend, apparently."

Kaitlyn studied her and shook her head. "Throw the turkey in already, and we'll finish this chat."

The bird slid into the oven, and the girls headed into the living room for a coffee break.

"I heard the tone in your voice."

"What tone?"

"Hmm… a weird sort of jealous sadness combination."

"I'm not jealous of Lucas."

Kaitlyn cocked a brow. "So, what are you thinking?"

She sighed as she fell beside Kaitlyn on the couch. "I miss him. Lucas, I mean."

"Yeah, I can tell."

"Don't get me wrong, I'm very happy to be with Nate, but something's missing."

A Cheshire Cat grin spread across Kaitlyn's face. "Like your daily dose of Lucas?"

"Maybe. But it's more than that. When we're all together, like last weekend at their house, Nate gets sort of… not possessive, because that's not the right word but it's like that."

"And you don't approve?" Kaitlyn cocked her head.

"Yes, and no. Whenever I need to deal with the anxiety, or mention how I'd dealt with an issue, Nate gets defensive."

Kaitlyn laughed.

"What?"

"Oh my god. He's super jealous."

"Nate? Or Lucas?"

"Both actually." Kaitlyn smirked. "Nate's jealous because you and Lucas spent all summer bonding. Remember how I told you a while back, you two had connected on a deep, emotional level? I'm not the only one to have noticed. Nate must've seen it too. And Lucas, yeah, we both know how he feels about you, so he's jealous that Nate has you, while he has to sit on the sidelines and watch. That's why he's out with a *friend* every weekend. He's trying to get over you."

"Lucas is a friend, that's all."

"You keep telling yourself that." The sarcasm was thick in her voice.

"Kaitlyn!"

"All I'm saying, is if I had an eighteen-year-old ogle me the way Lucas looks at you, I'd consider it. Besides, he's kind of cute. For a boy."

For a boy. He was barely legal. A year and a bit younger than herself. She studied Kaitlyn, who was the same age as Nate. Both twenty-two, both finishing up their final year in university where she was technically in her second year, although it was the first term of a new program. And Lucas? It was his first year. Yes, one could argue Lucas and she had more in common, age, and school wise, but her heart belonged to Nate. It was because of Nate, she could fight hard against her demons and triumph. He filled her in a way she couldn't explain properly. To anyone, herself included. He was Nate. Loveable, charming, pushing her beyond her comfort zone Nate. "Lucas is only a friend. A really good friend."

Kaitlyn tapped her arm. "You believe that, if you want." Kaitlyn crossed her legs, tugging down on the hem of her skirt. "Remember, I was here the night you had the breakdown over your feelings for him."

Aurora's cheeks flamed up at the memory, and she quickly swallowed it down.

"All I'm saying is he looks at you as if he wants more."

"That's absurd. He knows how in love with Nate I am."

"Yeah, maybe so. But the heart can't control who it falls in love with."

"Tell me about it. I'm the girl with vehicular PTSD falling in love with a race car driver."

Kaitlyn laughed, the infectious sound filling the space around them like a hug. "Yeah, never would've saw that coming."

"And you… What about–"

"Tatiana." The name rolled off Kaitlyn's tongue with love and softness. "Two more days. I can't wait to see her in person again."

Over the summer, Kaitlyn had spent time back home in Russia, where she met and fell in love with Tatiana. In the passing weeks, both Kaitlyn and Tatiana had done everything they could to start planning the rest of their lives together. Tatiana was arriving in Canada in two days to set those plans in motion.

"I can't wait to meet her and see the woman you've given your heart to."

Kaitlyn giggled. "I can't wait for that either. You're going to love her. She's so amazing."

"Have you told your parents yet?"

Kaitlyn shook her and whispered, "No."

Her eyes bugged out. "Are you kidding me? When do you plan on telling them?"

"Years from now."

"Please let me you're joking."

Kaitlyn shrugged. "I don't know."

"She's moving in with you, right? Surely your parents can figure it out?"

"Right now, they think she's a roommate."

"You need to tell them."

"I'm not ready to be disowned, okay?"

"Does Tatiana know you've wimped out and hid it from your family?"

"Yeah."

She had no more words. It was an ongoing discussion between her and Kaitlyn. Her parents were in the dark about her sexual orientation, but on some level, they had to know, right? Parents just knew things about you if you never said them.

She sighed. "Anything I can do to help? Do you want to have them over here, and you can tell them on neutral ground?"

"No. I'll talk it over with Tatiana and see what she thinks. It's not like we're getting married or anything."

"Good, 'cause I'd need time to plan a bachelorette party." Aurora beamed at her friend.

Kaitlyn grinned, her warm smile highlighting her gorgeous

cheekbones. "What about you and Nate? Do you see a future with him?"

"Do I see a future with him? Like a forever future?" She took a long drink from her coffee cup and let the warmth drip down her throat. "That I don't know. I have a hard time stomaching the idea of him moving in because it's all so new. I know I love him, and I hope he loves me as much."

"He does."

A long pause. "But a lifetime together? I don't know. Kind of scary to think about."

"Not really."

"You don't think if I proposed to Nate tonight, he wouldn't run out the door faster than his car can drive?"

"I doubt it."

She cocked an eyebrow. "Let's give it a year or two first, before we start talking marriage and forever. I'm okay enjoying the here and now. Forever is too scary. I need to figure out what I want from life before I drag someone else into it."

"Coffee break over. Time to make desserts."

"Thank goodness you're here to keep me on track. Imagine the shenanigans I'd get into if you weren't." A deep belly laugh. "Let's get back to work."

***

"Happy Thanksgiving Johnson Family," Kaitlyn said hours later as Nate and his family entered the apartment.

"Hey, everyone," Aurora said, eyeing Nate.

He hung up everyone's coats in the closet and avoided eye contact.

"Where's Chris and Max" she asked, after seeing everyone but his sister and boyfriend.

Brenda piped up. "She's running behind. A patient contacted her and needed an emergency visit. She'll be here, with Max, as soon as she can."

Ah yes. I've had a couple of those.

Brenda walked ahead into the kitchen and pulled upon the oven door. "The turkey looks good, honey. May I?"

"Of course." She passed the meat thermometer over and as it plunged in, a trickle of juice ran down the side. She hoped it tasted as good as it looked.

"Done," Brenda said, extracting the bird from the oven.

Leaving the women in the kitchen, she waltzed over to Nate who hadn't moved from the entrance. Her hand tenderly stroked his whiskered cheek. "Everything okay? You look upset." Indeed, the bags under his eyes were full and dark as though as he hadn't slept for weeks, and she knew for a fact he slept damn well last night.

He planted a kiss into her palm. "Just a rough day."

She eyed him sceptically. "Things aren't going well at the site?"

He shook his head. "I'd rather not talk about it, right now." A long finger of his trailed down her cheek and cupped her chin. "It smells wonderful in here. I can't wait to eat."

As she surveyed the area, pride and a sense of togetherness bubbled up inside her. Everyone busied themselves as Kaitlyn doled out plates and cutlery, and Brenda dished the food into serving bowls. Lucas kept his distance from the kitchen, and his mother, by producing a couple of stacking stools to set up around the table. It was going to be a tight squeeze fitting in seven there, but she looked forward to being shoulder to shoulder with everyone.

Brenda spoke up from the kitchen. "The bird can sit for a minute while we get the rest of this onto the table." She smiled, the same easy going smile her sons had. "You ladies did a wonderful job. Everything looks so appetising."

Aurora's heart filled with love hearing the compliment. The Johnson's gave her something she hadn't had in a long time—family—and she was going to do everything she could to keep her family close together and happy. There were a few details, however, she needed to work through first.

Her stomach growled loudly.

Nate chuckled beside her as he approached. "Well, let's slice up the bird, and eat. You're starving."

Aurora opened a drawer and pulled out the sharpest knife she could find.

"I'm starving too." His voice was like music to her ears.

She spun and smiled at him.

He bent lower to her and his breath tickled his ears as he whispered, "But I'm starving for you."

The room felt too hot, and the heat rose fast in her cheeks. She didn't dare chance a peek behind her where she felt the weight of Brenda's smirk. "Is it hot in here?" Her shirt bellowing as she tugged on it.

Reaching the patio door, she opened it a crack and let the cool rush of October air race into the apartment. A melody played from the speakers as she flipped on the stereo.

"No top 40 please," Lucas said, walking over and reaching for the remote.

"And what do you propose I put on?"

He laughed. "Opera?"

She punched him playfully. "Not for dinner. That's music you need to sit and give your full attention to, like in a car. It's not background music."

"Where's the cord so I can hook up my phone?"

Digging through a box of cables and cords, she produced the one he needed and raised an eyebrow of suspicion at him.

"Trust me." He thumbed through his music, and the slow gentle beats of classical music rose from the speakers.

"Okay, it's acceptable." She giggled as she patted him while heading back to the kitchen.

The hacked-up turkey, because the sharpest knife she had wasn't sharp at all, sat in the middle of the table as the guests mingled about deciding where to sit.

Everyone in their places, Brenda spoke up. "No one's told me when we should expect Cole?"

Aurora pulled out a chair beside Nate. "He had to work but he'll be here next weekend."

"Too bad, I'd like to meet him."

"You will," Aurora said, as Nate gave her thigh a gentle rub. "Hopefully before Christmas."

Nate and Aurora had only been back together for a couple of weeks, but it was the third time Brenda had asked about him. It made her nervous because a lot of information had surfaced about him, and she wasn't entirely sure how much Brenda knew. Nate and Chris were the first to have put it all together, and Lucas wasn't far behind. Still, knowing your daddy was a recreational-drug pharmacist, as Kaitlyn called him, was one thing, having others know it too, made the situation more uncomfortable. Nate's family was the quintessential clean-cut variety, and the worst thing they could ever be pinned with was one too many speeding tickets. Apparently not all drivers got their need for speed out on the track.

The buzzer rang and Aurora jumped up to get it.

Brenda spoke up. "Well I'm glad someone from your family is here."

It didn't take too long before Aurora saw Chris and Max step off the elevator, hand in hand. Chris presented a pie to her. "Sorry it's store bought."

"You didn't have to bring anything." She smiled over at Max. "I'm happy you both made it." She closed the door as they entered the apartment.

Aurora introduced Kaitlyn to Chris and Max, as the couple found the two vacant spots at the table, squeezing in between Brenda and Kaitlyn.

When everyone was settled again, the serving platters passed around. Aurora's heart swelled at the gathering, surrounded by all she loved and held dear, except for her missing father. A cool breeze nipped at toes and music swirled in her ears. She couldn't remember being so content with how her life was.

Brenda dropped a spoonful of mashed potatoes on her plate.

"Kaitlyn, tell us a bit about yourself. How'd you meet Aurora?"

"We were dorm mates last year, until she moved here in May." Kaitlyn winked at her.

"Right on campus?"

"Lister Hall."

Brenda tipped her head as she asked, "So, you're from out of town?"

"Sort of. I'm originally from Tula, which is outside of Moscow but we moved to Bruderheim when I was a teen."

"Are you celebrating with your family tomorrow?"

"I'm celebrating with my family today," she said, waving her hand toward Aurora. "Besides, I'm working tomorrow."

"What about your parents?"

"They're busy."

"And siblings?"

"None."

"What about a boyfriend?"

Kaitlyn pleaded with her best friend, sheer panic crossing her face.

Aurora sensed the anguish and kicked Nate who sat on her right. "What is this mom, the Spanish Inquisition?" He laughed and passed around a basket of fresh buns.

"I was simply curious. Sorry, Kaitlyn, I didn't mean to be nosy." Brenda grabbed a bun and passed it on.

Kaitlyn held the basket as a pained expression briefly passed behind her eyes. "My girlfriend, my very serious girlfriend, Tatiana, arrives on Tuesday."

"Love it." Aurora mouthed in Kaitlyn's direction, as a huge smile grew on her face and she gave her best friend the thumb's up sign.

Kaitlyn shrugged playfully as the expression on her face morphed from fear to pride.

"Oh, wow." Brenda said, smiling. "How exciting."

"Yes, it is," Aurora said. "And you're the first people she's sharing it with."

"Well, congratulations, Kaitlyn." Brenda said. "That reminds me..." She pushed back from her chair and went to her bag beside the front door. "This calls for a toast." Wine bottle in hand, she headed into the little galley kitchen.

Aurora dropped her butter knife and swallowed. Another squeeze on her thigh. In shock, she took in everyone's faces. Kaitlyn stared open-mouthed in Brenda's direction, and Lucas' widened gaze darted between his mom and her. Chris kept her focus in Aurora's direction. Her mouth dry as cotton, she searched for Nate's eyes, hoping he'd see the fear in hers. It registered.

"What are you doing, mom?" Nate kicked back from his seat and walked to the kitchen.

Cupboard doors opened and closed. "Looking for wine glasses."

"There are none," Aurora said, her voice strained with control as her hands curled into tight little fists.

Alcohol had poisoned the mind of the idiot who ran the stop sign and plowed into the car Aurora had been driving, forever changing her life. His stupidity killed her mom and sister instantly and in its wake, left Aurora with post-traumatic stress disorder. It took her over two years before she could venture back into a vehicle again. Never in her whole life had she ever tasted the bottled poison, and it curdled her blood to have it in the apartment. It was that asshole's stupidity who took away her family. Her girls' weekends. Her family celebrations.

Lucas tipped his head and narrowed his eyes, shooting a confused look toward her. Aurora shook her head. Dinner was supposed to be magical, filled with laughter and bad jokes, and complaints of stuffed bellies, not a hacked-up turkey, an inquisition, and alcohol. Is this what every gathered family tradition would turn into?

Low mumblings came from the kitchen behind her. Turning in her chair, she swallowed her pride and pasted on a big fake smile. "It's okay, Nate. If she wants to have a glass of wine, I'm not going to stop her. There are smaller glasses in the cupboard beside the fridge." The napkin fell from her seat as she stood. "Give me a minute."

She walked to her bedroom as calmly as she could muster and grabbed at the Xanax container on her dresser. She needed an out—a way to escape the hurt building. Thanksgiving dinner without her momma, her sister, or her daddy all because alcohol ruined her life. It wasn't the time to freak out, but she didn't know how she could handle sitting at the table surrounded by wine. The Xanax would help a lot; help her not to care about the poison. Help her not give a fuck how Brenda inconsiderately brought it into her home.

Opening the pill container, she poured the contents into her hand, but nothing poured out. "What the fuck?" Peering into it, she stared hard. "Fuck." The empty container pinged off the far wall, and landed on the floor, sight unseen. "What god damn good is it to only have access to two fucking Xanax a week?" She ran her fingers through her hair, tugging out a few weak strands.

"Because that was the rule you helped implement." She spun on her heels when Lucas' voice spoke from the doorway.

"Yeah, well it's a shitty rule."

"You don't say." A smile tugged on his lips but it wasn't a true smile. It wasn't one to break down her anger and relax her.

"Everything was supposed to go perfectly today, and instead it's falling apart."

"It's not. I promise."

She crossed her hands over her chest. "But…"

"Stop. You're over reacting a tiny little bit."

"The turkey is all hacked-up…"

"So, what? It'll look even worse as it digests."

She scrunched her face up. "And the inquisition?"

"Mom does that to everybody. She's not like Max around strangers, who completely clams up and says all of two words. She probes, to break the ice and learn about someone. She did it to you, if you'd remember."

"I think I was drugged."

"Perhaps. But this is normal. Didn't you ever have a Thanksgiving dinner with your family?"

"Yeah, but it was different than this. It was happy and full of laughter."

"And this will be too. Everyone will remember the love and the excess food and all of that, unless you continue to make a big deal out of this. Then that's what they'll remember. With your family, I'm sure things went wrong, but you don't remember them because they were brushed to the side." His hand waved in the air. "Now listen to me. Take a deep breath."

She raised an eyebrow.

"I mean it, Aurora, take a deep breath."

She inhaled, counted to three and exhaled. "There."

"Yeah, right. Do it again."

Another inhale, this one she breathed in for a count of three, held for two and exhaled for three.

"Better?"

"Yeah." She had to admit it did wonders to focus only on the breathing.

"Nate's talking to mom. Not sure what she was thinking. She knows better. Other than that, everything else has been perfect. This is a little hiccup." He ran her hands over her shoulders. "Breathe again."

As he instructed, her breath sailed out, and she felt more in control of her emotions. "It'd still be helpful if I had a pill."

"Yeah, well you need to wait until when? Tuesday?"

A slow nod. Tuesday. Three days away.

"You've got this. You're in control. Now come on. Let's eat and not let this delicious food go to waste."

He held her hand down the hall to the eating area where four sets of eyes welcomed her back, and one set stayed firmly glued on her and Lucas' hand.

She pulled away from it and resumed her spot between Brenda and Nate.

He leaned over and whispered, "What was that all about?" There was no mistaking the undertone in his voice.

"It's grounding." A quick glance across the table to Lucas who dropped a huge dollop of mashed potatoes onto his plate. She met Kaitlyn's raised eyebrow and focused back on her own plate.

"Aurora," Brenda said, "I'm really sorry."

"It's okay. I promise." The biggest smile she could muster forced its way onto her face.

"No, I've triggered something in you. I was a completely insensitive jerk. Please forgive me."

She turned to Brenda. "I promise you it's already forgotten. I'm sorry for needing a minute to get myself under control. Let's move on, shall we? How's the cabbage salad tasting, Max?"

"It's delicious," Max chimed up as he reached for the serving bowl.

"It must be good. This is your second helping," Chris said with a smile on her face.

The air was thick and for a few minutes only the sounds of forks scrapping across plates, the chewing of turkey and the crunching of salad filled the air. It drove Aurora insane. It wasn't supposed to be like this. This should've been a meal of happiness, endless chatter, and laughter. Instead, she saw the awkwardness on Kaitlyn's face, who picked at her food. She wondered if she'd be more comfortable sitting with her parents.

She was surprised by the expression on Lucas' face. He held very little emotion, and studied the turkey bun concoction he held between his spindly fingers, not at all bothered by the absence of talking. However, he attacked the sandwich as if he hadn't eaten all day.

Nate on the other hand, looked borderline pissed off. His brows were furrowed, and he attacked his potatoes like they'd done a huge injustice to him by simply being on his plate. Surely, the hand holding thing wasn't bugging him, and she hoped deep down it was whatever incident happened at work. But the more he attacked his food, the more she worried. Was Kaitlyn right? Did Lucas see her with the same eyes as Nate? But it was innocent. Totally innocent. Nate *had* to know that. He had to know she was true to him, and him only. She hadn't been with anyone since their breakup, where he had.

Brenda broke the silence. "This was really good, ladies. You've put on a splendid meal."

Kaitlyn smiled with pride. "Thank you, Brenda. Aurora handled the turkey though."

"Only because you were gagging as I cleaned it." A giggle bubbled out of her as she shared with them the cleaning episode.

"So, I'm squeamish around bird violations," Kaitlyn said as the story quickly wrapped up. "That's why I'll never make it in medicine."

The food clearly was delicious as Aurora checked out everyone's empty plates. Even the serving dishes in the middle had dwindled down. She was impressed.

Brenda swallowed down a drink of water. "Wait until you have the meal next weekend at the banquet."

Aurora put her fork down. "Banquet?"

"Yeah. Every year, after the season wraps up, there's the awards banquet. It's a big fancy night, where you get to dress up and be totally catered to."

She twisted in her seat and smiled in Nate's direction. "Were you planning on telling me about this?"

"I hadn't decided yet if I was going." His eyes remained focused on his emptied plate. "It wasn't that good a season."

Which is my fault, I assume? Her gaze bounced back and forth between Nate and his mom. "You could've said something." She connected with Lucas who shrugged.

"I figured he would've." He thrust his chin in his big brother's direction.

Brenda wiped her mouth. "A lot of big wigs will be there, Nate. This could be your chance to get a few sponsorships for Northern Lights Racing."

Nate lifted his head and took a long look around the table. "Maybe. Would be nice to get a deal or two secured before the end of the year." Nate's eyes finally connected with hers. They held her for a heartbeat before dropping back to his plate.

Was he holding back on my account? She grabbed another bun although she was stuffed to the brim and didn't think she'd be able to get it down. "It could be fun. A night away. No studying, no demands, just us all dressed up being catered to."

"She makes a valid point, Nathan."

"You're glamourizing it." Sighing, he twisted toward her. "They're kinda boring. We sit around the table watching video segments. Everyone collects their major trophies and cash prizes."

"Like Lucas?" Her gaze shifted between the two brothers.

"Yes, he'll get a trophy of some sort." His tone sounded light but she heard the pride in it.

Brenda laughed. "Yeah, he'll be collecting a trophy. His first place award."

Aurora tuned out Brenda's pride bursting explanation and focused on Nate. *Was he jealous that Lucas was receiving a trophy, and he wasn't? That wasn't very Nate-like.* But he sat there, shoulders rolled in, dragging his fork through a leftover puddle of gravy. She needed to diffuse the buildup of tension again. "Will there be dancing?" Excitement rose in her voice.

A broad smile broke out as Nate nodded. "Always."

Her smile and raised eyebrow matched his. "I like dancing."

"Fine," he said, never taking his eyes off her. "You sold me. We'll go."

She tucked a strand of dark hair behind her ear and smirked in his direction. "So easy to convince. I'll need to remember that."

♥Chapter Five♥

"Good afternoon, Aurora." Dr. Navin closed the door to his office. "Make yourself at home."

She slumped down on the sofa and kicked off her shoes. "It's nice to have you back."

"You didn't see anyone in my absence?"

"No. I'm not really comfortable with anyone else."

"I'm flattered."

"You should be. I've seen enough shrinks to last two lifetimes but I like how you make me think after our appointments have ended."

Dr. Navin sat on the couch in front of her, his mass causing the cushions to wrap slightly around him. "Do you want to catch me up on things?"

"Not much to say."

He leaned back after tossing her folder onto the table. "You made it to the track?"

"Yes."

"Do you want to tell me how that went?"

"It went well. Minor issues, but we handled it."

"I'm pleased to hear it." He shifted and leaned his head on his hand. "And the ride home?"

"It was different, but we managed."

"Talk to me about why it was different."

Aurora wiggled in her seat, and pulled her legs under her, readjusting to soothe a minor ache in her hip. She tugged down her sleeves and covered the palm of her hand. "I came home with Lucas and Nate. Nate tagged along on the first leg and commandeered the ship, as he later said, for the next two legs. He was nervous about driving me since he never had. Well, without the magical drugs."

"Go on."

"I could feel his tension, like he was trying too hard. Lucas filled him in, but it was completely unnatural."

"You and Lucas had time to work up to that. This was all dropped on Nate's lap. I'm sure he did an excellent job considering you made it home safe and sound."

"Oh, I'm not faulting Nate, so don't take it that way. All I'm saying is it was weird. The comfort I was used to was gone."

"Where was Lucas?"

"In the backseat. It was weird though when we got to my apartment."

"Because?"

"Well, I did it. There were hugs all around and then it got awkward." She pulled harder on her sleeves. "Lucas didn't think it was smart to stick around. Besides, he had a late-night coffee date." A snotty voice rolled out with her statement and she swallowed back her bitter words.

"What are you thinking?"

Her focus jumped around the room. To the wall where she tried in earnest to read his certificates. To the window, hoping to focus on anything but the elephant in the room she accidentally unveiled. She didn't want to think about… Things. "It's complicated." It was the best she could come up with.

"Tell me. Perhaps I can help uncomplicate it."

She sighed as the tears built and she closed her eyes for a breath hoping that would make them disappear. "I can't make sense of it." As her eyes opened, the tears fell. *Why am I crying over this?*

"Aurora," he said, scooting himself to the edge of the sofa. "Whatever you're thinking, this is a safe space."

She grabbed for a tissue, dabbing under her eyes.

"Are you and Nate back together?"

A nod.

"So, everything you worked hard for, you achieved, am I correct?"

Another nod. Another dab.

"You gained a remarkable friend in Lucas, you tackled your PTSD enough to drive forty minutes away, and come home with the man you set out to win back."

Another nod with a sniff this time. "But things have changed since."

"How?"

"Who do I start with?" She stretched out her legs and pulled her hands completely into her sleeves, balling up the tissue. A long, painful sigh. "I'm thrilled to be back with Nate, like over the moon, but I miss Lucas. I was with Lucas daily for nine weeks and it's hard to quit him cold turkey. Even when Nate and I were together, we weren't together that often. And now? Nate drives me to the U most days, but he's got his own classes, and he works two evenings a week. Plus, he has karate one evening a week. Did you know he helps teach a kid's class?"

Dr. Navin shook his head.

"Yeah, I didn't either."

"It's great you are learning about each other."

"We are. In many ways, it feels brand new, and yet it's not."

"That's expected. It *is* a fresh start."

She sighed.

Dr. Navin tipped his head as he readjusted himself. "But there's more, isn't there?"

"I miss Lucas."

"Yes, I understand that. You've mentioned it."

"Nate's gone most evenings, and Lucas still comes over, but he leaves early. Then I'm all alone. Nate stays over on weekends only."

"Why's that?"

"He and Brenda get along great. He figures with classes, work, karate, and everything else he has going on, it's easier to crash at home, where he can come and go as he needs. There's no worry on his part to wake anyone if it's late at night."

"He told you this? Or are you guessing?"

"No, we talked about it. And it's sweet that he thinks I'm in bed at ten, which so rarely happens, and his arrival to my place would keep me up. At his house, he lives in the basement which has a separate entrance, so he can come and go without disturbing anyone."

Dr. Navin sighed. "And Lucas? Does he still fight with his mom?"

"Yeah, but they've reached an impasse I guess. She's not going to change her stance on him staying in engineering, but he's already set everything in motion to switch faculties in January, and I suppose I helped with that."

"How?"

"I gave him a boat-load of money at the end of our training. The night he drove me out to the track, I gave him enough money to get through a year's worth of university."

"Wow, Aurora, how generous of you."

She blushed. "I didn't do for the accolades and I didn't do it to help him transfer. I gave him that money as a small token of my appreciation for everything he gave up helping me."

"I'm sure he was tickled pink."

"Actually, he was a little pissed off and said he wouldn't take it. But after a lengthy discussion, he finally agreed. He's now enrolled in psych for January."

"Ah, another doctor." Dr. Navin leaned back in his chair. Chris Johnson, Lucas' older sister, was a psychologist in Dr. Navin's office. "Well, I'm sure his mom will get over it."

"You see, that's the thing. I'm the reason for the change in Lucas. I'm the reason he can now afford to switch faculties and not ride on his brother's coattails. But there's a family history. The scholarship that afforded Lucas to take engineering is named after their grandfather."

"I see."

"So, you see where I'm going with this?"

"Not really."

"Lucas didn't try to fix me for any reason other than because I asked. He didn't swoop me off my feet and decide to heal me."

"Like Nate did."

"Exactly, although I love Nate for doing that. He really did jumpstart a process. But I needed Lucas' help. In a way, he needed me too. Needed to see that there was life beyond what he thought was a pretty straight and narrow path. He had blinders on, just as much as I did. He knew about the PTSD, but he taught me to trust and depend on someone else. Completely. Without worrying about what they'd give me in return. And that's something I never knew I needed so much."

"We're back to your feelings for Lucas."

"I've reached the conclusion that I do love him. For many more reasons than I'll ever admit. But it's not a romantical love. But no one else sees it."

"What do you mean?"

"I suspect Nate's jealous of Lucas because he knows how to calm me in a heartbeat or two. We have this natural closeness and it rubs Nate the wrong way."

"And you don't understand that?"

"No. Because there is nothing romantic between us."

"I remember you saying in a previous session how Nate had a girlfriend."

Her blood instantly boiled and her hands rolled into tight little fists. "That was different. There was kissing and sex between them."

"And you know this how? Did you see it?"

"No. Lucas told me they were together."

"And you believed him?"

"Dr. Navin, last time you tried to place a smidgen of doubt into my mind about Lucas, it almost worked. But I'm not going to doubt

Lucas. I saw the way Marissa acted around Nate when I was with him."

"My point is, you are getting all riled up about this Marissa and she's not in the picture. Nate's little brother is your security blanket. Nate's *brother*." He left the word hanging in the air. "You don't think *that* would bother him? We're not talking about a guy friend you work with, and you share a few secrets together. We're talking about a brother. And a brother's bond is a tough bond."

♥Chapter Six♥

Aurora slumped her shoulders as she walked into the waiting room.

"All done?" Nate said, dropping the magazine onto the pile atop the table as he stood.

"Yes." She walked passed him to the receptionist.

"Do you prefer the same time slot for your next appointment, Ms. MacIntyre?"

"Please." She grabbed her coat from the coat rack as the lady typed on the computer.

"All booked. See you in two weeks."

Aurora asked Nate, "Been here long?" Since the temperatures had dropped in the days following Thanksgiving, he'd offered to drive her to her appointment rather than have her walk. However, he had no desire to sit in a waiting room for an hour, especially in one where his sister also worked.

"Got back about ten minutes ago. Needed to pick up a suit for the banquet."

"Good. I'd hate for you to have waited for me."

A broad smile played on his face. "You're worth waiting for."

She raised her eyebrow, but said nothing, her mood shifting to the positive with his grin. They emerged from the building, tightening up their coats. "Brr..." she said, glancing to the sky. "It looks like it's going to snow."

"It's supposed to."

"The skies are very white."

"How was your therapy? Am I allowed to ask?" he asked.

She breathed in a quick inhale of the biting cold. "It's good. The thing about Dr. Navin, is he cuts right to the bone. He doesn't sugar coat anything. Sometimes that stings." *Like today.*

"Is that bad?"

"A few months ago, I would've said yes, but now…" She stopped at his car and shrugged while opening the passenger door. "Now, it doesn't really bother me. He tells me how it is. I like that. I can handle it."

"Have you been seeing him long? Chris has never mentioned him." Following her lead of getting into the car first, Nate slipped into the driver's seat.

"A few weeks after our breakup. I went through a few interesting doctors, but I settled with him. At first, he was a dick, but his words hung on me. Found myself really listening to him. Then he gave me homework."

Nate laughed, the most joyous sound filling the interior of his car, and filling her soul. "Homework? For real?"

"Yeah. Remind me, I'll show you when I get home."

Nate dangled the keys. "Ready?"

She took a long, calming breath. "Ready." A quick buckle up, and a glance at Nate before she closed her eyes. The vehicle rumbled to life beneath her.

Thankfully the ride from the clinic to home was a relatively short trip of five minutes. Totally doable now. But a couple months ago, it was sheer panic. Now, she counted each of the four stoplights, as the road was too busy to make any of them. So much for free-flowing traffic. At the fifth light, they turned right, only a half block from her parking stall.

The vehicle quieted, and she popped open her eyes.

"You're getting better at these."

"I'm trying." She forced a smile. Not her favourite mode of transportation, but it worked. That drive would equal a twenty-five-minute walk, so there was a plus to be able to face fear to save twenty minutes. There was a lot you could accomplish with twenty extra minutes.

"You know I've been thinking..."

"Can we talk about this outside the car?" She opened the door and put her feet on the asphalt.

Nate joined her. "Anyways," he said, alarming the car. "What would you say to sitting in the driver's seat?"

"Is that a joke?" Her voice pitched. She *was* in a good mood.

He flinched. "No."

"Seriously? I'm just getting to the point of tolerating a car ride without too much anxiety, and you want me to sit behind the wheel?"

"It was a thought."

"Well," she said, giving him a once over.

He stood seven inches higher than her, radiating confidence and a give it a try type attitude.

"It won't happen. I'm sorry."

"You wouldn't be driving. You'd be sitting there. No keys in the ignition even."

The mere idea of it caused her heart to pound, and her limbs to tingle. "I... I can't."

"Okay," he said, but he didn't sound convinced. "I'll re-work Operation Baby Steps." He smiled, and seeing the dimple in his cheek, warmed her heart. "I'll figure something out."

They entered her apartment a few minutes later, and she spotted one of Lucas' jackets hanging in the closet as she hung up her own. Ever since her reunion with Nate, her apartment lacked its usual warmth. Different. It was still her home, but it felt less so without his jovial laughter and his constant companionship.

Her backpack dropped to the floor by the door. "Hungry?"

"Only for you." He closed the door and tossed his coat on the nearby kitchen chair. His eyes lit up with playfulness.

"Well then," she said, grabbing his hand and leading him down the hall to her bedroom.

The twenty minutes saved by driving would work to her benefit.

"Okay, after that workout, I'm hungry for food now," she said, emerging from the bathroom. The damp cloth cooled her heated body as she ran it over her shoulders and breasts. Strutting over to her dresser, she pulled out a fresh pair of panties, and slid them up over her long, thin legs.

Nate eyed her as she got dressed. In haste, he grabbed his jeans off the floor and hopped into them. "Yeah, me too."

Dressed in pair of leggings and a long pink top, she led the way down to the kitchen. "What shall I make?" She opened the fridge and peered in.

"What's quick?"

The door closed. "Quick?"

"Yeah, I have lecture that starts in–" A glance to his watch. "Half an hour."

She sighed and leaned against the counter. "Well, I can make you a sandwich for the road."

"I'm sorry, I didn't realise how much time had passed." He bent down and brushed his lips against hers. "I'll pick you up in the morning?"

"You're not coming back tonight?"

He straightened up. "No. After the lecture, the guys and I are going to play basketball for a bit."

"Oh, okay."

His phone rang and as he looked at the display, he growled under his breath.

"Everything okay?" She reached out and touched his arm.

"It's just Marissa. She doesn't understand that you and I are back together. She wants to get back together."

"Oh," she said, trying desperately hard to keep her feelings under wraps.

"Hey," he said, lifting her chin and making eye contact with her. "It's you I want. It's you I love."

"Love you too." She didn't watch him leave. Not until the door latched in place, did she glance toward the exit.

♥Chapter Seven♥

Waking up in Nate's strong arms was the best way to greet the morning. She only wished it happened more often; like during the week. Weekends were her favourite for that reason alone. Breathing him in, she rolled over and stared at his handsome still sleeping face. The whiskers on his face shadowed the chin and gave him a rugged, sexy demeanour. His dark hair, a little longer in the off-season, hung above his eyes. Those perfect lips begged to be kissed.

"It's creepy when you stare at me like that."

She jumped. "I didn't know you were awake."

"I noticed when you moved. And your breathing wasn't like it was before."

"*That's* creepy."

"Says the girl who stares at me when I'm sleeping."

"But you weren't sleeping."

"Touché." He pulled her closer. "Good morning, beautiful." He popped open his dark eyes—irises like melted chocolate with flecks of crushed up peanuts.

She placed a deep kiss on him. "Morning." His bottom lip tasted so good as she sucked it between her teeth.

He pulled back a bit. "How'd you sleep?"

"Really good. Solid for once."

The tongue piercing of his ran over his teeth. "What's on the agenda for today?"

Fingertips trailed down his chest as her own heart sped up in anticipation. "I'm meeting Kaitlyn and Tatiana—"

"You mean those two have finally come up for air?" He laughed.

It was true. Since Tatiana's arrival, she'd barely got more than three words from Kaitlyn. However, after a desperate plea for help, Kaitlyn responded with something other than *can't right now.*

"I still haven't found anything for the banquet."

"You know the banquet's tonight, right?"

"Yes, but I want a sexy and yet respectable dress. It's a tough find." She winked. "I am the girlfriend to the owner of Northern Lights Racing, after all."

"Don't forget I'm a racer too."

"Will you be racing the late stocks next season?"

Nate's laugh bounced the bedroom walls. "Late model super stocks, but you almost got it." He tugged on a strand of her hair. "I'll have to see. I have a meeting with Jefferson Racing Monday evening to talk about the beast."

"Why?"

"It's not mine. I've been driving under Jefferson's banner, and the beast belongs to him."

"So, if you can't get the beast, you'll need to invest in a new car?"

"Yeah."

"And that costs lots of money."

"Exactly."

"So, sponsorships are huge."

"Now you're getting it." The dimple on his left cheek deepened.

She twirled her fingers down his naked chest and circled his belly button. "So, tonight could really be a big deal, if you get to meet with these big wigs your mom mentioned? How big are these big wigs?"

"Not as big as she'd have you believe. Mom's always making a mountain out of a molehill, but there are a few scouts sent up on behalf of the big US teams. Nothing's ever come out of that though. They basically get invited up as PR for our track."

"Oh."

"We're not big enough to attract the likes of Jimmie Johnson, Jeff Gordon, and company."

"Oh, that's too bad. Jeff Gordon's kind of cute."

"You think so, huh?"

"Yep, he's got dark hair…" She ran her fingers through Nate's hair. "Dark eyes. Five o'clock shadow." Her fingers trailed over his cheek. "Soft lips."

He pulled back, smiling. "How do you know they're soft?"

"They look soft."

"I didn't realise you had such a fan-crush on him." A quick glance around her room. "I don't see any posters hanging up."

She kissed his chest and nonchalantly added, "It was part of my training."

"To stare at Jeff? I may need to discuss things with Lucas a little more in-depth."

She laughed. "He insisted I watched a few hundred car crashes and interviews with the drivers. Kind of like a desensitising thing."

Nate nodded and stayed quiet.

Sensing a moment of hesitation, she kissed down his chest toward his belly button, leaving sweet little wet spots. "But let's not discuss Lucas right now."

Nate was lying in her bed, partially naked. She'd be damned if she was missing out on this.

A while later, they rolled out of bed, happy, sated, with a healthy flush over both their cheeks. Fresh from another romp in the shower, a scantily dressed Aurora barefooted into the kitchen to start breakfast. She had an hour until she needed to meet up with Kaitlyn and her girlfriend.

She balanced her weight on one foot, lifting and twisting the other.

"Are you sore?"

"Not at all. If anything, I'm quite relaxed."

His gaze fell to her lifted leg.

"Oh, just working out a little kink while the oil heats."

"You're really working with hot grease wearing only that?"

There was nothing wrong with her... outfit. Yes, her nightshirt was thin, but it was silky and comfortable, and at least it covered her from neck to her feet. Nate was dressed only wearing a pair of jeans. His naked chest, although not a model-sculpted body, was perfect to her and it begged to be touched. Again. She sized him up in comparison.

He poured himself a cup of coffee. "I'm not complaining."

"Yeah? Says the one barely dressed at all."

"At least I'm wearing underwear." A finger slipped under the spaghetti strap of her shirt, lifting it an inch high. "You've got nothing on under this."

"You were hungry, and it was quick to pull on."

"And will be easy to slip off when I have dessert."

A smiled leaked from her lips. "Stop it. I hear the growling in your tummy."

"Well, it was quite the workout this morning. That's two before we even eat."

A flush exploded on her face as she recalled the start to her day. "Yes, it was. I like starting my weekend days like this."

"Me too." He planted a kiss on her cheek and grabbed a couple of plates. "Just us for breakfast, or is Lucas joining in?"

"Just us."

The nearby drawer opened and slammed shut. "Sorry," he said, but he drummed his fingers on the counter. "You know, I've been thinking about the car, and Operation Baby Steps."

"Way to kill the mood."

"By talking about the car?"

She knew where this conversation was headed. Exactly which

road it was travelling down. It was a conversation Nate brought up on Tuesday, and Wednesday and Thursday. She assumed it was over when he was mum about it yesterday. "I'm sorry, Nate. I'm not ready to sit behind the wheel. Fuck, I'm barely able to sit in the passenger seat." Her words raced out of her, scared to even think what sitting in the driver's seat would do to her.

"You're doing great though. We make two trips a day."

"Yes, I'm aware." One trip to the university and one home. More than enough. Sometimes more, but not very often. "Isn't that enough?"

He screwed up his face. "Of course, it is. But…"

"But what?"

"I want the fear to be completely gone."

"But I'm not ready to drive again."

"And you weren't ready to be a passenger either and look what happened."

"Geezus, Nate. There's no desire for me to drive. I don't know why you can't understand that. I get that it's *your* livelihood, and you'd be helpless if you couldn't drive, but I'm not you. I'm perfectly okay being a passenger for you or Lucas or Dad on occasion, but that's it."

"I just don't understand…"

"What don't you understand?"

He backed up a little and sighed. "I don't get why you can take that big step in getting yourself into a vehicle for Lucas, but you can't get behind the wheel for me?" He spoke softly, keeping his voice calm and even.

Aurora lost her cool. "Oh my god, is that what you think? That I did it for him?" She dropped the flipper on the counter. "I did that for me, to prove something to you. To stop you from retiring. One might say I did it FOR YOU."

"So, you'll only get behind the wheel if you have something to prove?"

"Do you listen to yourself? Really? How do I put this in a way you'll understand? Losing you, having to push you out of my life was the second hardest thing I've ever done. But I couldn't do it. I couldn't stand to be away from you. Every day was a knife in my heart, twisting a little bit. But I forced myself. Made myself touch a car, get into a car, buckle myself up and go somewhere. That took a lot of time and dedication. But hear me out on this, Nate. I have no desire to ever operate a machine that could kill anyone. I drove that night. It was my fault that Momma and Carmen died." Her body shook from the ache she forced deep down. A soul-wrenching ache always surfaced with the recall of that horrible night. In a whisper, she said, "All my fault. I was in charge of their safety and I blew it. I should've checked to make sure no one was coming. I don't ever want that responsibility again. Never again."

His tone softened, just like the expression on his face. "It wasn't your fault, and the witnesses agreed."

"But it was." Her voice weakened. "I was the driver. And I failed. I paid heavily for that mistake too."

"Oh, Aurora." Strong arms wrapped around her. "Have you ever gone back there?"

"Back where?" she asked, shaking out of his embrace and flipping the French toast over before they burned to a crisp.

"Back to the scene of the accident."

Her fingers gripped the flipper tighter. "No, never."

"Why not? It would be good for you, I think."

"How would it be good for me?"

"Help you see how everything moved on."

"Of the five people directly involved, only two people survived. One's in jail though so I don't think that's moving on."

"But you're moving on. You've been doing so well. It would be closure for you."

"God, why does everyone keep telling me that. I know how they died. I was there. I know why they died. Because some asshole had a bloody brilliant idea to pound back the beers and drive. I know all the people involved. I don't need closure, Nate. I lost my momma and sister. I'll never get closure from that. I live with it every day."

"I think it would help a lot," his voice a whisper from behind.

Visiting the crash site wasn't interesting to her in the least. There were pictures—a quick Google search yielded a few—but she lived it entirely different than they'd have you believe. A part of her heart died in the wreck and never healed. Nothing would ever heal the damage. Seeing the scene would only make things worse, she was sure.

"Here's your breakfast," she said, dumping a couple pieces of blackened French toast onto his plate. She glanced at the clock. "I need to go if I'm going to meet the girls on time."

"I can drive you, if you give me a few minutes."

"No thanks. I'll walk." *I need to cool down.* "What time do you need me ready for tonight?"

He stood pressed against the counter, a sadness creeping onto his face. "I'll pick you up at five?"

"I'll be ready."

***

Aurora leaned back on her chair. "I'm so stuffed. I can barely move, how am I going to dance?"

And she wanted to dance. Her dress was made for movement. In the dressing room, after she slid the ice-blue satin straps over her shoulders and Kaitlyn zipped and hooked her closed, she did a twirl. The bottom of the satin and chiffon dress billowed out, giving her an ethereal princess feeling. Thankfully the dress was a stunning empire waist style and afforded her an overindulgent tummy-expanding space. "Check out my food baby."

Nate followed the gentle glide of her hand, horror creeping across his face as she patted her rounded middle.

"Told you the food was amazing." Brenda, who sat on her left, gave her a little nudge. Her boyfriend, Bill, sat on Brenda's right. "The dance starts after the awards, so you'll have time to feel better." Brenda had really outdone herself, to the point she was barely recognisable. Her normally flat chestnut brown hair was poufy with a tinge of a curl in it. Her beautiful, warm face was highlighted to bring out her high cheekbones and decadent eyelashes. It was weird to see her not sporting jeans and a hoodie. In a slimming dress, the loveliest shade of lavender you'd see in a perfect sunset, it easily took ten years off her, and she was already young.

Lucas kicked back from his chair, across the table. "They really outdid themselves this year. That steak was ah-mazing."

"It all was. I can't believe I stuffed down a dessert," she said, licking her lips and tasting a sprinkle from the cheesecake.

"Do you want anything to drink?" Nate asked.

"A peppermint tea, please. I need to de-bloat."

He leaned closer. "We'll work it off later, I promise." His whisper a tickle against her ears which warmed slightly with his comment.

Glancing at Lucas, who abruptly dropped his connection with her and fiddled with his napkin, she asked, "Where's Taylor?" Lucas' arm candy for the evening. His *flavour of the week* as Nate called the rotation of dates.

That brought his blue-greys back to hers. "Sitting with her family. I'll see her after the presentation."

Lights flickered above them and a tall, lanky man walked across the stage.

"Now the awards," Nate said after a drink of coffee.

The lights dimmed in the hall, and the presenter continued over to the podium.

"Anything we should be watching for?"

"Not for me," he said, his tone light, but she heard the sadness underneath it all. "But Lucas will get his award in a bit."

She was very proud of that, as he nicknamed his car *the Chaser*, always chasing first place. Not this year though. This past season he totally kicked ass. Although she hadn't watched a single race in person, she checked the app he'd shown her once. Or twice. "What about you?"

He whispered, "I didn't have the points to rank high enough to get any award."

"I thought you had placed a few times?"

He sighed and pulled his chair closer to hers. "Yeah, but I was sidelined for a couple of weeks with the crash you saw and I was out for another couple with the ones you didn't."

Her eyes widened, and the blood drained from her face. "Ones? As in plural? You were in more crashes?"

"Yeah, but they weren't my fault."

"When?" Her voice barely squeaked out the words.

"It doesn't matter." He didn't meet her eyes.

Curiosity took over, and she shot a quick you're-going-to-explain-yourself look to Lucas. "Before or after that day you burned out of the parking lot?"

Nate's narrowed eye studied her. "Both. But don't worry about it."

How could she not worry about it? Lucas had never mentioned anything to her about it all summer, in fact, he'd told her everything was going well. She was going to have a stern talk with him later about this. She'd demand an explanation, but he had his back to her.

Nate jumped his chair closer to her. "I can see the look on your face and the daggers you're shooting at him."

Resuming her focus on her boyfriend, she kept the distance between them snug.

"Whatever you two did this summer, I certainly wasn't aware of. I'm sure it must've gone the other way too."

Apparently.

"What's good for the goose, is good for the gander."

"Yeah, whatever. It was serious enough to take you out of racing for a couple of weeks, so I should've known."

His voice was low and deep, firing up her insides even though she was agitated. "What would it have accomplished? Absolutely nothing, aside from setback or two, am I right?"

Totally. A weak nod. "But–"

"No buts about it. It's done, over with. I had no injuries. The beast got fixed. Life moves on."

Nate gave his attention to the man on stage, who pandered on about the future of stock car racing and how some of the best NASCAR drivers had their start at a small track, like the one they raced at. The presenter glanced around the room adding that perhaps a future XFINITY racer sat amongst them and he pressed play on a video presentation.

She tuned both guys out almost completely, seeing a picture of Nate as he collected one of his wins. Feeling a little devastated about the crashes she didn't know about, she understood knowing would've set her back. Days if not weeks of her training. Resigned that 'what happens at the track, stays at the track' was a mentality she was going to have to get used to, especially being the girlfriend of a race car driver.

Around her the crowd broke out into applause as the season's third place winner's name was called—Marissa Montgomery. The beautiful brunette, who stole the show in a stunning two-piece bubble gum pink floor-length gown, ascended onto the stage to collect her trophy and cash.

A glance at Nate was all Aurora needed. Although he clapped along with the others, a sadness washed over his face that it wasn't him collecting the award.

She squeezed his hand. "Next year?"

"Maybe." He shrugged but didn't glance in her direction.

"How far off were you from a trophy?"

"One point. Our crashes and subsequent DNFs kept us from getting higher in the standings."

"Oh, wow." She hadn't realised it was *that* close. Nate missed out by one measly point. Would he have ranked higher if he hadn't been involved with Marissa? Lucas had shared with her how Marissa would be a distraction on the track, instead of a fierce competitor.

Another round of applause as Marissa was joined on stage by the second and first place winners; a guy named Chad, and a lady named Kendra. Someone in the back of the room whistled loudly. As the winners descended the stage stairs, closer to their table, Marissa's gaze hardened as she focused on Nate.

"Don't worry about her," he said to Aurora, but his eyes were focused on his ex-girlfriend.

Don't worry? Yeah, right. She watched as Marissa turned away from them and holding her trophy in her left hand, sauntered through the crowd, weaving her way to the bar. She leaned against it seductively as she openly flirted with an older man in a grey tux.

"Hey," Nate said, nudging her out of her staring. "This is Lucas' category."

Well this she wouldn't miss.

The presenter talked about how there was no pressure on the Feature class drivers to excel to the big leagues, and how most of the drivers made it their weekend hobby to race hard and play harder. While he spoke, a short video of highlights ran on the screen.

"There he is," she said with a hint of excitement in her voice. It was neat seeing Lucas up on the big screen for a few brief shots. She'd only watched him race twice; both times at the start of the season. As the video showed shots of the pit area, you could tell Lucas had a lot of fun. In most of the pictures, he was smiling, or photo bombing or holding a tool in his hand.

A few lingering words from the presenter. The third place and second place were called. "Our first place winner is Lucas Johnson."

Aurora cheered and whistled as Lucas took the stage to collect his trophy.

"Gee, if I knew you'd get that excited, I would've tried harder," Nate said, a trace of jealousy in his voice.

"Wait until next year." She winked. "And imagine it tenfold."

"I do like a challenge." His lop-sided smile warmed up his face.

Lucas re-joined them at the table, the sizeable trophy placed toward the middle.

The awards ceremony carried on through a few more classes, Nate trying his best to explain and fill in the gaps the announcer didn't explain fully. As he finished, the lights dimmed further, and the disco ball threw out colours all around them as the DJ took over the mic.

"Now, we can dance," Nate said, rising and extending his hand to her.

"Ladies room first?" she asked and headed to the back of the hall.

Relief settled over her once her bladder was drained, and she powdered her face lightly. After tucking in a stray strand of hair, she walked back out into the banquet hall. Music poured out from the open doors, and flashes of reds, blues, and yellows sprinkled the room like confetti.

She passed by racers holding their trophies, posing for pictures with the track logo behind them. *Wonder if Lucas got any pics?* She weaved her way through the tables, heading for her tall, dark-haired man.

Nate stood twenty feet away, talking animatedly with a guy she did not recognise. Nate's hands were flying all around, and even from a distance, a huge smile was plastered on his face. Mr. Unrecognisable consumed every word Nate spoke. Was he an up and comer? A rookie looking for advice? A sponsor? Whatever they were discussing, it brought sheer joy to Nate.

Lucas intercepted her. "How about a dance while you wait for Nate to finish up with that guy?"

"What would Taylor say?"

He searched the area and pointed. "Probably nothing. She's dancing with her dad right now. I can dance with her later."

Her gaze flittered back to Nate and the stranger. They were deep in conversation, based on the lips moving and heads bobbing. "Yeah one dance shouldn't hurt."

They had a lot of fun last time they danced. Until it went too far and made her second-guess everything. There was no way that would happen here, surrounded by a hundred or more people in a very public setting, would it? She nodded, and they pushed their way to the dance floor.

His hand, slightly rough and calloused, held hers tight.

"Have you been taking lessons?" she asked as he two-stepped her around the dance floor.

"Not at all, why?"

"Last time, you weren't this good." She laughed.

"Yeah, well last time we weren't dancing to a country song. It was that Top 40 crap you like. This is real music."

A giggle escaped her. "There is nothing wrong with Taylor Swift." She gave a playful smack to his shoulder.

"She was country music's darling until she crossed over to the other side."

"The other side?" She laughed harder. "T-Swizzle has always been Top 40."

"Nope, not always." He spun her around, his grip on her lower back tighter, but the giant smile on his face said otherwise.

"Well, she's definitely no Guilana and her operatic voice, but at least you can shake to her music."

"You listen to Guilana?"

"Every night. I can see why you enjoy her. Her voice really is remarkable."

"I'm impressed. Maybe there's hope for you after all."

"Perhaps."

"How'd you know how to two-step if you're so anti-country music?"

"I'm not anti-country. But you're a good leader, and dancing is dancing. If you can move and shake it, it counts."

They reached the stage where a sea of people, old and young, milled about surrounding them in fluid movements. The tables they had sat at, were lost to her. A small disco ball flickered with multi-coloured lights, bathing them in shades of red, blue and green. The beat from the music matched the tempo in her body as they sashayed and twirled–her dress billowing out around their feet.

"Who's Nate talking to anyways?"

"I missed his name, but he said he was a rep from Rooker Racing."

"You say it like it means something."

"Not really. Rooker Racing is a small organisation under a

larger umbrella one. Ever hear of Whitewood Motorsports?"

She shook her head as she two-stepped backwards.

"It's strictly a PR thing for them to be up here. They're always looking for talent and like to inquire about new blood."

"Is Nate considered new blood?"

"Could be."

"What would they do with him?"

"Depends on what their goal is and who started the conversation. Maybe Nate approached him to inquire about being a sponsor, or how to acquire sponsorships. Maybe it's more than that. We'll ask in a few minutes."

She twisted her head, trying to find Nate. It was impossible. There were too many people, and she was smack-dab in the middle of them all. Giving up the search, she focused on the music, allowing it to infiltrate her soul. "So, what do you get for first place?"

"Bragging rights."

"No seriously?"

"I get a nice prize for next season. All my track fees and racer registrations are paid for, plus deep discounts on parts and accessories from Bradley's Motors."

"Seriously? That's not much."

"It may be no cash prize, but it really helps out in the expense department. At least I won't have those fees to worry about. Any spare income I get, I can put toward the car, or other expenses. There's not as much cash for features as there is for the super stocks."

"Why is that?"

"There's big money in super stocks, as it's a NASCAR thing. That's why the PR guys are here. To meet up with the stock drivers and see if they have a shot at driving on the big tracks."

She searched again for Nate and spotted him. He was still chatting with the other man.

The music changed tempo and slowed down as a familiar voice crooned through the speakers.

"Want to sit down?" Lucas asked.

"Nah, I'm good. If you are." She cocked an eyebrow.

Lucas pulled her close, his hand slipping from her waist to her lower back. He didn't make eye contact. "I can dance all night."

"We'll see about that." She laughed. "Hey, this song…" The lyrics floated around her, transporting her back in time. A cliff-side lookout. A mesmerising sunset.

He twisted and spun her out, reeling her back in. Her dress billowed at her feet with the spin. "Yeah, *this* song."

She couldn't figure out his tone. Was it sarcastic or sweet? She lightly squeezed his shoulder where her left hand rested. Did it remind him of that summer night at the ravine where they danced in perfect synchronisation in the twilight? A search over his face revealed nothing. No smile, no sadness. It was a blank slate as he gazed out over her head into the crowd.

The song wrapped up, and they separated. As she stepped backed, she thanked him. To her right stood Nate, a hint of a smile contrasting the arms crossed over his chest.

"There you are," she said, walking over to him.

"When I said there'd be dancing, I meant with me." He winked.

"Oh stop." She pushed playfully on his shoulder. "We were killing time while you talked with that guy."

That guy walked by and clapped Nate on the back. "See you Tuesday."

Her hand snaked around Nate's waist, but her gaze followed the man as he twisted around the tables, exiting the banquet hall. "Who is he anyways?"

"Colton Rooker."

"What's going on Tuesday?"

"A meeting," Nate said as a broad smile split his face in half. "He wants to discuss me driving under his label."

Her forehead creased. "How does that work? How can you can drive under his label and your own?"

He laughed. "I can't do both. Remember when I told you how I call the beast mine, but it belongs to Jefferson Racing Enterprises?

Monday's meeting is to see if I can buy it out. Well, Tuesday I have a meeting with Rooker. If I can't get the beast, I may have a strong back up plan."

"So, this Rooker guy is better?" She was so confused. Maybe she should've spent more time learning about the politics and the behind the scenes to better understand, in place of watching crash videos.

"Not better necessarily. Just different. I know he goes to a lot of tracks around the country scouting out talent. He was responsible for getting Tad McMurtle signed."

"Who's that?"

"A NASCAR racer."

"Never heard of him."

"It's not important. It's that Rooker Racing has that connection."

"So, you're saying if this Rooker guy is interested in you, you could be racing someplace else?"

"The possibility exists, yes." He picked her up and twirled her around. "I'll know more on Tuesday."

Like a mic drop to the floor, her smile fell off her face. *But I just got you back.*

"What's with that face?" he asked as his thumb stroked her cheek.

She brushed it off to the side. "I don't know. A feeling I have."

"Are you okay?"

"Yeah. But I can't help feeling like I'm going to lose you. Again."

As he held her close, he whispered in her ear. "I can't see how you would as I'm not going anywhere."

♥Chapter Eight♥

By the time the clock struck midnight, Aurora's feet were sore and a tad swollen, and her hips ached. "We should go home. I won't be able to move very well if they seize up on me." She rubbed her hips and winked in Nate's direction. "Right now, I'll need a full body massage and a long soak in a tub."

Nate's eyes twinkled. "Alright, let's say goodnight."

Brenda had already left with Bill, so it was a matter of locating Lucas.

"He's out on the dance floor."

She scanned through the crowd, stopping on her best friend dancing with his date for the evening—Taylor—a petite blonde in a green dress.

Lucas turned in her direction. When she waved goodbye, he whispered inaudibly to the blonde, and ran up to Aurora. "You leaving?"

"Yeah, it's time. My hip's starting to ache."

Alarm crossed his face.

"Nothing a hot bath can't help."

"You're sure?"

"Yeah." She wanted something stronger, like a Percocet, but those were banned, and she'd tried exceptionally hard to not crave one. But it proved impossible to not want to fall back on her old habits. She'd make do with the Advil she kept buried and hidden.

Lucas studied her, his gaze hovering over her eyes as though he could read her mind. “Call me tomorrow?”

“You bet.”

Lucas nodded to Nate. “See you later.”

“Tomorrow.”

She linked her arm through Nate’s as they left the banquet hall behind them.

“I’ll go grab our coats,” Nate said.

“Great. Meet me at the bathrooms.” Clutch firmly in hand, she made her way over to the ladies room.

She checked the area, dipping low enough to peek for shoes in the stalls. No one was in there. Sighing, she opened the tiny purse and unzipped the hidden compartment. There in all their glory were two aqua-coloured extra-strength Advils. Sweet, sweet intoxication.

But do you really need them?

She rubbed her hip. It ached with a persistent throbbing, and periodically a sharp pain from the sciatica shot down her legs.

Guess that answers that.

She cupped the pills in her hand.

It’s just Advil. An over-the-counter medication. It’s not bad. It’s not addictive. Anyone can get them. And I can quit them at any time.

She laughed. As if reasoning with herself was something a sane person did. Another glance around the bathroom. The quietness was unnerving. She cupped her other hand with tap water. Drinking from her hand, the cool liquid filled her suddenly dry mouth, and she popped the two pills in and swallowed.

It had been so long—weeks even—since her last Advil taken after a particularly gruelling physio appointment. On her empty stomach, it didn’t take long to feel the effects tonight. By time they reached his car in the parkade, the ache had diminished greatly.

He held the door open for her as always. “Whenever you’re ready.”

Rearranging the bulk of her dress into the car, she said, “Let’s go." Her seatbelt clicked into place.

They drove out of the parkade, and onto the city's main drag. Lost in her own hazy reflections of the evening, the trip passed by quickly until the car's gentle hum disappeared.

"Where are we?" The area was as unfamiliar to her as politics in racing.

"Thought we'd make a stop first and check out the moon."

She craned her head, scanning the skies. "Where is it?"

He came over and opened the door, helping her from the confines. "Over there." A long finger pointed south-east.

They walked over to a park bench, and as they passed the building, the partially full moon hung above the bridge.

"Wow."

"Yeah, it's gorgeous when it hangs over the High Level Bridge."

"Where exactly are we?"

"Below us, is a golf course. I want to say the river valley one, but since I'm not a golfer, I'm not sure." His finger raised. "Those buildings over there, across the river, that's the university."

"Really?" She'd never seen it from this viewpoint. So many large buildings scrawled across the campus but from this distance they resembled a child's building set. Most of the interior lights extinguished, the area mirrored a postcard image as the rising moon created illustrious shadows.

"The engineering quad is on the right."

That faculty was housed in the north-west corner. Her department, and Lucas' future department were situated on the south end, far from the river. "I really should walk around campus more often."

"Yes, you should. It's beautiful."

She shivered under her dress coat; it was barely thick enough to keep her covered as she dashed from building to building. It wasn't hers, either. She'd dug it out of Carmen's closet. "It's cool. But why are we here? We could've seen the moon from my apartment."

"You'll see."

She nodded and narrowed her eyes, not fully convinced.

"Come on, let's go for a walk. Your hip's not bothering you so much it would impede you from taking a moonlit stroll with your boyfriend?"

A quick check. *Nope.* Everything felt damn good. "Still looking forward to a full body massage when I get home though." She gave him a subtle wink.

They walked hand in hand to a set of lights and crossed over. Down the road and past a building, she leaned into him, his arms wrapping tightly around her shoulders. They crossed a small one-way street. He led her over to a railing and glanced over.

She stopped in her tracks. "Where are we?" Taking a couple steps, she inched closer to the post where black signs with white lettering were raised above them.

Underneath the sign, she shivered unexpectedly. The street names were all too familiar. "Nate?" she gasped, the air around her freezing her to the bone with each rapid breath.

A car zoomed passed her down the one-way road.

"I pulled the report. This is the street the–" he coughed, but it sounded like asshole, "–drove down." Pointing to the right, he said, "You were headed in that direction." His hand moved across the horizon.

Firmly gripped in his hand, they crossed the quiet street. "I don't know, Nate. Something isn't right."

"What do you remember?"

The building anxiety changed her view. The area became blurry and indescribable. "I was wearing jeans and a long sleeve white t-shirt. My hair was in a long braid and I had on ballet flats. Something easy to shop in." Her breathing sped up. "We'd finished up supper at Bucatini's. Carmen told me to drive and to take this scenic road back to the hotel." Her eyes roved about as if by searching for it, she'd see it through the buildings. "I didn't want to drive as I wasn't familiar with the city, but Carmen insisted as she'd and Momma had had too much to drink."

A pounding deep in her chest threatened to break its confines.

A seatbelt clicked. The engine started.

"I remember laughter and singing. We were singing to a Martina McBride song." The melody sang clearly through her head. "Carmen told me to stay to the right, otherwise we'd be going down into the river valley, so I did."

A flash of lightning on her left raised the tiny hairs on the back of her neck. Thunder cracked loud enough to be heard over the music.

"I'd been driving for less than five minutes."

Brilliant lights beamed from her right side. She whipped her head around and in a sick slo-mo watched them grow larger and larger until they blinded her completely.

"We were crushed against a brick wall. I distinctly remember there being a brick wall."

A head shake to erase the vision like one would do on an Etch-A-Sketch, and similar to the toy, a faint image always remained. No matter how many times you shook it, it was still there. A loud sigh escaped her lips. Her system felt hyper-stimulated and although she knew she couldn't run miles, her body produced the energy for it.

But the memory didn't match up with the reality of her view. Glancing down the road, there was no brick wall. Concrete pillars with metal railings as far as the eye could see, but no brick wall. "I was pinned between it and the other car." She walked a few paces, checking the area. "This isn't the place." A sigh of relief, a slump of the shoulders.

Nate leaned against a metal railing. A breeze fanned his hair, and he tightened his jacket. "This is it. I've checked."

"You're wrong. There was a brick wall. I distinctly remember a brick wall."

The accident was earlier at night during a summer thunder storm than the current time, but still, something about the area should be familiar, right? Why could she recall the mundane clothing she wore, but not remember the big buildings around her? She hadn't heard the song since that night, yet she remembered the lyrics and who sang it most off key.

Carmen.

So why was she remembering a brick wall when there wasn't?

Stepping over to the railing, she continued to examine the area. No, he had to have the address wrong, a number mixed up. This clearly wasn't the place. The scene of her life-altering accident.

"I guess when the city repaired this, they changed it. Made it better and stronger."

"Why would they do that?" She gave him a quizzical look. "You've got the wrong place. You have to."

"I don't. I can prove it."

"How? You weren't there. Maybe the report you got had an error."

"I'm in the right spot."

She followed his gaze over the area. The street lamps bathed a blue structure in a soft glow, and a step to the right made part of it wink at her. Stepping onto the concrete riser, she stood in front it, her eyes squinting to read the details on the shiny plaque.

The words sharpened under the light from Nate's phone.

In loving memorial of Angelica, Carmen and Rebecca whose lives were cut short on May 24, 2014. Forever in our hearts.

"What?" Her clutch fell to the ground as her fingers traced the names, the cool of the metal nipping at her fingertips. The letters became blurry as tears formed. Stepping back, she stumbled and found Nate standing right behind her. "How'd you…?"

He shrugged and said nothing.

"Who?" The tears warmed up her cheeks as they flowed.

"I don't know, but I have my suspicions."

Oh my god. This was *it. This was the spot where my family died.* The more she surveyed the area, the stronger the waves of flashbacks.

One crashing on top another. The sounds of crunching plastic, grinding metal, snapping glass. The pain crept in fast and furious. It settled deep in her bones as the memory recalled her pelvis crushing as the console slammed her into the arm rest of the driver door. Pain arched through her leg as it bent and snapped. The air bag exploded in her face and broke her nose. The cracking of a rib or two she heard microseconds before it tortured her chest. In the world's quickest thought, she wondered if it punctured her lung as each breath stung. Her arms no longer felt attached. The agony was as real to her now as it was on that fateful night. Her mind physically transported her back in time. Knees weakened, and she tipped, Nate preventing her from reaching the ground.

"I got you."

Through her tear-stained view, she focused on him. "It hurts."

"Where?"

Unable to see beyond the tears, she closed her eyes. "My hips, my back." A skip in her breathing. "My heart."

"Okay, let's go. Can you move?"

She murmured as she tried but it was like learning to walk all over again. The pain was nauseating. Suddenly, she was lighter than air, and the cool breeze over her face freeze-dried the tear trails. Her mind as grey as the morning sky, each step getting darker until everything became black.

❤Chapter Nine❤

Aurora felt as though she was coming off the Isas—special pills her father gave her for road trips. Everything was hazy. Nothing sounded crystal clear. She blinked and tried to focus on her surroundings, but it was useless.

She wanted to move, but her body weighed a thousand pounds.

Soft breathing came from her left. A TV was on but it was faint and far away.

Where am I?

Familiar smells surrounded her, so she assumed she had to be in her apartment. But how did she get here?

As she twisted, someone moved beside her. "Nate?" Her voice cracked and sounded gravelly as if a cheese grater had scratched up the inside of her throat.

"Aurora." His hand softly caressed her cheek.

Not wanting to be touched, she pushed hm away.

"She's awake," he yelled, his voice directed away from her.

"Stop yelling," she whispered, rolling and covering her ears. Things were still foggy. Her legs dropped over the edge of her bed and she scrambled to sit, but a dizzy spell washed over her. "What happened?" Her head fell back against a pillow.

Footsteps, belonging to at least a couple of people, came from her left. "How are you doing, Aurora?" A familiar female voice. Chris.

What's she doing in my apartment?

A long exhale. "I'm dizzy." Her hand covered her eyes, not that it mattered, they were closed anyways. She quickly and gently rubbed her face. Everything was intact.

"Okay."

The last thing I remember is the monument and the pain. Everything after that is blank.

With great trepidation, her hand moved to her hip, and she gave it a little rub. It was in one piece and it didn't hurt, thank god, but she could've sworn it was smashed. Again.

"Tell me what you're thinking," Chris' voice said beside her.

She opened her eyes and surveyed her surroundings. She still wore her beautiful blue dress. Light flooded in from the hallway, making the room brighter than she would've expected, or liked. The clock flashed 4:38. It was the middle of the night as the curtains were open, the blackness beyond them. Nate sat beside her on the bed, Chris knelt on the floor on her other side, and Lucas hung back a bit, closer to the door. All of them, however, had one thing in common. They each bore concern. "Right now, I'm curious as to why you all look worried."

"What were you thinking about when you rubbed your hip?" Always the professional, always so soothing, always hard to refuse to answer. Especially when she looks at you with love and genuine friendship.

She exhaled again. "I was relieved it wasn't hurting anymore."

"It hurt before?"

"Yes and no."

The faces all stared at her.

"I mean when we first got to the place where Momma and Carmen died, it didn't hurt." *Anymore.* But she wasn't sharing *that* with anyone. "After walking around and seeing the monument there, everything started hurting. And not like a dull back ache. Like I was being crushed again."

Chris said softly, "That must've been awful."

"It really was."

"And how are you feeling now?"

"More than a little confused." Her eyes jumped from Chris to Nate and over to Lucas. "Why are you all here?"

Nate spoke first. "You fainted, and I was worried. She's the first one–"

"The first person you call when there's an issue with me. I know." Tendrils of hair fell in her face as she sat up.

His finger lifted her chin. "Because we all care about you."

Turning her head to Chris, she said, "So what happened?"

"You blacked out. Your body became overwhelmed, and this was the best way for it to handle it." Chris patted Aurora's hand. "It's not ideal, obviously."

"So, what does that mean? I'm suddenly afraid of cars again?"

"You tell me."

Unable to meet Chris' gaze head on, she twisted away. There was no way she'd consider looking at Nate as she sensed his tension and didn't want to see it on his face. Lucas seemed a safe bet, but she wasn't about to chance it. Ignoring both men, she firmly placed two feet on the floor and stood.

Hands all rushed to crowd her.

"I'm fine," she said as she walked to the bathroom and closed the door. Did they expect her to fall or something? She shook her head in disgust.

She lowered the lid on the toilet and sat. What the hell was going on with her? Why would her mind betray her? The night had been perfect until the monument. *Am I afraid of cars again? I don't think so. I got into one last night. I didn't even take a Xanax, although I really could use one right now. My fucking heart feels like it's running a marathon.*

She waited a few minutes before splashing cool water on her face, washing away her raccoon eyes and mascara stains. Hoping the coast was clear, she inched open the door and peeked out.

"Hey, you okay?"

Feet moving slowly across the floor, she leaned against the wall nearest her bedroom door. Voices echoed down the hall. A sigh louder than she expected, escaped from her mouth.

"Of course, why wouldn't I be?"

"You can try fooling them, which I don't think would be possible, but you can't fool me."

"I know. I'm just so confused about the whole thing." She walked over and sat beside Nate on the bed. "My body and mind betrayed me. Why would it do that?"

A warm arm wrapped around her shoulders and she leaned into him. "I don't know, but I'm truly sorry. I shouldn't have taken you there. I should've listened to Chris."

"Yes, next time, please do."

"Next time? You mean you want to try that again?"

Her head whipped up to stare him in the eyes.

"Gotcha." He smiled and gave her a squeeze. "I'm not ready for that anytime in the distant future. Plus, Chris is really pissed with me."

"Because you didn't listen?"

"Yeah." He shifted. "Nothing hurts?"

"No."

Nate sighed, as if all the terrible feelings he'd been holding back could escape with one sound. "I'm so glad. I really am sorry."

"What were you thinking?"

"That it would bring you closure?"

"Nate, how many times do I have to tell you, I don't want nor need closure?"

"But I thought I could–"

"The only thing I need right now is a Xanax, or a perc. Something to help me forget that the whole thing even happened."

"You don't seem like you're having an anxiety attack, and I'm super, super hesitant of you getting your hands on a perc."

"Fine." But it wasn't fine.

It didn't matter if she'd gone through a detox of sorts, it always hung over her. It was always there. Like the sun shining. Just the thought of it in her system excited her. But it had been a long time since she'd had a perc. Advil on the other hand…

"Can I have one anyways?"

His face twisted. "Do you really need it?"

"No, I don't *really* need it. I just want one to relax and drift away." Her shoulders slumped, and she rolled her head forward. "That's bad, right?"

"Bad? No. Concerning? Definitely." He stood and looked at her with love. "I'll talk to Chris." Nate left the room.

She knew better. Chris wouldn't have anything on hand, she wasn't stupid. Besides, she'd tried that trick over the summer during the training sessions. When they were practising, Chris carried meds for her, but Aurora had to get the order filled at a pharmacy and pass the pills directly into Chris' hand. That was the only way she'd have access to pills. Chris wasn't a walking pharmacist. Getting her to write a prescription was next to impossible–those orders came from her main psychiatrist. She was screwed before Nate walked into the room. She'd have to find another way.

♥Chapter Ten♥

"Everything alright?"

"Yeah, it's time to get up. I don't want to sleep all day," Aurora said to Nate as she rubbed her sleepy eyes. Covering them from the bright light streaming in, she stole a peek to the clock. It was 10:47.

"But it's Sunday. We're allowed." He pulled her close.

Giggling, she pushed out of his embrace. "I'm putting on the coffee."

Unsure if she still had company, she donned a housecoat and tiptoed down the hall to the kitchen. The spare bedroom door was closed, so she assumed someone was still around. The couch was empty though, so only one person stayed. Likely Chris.

Nate snuck up on her. "Chris left after you fell back asleep. But she wants you to call."

"I will. In a bit." She tipped her head to the spare room. "Lucas stayed?"

"Yeah. Did you honestly think he'd leave?"

No. She shook her head as relief filled her. "What about his date?"

"Hell if I know."

The kitchen was quiet, aside from the coffee dripping into the pot, and she wished her head would join in the silence. She hated how her mind took opposing sides. When she did well, the cheering was enough to rival huge stadiums, but when something went wrong…

All she heard were 'weakling' and 'can't handle a little visit'. The PTSD had made another mark on her heart and she was unsure if it would ever be erased.

Nate rubbed her shoulders while she braced herself against the counter. His strong hands firmly started at her shoulders, stroking downward until he reached her hands, when he'd begin again.

"That's nice, thanks." She closed her eyes and focused on the soothing motion, matching her breathing to the rhythm. The voices quieted, not a lot, but enough they became background noise. Coffee in hand, she ambled across the carpet and slumped down on the couch.

Nate sat beside her and gave her knee a rub. "What are you thinking?"

"Nothing and everything."

"You do that a lot, you know."

Her shoulders rolled inward. "It's complicated. My thoughts are very negative right now. I'm in shock how my mind and body can do that—that pain last night felt real, and yet, I know it wasn't. I don't understand. I was doing so well. I was making progress, and after a visit, my mind became so overwhelmed it shut down my whole body? Ugh. I'm so confused."

"I can't understand what you're thinking, but I agree with your frustration. And again, my apologies. I honestly thought it would help."

"How? How did you think it would help?" A fire burned in her core and she readied for a fight.

"I figured it would help wrap up your success. To show you how far you've come."

"I don't need to visit the scene of the accident to have grasped my little success. I drive with you every day."

"I kept thinking it would give you closure and help you move on."

"Nate, I was moving on. I've accomplished more in the past six months than I had in the past two and half years. Closure to me, would've been the opportunity to say goodbye to Momma and Carmen. But I'll never get it. The last time I saw Momma…"

An image flashed in her mind. Momma's head on her shoulder, blood dripping from a gash in her forehead. She shuddered. Unexpectedly another picture, via the rear-view mirror, floated to the surface—her sister singing along without a care in the world.

"I'll never get them back. They were taken from me, from everyone. And there's no closure on that. Besides it's such an overused word."

"It is," Lucas' voice carried out from behind the wall separating the living room from the kitchen.

She rose from the couch and headed to pour him a coffee. "Did we wake you?"

"Sort of." Lucas was bent over, staring at his reflection in the chrome coffee pot. He ran his fingers through his hair in a weak effort to tame it. "But it's no biggie. It was time to get up anyways." He poured himself a cup before she did, adding in a sizeable amount of milk and a spoonful of sugar. Tipping his head, he motioned for them to head back to the living room.

Nate hadn't moved from his spot, and she sat beside him.

Lucas grabbed a kitchen chair and brought it into the living room, turning it backwards as he straddled it. He set his cup on the side table by Nate. "So, what's the deal for today? Should we encourage you to get into a car and go for a ride to prove to yourself you're not having setback issues, or should we give you the day off to process it, and start fresh with class tomorrow?" He glanced at Nate.

Nate shrugged. "I'm on board with getting you into the car."

"Those are my only options?"

"You have a third plan?" Lucas squinted at her.

"Well… maybe. Give me a moment."

It was either face it or not, there really was no third option. Could she hide out in her room all day? Watch tv and pretend nothing happened last night? No. Neither of them would let her get away with that, and besides, it would be a terrible way to enjoy the day.

She rose and stood at the patio door. Far below, a small sea of vehicles reflected the sunlight, making the windows sparkle like diamonds.

Does the thought of sitting in Nate's car scare me?

A quick run through of any symptoms. Aside from a skip in her heartbeat, it didn't rattle her more than usual. But the idea of not tackling it today, calmed her more than it should've. It would be nice to sit around and enjoy a lazy Sunday, with a nice brunch where they'd all laugh and enjoy themselves. Reality could be what they watched on tv.

Her gaze flickered between the brothers who were as different as night and day. Nate was the epitome of nervousness; hands wrung together, and he gently cleared his throat as if he were sure she'd choose the uncomplicated way out and he'd need to put together a quick defence. Lucas, on the other hand, wore a calm façade, and rested his chin on top of his hands, which balanced nicely on the back of the chair. Always ready to go with the flow.

She opened her mouth and paused, closing it back up. What was it she really wanted to do? For starters, pleasing both guys, but more importantly, she wanted to prove what happened last night was an anomaly–unlikely to happen again.

"Okay. Let's meet in the middle. We'll go for a quick drive later to the sport pub down the street for chicken wings or something. But it will have to be around supper time. Deal?"

The guys looked at each other and back to her.

"Yeah. That works." Nate nodded in agreement as he rose from the couch.

Lucas said, "If you think that's best, I'm on board."

"I do."

"Great," Nate retrieved his chirping phone and gave it a once over, re-pocketing it hastily. "Do you mind if I run home and grab a few things?"

"I don't mind at all."

"Do you have a printer here?"

Her heart sunk a bit. Here, she'd hoped he'd wanted to spend the afternoon watching a movie or playing video games, not do boring school work. "Behind the cabinet doors." She pointed to the bookshelf in the corner of the living room, and remembering what she had strategically hidden there, decided to show him herself. Hunching down, she opened the doors and waving a hand across like a show girl, she pointed out the obvious. "It's not fast, but it works well enough."

He checked it out. "Wireless?"

"I sure hope so."

"Great."

"If you're nice to me, I may even give you the password." A sweet little laugh escaped her as she locked eyes with Nate.

His phone chirped again, and he gave it another glance.

"Go ahead and answer."

He shoved the phone into his back pocket. "It's just a telemarketer. I don't recognise the area code."

"Those are the worst," Aurora said, shaking her head.

"Anyways, I'll run home and grab my iPad and a few things. But I'll be nice to you, just in case I need to print anything for tomorrow's meeting." His soft lips landed on hers for a long, lingering kiss. "I'll need to figure out my budget and see what the max is I'd be willing to pay to own the beast."

"Sounds like fun."

He rolled his eyes. "Oh, so much fun. But at least you won't be here alone."

Grasping at her necklace, she cast a sideways glance in Lucas' direction. Was Nate suggesting Lucas leave? "What do you mean?"

"I'm sure Lucas has better places to be."

That *was* what he meant. She stepped back and was ready to speak when Lucas walked closer to Nate.

"Did you forget? You were the one who texted me from the car right after she…"

"Yeah, I hadn't forgotten." Nate's tone was sarcastic and not of the light-hearted variety. "However, she seems okay. She's willing to get back into the car, so we're good."

"I don't think so. My spidey senses tell me otherwise, and I need to see what comes of it."

"Who said you were invited?"

"I did. As her best friend—"

"And as her boyfriend, I think you should—"

"Hey," she yelled out. "For the love of God, I'm right here."

The guys stopped and stared at her.

"Geezus, take your pissing match outside. This is my home and I won't tolerate this." She bridged the distance between her and Nate. "Go and get whatever you need, whether it's for the afternoon or the next week. I don't care. However, Lucas is my best friend, and he's quite welcome to stay in my home for as long as he likes. It's practically his home anyway."

"What?" Nate's brown eyes grew.

"He lived here over the summer. Slept on the couch. Almost nightly," she added for good measure. "You might've noticed if you yourself had been home."

Lucas' posture stiffened, and he shuffled back a step or two. His hands waved back and forth.

Nate spun in place. "You stayed here that often?"

"I needed to." He backed up a little further as he tripped over his words. "She was in a bad place and needed a friendly shoulder to guide her and lean on." His blue-greys searched out hers in pleading for help to tame the situation.

"And I was his friendly shoulder as well." She nodded. "Things between your mom and Lucas have been rocky at best, so this was a safe place for him to crash."

"You could say it was a mutually amicable symbiotic relationship." Lucas said, with hope in his voice.

"You could also say it's fucking weird. You're my brother, and you're my girlfriend."

The coffee machine hissed breaking the strange silence in the room.

She stepped closer to Nate. "And you should be happy we get

along so well. I never got along with Derek's siblings."

Nate reached for her hand. "I am pleased with that, truly I am."

It was there on the tip of his tongue, holding back, so she asked, "But?"

"But it's weird. You two are freaky close."

"Not as close as you think." She stretched up and whispered in his ear, "I don't share anything about you."

"Well, that's a relief."

"No, that would *really* make it weird." She smiled. "Now, go home and get your stuff. I'll clean up the table for you so you can work."

♥Chapter Eleven♥

The soft cushiony material was much nicer to sit on than the hard chairs in the auditoriums. For the first time today at the university, she was comfortable. She'd snuck an Advil or two after lunch, as her hip gave her a bit of grief, but it wasn't enough to reduce the ache completely. A physio appointment was in need. Desperately. As she scanned her calendar, she realised she hadn't had one in nearly a month.

She hung her coat on the back of her chair and waited for her girlfriends to arrive. It had become a Tuesday afternoon ritual since she finished her last lecture at 2:15 pm and neither Lucas nor Nate were finished until four. Unable to find another way home, she needed to kill the time, and meeting up with Kaitlyn was ideal.

A few minutes late, her other best friend waltzed into the common area looking flustered and exhausted.

"What were *you* up to?" Aurora asked, a smirk crossing her face.

"Oh stop. I was running late. The prof went longer than I would've liked and I had to run over here."

"Ah-hah, sure."

"Really." Her phone buzzed as she threw it on the table. "It's Tatiana. She's lost." After a few quick texts, she sat down, crossing her legs as she leaned back. "Okay, she'll find us now. I don't know how she can get lost though, the university's not that big."

"And your suite isn't far from here."

"This is truth." Kaitlyn beamed. "But we can't be perfect one-hundred percent of the time." She checked her phone again. "So, tell me, what happened last night? Did Nate get the car for the price he wanted?"

Aurora shook her head. "If he wants to buy it outright, he'll need to get a sizable loan. I guess the owner wasn't keen on selling it to Nate to drive under another banner."

"What'll happen now?"

"He has a meeting with this Rooker guy tonight. Nate was really bummed out about not getting the beast. He's had that car for the last couple of years and knows how it works. Sorry, I mean handles. He's used to the way it handles, since he knows how a car works." She rolled her eyes.

A moot point in their brief conversation last night, but after further discussion, she appreciated the difference, even if she couldn't care less. She understood the basics–the beast was a car Nate was used to.

"And what's Rooker going to do?"

"That's the thing, I have no idea. Nate thinks it could be a big sponsorship, or nothing at all. It was his fall-back plan if things with the beast didn't go the way he'd planned."

"He's not really happy, is he?"

"Seemed a little off this morning but I know he's got a lot on his mind. He's afraid Justin, the car's rightful owner, may fire him now and replace him with another driver. And if he gets fired, he's really up shit creek without a paddle and will need to dish out lots of money to buy a car for Northern Lights Racing."

"That's so cool that he's named the new company after you."

"It's very sweet, I agree."

Kaitlyn's face burst into a full smile, and her eyes sparkled as she peeked over Aurora's shoulder. Turning around, Aurora watched as the gorgeous Tatiana breezed into the common area.

Sporting a giant smile, the curvaceous blonde dished out cups heavy with sweetly scented coffee. She slumped down beside Kaitlyn. "Allo, baby." For good measure, she added a kiss to both of Kaitlyn's cheeks. "Allo, Aura."

Tatiana's grasp of English was decent, but when she annunciated her name, it always sounded more like Aura, since she skipped the middle sound.

"Sorry I late. I chat with Delia."

"Her middle sister," Kaitlyn said, filling in the blanks.

"She had baby last month."

Kaitlyn smiled and reached for Tatiana's hand. "A baby boy. Tatiana's getting baby fever."

"I have no fever." Always impeccably dressed, she smoothed out the creases on her pants and crossed her legs. She shrugged off her coat and folded it onto the nearby chair.

"Yeah, you do." Kaitlyn nodded and refocused her attention on her best friend. "But Liev is super adorable. It makes my ovaries burst a little to see his sweet little face."

"If your ovaries burst, you'll never be able to have children," Aurora said and winked.

Kaitlyn laughed, an infectious sound that gave your heart no other option but to enjoy it and join in.

The couple before her smiled sweetly at each other. They were truly in love and evidently, exceptionally happy. Neither kept their hands to themselves. They were the perfect couple. Aside from Kaitlyn's insistence on not being able to talk to her parents about said happiness.

"Did Nate like dress you wore?" The twenty-nine-year-old blonde leaned forward toward Aurora. "Did he smile?"

The memory of Nate's face warmed her heart. "Oh yes, he smiled."

"T'was beauty on you."

"Thanks. I want to wear it again someplace, but I don't know where. Seems like such a waste to leave it hanging in the closet."

Kaitlyn smacked the tiny table, and the coffees teetered. "New

Years. Let's plan a big party for New Year's Eve."

Aurora's eyes widened. "Do you know how expensive that would be?"

"Then we'll plan for it here, I'm sure there's a party happening somewhere on campus. There must be a party to crash around here."

"Kait, I haven't crashed a party in a long while."

"It's time to get you back on the horse, Tiger."

Tatiana lifted a hand to interrupt. "Party crash?"

"Crashing a party means going where we're not invited."

"Yes." She nodded as if she understood and gave Kaitlyn's thigh a gentle squeeze.

Aurora focused outside, searching aimlessly for Nate. She'd hope he would've popped over and said goodbye before sneaking out of class to head to his meeting, but judging from the lack of his presence, she figured he ran out of time. "Yeah, well I had help with those parties. Lots of percs to get me through."

"So, this time, you'd enjoy it naturally. High on love."

"I want what you're having," Aurora said under her breath.

She glanced around the public area. Groups of students clustered together, laughing and talking. Happiness surrounded her.

"What's going on with you and Nate?"

"Nothing. I'm overreacting."

"To what?"

She glanced at Tatiana, who had moved in closer, and automatically, Aurora slowed down her speech. Although she grasped English, it still needed to be spoken slower to be understood. At least that's what Kaitlyn reminded.

"I don't know. Nate's really focused on this car issue and this meeting with Rooker. There's school, and when he's not busy studying and getting amazing grades, karate, and basketball and work eat up a lot of his free time."

"You can't fault the man for having extra-curricular activities. When the term started, you weren't together. He needed *something* to fill the void."

"I know, and I'm not mad at him for that. I just–" She sighed. "There's always a morsel of tension around him. He keeps pushing me about driving and getting behind the wheel, and I'm not ready."

"It's the jealousy."

"You keep saying that, Kait, but that's not it."

"Oh my god, of course it is. Nate wants to complete his mission to heal you, but instead of him doing most of the leg work, his little brother took over–"

"Because Nate was gone."

"For whatever reason." She waved her hands in the air. "But he wants to finish what he started. He wants you as comfortable as he can get you before next season."

"But I'm comfortable now. I don't need to sit in a car and drive."

"And a few months ago, you said the same thing about sitting in a car and here you are today."

Damn it, the girl was right.

***

Aurora's phone buzzed as she unlocked her apartment door. "It's Nate," she said excitedly to Lucas.

"Thought he was still meeting with Rooker?"

She shrugged and answered. "Hey, we just got here. Come on up." Her backpack fell with a thump on the kitchen chair.

Nate entered a minute later, his face flushed with colour and his brown eyes twinkled more than usual.

"So?" she began, looking from Lucas to her boyfriend. "Did this meeting go better than the one with Justin?"

"It went…" He scratched his head. "A lot of things were discussed, not at all what I expected though. There's a few minor things to figure out, but if I agree to the details, signatures will be made."

Lucas punched the air. "They'd be a sponsor for Northern Lights?"

"No…"

She studied Nate's face, trying to read whatever he held back. "What's with the hesitation?"

"No hesitation, just a few things I'd need to figure out."

Lucas stepped forward and waved his hands about. "Tell us… What's the deal?"

A loud whistle sailed out of Nate as he breathed out but he didn't make eye contact. He shoved his hands into the pockets of his jeans. "I'd be a driver… Under their banner."

The air crackled from the tension.

"Which effectively ends my association with Northern Lights." A brief and bitter smile in her direction before turning his full attention to his brother. "I'd have to sever all ties as soon as the contract is signed."

Aside from the sound of Nate twisting and cracking his neck, the room was eerily quiet.

Lucas closed his mouth and ran his hands through his hair, the V between his brows deepening.

Nate's gaze flipped between the two of them, excitement and anxiety flashing in his eyes.

She broke the silence. "What? How can that be? You created it."

Nate shifted. "And Lucas will still be able to race under it. I can help run the business side of it—anonymously—but I'd be forbidden from any driving under it. It's all or nothing. No middle ground. If I sign the contract, it ends everything. I'd be a Rooker Racer."

Lucas stepped back and folded his arms across his chest. "Wow. That's a lot to digest and agree on."

"Maybe so. However, he wants to do what JRE's never done."

"What's that?"

She leaned closer to the pair of men having no idea of what JRE did or didn't do for their racers.

"He wants to go… Big."

Her gaze floated between the brothers, trying to decipher the raised eyebrow Nate shot in Lucas' direction as Lucas gave his chin a rub. They obviously knew what it meant, but she had no idea. "Big?" she asked softly, hoping someone would fill her in.

"Yeah. So that's something I gotta work out."

She shook her head and stomped her foot. "Hello? What does *big* mean?"

"They want me to race not only here at the local tracks, but everywhere. I'd be travelling all over the US and Canada. I may qualify for one of the lesser known cup series, if I train hard and do well."

She tried piecing together what he was getting at.

Nate moved cautiously as he approached her. "They're thinking in a few years, with the right training, I could be as big as Jimmie Johnson."

"You mean, you'd be racing in those really long races?"

One Sunday afternoon, she'd sat with Lucas and watched one. One of the crazy ones, with 250 laps. Honestly, she didn't see the appeal of driving the same thing over and over 200 plus times. Always turning to the left, no variety. And the heat had to be unbearable. The episode she watched the announcer said it was 110 Fahrenheit, the track had to be way hotter. This is how Nate aspired to spend his time? What was wrong with the thirty-five laps he did locally?

"Yeah."

Unable to fathom what it would mean, she walked into the kitchen, opened the fridge and stared blankly into it. With a violent shove, it slammed shut. "Not to be a Debbie Downer, but why you? Why not Marissa? Or someone else?"

"Who says they didn't ask?"

"But you said you didn't place well."

"I didn't. But they watched videos from the track and they like my style of driving."

There's such a thing as a style of driving? She slumped against the fridge door and closed her eyes. "Oh."

His footsteps sounded against the carpet as he neared her. "I haven't said yes, yet."

As her eyes fluttered open, a smile teased at the edges of her lips, whereas sadness clouded his.

"But I also haven't said no." His hands ran the length of her arms, stopping at her hands. "There are a few details I have to work out. One being how I could ever leave you." Tenderness filled his gaze.

"Maybe I could travel with you."

A wild laugh filled the room, but it didn't come from Nate. Both turned toward Lucas.

"Sorry, that just–" Lucas refused to make eye contact and checked his watch. "Well, I suppose there's time to work her up to flying or long-distance driving." He grabbed his backpack and walked to the door. "I'll leave you two alone. Aurora call me later and we'll talk. You too, bro. I want to hear the finer details."

After the door clicked shut, she asked, "When would you need to start?"

"The first race is in February, but I'd negotiated leaving right after Christmas for training as I can do some of the physical stuff here."

"Negotiated? So, you *have* already said yes."

"No," he said firmly, "but I needed to make it clear to them this was huge and I'd need time to sort things out here. I can't up and leave."

"I thought racing started in the summer?"

When she narrowed her eyes at him, he explained. "Yes, here the tracks don't open until May, but there… well the series starts in early February."

"Oh. Well… Well, that's a few months." She swallowed down the rising bile. "Workable."

"Aurora, you don't have to do anything you don't want."

"It's amazing what I can do under pressure." After shaking her head, she said, "So you'd go travel, and I'd be stuck here? What about school? You have a term and a half left."

"A detail I'd need to work out."

"What about your mom? She'd be devastated if you left." She was grasping at straws, but she wanted to lay it all out. Play devil's advocate.

"Probably, but she'd only ever be a flight away. I wouldn't be dropping off the face of the earth." He placed his hands on her shoulders. "I'd be gone February until November. Home for Christmas and a couple of weeks in the summer for sure. And hopefully more often."

"Great." She broke away and marched into the living room.

"What?"

"My dad used to do that, you know. Gone for three, home for one. Know what it did to their relationship? It killed it."

He sighed as he inched closer to her, but not close enough to touch her. "Like I said, I haven't said yes yet."

"But you're thinking about it."

"Why wouldn't I? It's a fantastic opportunity. I'd be crazy to say no."

Deflated, she slumped onto the couch. "I know you love racing—a lot—but I didn't think you loved it that much to do it full time."

"It's always been a dream, but never one I thought I'd actually achieve. I'm a local kid and this is the NHL calling." He winked.

The hockey reference helped. It was such a big deal to be drafted from a minor league hockey team as a draft pick for the NHL. A rarity as well. Probably have a better chance at winning the lottery. She studied him as her heart sank into her stomach. This was his winning lottery ticket–and he needed to cash it in.

Nate fell beside her on the couch and gave her knee a tender squeeze. "I love racing so much. The thrill of it. It's such a rush. But, and there's always a but, I need to examine all the details."

"How much time?"

"What do you mean?"

"When do you need to give this guy your answer?"

"He's back November fourth."

"I see."

"I know it's a lot to take it right now. I'm still reeling from it. We'll figure it out."

If you say yes.

♥Chapter Twelve♥

"Hey, Lucas." She tripped as she slipped into the seat next to him. The coffee shop on the main floor of HUB mall was busy; crammed with groups of students chugging their double nut soy lattes with half-foam and a sprinkle of cinnamon. She gave Lucas a nudge. "You look like hell."

"Thanks. I swear I haven't slept in days. It's like training all over again." His left hand rubbed his face.

Training. Their term for the agonising sessions they did repeatedly, acclimatising her to a car, and driving around. PTSD is a bitch and takes down anyone it can grab. Over the summer, it worked it's damnedest on Aurora, and occasionally it pulled Lucas into the pits with her.

"I'm tired of sitting in this stupid class, learning stuff I already know. I can't wait to be done with this and move over to psych."

"So why try so hard? Why don't you just give up now?"

"Very funny. I'm already getting grief from mom."

"I'm kidding," she said, her eyes getting wide.

"I know. I'm not a quitter, but good lord, I'm so done with this. How many weeks until finals?"

"Fuck if I know. I'm not counting."

He placed his head on his books. "I have an assignment due

Monday and one on Wednesday. What about you?"

"Yeah, they're never ending. I think there's a test next week. I don't know. I don't really care." She picked at the corner of her notebook. "I can't stop thinking about other things… What about this deal between Nate and the race company?"

"What about it?"

"I'm curious about your thoughts on it."

"No way. Not going there."

"Lucas, talk to me. If he accepts, do you really think he'll be gone all the time? Racing every week."

"No, he won't be gone *all the time*, but yes, he'll be racing a lot more than he does now. He'll race here once or twice over the summer."

"Once or twice?" She pouted. "It's really a great deal for him, isn't it?"

"From the bit parts he's explained to me, yeah, it really is."

"And he'd be crazy to say no."

"Completely crazy but it's more than that…"

"Would they pay him? Cover his expenses?"

"Probably a small salary, nothing even close to what the big guys make, and yes, they'd probably cover some of his expenses. Not likely all of it. I'm not really sure. I haven't seen the contract in person."

"But he talked to you."

"A little. He expressed minor concerns he had over a couple finer details brought up in the meeting. Mainly to do with Northern Lights Racing." A group of girls walked by, laughing and whispering, and it caught Lucas' attention. He shook his head slightly and refocused on Aurora. "I lack the business side of racing that Nate has in spades. I'm more a hands-on guy, handling the mechanical issues. Running the business aspect of it is creating a huge issue. He doesn't want to give it up, he's invested a lot in it already. But we both know I'm not the one to run it."

"But Nate said he could run it."

"Honestly, he's stretching. He'll be doing so much training in between races, and unless he plans on never sleeping, he won't have the energy to put into running a business."

"What kind of things would a person need to do to manage that?" Ideas floated through her brain. Could she take on that role? It couldn't be too hard, calling around getting sponsors, keeping a track sheet of expenses and income. "Maybe I could help out?"

"No offence, but you lack some necessary skills."

"Like what?"

"For starters, you'd need to be comfortable in the pit with the cars revving all around. You'd need to not freak out at a crash. You'd need to be able to chat with people."

"I talk with people."

"Right. And you almost got fired for your people skills at the library."

Well, he had her there. "But it was a library, and shelving books is boring."

"You honestly think you could handle the drive—every weekend—to the track and hang out there all day long?"

"I'd try." *I may need to have a chemical back-up plan to help me stay calm, but I could try.*

"It's sweet of you to think you could help out but I'm there all the time and I couldn't do it." A low groan sneaked between Lucas' lips, and a longer sigh followed. "I need an espresso. Want one?"

Right now, I'd love something stronger. Much stronger. The mere thought of a perc, or a handful of Advils, made her body giddy with excitement. It had been so long since the perc, but still she tasted the imaginary pill as it slipped smoothly down her throat. That incredible feeling of warmth as the magic spread to her extremities, relaxing her to the core. Her heartbeat slowing, rational thought abandoning her, and the total feeling of not giving a fuck surfacing. She missed all of it and wanted it back. Now. The harder she thought about it, the more her body craved it.

"Hey," Lucas said, snapping her back into the moment. "You okay? You disappeared on me for a minute there."

"Sorry. Lost in thoughts." *Of sweet, sweet chemical relaxation.*

His hand waved in front of her face. "Hey… you're doing it again. What's going on? This deal between Nate and Rooker, and everything surrounding Northern Lights really weighing on you that much? Or is it more than that?"

He was her best friend, she should be able to tell him. But what would he do? Scold her for wanting the drugs? Not likely. Talk to his sister? That'd be more like it. Although it wouldn't solve the craving she was having.

Admitting her craving was a good step, right? She didn't need to admit to having taken the Advils, which really weren't cutting it. They did a suitable job, but it didn't fill the void in her quite the same way as a perc would.

Sighing, she leaned closer to him, and although no one else was around, she whispered, "I need something."

"What? I can easily get you an espresso." Clearly, he was tired and missed the meaning of her words.

Poor guy. She shook her head. "Not caffeine. Something better. Something to take me away."

"Oh no. Really?" He knew. His eyebrows drew together, but she was thankful to see his expression carried more concern than disapproval. "What do we do about that?"

Her hands wrung together. "I don't know. But right now, in this very moment, it's all I can think of. I really want a perc. Like, desperately."

"Okay. Let's go."

"Where?"

"For a walk."

"Where to?"

"Just come on," he said, urgency in his voice.

Pulling her hair out from under the coat she zipped up, she grabbed her bag and followed.

Lucas was an affectionate guy, the kind who wore his heart on his sleeve. It was one of several things she adored about him. So, it meant nothing when he held her hand. It was a way of grounding her, of him helping her stay in the here and now. She supposed to outsiders it looked like more, like a young romance, but they both knew better. And neither cared what the outside world thought.

The first time he'd held her hand, it totally shocked her. They were on the fiftieth attempt on sitting in the car. When she failed—again—at keeping the dark scary shadows away, she jumped out and started screaming, drawing the attention of others in the parking lot. As soon as Lucas touched her arm and held her hand, the screaming stopped. And she buried her head into him. After that, when she'd start feeling like she was losing again, the gentle touch of his hand, whether he placed it on hers, or held it tight, always helped to ground her. It reminded her she was physically okay. And magically, it helped. Every. Single. Time.

As it did now, walking the university grounds. Lucas gave her hand a squeeze and tugged her along the sidewalk between the buildings. The surrounding air as cool as the newly fallen snow. More snow was in the forecast. Judging by the light, wintery grey clouds hanging above them, it could happen within hours. The joys of living far north of the equator.

"Where are we going?"

"Over to see-sis." Although it was pronounced phonetically, it was the CCIS building.

She frowned, but continued walking beside him. In silence, hand in hand, they walked the non-descript sidewalk, passing other engineering students. At least that's what she assumed, they were in the engineering section of the university after all. She slowed her pace and took in the view. This was a new part of campus for her, and she briefly admired the buildings and the way they were built.

Lucas slowed to her speed. "Hip sore?"

"Oh no, I've just never been in this part before."

"It's quite pretty here, and I imagine in the spring it's even better." He pointed out the various buildings and was either filling her with bullshit stories or knew what he was talking about as he described them.

They entered a building and Lucas came to an abrupt stop inside the entrance.

"What?" she said, searching his face for any kind of clue.

"Look up."

She faced toward the ceiling. The entrance was wide open, and she counted out six levels, all open to the main floor she stood on. Way above her, models of the planets hung suspended in the air in a random order.

"Cool eh?" he asked, his voice just above a whisper.

"What is this place?"

"At the top is the observatory. Well that part's outside. Come on," he said pulling her toward the elevator. He pushed the button for the fifth floor and the sensation of the floor pulling her down made her giggle as the butterflies surfaced.

The doors opened and beyond the railing, a model planet floated in midair. They stepped out and he let go of her hand as he moved away. She watched it fall to his side as the other readjusted his backpack. Fixing her own she walked over to the glass railing.

"Look down."

She did. On the floor, where they'd walked moments ago, was a constellation. It was clearly a map of the Big Dipper, with the seven stars in the shape of a pan, inlaid on the tile floor. There were other dots, but she didn't know what they formed. Her knowledge of astronomy was limited. A laugh breezed out of her. "I'd been amongst the stars and not known it." Taking it all in, she viewed the area from bottom to top. "Very neat place."

"Yeah, it's pretty cool." He rested and leaned his arms on the railing. "How are you feeling now?"

Stepping back, she tipped her head. *I'm okay. The desire is still there, but it's waning.* "I'm good. Thanks. I needed the distraction. But why here?"

"Well, obviously you've never been here before."

"Ah, no. None of my classes happen in this building."

"So, it was a great distraction."

"Yes, it was. Thank you." His hand warm in hers and she flicked her gaze up to his face. But he wasn't looking at her, Lucas glanced over her shoulder. Curious what caught his attention, she spun around to where a half-dozen female students sat around a table. She refocused on him.

Colour flooded his cheeks, all the way into his hairline, making the reddish-blond more prominent. "Can I talk to you?" His gaze fell to the floor.

She playfully punched him. "Of course, you can."

"It's really personal."

"I'm all ears." She leaned closer.

"Well, there's this girl, I mean woman…" He tripped over his own words. "And I want to tell her how I'm feeling about her…"

Her gaze flitted over to the group of ladies and back. "Ah, girl troubles." She laughed. "We're a tough bunch to figure out, aren't we?"

"Oh my god, you have no idea."

"Which one is she?" Trying to be casual, she turned and searched the group of females. Which one was he interested in? The brunette laughing with her head tipped back? The one shoving a muffin in her mouth? How about the blonde in fancy clothing, clearly out of place surrounded by yoga pant wearing ladies? Is it the super cute brunette who had her eyes narrowed ever so slightly in her direction?

"The brunette."

"There's two."

"Doesn't matter anyway."

"Of course it does. Why wouldn't it?"

He spun around, turning his back to her.

She dropped her bag beside the glass railing and closed the distance between them.

"Because she doesn't know I exist."

Oh Lucas. "The only way she'll know is if you make yourself known to her. Go talk to her."

Lucas nodded. "I have. Lots."

A giant smile crossed her face. "You're really smitten with her."

He nodded and scuffed his runner on the floor.

"She's not a flavour of the week?"

"What?"

"It's what Nate calls your dates of the week."

"Yeah, well what would he know of it. He's only ever seriously dated a couple of people his entire life. Sometimes you need to test drive a few before you know what it is you want." He stopped talking and turned to her, cheeks as red as flames. "Sorry, that sounded like I was taking a shot at you, and it's not what I meant. I'm not like Nate. I don't get things right the first time."

"Oh," she said, walking back over to her backpack. "Well maybe yours is sitting over at that table but you're too stubborn to make the first move?"

"Do you have any idea the pressure on us guys to make the first move?" He rubbed his eye. "What happens if I finally summon up the courage and tell her what I'm feeling, and she shoots me down? I'll look foolish and feel worse."

"What if she agrees?"

"What if she doesn't?"

"Lucas, you can't go your whole life without a little risk."

"Risk I can handle. It's rejection that stings."

"I understand that. All too well." Rejection hurt on both sides of the equation. It wasn't just guys who feared it. Girls did all the time. Probably why many didn't make the first move. "Then what? It's obvious you're more into this girl than a roll in the hay. Tell me more about her? Maybe I can present a way for you to easily talk to her."

The group of girls giggled, and she focused on them.

"She's beautiful."

Aurora nodded. "I can see that." She eyed the one laughing with her head tipped back.

"I imagine she's kind to her friends, as they always want to be with her."

"She does seem to be chatting with all of them. Is she in your classes?"

"No."

She shook her head. "How do you…"

He shrugged. "It doesn't matter. Girls never make the first move."

The brunette in question glared in her direction.

"What if she thinks we're a couple and saw us holding hands?"

"So what? Maybe it would make her jealous and want to come over here."

Pulling her head back slightly, she scrunched up her face at Lucas. "What? Why would you think that?"

"Doesn't jealousy push people to go beyond their comfort zones?"

Again, she screwed up her face. "No."

"Really?" He stared her in the eyes. "Marissa never brought out the green-eyed monster in you?"

"What?" *Oh god, I wish I could forget about that bitch. Laying her claim to Nate.* She shuddered.

"See?" He laughed. "Just hearing her name makes you green."

"What? It does not. She's an exception to whatever rule you're thinking of. We were over when she–" She couldn't say it. It made her sick picturing her and Nate *together.* It wasn't jealousy propelling her to go back after Nate, it was her desire to be with the man who brought her to life. Marissa had been a stepping stone as far as she was concerned. She was never jealous of Marissa…

"You can say whatever you want, but it's there. I can see it brewing underneath." He laughed, and a smugness played on his face, lighting up the eyes.

"Pfft," she said, and checked out the girl before glancing at her watch. "I'm going now. Nate will drive me home. I'm supposed to meet him by the main entrance of Rutherford." She patted his arm. "Good luck. Go talk to your dream girl. I want to hear all about it later."

As she walked passed the group of ladies, eyeing the brunette, she smiled and said, "In case you're wondering, he's single."

♥Chapter Thirteen♥

Nate pulled into his parking spot at the apartment. "You've been strangely quiet since we left the U."

"I'm always quiet when you drive. You need to keep your focus on the road." *And I've been thinking. Of you. That contract. If Miss Brunette and Lucas got together.*

"It's more than that."

She sighed and crossed her arms over her chest. "I'm worried."

"About Cole's visit?" Her father had texted her this morning he was coming for a quick visit tonight.

Let's run with that right now as it's the simplest problem. "Yeah."

"I'm sure it'll be okay."

"I'm so relieved you think so." She rolled her eyes. "Aren't *you* nervous about seeing him again?"

"Nah. We both have your best interests at heart, and that's all that matters. What he thinks of me, I can get around."

There were several times where Nate had slipped on any relationship with Cole. The first was failing to call him when they got home from their first trip to the track, a part of the deal of Cole providing him with the necessary drugs to get her safely home. Whoops. A mistake that cost them time together until Aurora begged her daddy to send more.

The second time had been leaving Nate. Although Aurora ended the relationship, Cole directed a lot of his anger toward Nate. She'd come close to overdosing to separate herself from him, and though it pushed her to get clean, Cole did not lessen his distrust of Nate.

Upon learning Nate had taken her to the scene of the accident and pushed her back into a mini relapse, he wasn't at all pleased. Not one bit. He'd slipped how worried he was about her not only relapsing her mental state, but also with her drug dependency.

"Yeah, well good luck with that." She leaned over the console and gave him a kiss. "Shall we?"

The key twisted in the lock, but it was already unlocked. She should've known he'd not lock it up.

"Hey, Daddy."

"Princess," he called out, and emerged from the spare bedroom. The one she'd left designated as the guest room. He embraced her and gave her a quick kiss on the forehead.

She stepped out of it and moved over to Nate.

"Nate," Cole said, a hint of a growl under his breath.

"Sir."

Sir? Is he trying to suck up? That'll never work. She flipped her gaze back and forth between the two men. Standing together in the same room for less than a minute and the tension was already thick as pea soup.

"I know it's early but let's go for supper. I haven't eaten since breakfast."

She glanced at the clock hanging on the wall. It wasn't even four o'clock yet. "That's like a really late lunch, Daddy."

"Well, whatever. I'm starving."

Aurora spun to face Nate. "Want to join us?"

He leaned in for a quick kiss. "Nah. I've got a tonne of studying to do." His rough hand caressed hers as she followed him over to the door. "Call me later."

"Sure you won't come?"

He raised his eyebrow, and a sly smile leaked out as he whispered in her ear, "Now, now. You told me I can't stay over."

A playful punch to the arm. "You know what I mean."

"Indeed, I do. But no, I won't join you for dinner. It's been a while since you've had a chance to visit with him in person."

Normally, her daddy came to town on his week off. He worked three on, one off, from his oil rig job up north. A lucky one who still had a job. The recession had hit and many oil workers lost their jobs, and he scrambled to cover the hit. It had been almost six weeks since she saw him last.

"Fine. I'll sulk without you."

"Call me when you get back."

"I'll miss you."

"I'll miss you more."

"I'll miss you most." She blew him a kiss and watched as he walked down the hall to the elevator. Turning around, she faced her father.

He rubbed his hand across his brow. The grey at his temples had expanded, and the salt and pepper hair held more salt than pepper these days. "Anything you care to tell me?"

Cole and Aurora had grown closer over the past few months. After her accident, they'd become distant with each other, although they both checked in on the other. But it was a relationship that only skimmed the surface. When Aurora ended things with Nate, and had come close to an overdose, that's when things start to change for them. A screaming match between the two had ironically brought them closer together, especially after they finally talked. About the accident. About her drug use. About being in love and losing it all. Only then was Aurora able to come clean, but she needed her daddy's help.

He'd removed everything containing anything that could be harmful as a drug, or mixed with a drug. There was nothing left. No Tylenols. No Advils. No cold meds. Nothing for an upset tummy. Nothing.

But she wanted to get clean. Needed to. Not for anyone else but herself. And it had been hard.

She swallowed but shook her head.

"I found the small empty bottle of Advils."

"Oh yeah? That was from Carmen's room." Relief sailed over her as the lie came out so easily. "You should see what I've done with it." She started walking down the hall and stopped when he hadn't moved. "Would you rather not?"

He hesitated and apprehension clouded his face.

"You don't need to. It's not a big deal."

He stepped closer to her. "No, let's see. It's been awhile."

She walked the remaining steps to her sister's old bedroom and slowly opened the door.

Cole's face morphed from shock to sadness to curiosity. "Wow. Where is everything?"

"Donated, mostly. A lot were old clothes that didn't fit me. Most of the paints from her art supplies had dried up, and the brushes were in terrible condition. I needed to toss those. I hung up a few more of her paintings around the place–"

"Yes, I did see a couple in my room."

"Other than that, it was mostly reorganised and shuffled around."

He inched around the bedroom. "You've been busy."

"Yeah. A little. It's therapeutic to say the least."

"I can imagine."

"Have you tackled mom's stuff?"

He shifted on his feet. "You should come up and see it for yourself. Why don't you come up for Christmas?"

Her stomach dropped like a concrete brick in the water. "I… I… I don't know, Daddy. There's lots going on here. Even if I did want to visit, I don't know how I'd get up there."

"I have a special pill for you."

"If I never take an Isa again in my life, it'll still be too soon."

The growling from his stomach was loud and clear. "You know what, let's discuss this over dinner. I'm famished."

A large intake of air, followed by a slow exhale. "Okay, but you have to listen to me. Remember? Go when I say so." Cole had only driven her once un-medicated. Days before her fateful trip to the track to win Nate back.

"Not a problem."

Locking up, they headed down to his gigantic truck. It was new, at least new to her. Last time he came for a visit in a more reasonably sized vehicle. "So, you belong to this monster. Do you really need something so huge?"

"Yes," he said without any emotion in his voice. "I need the power of this truck in and around the job sites."

She glanced at the passenger door. It had to be at least four feet above ground. "How am I supposed to get in?" Her eyebrow arched, and secretly she hoped they'd have to call the whole thing off. As comfortable as she was getting into a vehicle, she had yet to climb into one. Should anything happen to necessitate a speedy exit, this would be a long drop.

A beep came from the remote Cole pulled from his pocket. A black step extended down, readying itself for her.

"Seriously?"

Cole reached above her head and opened the door. "Whenever you're ready, Princess."

Her gaze travelled up the ladder to the door of the truck. The distance between the ground and the seat was remarkable. A deep breath for courage, and she pulled herself up and into the truck. The view was quite a bit different from Nate's car, or Lucas's, both of which sat near the ground. This felt like she was in the clouds. But not quite.

With the door closed, and Cole in the driver's seat, they took off. Cole beamed at his daughter. "This is really great. I'm proud of how far you've come."

"Thanks." She did not reciprocate the feelings. Too busy clutching to the seatbelt as the truck bounced down the main roads. Nate's car was much smoother.

Idle chit-chat between them, they pulled into the Milestone's parking lot, and parked near the back of the lot. With a table along the outside wall, they sat and ordered.

"I meant to tell you, I ran into an old friend of yours last week."

"Oh yeah, who?" It would have to be an old friend. She hadn't talked to anyone from up there since the accident as they all abandoned her when she was pinned to a bed resembling Frankenstein. Even her boyfriend took off, leaving her alone. *Jerk.* In her books, her Fort Mac friends were no longer considered acquaintances, since no one bothered to call on her. After they abandoned her in the hospital, she couldn't be bothered to try to get in touch when she'd finally left. She'd moved on.

"Derek."

A swallow of Sprite lodged in her throat and started to burn. A thump to her chest as the tears stung her eyes, and finally it went down. "Shut up," she said as she covered a small burp. Derek Thorvelson was no friend of hers. "When was this?" *Not that I care.*

"He was visiting his family and looked me up. We went out for dinner."

A laugh escaped her mouth. What a snake. Mind you Derek and her father always had a good relationship, apparently better than she thought. Which was weird because Derek never was *the one.* Who knew the Derek-Daddy relationship was stronger than hers and Derek's, but what did she know? She was a naïve seventeen-year-old who was going to go to med school and thought she understood how the world worked.

"He's good. Asked how you were doing."

"I'll bet."

"No really. I think he's grown up a lot." His knuckles cracked as he squeezed them.

"What? What are you not telling me?"

Cole's hands clasped together. "I don't know if I should tell you or not."

She leaned back against the booth. *This can't be good.*

"He's getting married."

Not what I was expecting to hear. Although she didn't *want* to hear more, she kind of did. "To whom? Oh, don't tell me. To Ruby?"

Her former best friend–until *that* night. As if it were her fault she had to bail on grad. It's not as if she planned it. All her friends had no issues moving on with their lives. They also had no issues doing it without her.

A gentle laugh from her daddy broke her thoughts. "No, not Ruby. As far as I understood, it's no one you know."

"Yeah, but Fort Mac is a small town, Daddy. Chances are…"

"He lives in Calgary now, and I assume that's where she's from."

A shrug. She didn't care. Not really. "She can have him, he's a jerk anyways."

"I disagree."

"Yeah, well you also thought giving me street drugs to help…" She air quoted the word help. "… with my fear of cars was a great idea too. So, we'll have to agree to disagree."

For two years she was the unwitting recipient of taking rhohypnols for him so he could transport her in a vehicle without her remembering and screaming in terror for the duration of the ride. It was Chris who discovered that tidbit of information.

Cole shook his head as the waiter placed food on the table. "Anyways," he said with a big sigh, "he was curious how things are going with you, and if you were seeing anyone."

"And you told him what? Because I know what you think of Nate."

"My thoughts about Nate did not enter the conversation. As much as I don't like Nate, I can see what he does to you. You're coming back."

"Huh?"

"The girl, the woman, the person, whatever way I can say it without sounding weird. Anyways, that person, she's coming back. You're more upbeat and have a better view on the world. You're willing to try things outside your comfort zone." He grabbed a fork and stabbed at the house salad. "And I know Nate's a big reason why. And I want to hate him. Believe me, I do. But I can't. He's bringing you out of the dark hole. And I can't hate him for that."

Wow. There were no words. This was not how or what she expected to be talking about tonight. Her relationship with her daddy had changed—strengthened—so much over the past couple of months, sometimes it took a minute to get used to the heartfelt honesty between them.

"I am very happy with Nate and I love him more than I can describe. His family is so essential to me. They are my family too. You really should meet them. You'd love Brenda, well maybe not love her because that would be weird. But you know what I mean." A deep breath interrupted her.

"Do you get along with her?"

"Yeah. Just the incident at Thanksgiving. Otherwise, she's been pretty cool. We have dinner at her place once a week typically." *Do I continue? How will he take it?* With a quick head shake, she said, "She's becoming a mother figure to me." A quick search of his face.

"That's great, Princess." A warm smile played on the edges of his lips but it pushed into his eyes. "I'm very happy to hear it. You and your mom were very close. I know how much you miss that connection."

"I do. She's definitely not Mom, but she's cool."

Cole squeezed her hand. "I'm relieved. A girl needs a mother figure in her life. This may shock you, but there are some things dads don't understand."

"Maybe so. But I'm not girly enough to truly need those things. Remember, I have no uterus."

Cole blanched and choked down his food. "It's not just that. Sometimes you need someone to discuss feelings and shit with."

"I have the shrink, remember?" She laughed. *And Lucas.*

"It's more than that, Princess."

"I know. I'm giving you a hard time. You really do need to meet them all. You should come here for Christmas? Please? I didn't kill anyone with my cooking for Thanksgiving."

Cole munched on a man-sized bite of his burger. Wiping his mouth, he said, "You know my crew usually want to spend time with their families, so I'm the one who works–"

"But you invited me up there."

"Yes, because I'm right there. Thirty-minute drive. Not the four and a half hours like coming here. My crew needs—"

"And for once, your crew can allow you to spend it with your family. With me. Please?"

"I'll honestly give it serious consideration. You have my word."

And that was that. At least he'd think about it. It wasn't a no, and not a confirmation, but at least it was a start.

"So, are your classes going well?"

Heat flooded her cheeks. "Not really."

"What's up?"

"They're hard, and it's hard to focus."

Cole raised an eyebrow. "What do you mean it's hard to focus?"

"What I mean is I can't focus on what the instructor is talking about when I'm still trying to figure out what he said originally. It's tough. I feel like I'm barely treading water."

"What's your average?"

"Overall, or per course?"

"Overall."

"Seventy-two."

"Aurora," he said, leaning back against the booth. The joy he had moments ago, receded. Now, disappointment hung over his face and in his tone.

"I know. I'm sorry." She focused on her plate, her burger untouched. "But it's difficult."

"And Pharmaceutical Sciences was easy?"

"It seemed that way." Shame coursed through her body.

Last year she'd completed a few courses, hoping to get a degree and be able to dispense drugs. However, once she went through withdrawal and came to her senses, she figured if she did get her degree, no one would hire her based on her past—if they ever discovered it. She switched into sciences, hoping to enroll into med school. She had been book smart. Once.

"But it's really difficult being there full time."

"It was easier when you did it from home?"

"Yes and no. It's just… I'm in it all day long. There's no real break aside from lunch. It's go go go. I can't handle it. It's too much. I've contemplated switching faculties."

Cole dropped his burger back onto his plate. "Again?"

"I know, I'm sorry." The material wasn't hard, mostly it was the focusing part. If she listened to the professor the whole time, maybe she'd get more out of it. As it was, her mind wandered lots, and she drifted in and out. Too many thoughts and not enough time to think them.

"Work through this term and we can reassess at Christmas. I don't want you becoming a permanent student."

"I never had any intentions of that. I haven't found anything I'm truly passionate about yet."

"You will."

"I worry I won't. Carmen always knew she was destined for the arts. Her talent was always there. Nate said he always knew he was meant to be in engineering. Lucas did too, until he discovered his passion."

"Which is?"

"Helping the sick and twisted get through their issues in life." A little slip of a laugh breathed out of her. "You know, like me."

"You're really too hard on yourself."

"I don't think I'm hard enough to be honest with you. The person I was before the crash was a pusher and did everything she set her mind to. I can't even focus enough on getting through a class."

"Take things one day at a time." He scratched his chin. "Are you feeling overwhelmed?"

"Constantly," she said without filtering.

"Why? What's consuming you outside of school?"

"Don't worry about it. I'll get through it."

"Princess, I want to help. Remember talking about it is beneficial, even if there's nothing I can do."

She sighed. It was true they were having a heartfelt conversation and as much as she didn't want to unload on him, he really was someone to confide in. Someone who wasn't necessarily on Nate's team. "Well, there's school."

Cole nodded and chomped into his burger.

"And things with Nate."

With a full mouth, she wasn't sure what he said exactly, but it sounded like, "Is he pressuring you?"

"About what?"

He wiped his mouth and took a sip of his pop. "Your recovery, school, family... I could go on."

"No. None of those things. He wants me to get behind the wheel, but I'm not there yet. I don't think I'll ever be ready for that. Too much responsibility."

"Based on what you've done already, I'd hazard a guess you'd completely relapse if pushed too hard."

Her stomach felt as if someone dropped a lead weight in it.

"With the drugs, Princess," he said as though she hadn't changed colour before his eyes.

"Well, yeah, I get that."

"You haven't been using?"

Advil doesn't count as 'using' does it? "No, Daddy."

"Not sneaking it somewhere?" He assessed her, tipping his head to the left, rubbing his chin in thought. "But you're craving it."

"Oh my god, yes. Daily. Hourly. By the minute." She avoided his eyes, afraid he'd see the shame within them. It was a terrible thing to be a recovering drug addict. "I thought the cravings would get less over time."

"I wouldn't know."

"Of course not. You only deal them out. You don't actually take them. You're a weird drug dealer." Her tone was harsher than she meant but she couldn't stop herself. Edginess washed over her.

"Hey, now you just wait–"

Throwing her hands up, she stopped him. She hung her head and took a deep breath. "I'm sorry, that was out of line."

"You're damn straight it was."

"I'm… Ugh. I don't know what I am. Overwhelmed mostly." *I so want to tell you about Nate and this new offer or deal he's contemplating. But I can't. Not until I know more. Like whether he accepts it or not. And if he'll be gone for chunks of time.*

Cole leaned forward and pushed his plate off to the side. "And what do you do about it?"

"Well… If I had my pills, I'd take them." She laughed an uncomfortable laugh. "But I've already used my weekly limit. I won't get more until Monday."

"Okay."

She swallowed down the question poised on the tip of her tongue, knowing the answer before she could give it voice. *I wonder if you'd give me anything. Or recommend something I can take to ease the nightmares and quiet my daydreams. To help me be the normal I used to be. This me, the one I am now, is totally lost without it.*

"Hey, what are you thinking?"

"Honestly?" She searched for a reason to not speak her mind. But there was nothing holding her back. "Can I ask you a personal question?" She waited for hesitation from him. Nothing. "With you and momma, your three on, one home work schedule, did it ruin your marriage?"

"What? Where is this coming from, Princess?"

"I'm curious, is all." Her shoulders fell. "Nate's been offered an amazing deal. To travel and race all throughout the states. This new owner wants him to go big."

"Big?"

She shrugged. "From how I understand it, like Jeff Gordon big. Eventually."

"Oh."

"So, he'd be travelling lots. And I worry about it because you were gone seventy-five percent of the time and it didn't help your marriage."

"Things between your mom and I were different. It's hard to

explain, but honestly it had more to do with expectations at home when I was there. Like she thought I should've understood what everyone's schedules were. But I didn't, and so I asked. I wanted to be a part of everything but didn't know how to fit in seamlessly when I was there. I'm sorry that it's not much of an explanation, but it is what it is. There's absolutely nothing I can do about it now."

"But if you could go back in time and change things, would you?"

Cole blew out a loud breath. "That's a loaded question. You change any one thing and it ripples into the future."

She picked up a fry and munched on it.

"But I get what you're asking. And no, I don't think I would change things. If your mom and I were truly meant to be together forever, we could've made it work. But our relationship wasn't important enough for us to save. We were in it together for you girls and I think that's the wrong reason."

"Oh."

"But don't read too much into it. Angelina and I wanted the very best for you both. We were happy to stay together and keep things amicable. And for the record, we loved each other. We just weren't in love with each other. And that's clearly not you and Nate."

She sighed and leaned into the back of her chair. That was a lot of information to take in. How long had they fallen out of love? Was there any reason for it or did it they happen to notice one day it was gone? Was it his job? Was it because most of child-rearing fell on Momma's shoulders? For a moment, she was thankful she wouldn't be able to have children. She'd never have to worry about sticking it out with someone she didn't love fully.

"I wouldn't worry too much about it, Princess. I know, easier said than done. And it's part of the reason why I probably want to hate Nate. He's your one. And everyone knows that." He winked at her.

There's hope for Nate. The thought of him being *the one* made a smile bubble up to her lips. "Thanks, Daddy." Not seeing him made her ache. She wanted to get home and at least chat with him. Fill him in and let him know things weren't as bad as they both thought. "I should get back home. I have mid-terms I should be studying for." *Even if all the studying in the world isn't going to make any more sense of it, I should at least try.*

"But you've hardly eaten."

"I typically don't when I'm being driven somewhere, remember? I'll eat it when I get home and I know I'm not going anywhere. But thanks for supper. I've really enjoyed this."

Cole squeezed her hand. "Me too, Princess. Me too."

♥Chapter Fourteen♥

It was early Monday morning, three in the morning and again she woke up from a horrific nightmare. Unlike her previous dreams, this one had nothing to do with cars and everything to do with falling. Falling down a long, dark crevasse. Nothing to grab onto. No one around to hear her screaming.

She wiped the sweat off her forehead and pulled at the nightshirt stuck to her body.

Yuck.

A glance to her left, to the empty space in the bed where he'd be. Sigh. Not tonight. She told him things were getting better, and they had been–sort of, thanks to the keeping the Xanax for bedtime. To help keep the nightmares away. In a way they worked, until she ran out. Thankfully she wasn't dreaming about car crashes and losing her boyfriend in a fiery accident. The falling dreams were better. Not. At least she wasn't having a panic attack.

Splashing cool water on her face, she listened to her heartbeat. It was quicker than normal, but not the racing it could be at. Even her breathing was in the normal range for 'just a bad dream'. She grabbed a fresh nightshirt and tossed the damp one into her hamper, making her way down the hall.

In the living room, she retrieved a book out from under a pile of magazines. It was about conquering PTSD, and seeing your fears for what they were. It wasn't light reading, but highly interesting.

Buzz.

Buzz.

Aurora shot awake from the depths of sleep and in surprise, the book in her hands flew out in a flash and connected with a glass of water. The clear fluid run across the table, trickling off the edges.

"Shit!" She glanced at the clock. It was after eight. "Damn it."

The buzzer sounded again.

Righting the glass and lifting the book from the floor, she raced over to the intercom button. "Hello?"

"Good morning, Beautiful."

She let Nate into the building, sliding the chain off the door. Grabbing a cloth, she wiped the small puddle on the coffee table and danced on the one she laid on the floor. In haste, she ran into her bedroom grabbing yesterday's jeans. They were rolling up over her ass when she heard his knock and his voice call down the hall.

"I'll be five minutes." She hoped her voice was loud enough for him to hear. Flipping through her drawers, she grabbed a fresh bra, slipping her arms into it as Nate entered the room.

"Did you sleep in?"

"Yeah, something like that." Nearly breaking a hanger, she yanked down a sweater. "Need to brush my teeth and do my hair, then we can go."

"Did you not sleep well last night?"

She shook her head and walked into the bathroom. Her head dipped low to clean her teeth, she saw him leaning against the doorframe, looking patient and relaxed as if they had all the time in the world. How'd he do that? She was so flustered her toothbrush went too far back in her mouth and she gagged herself.

Nate's beautiful laugh sounded behind her.

"Don't laugh. I have a weak gag reflex."

"It's not that weak." His eyebrow arched and a seductive smile inched across his clear face.

A quick brush through her hair, and she wrapped up the fastest braid ever completed. "Ready."

"Finally," he said, as he stepped to the side to let her pass. "Thought we'd never leave."

She rolled her eyes.

"Aw, what's the matter? You used to be a morning person." He spun her around so she faced him.

"Not when I'm running behind, I'm not."

"What's the big deal? So, we're ten minutes late. Probably miss the traffic rush this way."

"It's a big deal because punctuality matters."

He leaned down and kissed her quickly on the lips.

"Plus, I should have breakfast…"

"Relax. I've already taken care of it. Coffee and bagels await you in my chariot, my love." A full smile crossed his face. It tugged at the corner of his eyes and brought out that sweet dimple.

"Are you ready?"

"As I'll ever be," she said grabbing a jacket and her backpack.

At his car, he popped the trunk, and she dropped her bag inside. She walked over to the passenger door and went to open it.

"Wait," he said as the trunk slammed shut. "Breakfast first."

"Can't we eat in the car?" They'd already be more than ten minutes late.

"I don't like to eat while I'm driving, it's awkward."

She stared at him, tipping her head to the side. "So why didn't you bring them up?"

"Because I thought you'd be ready to go."

"And since I wasn't?"

"Now, we'll eat down here. Come on, let's go for a walk and eat at the park."

"Seriously? It's two degrees out."

"Yes, it is. It means we can hold hands and cuddle to keep warm. Besides, I have something I want to talk over with you and asking you in the car is really unromantic." His bright eyes sparkled and took the cool edge off the grey skies. He pulled out one venti-sized coffee from the console and placed it into her hands. "One maple macchiato for you." Once again, he reached into his car and when he stood back up, he held a brown paper bag and another coffee. "Let's go to the park."

Heart skipping along as she pondered what he wanted to ask her, she looped her arms through his, holding tight to the cup, relishing the heat it gave off. They crossed the street and made their way into the park area. Sitting on top of the table, Nate passed her a bagel.

"Your favourite."

Unwrapping it, she smiled as the scent of peanut butter filled her immediate surroundings. "PB and J."

"Of course." He sat next to her, pushing his hip into hers and keeping the distance between them to a minimum.

"You know," she said after swallowing down a bite, "this is oddly romantic."

"Oddly romantic, eh? I kind of like that." He finished the first half. "I figured, we're already going to be late."

Her head lowered a bit until his cool fingertip tipped it back up.

"But while I waited for you, I checked your schedule. Neither of us had anything pressing, so it's okay if we miss the first class."

Her eyes searched his, knowing what he said was truth. She wasn't writing an exam, and her first class she usually slept through anyways.

"So, we can enjoy a leisurely breakfast together without a worry, okay?"

"Okay."

"And after, we'll have a swinging contest."

"What's that?"

"Whoever can jump the furthest from the swing wins."

"What's the prize?"

"Respect." He laughed.

"Well, you win. I won't be able to jump very far. I don't think the ole hip can handle a jolt like that."

"Yeah, you're probably right." The paper crinkled in his hands as he squished it up. "But I've never known you to back away from a challenge either."

"Let me finish my breakfast first, and then you're on."

"That's my girl." As he took a drink, his eyes never left hers.

Within a minute, she'd put her garbage away and headed for the swings. "How about whoever gets the highest first wins?" She snuggled onto the swing and pushed back with all her might.

"No fair," he said racing to the swings, having tossed his coffee in the trash. "You got a head start."

"I'll take what I can get." Her feet cut through the air, enveloping her in coolness. Pumping as hard as possible, she soared higher and higher with each back-and-forth motion. Butterflies settled into her tummy as she fell back toward the earth, only to cement when she thrust herself forward. "I'm higher than you."

"That may be true," he said, laughing and swinging beside her. "But I will have the farthest jump." He readied himself, getting his arms on the outside of the chain. At the top of his upswing, he launched himself out.

The butterflies swirled in her stomach, watching him soar through the air, until he landed, and tumbled forward from the momentum of his launch.

"Tada," he said, turning with his hands thrown in the air. "Your turn."

"No fucking way," she said as her feet dragged on the ground with each passing swing.

"You can jump from there." He stepped closer to her. "I'll catch you."

"Yeah. As if I could accurately jump into your arms while swinging."

"Try."

What the hell. It's not like I'm that high up any more.

"I want to ask you a question. Before you turn me down, there's a reason why I'm asking."

Oh my god. Her arms went around the chain of the swing. If it was moving slower, then her heart was racing. She swallowed, afraid of what question he wanted to ask her. What question could he ask that he'd be afraid of rejection? *Not the marriage question?* Her heart plummeted into the depths of her stomach. *No, couldn't be. Shouldn't he be on bended knee? And it's like way too soon. I know Daddy said he was the one but... Oh. My. God. Did they talk behind my back? Is that why Daddy said he was coming around?*

The swing slowed. Total opposite of her racing thoughts.

Nate stood a few feet in front of her, a mischievous grin playing on his face. "Are you going to jump?"

"Are you going to ask?" She waited for it to go a little slower.

He winked. "Jump first."

A little slower. A little more. She pushed away and for a microsecond felt weightless. As her left foot hit the ground, it rolled, and by time the right foot landed, she was already on her way to the ground.

Thankfully, Nate managed to get his arms under her before she face-planted. "You missed," he laughed as he held her. "Were you aiming for four feet in front of me?"

The pain was crawling up her leg. "It hurts, Nate."

"Your hip?" Concern laced his voice.

"My ankle." The pain was biting, and she fought it back.

With one swoop, he scooped her up and carried her back to the table. Sitting, he squatted down. "I'm going to roll up your pants."

Her eyes rolled skyward, and she bit her lip as his fingers gently palpated her throbbing ankle. As he skimmed across her ankle bone, she screamed instinctively.

"Dammit," he said from under his breath. "Let's go to the ER."

"No, really, it's not that bad." She slid off the table and winced as she put her left foot on the ground.

"Great," Nate said, crossing his arms over his chest. "Let's see you walk to the car."

Determination on her face, she hesitated in moving forward. She did not want to lift her right foot and put any pressure on the left. A hop. A shuffle. *Maybe I can get there like this?* Her left foot slid forward, and pain like a hot knife lanced through her, causing her to throw back her head.

"Everything okay?"

"Just hunky-dory," she said through gritted teeth. *I can do this. It doesn't hurt too much.* She inhaled a huge gulp of cool air. It felt great against the heat burning within. A gentle tap and a quick shuffle. Left foot down, and just as quick she had it pulled back up off the ground. The stabbing sensations were too much to bear, and the tears quickly betrayed the confidence she had.

"Aurora?"

She whipped her head toward him. "It hurts okay? Happy now?"

"Not really." He wrapped an arm around her left side. "Would you prefer to walk or shall I carry you?"

"How about you get your car, and I'll wait right here?"

"You sure?"

"Trust me, I'm not running anywhere."

He kissed her quickly and raced off to get his car.

The moment he turned his back on her, the tears fell fast and furious. She had a minute or two at most and releasing the river felt good. She didn't want to acknowledge how much her ankle hurt. She wanted to fight through it, and internally swore to be strong, pretending the pain wasn't as intense as it was. But it ached and throbbed against the canvas shoes.

Her face in her hands, she heard the car enter the nearby parking lot and approach the spot she stood. Wiping her face, she blew out a breath of air watching it hang in the air.

"Hurts that much?" His soft voice calm and full of concern, the judgement in it tossed aside.

A simple nod.

"If I support you can you hobble over to the car?"

Another nod, and she was lifted, putting pressure on the good foot only. A few awkward hobbles, and she belted herself into the car as he drove off to the emergency room.

The nurse at the triage desk was kind and took all the info she needed before getting a wheelchair for Aurora. "It'll be awhile," the nurse said, patting her shoulder. "We'll call you when you're up."

Nate wheeled her into the waiting room, parking her against the back wall.

Tears she didn't want to cry, fell down her cheeks. With the tips of her fingers, she wiped them away, not wanting to see the sympathetic expression on Nate's face. She studied the mostly deserted emergency room. Three other patients sat scattered around, and naturally, none of them pretended to be pleased being there.

His soft hand rubbed the top of hers, causing her to turn toward him. "What can I do to help?"

"Nothing, right now." The pain continued biting her ankle. "Thanks for being here with me."

"Where else would I be?"

"In class? If I hadn't slept in…"

He shushed her with his finger. "We can't change the past, so there's no use dwelling on it."

The past–something she'd never forget. The gentle way she limped reminded her of a past she'd never escape. And dwell on it? It was always around her. In her thoughts. In her actions. It was who she was. It had defined her.

And without warning, an intense need for drugs roared to life. Where it had been content to remain on the vestiges of her mind, the throbbing ache in her ankle fanned the embers. Thinking of pain relief ignited the flames, and she knew she was in big trouble. And worse than knowing how she needed the pain relief, was how much she *wanted* it.

Afraid her thoughts would give her away, she tried to focus on the tv and allow it to absorb her with the mind-numbing reality show. She had no interest in it, but feigned it regardless.

Time had slipped away, and at the start of the second episode, she said to Nate. "In the park, you wanted to ask me something?"

"Yeah. But not here. Not now. Not like this."

She wished his expressions were as easy to read as hers apparently were. His face was blank, and nothing in those chocolate brown eyes gave away any feeling. A shudder coursed through her.

A nurse called out her name.

"Do you want me to stay here?" Nate asked.

She squeezed his hand. "No, I want you to come."

His sly little smirk did what she suspected he had hoped, it brought a little smile to her face. "Lead the way." Nate pushed the wheelchair, and the pair of them followed the nurse down the hall to an enclosed room.

Aurora repeated to the nurse what had happened, as she retook her vital signs and studied the swollen, discoloured ankle. "Well, we're going to send you for x-rays to be sure it's not broken and we'll get you all fixed up." The squat nurse scribbled in her chart and avoided eye contact. "What's your pain level at?"

She was too familiar with that question. With her time spent in the hospital it was standard. *Tell us your pain number and we can dose the medication to alleviate it.* The higher the number, the stronger the dose. A quick glance to Nate, who leaning closer, was very interested in her answer.

The debate warred within. She was no wimp, but it sure as hell hurt. If she played it less, it was a five or six. It certainly wasn't a nine or ten–she'd had those, and this wasn't it. It throbbed and ached, like it had its own heartbeat, but it was no ten. That alone told her nothing was broken. But she'd definitely twisted it, or stretched a ligament. Possibly tore it. Any of those would make it an easy seven or eight.

"Ugh." Her voice filled with sourness. "I hate the pain scale."

The nurse finally made eye contact with her. "It's standard."

"I know, but it still sucks. How about asking me how I feel? Where it hurts the most? Judge my pain that way rather than by a stupid number."

Nate moved a bit closer to her.

The nurse raised her eyebrow.

Aurora didn't want to be mean, but dammit, she was more than a number.

In a condescending tone, the nurse asked, "And where does it hurt? Your ankle, I suppose? And how do you feel? Like it hurts, right? You give me your number, and I'll get you the drugs and an x-ray, and we can both be out of each other's way."

Her eyes narrowed into thin little slits, and the nurse became fuzzy as she stared. "Eight."

"Thank you." The clipboard slammed shut as she marched through the door.

"Good lord," Nate said.

"I know, right?"

He shook his head, his eyes only on her. "Hurts that much, eh?"

"Yeah. I debated being all tough and strong and saying five. But I figure as soon as they touch it for x-rays and a cast or bandage, it's going to hurt a helluva lot more than an eight. I want, no I need to be prepared."

The nurse returned, knocking once before storming in. "They have an open spot in x-ray. We're taking you over right now."

"Now?" A wave of panic descended over her.

"Now." The nurse had a smug little smile on her face that worried her. Afraid Nurse Ratched would enjoy putting her into a nine or ten for pain first. The nurse spoke to Nate. "You can stay here until we're back. It won't be more than a few minutes."

Faith that everything will be fine, she nodded.

He kissed her cheek. "I'll wait here." He sat on the bed.

"You get the chair," Nurse Ratched said in a disdainful voice.

"That was my next choice."

She pushed Aurora out the door.

♥Chapter Fifteen♥

Nate

With Aurora heading over to get an x-ray, Nate got comfortable on the blue-padded chair beside the bed. He pulled out his phone and sent a text to Lucas, since they were going to meet up for lunch, telling him plans had changed. It was very likely he'd be taking Aurora home to rest and not to the university.

He wasn't expecting to hear back from him right away, so it was a bit of a surprise Lucas did text back. 'Tell her I'm sorry and to stop jumping around. □ BTW, what did she say?'

He sighed. It didn't go the way he'd planed, that was for sure. Fingers typing furiously, he texted, 'I didn't get the chance to ask her.'

Lucas replied quickly. 'Oh. Well then. Tell her I'll pop over and visit after labs.'

A quick shuffle in the seat, and he propped his foot over his knee, shaking away the tinges of a green-eyed monster. *Of course, he'd want to pop over. Why wouldn't he? I know they're just friends.*

He shook his head and tapped his foot. *He's my little brother. I need to get over this.* But the jealousy, it sat there in the shadows of his mind waiting to spring out at him. Since they'd gotten back together, he spent more time than he'd care to admit wondering about their relationship. Not his, but the relationship between Lucas and Aurora. They were very close. She leaned on him in a way he wished he understood. Lucas read her fears so well.

How *had* he helped her? What steps had he taken? When *he*'d been helping her, there was a lot of physical touching and whispers of encouragement. He'd tried to replace the negativity of the situation with a positive action. Had Lucas done the same? Had he caressed her arms? The thought made him shiver. Had he whispered sweet words in her ear while inhaling her intoxicating coconut smell? He truly hoped not. That seemed truly personal.

Stop!! She said there was nothing there. Truly platonic.

He needed to distract himself from his jealous thoughts. He had plans for them, ones she wasn't aware of. It was important to him she try getting behind a wheel again. Maybe not drive again, but he hoped. University was done for her in April. And if he agreed to the NASCAR team agreement deal, he'd be on the road. A lot. She'd need to be able to function without him, and without him around, hopefully she'd get herself to and from school. He could leave her his car. And besides, she needed to drive herself—or catch a bus—and not always depend on Lucas. He needed to break her dependency on him. But he was sure, with being on the road, Lucas would step up and help her because it was the right thing to do. *Damn it.* Why did all his thoughts swirl back to his brother?

A needed distraction from the green-eyed thoughts, he flipped through and answered a couple of emails. It only kept him busy for a few minutes.

The door opened and a very teary Aurora was wheeled in.

He jumped over to her and squatted down beside the chair. The pain was evident as her eyes were red, and her shoulders tensed as he placed a hand on it.

"Dr. Bishop will be here in a couple of minutes. I'll be back with pain relief. Her shoe." She placed the runner into his hand and disappeared beyond the boundaries of the room.

"Hurts more than an eight now?"

A fresh trail of tears. "First the shoe needed to come off, and they needed to move it to get a better picture." Her voice cracked.

"Yikes. Do you want to lie down?"

She nodded, and wheeled herself closer to the bed. The wheel locks went on, and she pushed herself out of the chair, putting all her weight on the good foot.

"Let me help you," he said, but didn't know how he could. She had control and knew what she was doing. Probably was used to manoeuvring herself after her accident. He stood beside the bed as she sat on it, and turning, lifted her leg.

She winced as the bad foot touched the surface of the bed but didn't have a chance to get comfortable as the nurse came back in, with a doctor steps behind her.

"Hi Aurora, I'm Dr. Bishop." Introductions were made, and he pulled up a chair to the foot of the bed. "I'm going to move your foot, and check for the severity of the injuries." To the nurse, he said, "Has she had anything for pain relief?"

"Not yet."

The doctor glared at the nurse. "Well, give her one." He jerked to a stand and narrowed his stance. The doctor stood beside the bed and spoke to Aurora. "It'll take a few minutes for it to take effect." He exited the room with a sideways glare toward the nurse.

The nurse busied herself, leaving and coming back in less than a minute with a syringe of relief.

"What are you giving her?"

"Morphine."

"Will that cause dependency?" He didn't miss the question on Aurora's face and in her tone.

The nurse glanced at him as if he were stupid. "Not with one dose."

Panic filled his veins. "She broke a Percocet addiction a few weeks ago. Will this..." He was torn. He didn't want her to slip back into her old ways but he didn't want to see her hurting so much either. And if she started to abuse drugs again... Well, he could kiss his deal away.

Rooker Racing had an image to uphold, and it stuck to the

highest standards. Not only did the drivers need to be drug free, but their immediate family as well. Aurora, as his girlfriend, was in that loop. It had taken a lot of convincing to get Colton Rooker to understand Aurora's *past* addiction. How she was clean and not going to relapse. He'd promised.

The nurse sighed in his direction. "We're not going to give her a prescription for this, if that's what you mean."

A low, inaudible moan. It's not what he meant. It was so hard to be blunt. "Will this trigger the cravings in her?"

"I highly doubt it."

"But you don't know?"

"Nate, please," Aurora said, reaching for him. "I'll be okay. I need it. For real." Her eyes begged and pleaded.

The nurse turned her back to Nate, probably inserting the drug into his girlfriend. He could almost feel the contract go up in flames.

"There you go." The nurse dropped the syringe into the lockbox and left the room.

He pulled up a chair and watched Aurora slip into a silent haze. He wondered what thoughts were going through her mind. He couldn't tell this time. Those breathtaking blue eyes were closed tight, but tears leaked through the edges of her lashes. Once tight with pain and worry, the unmistakable sign of relief washed over her and her face started to soften and relax. Her hands, in tight little fists, loosened as he wrapped his fingers through them.

Oh, Aurora.

♥Chapter Sixteen♥

OMG–I feel so fucking amazing.

The morphine coursed its way through her body. It flooded to her head first, at least that's where it felt the strongest. As she focused on it, her breathing regulated and her pulse slowed a touch. Tendrils of relief swirled around her ankle, like a vine on a trellis. Her eyes closed, she allowed the sweet chemical intoxication to fill her cells; drifting and floating in a sea of senseless thoughts.

When the doctor came back in after scolding the nurse, she wasn't sure how much time had passed. It didn't matter. She was more relaxed than she had been over the past couple of hours. Days even.

The doctor stood beside her. "How are you feeling?"

"Like I'm floating." She tried to focus on him but gave up as he swam into view.

"How much did the nurse give her?" Nate's voice sailed in from her right.

The nurse didn't sound pleased as she answered from behind him. "A standard dose based on height and weight."

"She's a recovered drug addict." The bed moved as he sat down. "Or was."

Dr. Bishop raised an eyebrow. "What did she abuse?"

Preferring to escape Nate's saddened expression, she melted

into the pillow as her eyes closed.

"Percocets, Flexeril and Xanax."

"Hmm…" A chair wheeled across the floor. "Aurora, the x-rays don't show anything broken, but I am going to assess your ankle and move it so I can see what kind of damage there is." He cleared his throat.

"Yes, I'm listening," she said. "I'm trying not to think about what you're about to do."

"Okay. I'm going to begin." His fingers were warmer than she expected as he tenderly wiggled her toes, and palpated the muscles, or tendons or whatever it was. A push here. A tap there. A finger dug in.

She growled. "Geezus, are you actually trying to break it?"

Silence. More tapping. More pushing. A turn. A twist.

The last one caused her to wince and involuntarily scream. "That hurts." The morphine lost its grip on her. It wasn't masking fuck all as far as she was concerned. Every touch disturbed her and pulled her away from the daydream-like sensations.

He set her foot down on the bed. "You have severely sprained your ankle."

She rolled her eyes. *I could've told you that, and I haven't spent seven years in med school.*

"You'll need to wear an air boot. As the swelling goes down, you can increase the pressure. Plus, you can take it off for personal hygiene and physical therapy."

She pushed herself up onto her elbows. "What? I have to go to PT?"

"Yes."

"I hate PT."

"You're familiar with it?"

"Extensively."

"Well, you're going to be one strong lady when you're finished."

Asshole. She didn't bother looking at him. *More physical therapy. Ger-rate.* "The morphine's wearing off, can I get another?"

"Aurora?" Nate stroked her hand. There was something in his

voice she hadn't heard before. It wasn't concern so much as it was fear. What did he have to worry about?

"Seriously. The aches and pains are coming on strong." She searched deep into his eyes. Was he worried she'd go back to her old ways? It wouldn't happen. He had to believe her. She needed him to believe her.

The doctor jumped in. "Your dose will provide relief for the next few hours."

"Are you calling me a liar?" Suddenly defensive, she propped herself back up on her elbows.

"Let's give it a minute or two. If, after Nurse Claudette fits you for your boot, you are still feeling severe pain, we can reassess."

"Which is code for not going to happen." Her eyes slammed shut to the shock on Nate's face.

"I can write you a prescription for…"

When he stopped talking, she opened her eyes. Nate was shaking his head.

The doctor stood with his hands resting on the counter, pen tightly squeezed in his hand. "She can take over-the-counter ibuprofen, but it won't be as effective in her pain management."

Aurora rolled her eyes, hating when people talked about her instead of to her. "Yeah, I'm not allowed that either, although maybe there will be some concessions to be made." Eyebrow raised she gave her full glare to Nate.

"I'm not your warden."

"You sure as hell act like it."

Nate jumped off the bed. "Hey, I'm only trying to help. You know what can happen, what did happen. I don't need to bring up Matthew, do I?"

"Well, you just did. Seriously, are you ever going to let it go?" She rolled over to face him, wincing slightly as her foot moved.

"You made your bed, you need to lay in it."

"So, by that pearl of insight, you're essentially going to throw it back in my face for the rest of my life." She fell back against the bed.

"How many times do I need to tell you I was HIGH that night?"

"Precisely my point." His feet slid across the floor. "And what about the time I followed you home? You were out of your mind."

"Geezus, Nate, I've gotten help since."

His tone softened. "I know you have. And you've come so far." He paced and sat beside her. "I'm trying to help you not go back down that path. I need you to stay clean. For you. For your health. Can you understand that?"

She nodded, and resigned that he was right, she sighed. "So, my question should be, how do I manage the pain when I can't take anything?"

They both focused on the doctor, who acted as if he'd prefer to be anywhere than where he stood.

"Well..." He swallowed and pulled out a notepad. "A prescription will only get you so far. Whereas over-the-counter meds are readily available. I suggest the prescription for a few days to get you over the first hump. Then, if the pain has not reduced, although I suspect it will, you can visit your doctor for a few days more. I think it's the best option, aside from toughing it out, which will be murder. The drugs are available to help you."

Nate crossed his arms over his body, an indignant expression on his face. "I suppose I could control the pills? Give them to you as needed."

"Would you be moving in?"

A flash of excitement lit up his eyes. "Well, you may need some extra assistance."

She flipped over the thought in her mind. It wasn't hard to forget how difficult it had been when she came home from the hospital after the accident and tried to manage all on her own. Although she wasn't nearly in the same predicament, it would be helpful having someone there, at least for a couple of days until she got her bearings straight. And she'd have easy, or easier access to her meds.

The idea warmed to her and giving in, she said tersely, "Fine. We'll take the prescription, and you can be in charge. But only for a couple of days. After that, I'm on my own."

A small smile formed on his face. "Fair enough."

The doctor scribbled on his notepad and thrust the paper into Nate's hand. "Follow up with your regular doctor for management of care." He mumbled incoherently as he walked out of the room.

Her foot atop a small mountain of pillows in her bedroom, she woke up. The residual haze from the injected drug long gone, she was angry. And her ankle throbbed. It was a close tie as to what had stronger feelings–her anger or the throbbing. She reached for the crutches beside her bed and swung her unevenly weighted legs over. Righting herself and standing on the good foot, she hobbled her way to the kitchen where the delicious aroma of spice and chicken hung in the air.

"Hey, you're up," he said as she came into the eating area.

"Yeah, and I'm mad as hell."

He dropped the flipper on the counter. "Why? What's wrong?"

"I just hurt. And when I hurt, I lash out. And I feel like lashing out. A lot." She slumped into the chair and stared at Nate bustling around in her kitchen.

"Anything I can do to help?"

"Give me something to take the edge off."

He checked his watch and braced himself against the counter. "Not for another forty-five minutes."

Under her breath, she growled.

"What about a drink?"

"No, I want something to take the pain away."

He turned his back. "I can't give that to you."

She wondered if it hurt him to refuse her because he wasn't making eye contact with her. In fact, he was avoiding her as he focused on the food.

"Nate, please," she asked in her sweetest voice.

There was no answer.

"Really? You're going to ignore my pleas?" She slammed her

hand onto the table. That got his attention.

Sadness in his eyes, he said, “I don’t know what else to do. You can’t have anymore right now, and I don’t want to listen to you beg for it.”

But I want it. I need it. I’ve had a taste for it and it was so good. I need more.

She needed to distract herself, or at least find a way to get through the next forty-three minutes. Pushing herself to a stand, she hobbled herself into the kitchen. “I’ll set the table.”

♥Chapter Seventeen♥

"Nate."

A small grunt but no movement otherwise.

"Nate." She poked him in the back. "Nate, please. Wake up." With her hand firmly on his arm, she shook him awake.

"Wha? What? What's wrong?" His voice raw and dry.

"It hurts."

"Your foot?"

"Yeah."

"What time is it?"

"Time for pain relief."

"You need to–"

"I've been watching the clock for the last twenty minutes. It's been eight hours now." She twisted slowly and deliberately.

A grunt as he pushed himself up into a sitting position and rubbed his eyes. "It's two-thirty in the morning."

"I know. I'm sorry. I couldn't wait anymore. Sucks I had to wake you up, but if you'd leave me the–"

"Not going to happen, and you know that."

Was that look a judgy one?

"I don't mind doing this for you."

She wished she could read his mind and know exactly what he

was thinking. In the dark of the early morning it was impossible to read his face.

"I'll be right back."

"Thanks."

He stumbled to his feet and shuffled to the bedroom door. "Do you need water?"

"Sure."

The ache in her foot throbbed. The most intense pain gravitated naturally around her ankle, but the achiness slithered up and down her calf as well. Lifting her foot off the pillow to readjust was a nightmare.

She grunted and groaned, but with serious concentration, sweat and a tinge of tears, she managed to push herself into a reclined sit.

Nate walked in with a glass and set it beside the bed.

She opened her hand, and he dumped one little pill into it. "That's it?" she whispered.

"That's it."

Not wasting any time, it slipped smoothly down her throat as the water chased it.

"Can I get you anything else?"

She shook her head no. "Wait," she said, as he stepped toward his side of the bed. "Can you help me? I can't sleep on my back, and it's all in knots. I need to turn onto my side, or my stomach ideally."

"How do you plan on sleeping on your stomach? That won't be comfortable at all."

With a groan, she slid down and rolled onto her left side, facing Nate's side of the bed. "No this won't work." She sighed.

"Wait, it could." He walked to the hallway. An agonising moment later, he returned with the throw pillows. "Here," he said as he lifted her leg and slipped a pillow between her knees. Before she rested her leg, another pillow sat atop her foot, cushioning it from the air-boot. "Does that feel better?"

"Much." She reached for a third to wrap her arms around.

Nate rolled back into bed, turning to face her. "Do you want to stay home tomorrow or head to class?"

"I'd like to stay home. Another day off won't hurt me." *Ha-ha. I hope. I'm struggling already. What's another day?* She grunted a bit as she readjusted herself. "So, tell me about racing."

A gentle laugh, with a smile stretching across his face. It wasn't hard to miss in the glow of the room. "What do you want to know?"

"Why do you like it?"

"Because it's fast."

"But you don't seem like a daredevil."

"What do you mean?"

She gripped the pillow tighter. "Well, you're not a skydiver. You don't take unnecessary risks."

"Doesn't mean I can't enjoy racing a well-tuned car at high-speeds."

"I suppose. I still don't get it, but I suppose."

"Why do you like dancing?"

"Well, it's calming. When I hear the music, it's more than surface level. I feel it. Everywhere. It's in my soul. It tells me what to move and when to move it."

"That's how I feel about racing. It's instinctual, if you will. It's in *my* soul." His finger tenderly touched her cheek. "It's a part of me. It's who I am."

A sigh blew out from between her lips. "I just…"

"What?"

"I just worry."

"Anything in particular? The safety issue?"

"Yeah, to a large degree. But it's more than that. I've seen the safety equipment up close, I know how it works. Lucas gave me a very long lesson." She did not miss the sound he tried to withhold. "What?"

"Nothing."

The air between them shifted. "No, it's more than nothing. Whenever his name comes up, it becomes something."

"He's my brother."

"Thank you. I wasn't aware."

"You know what I mean."

"No, actually, I don't think I do."

"It bothers me."

"What? My friendship with Lucas?"

"It's more than friendship."

"Um, no it's not."

"I see the way he looks at you."

"Which is what way exactly? Because he doesn't, and has never, looked at me the way *you* look at me. You see me as more than I am, and you always have. Lucas sees me as someone who'll give him a hard time and call him a dork. Not someone to take to bed."

"No, there's more there."

"Well, you're reading way more into it than there is."

A huff and a sigh filled the weighted space between them.

Without any hesitation, she asked, "Nate, are you jealous?"

"What? Of Lucas? No. Why would I be?"

"I don't know, you tell me."

Nate rolled onto his back and closed his eyes against her stares. "Lucas has never had to fight for anything."

"So what?"

"I had to fight for you. I was willing to give up my second love to be with my first."

"Yeah, and Lucas was in your corner for that. He did everything in his power to make sure you didn't have to give up your love of racing. That you got your glory *and* the girl. He worked hard, and tirelessly, to make sure you didn't lose. Instead of being jealous of him, you should be proud. I don't know many siblings who would go so far out of their way to help another. He sacrificed a summer of hanging out with his friends to spend time helping me."

"And that's what I mean. In a way, he was intimate with you."

She couldn't help it, laughter burst out. "Shut up. He was not."

"He didn't have sexual relations with you, I get that. But he was in your head. He knows what makes you calm, what revs you up. He knows how to bring you back from wherever it is you go when you zone out."

"So that means we had an intimate relationship?"

"Yes. He knows things."

"And it pisses you off?"

"A great deal, actually."

There were no words. How does she respond? Nothing she'd say would make it better. She and Lucas were best friends although maybe it was a little more one-sided. After all, yes, he could read her. Exceptionally well. He knew what helped, and what hindered. She'd leaned on him hard all summer, so it was only natural there would be a great connection between them. But that's all it was. Friendship.

Sure, she had feelings for him, loving feelings, but she'd never admit it to anyone aside from Kaitlyn. Her future was with Nate. She knew. Lucas knew. Everyone knew. Those *feelings* for Lucas were pushed down low. Besides, he had only ever said it was friendship. It was her who had read more into it than there was. He'd made *that* perfectly clear. If she did have feelings for Lucas, and Lucas did feel more for her than he said, which she knew he didn't, it would never work out. It was against bro-code. Besides, she was madly in love with Nate. Why didn't Nate understand that?

"So, you're jealous not necessarily of our relationship but because it was him that helped me?"

Nate stayed quiet but his eyes never left hers.

"Why does that bug you so much?"

"Because it was something *I* started with you. I wanted to be there as you crossed the finish line."

"Oh, Nate," she said, reaching out to touch his arm, "you were *at* the finish line. You just didn't know it at the time."

"I wanted to be the one you ran to when you were overwhel–"

"What do you think I've been doing? I run to you all the time."

"But it's different now."

She leaned her head harder into the pillow. This wasn't going well. She needed to smooth over the dent to his ego. But how? "Is there anything that would help you believe… I don't even know if it's to make you believe anything. I didn't do anything wrong. Lucas didn't do anything wrong. You didn't do anything wrong. And yet, I'm supposed to feel guilty for Lucas helping me win you back."

"I was always yours."

"That's a lie and you know it."

"Total truth." He crossed his heart with a finger.

"Really? Explain Marissa."

"Only after you explain Matthew."

Ugh. Matthew. Arguably the biggest mistake in her life. "Matthew was nothing. Nothing important anyways."

"But?"

"Like I told you, it happened before you and I were serious."

"Not *that* incident. I want to know about the summer. I saw him… touching you." He shuddered violently.

Not unlike the nastiness she felt herself when she recalled that day. "We were nothing. He wanted more, which I never understood because there's like this huge age gap between us, and he's widowed. But that day, well I cracked. I was fighting a huge craving for the drugs. Like the worst craving I'd had in two weeks. I was emotional. I was wrecked. The sentencing was happening, or had happened."

"For the drunkard who ignored the stop sign?"

"Yeah. So, when he, Matthew, told me about it, I broke down. And like the idiot he was, he took full advantage of it."

"There was never…"

"I *never* had feelings for him. Never ever. Aside from the crazy, wild-eyed fan girl crush he easily wrecked for me. I stopped fantasising about him about thirty minutes into our date. He didn't do it for me."

His eyebrows rose.

"And even that, I swear to God I thought was you." A shudder shook through to her fingertips. "I really hate talking about him. Can we stop?"

"Sure."

"Tell me about Marissa."

"What do you want to know?"

"Why her?"

"In all honesty?" He laughed, but it wasn't a happy laugh. More like a sad laugh. One she understood completely. "Because it was convenient."

"What?"

"She wanted me, so I gave myself to her. But it was awkward."

"Yet you stayed with her for weeks."

"I needed the distraction, but it didn't work."

"Why not?"

Nate rolled onto his back, shuffling closer to her.

She snuggled in close and placed her cheek on his bare chest.

"To be honest, as much as I enjoyed being with her, she wasn't you. For a while it was nice to not have to explain everything and to know she wasn't going to worry about me on the track, even if she was trying to take me out most of the time."

"You have a gift with words."

"But it bugged me. I like explaining the car stuff to you. I like it when you worry about me, even if you shouldn't." He pulled her close. "It makes me feel good knowing you care and are curious about how I spend my time."

"I figured being with someone who shared your interest would be better."

"Better than what?"

"Better than being with someone who was afraid of all that."

"But that's what makes you you. It's part of the reason I enjoy being with you."

"You're a strange man."

"Not strange. Lucky."

She sighed a peaceful, contented sigh.

"How's the leg?"

"It's much better, thank you."

He kissed the top of her head and she nuzzled into him further.

♥Chapter Eighteen♥

"How are you doing, gimpy?"

"Oh ha-ha, Lucas," she said, dropping her phone onto the kitchen table. "In my sorry state, I'd completely forgotten about my appointment with Dr. Navin. Thankfully it was easy enough to reschedule."

"One less thing for her to worry about," Nate said from the kitchen.

"Obviously swinging is more dangerous than racing." Lucas let out a huge laugh.

She threw a pen at him. It was the only thing within tossing distance.

"Missed," he said as he laughed louder. "How's the leg?"

Once comfortable in the chair, she tugged another closer and lifted her leg up on it. "Hunky dory. Should've done this weeks ago to avoid going to class." She rolled her eyes.

"When are you going back?"

"Tomorrow." She cocked her head toward Nate. "Boss says it's time."

Nate placed a steaming mug of apple cider in front of her. "Yeah. She's had two days off. The pain is manageable now. Time to refocus the energy."

She rolled her eyes again.

Lucas stared at her, raising an eyebrow.

"So, how's miss observatory?"

"Still unattainable."

Nate stopped and stood behind her, giving her shoulders a gentle squeeze. "Who's that?"

She faced up at her boyfriend. "This brunette from cee-sis."

"Oh yeah? On the prowl, are you?"

"Not for her," he said, avoiding Aurora's eyes. "Reaching for the stars isn't all it's claimed to be." He shrugged. "I'll always have my dreams though."

Aurora took a sip of her hot drink. "You've really got it bad for her, eh?"

Colour flooded Lucas' cheeks.

A knock on the door prompted Lucas to rise in a rush. "I'll get it."

Kaitlyn sauntered in. "Hey, Tiger," she said first to Aurora, before addressing the men in the room. "Hey, guys." She grabbed a chair and sat near her friend. "So, your inner klutz fell out of you?"

"More like jumped out of her," Nate said behind them, from the kitchen. "Want an apple cider, Kaitlyn?"

"Sure."

"I'd love one too," Lucas said, heading over to make his own.

"I got it," Nate said.

Lucas excused himself and walked behind Aurora. His voice was low, but she heard him whisper to Nate. "Have you asked her yet?"

The silence was deafening. She could only imagine what was going on between them. Why hadn't he asked her yet? And more importantly, what did he want to ask her?

Aurora gave a helpless smile to Kaitlyn, who was clearly confused about what was going on. There was so much to fill her in on, and yet there hadn't been any time. She desperately needed girl time, one on one. No Tatiana. No Nate. Nobody.

"Where's Tatiana?"

Kaitlyn shook her head, and removed her jacket, hanging it behind her on the chair. "Being all miserable. She caught a nasty cold and hopped herself up on cold meds so she's probably sleeping. I told her I was running out for a bit to see you and pick her up some soup." Her cheeks flushed and Aurora was thrilled to see her best friend so happy, even as she attended to her sick girlfriend.

"And how are things going, other than that?" Nate asked.

"They're good. Really good." Kaitlyn didn't smile, she beamed. The girl was madly in love. "I need to talk to you." She leaned in closer. "After supper?"

"Sure," she said not missing the wink Kaitlyn gave her. She turned to Nate and Lucas. "Maybe you guys can run out and get dessert or something?"

Lucas laughed. "Way to be subtle."

"What?"

Nate set a bowl of spaghetti in the center. "I know you probably need it. Been cooped up in here with me for the past two days."

"I'd never say I was cooped up. I rather enjoyed it."

"Sure you did."

Okay fine, she didn't really enjoy it. It was a pain filled couple of days, but yet enjoyable, because she wasn't alone. Nate stayed with her and never left. He cooked for her, cared for her, standing patiently in the bathroom while she had a shower because with the air-boot off, she didn't dare put any weight on the bad foot. He waited and dried her foot before helping strap the blasted boot back into place. It was beyond comforting having him around. Slowly, she had begun to depend on him, which a few months ago, she never would've believed she'd be capable of.

"And he could be gone for days, maybe weeks at a time," she found herself telling Kaitlyn as they cleaned up after dinner. Taking the request for ice cream to heart, the guys left right after supper finished.

"He hasn't said yes yet?"

"Not yet. Still a few details he needs to iron out. Like school. His job. If he takes this offer, he won't be able to work in the summer."

"What will he do for money? Racing is expensive."

"I don't know."

"They don't pay him at all?"

"I'm not sure. Maybe they pay all his expenses in place of a salary? I have no idea. He hasn't said anything and when I go to ask, he changes the topic."

"When does he need to decide?"

"Soon. Next week."

"That's not a lot of time."

"I know, right? And the thing is, I don't want to be the reason he doesn't go."

"He loves you, and any fool can see that."

"I don't want him choosing me over this opportunity. And yet, at the same time, I don't want him to go. Is that weird?"

Kaitlyn laughed and grabbed a fresh cup of cider. "No. I get what you're saying. You two just got back together a month ago, and here is this golden ticket sitting in front of him. Either he goes and tries what so few people could actually do, or he turns it down and stays here with you, leading a normal, unexciting life."

"Gee, Kait, when you put it like that, why would he want to stay?"

"It's such a dream, why wouldn't you want him to go?"

"Because I'm selfish I guess. I'd prefer having him here, where I can see him all the time. Where I know he's safe. Those tracks down south, they're bigger, longer and faster. I'd worry the entire time." She swung herself into the living room and sat on the couch.

Kaitlyn set down a couple mugs of steaming drinks and helped readjust Aurora's heavy foot onto a pillow. "I don't know what to tell you." A bump to the foot as Kaitlyn rearranged the pillows.

Pain racked across her face, narrowing her eyes. "Ow. Ow. Ow."

"Oh god, sorry." Kaitlyn jumped up.

"It's okay. It'll go away." She pushed into the back of the couch trying to press the pain away. A few deep breaths later, she opened her eyes.

"I'm really sorry."

"Kaitlyn I'm fine, really." And she was. The sharp, stabbing pain was starting to subside. However, it was being replaced by an intense ache. Not a good sign.

She glanced at the wall clock. Still had a good thirty minutes until her next pill.

"You don't look fine."

"I'll have to make due until Nate comes back. He's in charge of my drugs."

"Ah."

"Well, he thought it would be best. He was really leery of me getting any morphine in the hospital."

"That doesn't surprise me."

Aurora raised her eyebrow. "Oh, come on."

"You were a such a…"

"Bad person?" Shame covered her faster than any blanket ever could.

"No, never. I wouldn't say that."

"Then what?"

"You weren't bad. Messed up I'll give you. But you weren't bad. You didn't harm anyone. You never stole anything to support your… habit. The only person you damaged was yourself."

She had. Her drug habit had been a low point in her life, and sadly, she remembered most of it. Deep down, she wished she couldn't remember it. Then it would stay tucked away in the dark folds of her brain.

Kaitlyn held her hand. "And you've come so far. I've known you for a while now, and this is the happiest I've seen you, forgiving your present state." A quick nod to her gimped-up foot.

"That's what Daddy said too. Says I'm coming back to who I was. But I feel so lost."

"How so?"

"I'm not the same person I was before the accident. Not even close. That person, she was a child really. She knew nothing about life. And yet, I'm becoming her? Trust me, I know a lot more about how the world works."

"I think you're missing the general point. Cole probably means your outlook on life is changing. You're making plans, or at least thinking about it. A few months ago, you could barely make plans for the weekend, and now… Well, a lot of your long-term plans include Nate. You've got a family again, complete with crazy siblings. Yeah, you're changing. But it's a wonderful thing to see you go through. Not like the detox." Kaitlyn shivered, and it rippled over to her.

"Yeah. A low point."

"Hey, we all hit low at one point or another."

She heard the underlying tone in Kaitlyn's comment. "They'll come around, Kait. They have to."

Kaitlyn's eyes filled fast with tears and she wasn't a person to cry over much. The fact her parents were giving her the cold shoulder over her sexual orientation clearly hurt her. "What if they don't?"

"They're your parents. They will. They must. It's law or something."

She tried to smile to take the edge off, but it failed. Kaitlyn's tears streamed down her cheeks. "It's not like I choose this."

"But you choose happiness, right? And you and Tatiana are so happy. Am I right?"

Kaitlyn nodded. "We are so happy."

"And your parents, all your life have told you all they want is for you to be happy?"

Another nod.

"Well then, you show them. Be the happiest god-damn person you can be. You graduate top of your class and get the best teaching job. Turn your rental into your home, a sanctuary if you will. Show them you can be everything *you* want to be. Do what makes you happy. Your happiness is contagious. It always has been. And they'll see that and hopefully come to understand this amazing person they created is in love, and they'll have no choice but to embrace you. Because you are wonderful beyond words."

"Gee," she said, wiping away her tears, "when you put it like that…"

"I'm serious."

"And I love you for it." Kaitlyn leaned her head on her shoulder.

"I love you too. Is there anything I can do?"

"Will you stand beside me?"

"You know I will." Her eyes widened, and she ducked out from under Kaitlyn. "Wait a sec… Does that mean?"

Kaitlyn beamed. "Yep. I asked her to marry me."

"Oh my god, I'm so happy for you!" She squeezed her best friend. "When? How did you do it?"

"As for it being romantic, I'm sure it's the furthest thing. We were walking in the mall the other night and stopped in a jewellery store. Tatiana wanted to pick up new sleepers for her ears. So, as she was looking for them, I checked out the rings. She joined me and we tried on a couple for fun. This one she tried on was stunning, so I told her it looked great on her finger. She laughed but kept looking at the ring and me. I said it would be great if I could afford to get you something so beautiful for our wedding. It sort of slipped out, but she turned to me with this huge smile on her face. 'Yes,' she said. I of course gasped because I hadn't really asked, so I asked her if it's what she really wanted. When she nodded, I officially proposed. The clerk watching us clapped and asked for the ring back." Kaitlyn laughed. "Totally unromantic, but totally us."

"What a great story."

"Thanks."

"Do you have a date yet?"

"No, but we want to do it soon. Nothing big. Probably have the reception at Urban Dance or we can throw the party at our house since there won't be many people. Except we'd have to kick you out early, 'cuz you know..."

"That could be fun. Why so soon?"

"She needs to go back home in February, and we need to get all the immigration issues handled. Plus, she wants to have a baby."

"What?"

"Well, even though she'll be thirty in the spring, she says she's no spring chicken. Her clock has started ticking."

"Must be nice to have a ticking clock. Mine never got the chance." There was no jealousy in her tone. The statement was that—a statement.

Kaitlyn's gaze lowered to Aurora's tummy. "Nate knows, right?"

"Yeah and he's okay with it, or so he claims. But who knows? It's the furthest thing from his mind. He's knee-deep in reviewing this contract and trying to figure out the next year. Beyond that… It's this grey void."

"That's no fun."

"You know, I get the feeling there's more to this contract deal than he's letting on. He's not very forthcoming with many details."

"It's probably a lot to take in. You two recently got back together and he may be leaving you behind. I'm sure he's worried about that. And now with your busted-up leg."

"It's sprained, not shattered."

"Still…" Kaitlyn said, patting her arm. "He's got a lot to think about. Give him time and a little bit of space. Has Lucas said anything?"

"No. I think he's in the dark just as much. But who knows? He was so good at keeping Nate in the dark about what we were doing, maybe the tables have turned and he's keeping me in the dark."

Kaitlyn twisted. "You don't really believe that, do you?"

"I don't know what to believe anymore." She sighed and rested her head against the back of the couch. She eyed the clock. "I do know Nate will be here very soon and I'll get my pill."

Ah, sweet relief will be mine soon.

♥Chapter Nineteen♥

Bam. The books slammed onto the table, making her jump. "Lucas. What the hell?" she said, shooting daggers at him. "Do you need to do that every time?" The jolt caused her to knock a textbook onto the floor, so she bent over and snatched it off the floor.

"Yeah, I do." He laughed and grabbed a nearby chair, its legs scratching against the floor as he dragged it over. "Aw, c'mon. I'm playing with you." He reached out to touch her arm.

"I was trying to take a nap."

"Here? It's crowded."

"I got my official zombie notification this morning."

"Just in time for Halloween." He winked and gave her a gentle push. "Why not nap at home?"

"It's white noise here."

"You're not sleeping much, are you?"

She shook her head, watching as a butterfly, a giant M&M, and a small group of Monster High Barbies walked by, although the girls dressed as Barbies could pull those costumes off at any time. It didn't need to be Halloween. She gave her eyes a rub. "Nightmares, again. Plus, it's hard to sleep when I can't get comfortable."

"Nightmares still?" He cocked his head. "Here he comes."

A smile spread across her face, the anger leaving in a heartbeat when she spied her own personal sex-on-a-stick coming toward her, not that she was getting any lately. "But don't say anything to Nate. I'll tell him later. He has enough to worry about right now." Her eyes lit up as she faced him.

"Hey, Beautiful," he said as he bent down and kissed her. "Do you want to go home, or can you give me an hour?"

"I'd love another hour."

Lucas mocked her with a yawn.

"I'm supposed to meet someone here in a little bit. She's got study notes for me."

"Great. I'm going to run over to the gym for a quick game of hoops with the guys, and I'll be back at four?" To Lucas, he asked, "You're welcome to come play if you want?"

"No thanks, Bro. I have a huge assignment to work on. Mom wants to know when you're going to grace us with your presence." A smile etched his face as he glanced over to her. "Says she misses you."

Playfully, she smacked him. "Lucas."

"What?" A Cheshire grin spread between his ears. "That's what she says. It's the only thing she says, really."

"Whatever," Nate said to Lucas before giving his full attention to her. "I'll meet you here in an hour." He brushed his lips over hers.

"Right here?"

"This very spot, smartass."

"You know it."

"See you in a bit." He jumped from his chair and ran out of the open area toward the gym.

One gone. One to go.

"Hey look, it's starting to snow again," Lucas said, interrupting her thoughts.

She whipped her head around as the large snowflakes danced to the ground. "Oh," she said, her voice falling into her stomach.

It didn't matter how pretty it was. All she could think about was how it would freeze on the ground and make walking with the brick leg treacherous. Slippery. Angst-ridden. The previous snow fall had mostly melted away and hadn't caused any icy buildup, but if it stayed… She shuddered how much more limited her cruising would become.

"Earth to Aurora, come in please."

"Huh?"

"What's got you all worried? So, there's a little snow falling."

Unable to take her eyes off the flakes, she stared out the window. "Yeah, but…" *Calm down and breathe.* She turned to Lucas.

"Hey, you look like you've seen a ghost." He reached for her hand, warm against hers.

"Perfect, I'll blend in with all the others tonight."

"Everything will be fine. You worry too much."

"I don't think I worry enough."

"Should I call Nate?"

The thought had crossed her mind. But then again, she *was* meeting someone here who had a package for her. Latching on to Lucas' eyes, she forced a smile. "I'll be fine."

His eyebrow raised and his head tipped to the side. "You sure?"

"Yeah. I promise. I'll figure it out." *You can go now.*

Scanning across the public area of SUB mall, she spied someone. The person she anticipated all afternoon. The one who fit the description in the text.

"Sorry, Lucas, I need to go see her." She rose and grabbed her backpack, flinging it over both shoulders before grabbing the crutches.

Though it had been less than a week since the fall, she'd foolishly hoped she wouldn't need the crutches. But she couldn't put more than a second of weight on her foot before it screamed at her to relieve the pressure. It drove her crazy how painfully slow her body was at healing itself. After a full day of hobbling between classes, she ached everywhere. And the over-the-counter meds Nate kept around didn't work very well. She suspected he counted them before he crawled into bed, so she wasn't going to take more than recommended. But she ached and needed something stronger.

She swung off and crossed the space, meeting up with her classmate. A quick glance behind her. Lucas watched her sceptically.

She needed to be sneakier, and less excited about meeting a classmate she'd failed to mention previously.

"You got the money?" The heavily black-lined eyes stared through Aurora. Her jet-black hair hung limply in her sickly, pale face. Long black clothes covered her from neck to the floor, and a tiny symbol was painted between her eyebrows.

Casually, Aurora pulled out the folded twenties and slipped it into the girl's outstretched gloved hand.

The girl–the classmate–handed her a stapled package of papers she'd pulled out from her black bag. "Inside. Five, ten, and ten."

"Thanks." Aurora put her backpack on the table and placed the package inside.

"When you need more, text 'need chemistry help'."

Leaning heavily on her crutches, she kept her back to Lucas.

The girl stared at her as the zipper zipped shut. "Is there anything else you needed?" Her face was devoid of expression but her tone was sharp and critical.

Aurora wasn't sure how to answer and stalled for a breath. "No, just my friend is watching and I'm trying to pretend I'm getting homework help."

"Not my circus, not my monkeys." The girl escaped into a sea of other similarly dressed students, leaving Aurora stunned and flipping through options on how to explain the haste to Lucas.

With what she was sure was a loud swallow, she spun on her heel and proceeded back over to Lucas.

"That was quick."

"Yeah," she said unable to meet his gaze. "She gave me her notes. I'll give them back on Monday." She tugged on the backpack straps, tightening them against her chest. Had his eyebrows ever dropped?

"Everything all good?"

"Eventually."

"Oh hey, there's the guys." He smacked the table as he stood. Tipping his head slightly to the right, his blue-grey eyes narrowed at her;

enough to suggest he was curious about the transaction. "Call me later."

"Kay." Relief floated over her as he sauntered to his friends.

He turned back to connect with her. Twice.

Once out of sight, she pulled the papers from her backpack, and flipped through. A smile spread across her face as she spotted the contraband.

There in the middle of the packet of pages was a baggie with the three… four… five Ks–something like the Xanax, but stronger. Much stronger.

Her eyes darted everywhere. No one watched her. No one cared.

Another baggie contained ten Xanax and the last bag, held ten sweet little Percocets. Relief washed over her. She paid a pretty penny for all the drugs. They averaged four dollars apiece, but whatever. She needed them, and two right away for tonight's trip home.

She divided the Xanax lot in half, putting five into a regular pill container and the other five she left in the baggie and hid it deeply into the coin section of her wallet. For now. The bag of Ks she shoved into the depths of her track pant's pocket. She'd need to think of a better hiding place for those. But where? Someplace, no one would think to search. Hmm…

Another glance around to ensure her privacy, she removed a pen from bag and took it apart. Tossing the ink portion to the side, she extracted the precious bag of percs, and tucked them into the cavity of the pen. A small giggle escaped as she did it. No way anyone would search in there unless they needed a reason to search. Which they wouldn't. She's still clean and sober.

Well, not really.

And a sly smile tickled at her lips. The shot of morphine in the hospital derailed that, and the ten prescription pain killers kept it firmly off track.

However, she planned on keeping up the appearance of being clean. The Academy Award would be hers if she could figure out how.

♥Chapter Twenty♥

Aurora buckled herself into Nate's car. Breathing deeply, she melted into the seat and zipped her jacket up higher. She took a coveted pair of Xanax a few minutes before he was to meet her.

A long sigh escaped her lips as the pills raced through her system, and as if going through a checklist, ticked off one problem area at a time.

Slow down the heartbeat. Check.

Relax the breathing. Check.

Calm the racing thoughts. Check.

Feel good and warm all over. Check and check.

"What's on your mind?" Nate grabbed her hand.

Not much now.

She fought hard to have a normal smile, instead of giving in to the lazy, loose one her body wanted her to show. "Just worried about the snow falling and how icy everything will be."

"Nothing I can't handle. Tomorrow will be different if it keeps up." He pulled her hand up to his lips and gently brushed a kiss across it. "I'm sure we can find a spike or grip to attach to the bottom of your crutches as well."

Closing her eyes, she rested her head against the seat. Truth was, she was worried about the roads, but she wasn't feeling so uptight about it. But rather than give away anything by speaking or gesturing or making eye contact, she refused to glance in his direction.

The vibrations in the car soothed her, lulling her into a sleep. The car ride was quiet, but comfortable. For her at least. Judging from the amount of love squeezes, Nate didn't feel the same.

"Aurora."

"Yeah?"

"We're here."

"What? Already?" *Fuck.* How did they get here that fast?

"Yeah, you fell asleep."

Oh, well, that would do it. "Sorry. I didn't sleep very well last night."

"Anything you want to talk about?"

"No." Her gaze fixated on the newly fallen snow. The parking lot was mostly white, with the occasionally set of tire marks as someone drove through. "How were the roads?"

"Wet but not slippery. Yet. Tomorrow will be different." Nate grabbed her backpack from the trunk and passed it over. "Come on," he said, giving her the crutches and pulling her to a stand.

His rough hand fit hers perfectly and they walked silently into her apartment.

She kicked off her shoe and deposited her coat on the back of the chair, trying in earnest to be neater. Flicking the light on in the living room, she swung over to the couch and set herself tenderly on it, lifting her aching foot onto a plushy cushion. Sprawled out like she was, she took up the length of the sofa.

Nate crossed the room and stood in front of her. "You're awfully quiet today."

She relaxed further and closed her eyes, laying her hand across her forehead. "Sorry. I have a lot on my mind."

"Share with me."

Her eyes popped open. "Well, there's the finals coming up for which I feel totally unprepared. I used to be an A student in high school and now? I'm barely keeping my head above water. I think about your contract thingy. Have you made a decision yet?"

A head shake. "Not sure what I want to answer yet. I used to dream about this. Wonder what it would be like to be a part of the circuit, touring around. Racing was such a dream. When I met you, the dream, well, it shifted. It's not only me I need to think about, there's you too. My decision affects us both."

Yes, it would. And I want you to make the best decision. I can't tell you how I don't want you to go, because I don't want you to give up on a dream. You nearly gave up racing entirely because of me. I can't have you give up your dream either. But how to tell him. She didn't want to be selfish.

Tension hung in the air between them, this unsigned contract the wedge. Something prevented him from signing on the dotted line, she wished he would tell her what it was.

"Are you any closer to making a decision?"

"No. There is still a major kink I need to work out, but I can't figure out how."

"What are you trying to solve?" Ah the double dose of Xanax felt nice, and she allowed a long, lingering sigh float out of her. Each heartbeat she relaxed more. "Is it me?"

Nate ran his fingers through his hair. "No. It's something else I need to work out. A new problem has come to my attention I need to deal with first." His chocolate brown eyes darkened.

"Is it work?"

"No. That'll be easy enough to let go, especially considering there isn't a lot of construction work in the winter."

"School?"

"No, they want me to finish up. Instead of a full course load though, I'll be doing a class or two at a time. It's a much slower pace."

What was holding him back? What wasn't he telling her? He said it wasn't her, so what was it? Lucas? Was he worried Lucas would be hanging around?

"Is it money?" She could help with that. After all, she'd provided Lucas with a nice little padding to his bank account for school.

Surely, she'd do the same for her boyfriend in a heartbeat.

"Don't worry about it."

"But it's troubling you, and it worries me to see you so frazzled."

"Right now, all I want you to worry about is getting better."

As he turned her head, she closed her eyes to him, and his sweet soft lips brushed her own, while his fingers moved through her hair.

She wanted to pursue this, to escape in his passion but she couldn't do it. With a hand firmly on his chest, she pushed him away. "I can't."

"What's in you today? You're acting so different." His eyes got wide as he cupped her chin. "Aurora, look at me."

Her heart skipped a beat, and not in the romantic way. Taking a deep breath, and a longer exhale, she slowly opened her eyes.

Totally. Busted.

The hurt was evident in his eyes and disappointment loomed. "What did you take?"

Abruptly, she pushed away again and hobbled into the kitchen. *Avoidance. Yes, avoidance solves everything*. Time to start making supper. She pulled out a head of lettuce, a tomato and a cucumber, plus a new bottle of salad dressing.

"Talk to me." His voice came from the edge of the counter.

Although he sounded mad, he wasn't. Disappointed maybe, but not angry. "Tell me." His voice warm and comforting.

Refusing to answer, she filled a pot with water. "Spaghetti for supper?"

"I don't care what we eat." He stepped closer to her and pulled her close when she set the pot down. "I do however, care about you." He brushed the hair from her eyes, tucking it gently behind her ears, snagging it on her earring. "What did you take?"

"A couple of Xanax." The truth rolled off her tongue. It used to be so easy to tell him. In fact, until she got everything under control he encouraged her to take the drugs to settle her down. But since their summer breakup, where she adjusted to her PTSD and her subsequent withdrawal from the drugs, she'd been relatively clean. A set back here and there. But otherwise…

"From where? You finished off your weekly supply already."

"Do you check?" But she already knew the answer. Probably in cahoots with Daddy, his way of trying to get on his good side. She imagined the conversation the two of them had about this.

She wasn't stupid and knew better than to keep any Advil bottles around—in an easy to find location, anyway. Those were hidden in an unsuspecting spot not ten feet from where she stood. On her bookshelf was a copy of a wildly popular book she couldn't get into. Painstakingly, she'd cut out a nice little hiding place between the smut-filled pages. An inch thick and three inches wide by four inches tall. She planned to add her newest assortment to the cache.

"So where are you hiding these?"

"They're not hidden." She pushed free from him. "I bought five from someone in my OC class."

"Ironic, isn't it? You getting drugs from your organic chemistry class?"

"There's nothing ironic about it." She shifted, taking the weight of her good foot, and as quickly, put her full weight back on it. In frustration, she folded her hands across her chest. Damn foot was never going to heal.

"As much as I'm curious *who* sold you the drugs, I'm more curious as to why you thought you'd need them? You've been doing so well, or at least I think you have."

The doubt was loud and clear in his voice and she chanced peeking in his direction. "I'm not going back to my old ways, Nate. I can quit them any time I want."

"So why take one, if you truly didn't need it?"

"Just like you, I have a lot on my mind and sometimes it's nice to get away from it all."

His sign echoed in the small space. "There are other ways to deal other than drugs. Remember, Chris gave you some techniques. Do you need to see her, or do you want her to come over right away?"

Her shoulders rolled forward. "No, I don't want to see your sister like this. I simply needed to relax today. It's like…" She drifted off, lost for a moment in the sensation of her mind, which was a dark void of emptiness, rather than a dark mass of twisted thoughts. She much preferred this.

"Tell me…"

"It's like chocolate." His face twisted into a bizarre smirk. "Okay, so chocolate won't work. Sex," she said, her face lighting up. "Imagine if you went months without sex."

He smirked, and his sweet, intoxicating dimple showed up.

"Imagine I withheld that from you. Denied it to you. For months." She watched his expression slacken. "You'd want it pretty bad, right? Like it showing up in your dreams, dancing in front of you, reminding you of everything you're missing out on."

"Is that what your dreams are of?"

Fuck. Well, she walked into it, didn't she? She nodded.

"I'm sorry."

"It's not your fault."

"I get that. But I'm sorry it's haunting your dreams." He placed his hands on her shoulders. "What can I do for you?"

"I don't know."

"Did it feel good?"

"Huh?"

"The Xanax. Did it do what it was supposed to?"

Her head tipped up toward him. "Yes and no." She sighed. "Apparently it comes with a fucking large side of guilt."

If he tried to keep his grin under wraps, he did a terrible job.

"What?"

"Nothing." He wiped away his smile. "Guilt is an amazing thing. It lets you know when you've done something… umm…"

"Wrong?"

"Yeah, but I don't like that word, because it implies more than what I'm mean. There's a right and wrong time to use that type of drug. I think I mean your guilt was reminding you of how far you've come."

Tracing the lines on his shirt, she followed them down his chest.

"You've come a long way. And this is a minor setback. It's the only thing you've taken, right? No percs? Nothing harder?"

She shook her head. *Not right now.* "Just what the doctor gave us for my foot."

"Well, we can deal with this but I don't want you falling back into your old habits. How many did you buy again? Five?"

The lie came with the nod. Instantly her thoughts flashed to the other eight Xanax hidden in her purse, with the five percs. Discretely, as if she was brushing lint off her shirt, she moved her hand over the pocket in her pants, feeling the other—the new drugs—snuggled within.

People used Xanax and Percocet all the time, right? It shouldn't be such a big deal. And it really wasn't a problem for her in the past either. Until she combined them together or with other prescribed medications. That's when things went south. And when her prescription drug abuse started. Or escalated. It really depended on who you talked to about it.

"May I have them please?"

"What?"

"The other three Xanax. Can I have them please?"

"No."

His eyes jumped wide open. "What?"

"Well, what if I need them?"

"Then you ask me, and I'll give you one."

"But… but… what if you're not around?"

"Aurora, honey. I've practically moved in lately. When would I not see you?"

"But, what if…" Her mind ran laps trying to think of a way to get him to leave the pills with her. *Think, Aurora, think.* Every query she thought, he'd have an answer for. *Aha! Distraction. Move on to another topic.* She glanced around the kitchen. The water in the pot was boiling. "'Scuse me. I need to make supper."

Nate turned the stove off and moved the pot to another burner. "And it can wait."

"But I'm hungry," she pleaded, and instantly hated herself for sounding like a child.

"Five minutes isn't going to harm you. You not turning the pills over to me though is really starting to worry me."

"Don't be worried. Please."

"Hand them over."

"But I'm afraid. What if you're at your home and I need them in the middle of the night, but you're not here? Or in the middle of the afternoon when I'm in class and start to panic?"

His hands ran through his dark hair. "Well… how about I hide a pill somewhere? If you need it, text me and I can tell you where it is."

She narrowed her eyes at him, but had to admit it was an acceptable answer. Damn him for always finding a solution. All she wanted was the fucking pills to take as she needed them. Not when someone else dictated she could. She hated someone having control over *that* part of her life. At least he wouldn't be able to get them all.

Ha. I bought ten, used two, and will turn three over to you. So that leaves five for me. No four. No wait, six. What the hell. Ten minus two is eight. Eight minus three is five. Ha. Five. I'll have five to myself.

Inside she was cheering, but she kept the pissed off child-like frown on her face. "Fine," she said, swing-stomping over to her bag. Her foot screaming at her with each step. Angry, she extracted the pill container and thrust it into Nate's hand. No words escaped her.

Nate held the container, and after a few heartbeats, opened it up counting out the three remaining pills. Satisfied with the count, he closed it up and pocketed it. "Thank you." He held her hands, but she pulled away from them.

She grabbed the nearby crutches, and without a word, swung down the hall. For full effect, she slammed the bedroom door, stewing as she crashed on the bed. Too angry to think properly, she sighed as loud as possible.

"One, two, three. One, two, three." A quick inhale and she blew it out in haste as she counted again. "One, two, three," she said with firmness. "Fuck, it's not working." Arms crossed tightly over her heaving chest. "One, two–"

A knock on the door.

"What do you want, Nate?"

He opened it, leaning against the frame. "I'm curious why you're mad at me."

"Because."

"That's the best you can come up with? Really? You used to have some pretty good zingers."

A sigh. "I'm not a child."

"Thank god. Imagine the laws I'd be breaking if you were."

Damn him. His wisecrack made her smile. And she wanted to be mad.

"There it is." A smile formed on his lips. Not enough to make his dimple arrive, but enough he wasn't completely disappointed with her.

"I want to be mad, you know."

"I figured."

"So, can you leave? It's easier to be mad at you when you're not looking at me like that."

His eyes, those warm chocolate eyes with flecks of nuts, gazed upon her. With concern. With a touch of disappointment. But most of all, with love. "Not a chance." The bed moved beneath her as he sat down. "I've hidden them already."

Already? Where? She flipped through images in her mind thinking of all the possibilities. He wasn't out for more than a couple of minutes. "Thanks." She couldn't think of anything else to say, her mind focused on the location of the hidden pills. He was in the kitchen last, where would be a good spot to keep them accessible but out of sight?

"So… back to my question, Miss Avoidance. Why are you mad at me? I didn't make you buy the pills. If you needed more, and were that desperate, you could talk to Chris or Dr. Reynolds. No one wants you to suffer."

Her chin fell to her chest, and her hair hung beside her cheeks like a curtain. "I just wanted them for sleep. I'm afraid of the dreams.

I'm afraid to fall asleep because of them. When I wake up lately, it's been in a cold sweat." Her focus remained on her lap where she wrung her hands together.

"How often?"

"Often enough."

"Why didn't you tell me? I thought it was more sporadic than that?"

"I wish."

"Oh honey." He tucked her hair behind her ear and reached for her hand. "Please tell me. Talk to me. Talk to Chris. Talk to anyone. But don't hide it. Please."

"Okay."

"Promise?"

Words failed to sail past her lips as she searched deep into his eyes. Giving his hand a gentle squeeze, she leaned into his chest. "Thank you."

"For what?"

"For caring."

His arms wrapped tightly around her, and his chin rested on her head. "Of course. How can I not?"

♥Chapter Twenty-One♥

"What are we doing at the mall?" Aurora asked as Nate pulled his car into an available stall.

His eye twinkled with mischievous joy. "We're going to have a lot of fun."

"We could've stayed home and had lots of fun." She eyed him seductively. Damn, he was sexy. If only her stupid foot would stop ruining her life, they probably would've stayed home. But oh no, every little bump or twist shot up her leg and pretty much killed the mood. Too. Many. Times.

A wink from Nate. "And we'll try again later." He ran around to open her door before she had a chance to. "This will be a lot of fun. Something totally different. Something to get our minds off everything. Mid-terms, the contract..."

"My mind hasn't been on mid-terms." She gave him a quick kiss after she stood her good foot on the ground and grabbed her crutches. "It's always on you."

"I'm flattered, but I know better."

Inside the mall, she removed her hoodie. Wrapping it around her waist, it slipped free with her first swing.

"I'll carry it for you."

"No, it's okay."

"Aurora, I've got it." The hoodie looped over his arm. He kept pace with her as she swung herself into the mall.

"Are we going to watch a movie?"

"Nope."

They walked past a few clothing stores, a book store, the skating rink. "We're not going skating, are we?"

He laughed. "As much as I would love to see you on skates, it's not going to happen today or in the next few weeks. With your gimpy ankle and all."

Thank god. My hip's aching just thinking of it. A shudder coursed through her veins.

"What was that for?" He gave her hand a gentle squeeze. "The possibility of skating someday?"

She nodded and looked up to him. "Yeah. I worry more about what it would do to my hip though."

"Well, mention it at your next PT appointment. You have one next week, correct?"

"Monday or Tuesday. I'd have to check my calendar."

"Well, ask. Could be a fun date before New Year's."

"But what if I fall?"

"I'll catch you." He spun her around so quickly, it caught her off balance.

Her crutches crashed to the ground as she fell into his arms.

"See?"

Heart racing, she managed to smile up at him. "You're lucky you did."

His lips brushed hers as he wrapped his arms tighter around her.

She pushed back a little and righted herself. "Hey, Romeo, easy there. We're out in public."

"Afraid of a little PDA, are you?"

"I'm not afraid of it. I think out in public we should–"

"Aurora, my love, I don't care what any stranger thinks. I love you, and I'm quite content in letting the entire world know it." He tightened his grip on her and spun her around again.

"You're hopeless," she said.

"Yes, hopelessly in love with you." As he spoke, beneath the twinkle of his eyes was the truth. However, she was as much in love with him as he was with her.

With her weight on her right foot, she stood there as he bent over and retrieved the dropped crutches, waving away stares and glares from by passers. Placing them back underneath her armpits, she leaned on one and wiped the sweat from her forehead. "You sure do know how to sweep a girl off her feet."

He laughed but said nothing.

"I really wish I could hold hands with you. That would make your romantic gesture more romantic."

"Will this work?" Gently, his fingers grazed the small of her back, where heat emanated from it, warming a patch of cotton-covered skin. It was the next best thing to touching his hands. This was deeply personal. "So, no to skating obviously. No to the movies. Are we going dancing?"

"Could you dance with those?"

The crutches supported her well, but they'd never work. "Not in a month of Sundays."

Sporting goods stores passed by on her right, more clothing stores on her left.

They turned into the start of a collection of restaurants.

"You're taking me to a food court? Is my cooking so bad you think this is better quality?" Her eyebrow raised in questioning.

"No, not the food court. It's inside the food court."

"What?"

"You don't come to the mall very often, do you?"

"I come for the dancing, that's about it. Everything else I can order online."

"Well, I think you'll enjoy this."

She scanned the food court. There were many restaurants on either side, and the noise level increased the deeper in they walked. A fountain in the middle blasted streams of water ten feet high. Diners of all ages sat at the various tables scattered around, munching on cheap take out fare. As they walked around, she spotted an oddity within the heart of the food court.

"We're going to the arcade?"

"Mighty perceptive of you," he said as a low laugh sounded. "I thought it might be different than all the video games you have in the apartment."

"I've never been to an arcade."

Nate stopped dead in his tracks. "For real?"

"For real."

"Not even when you were in high school."

"I guess never being to an arcade would exclude high school?" She laughed.

"It's a rite of passage."

"Not for me. Besides, I was doing other things in high school."

"Like what?"

"Like studying for one thing. Once upon a time, I was an honours student trying to make top grades. I wanted to be a doctor."

"Doctor MacIntyre. I like it."

"Yeah, well it'll never happen." She pushed away the lingering thought. It was a long time ago. In the before times. When life was simple and carefree. When her biggest worry was the penultimate decision of what to wear to her upcoming graduation. If only she knew then what she knew now. Life had a way of throwing the shittiest curve balls and taking your dreams away in a heartbeat.

"It could."

"Sure. They'd love to hire a doctor who has a documented addiction to painkillers and anti-anxiety drugs."

"Had an addiction," Nate said, giving her a solid eyebrow raise.

They pushed to the middle of the arcade, past seas of people, to a non-descript circular counter with cheap, plastic toy prizes and a cash register on the one side. All around her were buzzers and bleeps, music and laughter, and a multitude of coloured lights. It was borderline sensory overload. As she checked out the crowd, she noted there were other couples her age. And younger teens. And kids with parents.

Every section had a specific set of games. Shooter games against the wall. Dance games at the front. Pinball. Old style Donkey Kong. Skeeball. Air hockey. Like a child in a toy store, she was excited to go and try a few out.

"Here," he pressed a small bucket of coins into her hand, "these are yours. Let's go play."

"Skeeball first," she said as she headed over to it.

"I thought you've never played?"

"I have." She winked. "I have this on an app."

Nate let out the most heart-warming smile, and with it, his dimple appeared. "You'll find it's a lot different to play it for real than swiping your finger across a screen." He loaded a token in, and the dropping and rolling of the balls to play made Aurora giddy.

After royally handing her ass to her in Skeeball, they played pinball where Nate continued to dominate her game playing abilities. However, she kicked his ass on the shooter games, to which he said he was surprised and fearful of. For over an hour, they dropped token after token into various machines, getting lost in belly laughs, laughing so hard their stomachs ached and shouting to hear themselves over the blasting music.

When her bucket ran empty, she frowned. "Aw, no more."

"Come on, there's one more game I want to try."

"You still have tokens left?"

"I've been saving them for this."

Turning her head left and right, she searched for an unfamiliar and unplayed machine. "I think we've tried every game here."

"Not this one." A spark flickered across his face but under the streams of flashing lights, she didn't read it in time.

A quick glance around the arcade. They had literally done every game except… "Oh no, no racing games, Nate."

"This one is different."

"How?"

He led her to the back area. The music was not as intense here, and the crowds had thinned out. "These machines are older. Like way older. The graphics suck actually."

"Encouraging."

"My point is, they're not even close to being real. Playing Death Commander Six was graphic. This is like a cartoon." He'd pulled her closer to a driving game. "See–shitty graphics."

As she stared at the screen, he was right. It was like something from before she was born. Very two-dimensional graphics, if they could be called graphics.

"You want me to play a racing game?"

His head tipped from side to side. "Sort of. Really though, I just want you to sit behind the wheel. Baby steps."

If her heart wasn't beating so fast from hearing the words—behind the wheel—she may have smiled at hearing the rest. Baby steps. His idea of getting her accustomed to touching a car and eventually sitting on it. Little tiny things that used to freak her out and now she'd adjusted to. But sitting behind a wheel?

"I thought I made it quite clear I wasn't interested in driving again."

"This isn't the same thing. Not even close. It's not real. There's no danger here. These seats don't vibrate when you smash into another car." Seeing the disappointment on his face must've meant a shaking seat was a great perk to playing a great racing game. This version apparently was for toddlers.

"I don't know, Nate."

He stepped closer to her, wiping away a wisp of hair, and gazing into her eyes. "We'll give it a fun name. Call it Operation Bigger Steps."

"Not catchy at all."

"Well, Operation Baby Steps has already been used, and quite successfully I might add."

With a knot in her throat, she stared at the child's game. The display was much smaller than the screens on the other games they'd passed by. The steering wheel was well used; sections of black were worn off revealing the chrome beneath. The flat, fibreglass seat was worn in places, and looked as comfortable to sit on as the floor. In fact, sitting on the floor would likely be more enjoyable. Actually, it would, because then she wouldn't be driving.

"Who's the craziest one here? You for thinking this is a good first step in what will arguably be hundreds of steps, or me for thinking maybe it's just fucking possible?" Her focus shifted from the two pedals up to him.

Nate had the biggest grin she'd ever seen.

"What?" she asked. "Say something." All he was doing was standing there, and it was making her nervous.

"You."

She placed her hand on her hip and was about to lean on the game when she caught herself. "What about me?"

"Did you hear what you said?"

"Yes…"

"The first of many, which gives what I'm trying to do, hope. And, the fact you're even thinking about it." That Cheshire grin of his remained plastered on his face.

"Sometimes I really hate you," she said in jest.

"I know."

It should be easier to slip into this seat than it is to get into a car. There are no doors, no seatbelts to pin me into place. Swallowing down a lump of fear, her eyes darted between the seat and Nate's still smiling face. Always the patient one. She was sure he'd stand there for an hour with a smile plastered onto his face if it meant trying this out. There was admiration in his patience, but right now, she wasn't feeling so charitable.

A swallow.

A knot in her stomach.

She passed him the crutches which he leaned against the wall. About to lift her foot and slip into the shitty-looking seat, she paused. "Wait." She turned to him. *Focus on his eyes. The way his ear to ear grin brought out his sweet dimple.* "How are we going to make this positive? You know, like we did with Operation Baby Steps?"

"What would help?"

"Fuck if I know. You're the one with the crazy plan." She hopped away from the machine.

"Okay, I'm thinking."

"You're thinking? Like right now? On the spot? You mean you didn't think this through?"

He sighed. It was probably not intentional, but it pissed her off.

Instantly.

Like a bat out of hell, she spun around and grabbed for the crutches.

"Wait," he said, grabbing a hold of her hand. "I'm sorry I wasn't more prepared. But I didn't think you'd be so–"

"So what?"

He shifted on his feet, but never let go. "I know you're stubborn, but I figured you'd at least try it."

"And I was about to."

"I know. I…"

Before he finished his sentence, his lips were on hers, pushing with intensity and yearning. A desire for connection in the vacuum of space they were in. She kissed him back, pushing up with her strong foot, pressing into him for all she could. She needed it too.

Breathless after a few dozen heartbeats, she broke away first and rested her head against his chest. "Okay, let's do this."

"Seriously? We can try another day."

"We're already here, aren't we?" Smugness crossed her face as she let go and faced the game. Or machine. Or the weak attempt at restoring her back to the old days where she took driving a car for granted.

With a few huffs and very little time to second guess herself, she closed her eyes and slid into the seat. *Not quite so terrible. It's like being a passenger. With a wheel in her face.*

His hand touched her right shoulder, and her left hand reached up, holding it tight.

"You're doing it."

"Yeah, I'm sitting in the seat. Congratulations are definitely in order," she deadpanned.

A tender squeeze meant to be reassuring only solidified the intense fear bubbling up inside her. It never ceased to amaze her at how fast the anxiety built when a heartbeat ago it wasn't there.

Where her stomach soured and rolled, her heart sped up and a cool sweat settled over her. *Just get it done and over with. The sooner the better.* With a shaking hand, she blindly reached out and felt for the cold hard metal of the steering wheel. Her fingertips touched first and she crawled them up and over, curling around the curved bar.

"Breathe," his voice whispered in her ear, closer than she expected. "You can do this."

I used to be able to. I used to have a perfect driving record. No tickets. No fines. No accidents. Until that night...

Her eyes snapped open. In front of her, the screen played; pink and red and green and yellow cars moved around on a grey road. The faster cars zipped onto the grass to pass the slower cars.

Her hands were still attached to the wheel.

All around her, sounds of bells, laughter, shouts and giggles mixed in with music. Lights flashed around, golden hues of orange and red lighting up the walls. Bright greens and vibrant blues danced on the floor.

Her hands were still attached to the wheel.

A semblance of a smile tugged at her lips. "It's not real," she said in a low, muffled voice. "It's not a real car, it's not a real wheel."

"And yet, you are really doing it."

"But it's not real. Not even close." Her heart thumped in her chest, slowing down to a normal speed with each deep inhale and release.

"I'm proud of you."

She considered his words and rolled them over in her head. Here she was, hands on a wheel, doing what she never thought she could. Deep inside, she had it too. *Pride.* Even if it wasn't quite the same thing. You got to crawl before you walk.

♥Chapter Twenty-Two♥

Nate's deadline dangled in front of her. A date circled on the calendar in red although she had no idea what his response would be. Even her response to him accepting the deal changed from moment to moment.

Yes, he should take it. It was a grand opportunity that would never come again.

No, he should turn it down.

But her reasoning for his refusal wasn't a solid enough answer because she had none. He needed to accept it. It didn't matter if it separated them for months at a time, that's what Skype was for, right? This was his dream, and he'd be foolish to turn it down.

The day of the deadline, Nate planned a romantic weekend for the two of them at a swanky hotel downtown. She figured it could only be for one of two reasons. Either he accepted the deal, and wanted to soften the blow, or he rejected it and needed a break from reality, with a weekend full of naked bodies and tangled limbs.

A small part of her hoped for the latter as sexual repression was starting to be a very strong emotion. It rivalled the need for painkillers. And if she could take a wicked painkiller and numb her foot, the sex would be amazing. She's make sure of it. Eleven days without it, and a man as sexy as Nate, well… it was brutal.

But first, they were having supper at Nate's house, and everyone would be there. Normally this would be no biggie as it happened on a weekly basis. However, today was *the day*, and she'd been waiting with bated breath to hear his answer. Apparently, he wanted to tell everyone all at once.

She loved being in Brenda's cosy living room. Although it looked like a picture right out of a magazine, her space was warm and inviting. Decorated with impeccable taste, she often wondered how one of Carmen's darker paintings would look on the walls. Regardless, the room always filled her with peace. Whether it was the beige leather couches, each decorated with jade-green throw cushions, or the dark wood end tables with elegant wrought-iron candle holders, she wasn't sure. Perhaps it was the lingering fruity-scented candles that filled the cosy space with hints of honeydew and lime. Whatever it was, it made her feel at home.

Plants stood tall in the corners, flanking a built-in bookshelf. A sprinkling of sci-fi titles and horror books were tucked amongst the many self-help books, which focused on healing and finding your inner peace. On the bottom shelf sat a vintage set of encyclopaedias. The gold lettering on the spine gave away their age, and the dust, their lack of use.

"Make yourself at home." He pointed toward the long sofa. "I'll get you a drink."

Yesterday she finally ridded herself of the crutches, but the payoff was an extremely sore hip and leg from the height difference between the air-boot and her normal foot. Until her foot was fully healed, there would be no satisfaction. Giving her lower back a rub, she walked over to the sofa and stretched out her good leg.

Nate emerged from the kitchen sporting a hot-water bottle. "For your back. I saw you rubbing it."

"Thanks." She happily accepted it, the warmth seeping into her aching bones.

He left the living room but returned a moment later with two cups of hot brown drinks. "My speciality."

She lifted the mug and placed it next to her lips. The aroma of chocolate and cinnamon aroused her senses. "OMG, it smells great."

"I figured I'd sweeten you up."

Eyebrow raised, she allowed the lightest touch of hot cocoa to pass her lips before she set the mug down. "Why are you trying to sweeten me up? Have I soured?"

Before leaving the university to head home and pack for the weekend away, she'd managed to discreetly sneak a perc when Nate wasn't looking. It greatly reduced her pain and made her feel damn awesome in the process. There was no souring that she was aware of and she hadn't felt like she'd gone down a wrong path.

"Hardly." He set his own mug down. As he reached for her, there was no denying the tremors in his hands.

"Are you cold?" The hot-water bottle soothed her back, but also kept her nice and toasty. The temperature hovered below zero outside and they were both freezing when they walked into his house.

"Nervous." His tone fell flat, and he didn't make eye contact.

The butterflies flitted around in her stomach, and her heart sped up in anticipation. She swallowed.

"I need to talk to you before I tell my family at dinner. Remember how I've been wanting to talk to you about something? Well, it's huge." His rough thumb caressed the top of her knuckles. "After talking with Rooker Racing, I needed to assess if it was the right thing. Then you had your fall, and I wasn't sure if it was the right time, but really, how often does a chance like this come around? And now, after being together all the time, I figured I just needed to come out and ask. Things are going to change so much over the next few months…"

Her stomach flipped. *Oh my god, he accepted the deal.* A tender squeeze on her hands and she found herself searching his eyes. They carried the weight of a thousand men in them and only had a fraction of the sparkle they normally had.

"Did you?" The rest of the words formed a lump.

His expression a curious mixture of excitement and sadness as if undecided about what he wanted to show off more. "I signed the papers at lunch."

"Oh… wow. Congrats!" Surprise cracked out of her voice as she bestowed out her regards.

"It's everything I wanted, or could dream of. They'll cover everything—all expenses—and I'll get a small salary on top of it. I'm on probation though, and they can turf me at any time, for any reason whatsoever, during the season."

"Which runs until?"

"Early December."

She swallowed. Hard. That was over a year from now. "And you'd start the season when? End of February, right?"

"Training starts January second."

Her stomach flipped again. Too soon. Two months and he'd be packing up and moving? Or travelling? "Would you be gone all the time?"

"Not *all* the time. Rooker's putting together a list of track dates and locations. He'll email me in a couple of weeks with the complete list, and we can check it out together. He did say I'd be driving in Alberta a couple of times."

"There's like one track here."

"Yeah, and I'll get to be on it." He smiled, but not enough to release his dimple.

"So, you'll be gone a lot?"

"A bit, yeah. But I can fly home on occasion. And you're always welcome to come visit me."

Visit you? The colour drained out of her face. "No breaks at all?"

"Not really, just the couple I've already booked."

Well now she needed to be sweetened up because she certainly felt like she was souring. She pushed the drink away, swallowed down her selfishness and plastered on a fake smile. "I'm glad you accepted."

"You are?"

A deep breath. She could do this. "Totally. This is a dream come true for you and I'm very happy for you."

The dimple showed itself. Not only did his smile deepen but his eyes sparkled. He was all lit up and it radiated from him. "I'm so glad you think so. It makes what I'm about to ask easier."

She tightened her grip on his hands as her breathing quickened. *Oh yes, that. The question.* A deep breath. Most people knew exactly how to answer *that* question, usually with a resounding yes. However, she thought most were asked some place public so the deck was stacked in favour of a positive answer. Perhaps Nate was confident of her answer. But would she say yes? It was so soon. Lately, her future—their future—weighed heavy on her mind, but a forever future? She was still young, too young really. Fear raced through her, and she wished she was more confident in her answer.

He released her hand, and she watched as it went to the pocket of his jeans.

Oh my god. She could hardly breathe.

He dug deep into his pockets.

Never pictured it this way. Thought he'd be on bended knee.

"I figured it would make it easier on both of us if I gave you something." His voice cracked a tiny fraction, and she worried he felt he was rushing the question. Shouldn't he be more confident instead of shaking?

His hand became visible. "Aurora, would you–"

"Yes," she blurted out, surprised at her answer.

He opened his fingers, revealing a shiny key.

Oh! Oh. She stared at the silver-tone key and saw a little racing flag on the head of it. Disappointment replaced her excitement.

"I was hoping you'd say yes." He held up the key, flashing it before her eyes.

"I'm surprised I did," she said, her filter not working. Her lips moved to say more, but her brain didn't register words. It was so not what she thought he was going to ask.

His brows shrugged together, and he studied her. "You weren't thinking…"

"Oh god, no."

"Because that would be quick."

A nervous giggle erupted from her. "Very quick."

"And this is a big enough step as it is."

"I agree." She laughed, taking the key from him and studied it. *But?*

The air between them hung around, little icicles forming in the air. "I thought it would make sense. With me being on the road, you could move in here. My room's in the basement, so there are a few stairs, but you'll be all healed before I go." He sighed as he tried to sell her on the perks of moving in. "There's always someone around."

Umm, yeah, because Lucas and Brenda live here.

"It's closer, in a way, to the U of A. You could catch a ride with Lucas, or take the bus or, hear me out, even drive yourself?"

Her mind went blank and her head bobbed slowly as she took in everything he said.

"I can still take care of you while I'm gone."

"How's that?"

"Well, you'd be in my house, sleeping in my bed."

"And what? Be roommates with your mom?"

"Yeah but not really."

She leaned away from Nate, pushing harder into the hot water bottle on her back. "But I have an apartment. One which gets paid for me and the lease isn't up until April thirtieth at least."

"You can live rent-free here."

"But I'm given an allowance to cover my living expenses. I hardly think Dad will continue with that if I'm living here."

"Actually, I think he will. It'll probably give him a huge peace of mind to know you're not living on your own and–"

"Do I need to be monitored?" Her tone pitched and matched the roller coaster in her stomach. The key cut into her finger as she tightened her grip.

"That's not what I'm saying at all."

"But it'll be safer for me."

"You're reading too much into this. It gives *me* peace of mind to know you'll be here. I'll have enough on my mind already."

"Because again, you think I need to be under watch and key."

"You're not hearing what I'm saying."

She tossed the key on the coffee table. "Not interested in moving in with your family."

"But…"

"Not when it's because you feel a need to keep watch over me."

"Aurora. There's more to it than that."

She shifted her tightened up body and glared at him.

"Things are going to change so much here while I'm gone. I need to know you and I won't."

Her eyes narrowed at him. "And by keeping me here, you think that'll help?"

"It'll help me."

"How?" Her voice terse and bitter. "The only thing changing is you."

"That's where you're wrong."

The sourness increased, and she swallowed back the bitter taste of bile.

"She's pregnant." The colour dropped out of Nate, turning him as white as the falling snow.

"What?" She had to have heard wrong, there was no way this could be true. It couldn't be. It was wrong on so many levels.

"She's due in May, right near my birthday."

"This is…" She stood and wobbled across the room.

The back door slammed and footsteps sounded up the stairs.

Lucas jumped into the living room. "Hey guys."

Aurora faced the corner, fighting the tears forming.

The air became ice cold. Perhaps it was because she was away from the warmth of the hot water bottle. No. That wasn't it. Despite the red-hot anger building in her, it wasn't doing a damn thing to warm her up.

"What's going on?" Lucas said.

Aurora hung her head and let the tears fall. She balanced her weight on the bad foot and quickly spun around.

Nate's face bore an unhealthy shade of grey. The sparkle long gone from his eyes as he held her gaze. His hands twisted tightly in his lap.

Lucas watched them both. The chill in the air froze him to the spot.

"I think you should leave, Lucas," Nate finally said, burying his head in his hands.

Lucas spun toward Aurora.

She wiped the tears away. "Does he know?" Her question directed at Nate who glanced up.

He shook his head.

"Marissa's pregnant," she said in Lucas' direction.

Lucas' mouth opened wide, and he snapped it shut. "You knocked her up? How could you?" He stormed over to Nate, hands outstretched ready to grab him.

Nate jumped up and out of the way. "It was an accident."

"God, that's gross."

"It's not like she's thrilled about this either. She had to give up a shot at the big time too."

"What?" she said, as her legs gave out and she collapsed into a chair.

"Rooker offered her the spot first. She turned it down because of the baby."

Baby. Nate was going to be a father. Marissa held the trump card. No matter what happened between her and Nate, Marissa would always be connected. Any family gatherings, his child could be present. Their child. The one thing she could never give him. Blood family. She'd lost- no matter what she did, she would never win.

She glanced at the key on the table. It reflected the lights, sparkling as she shifted in her seat. "I don't understand why you'd want me to move in if you knew she was pregnant."

"You don't get it."

Her eyes widened, and she stared at him, searching his face for the truth. "Please enlighten me."

"Fine, you want the truth?"

"Yeah."

He glared at her. "Yeah, because you've been so truthful with me." His hands went up in the air. "Does Lucas know you purchased extra drugs from someone in your OC class?"

From the corner of her eye, she saw Lucas drop his arms in shock as he confronted her.

"So, yes, there was some truth to keeping an eye on you. Rooker Racing prides themselves on being a drug-free organisation. They expect their drivers to be clean." A long pause as he placed his hand on his hip. The other pointed in her direction. "They also expect the driver's families to be clean." He stared at her with such an intensity, it took her breath away.

"Yeah, well…" She stared back at him. "Well, fuck that." Grabbing her coat and bag, she stormed out the front door and into the cold.

♥Chapter Twenty-Three♥

The air was colder than she expected and she hadn't worn proper winter attire to be out walking in the weather. Sizeable snowflakes fell all around her, and if she wasn't in such a foul mood, she would've delighted in watching them dance around her. Thrusting her hands into the depths of her pockets, she marched as fast as possible with the fucking air boot weighing her down and making her march more like a step and swing before starting all over again. She'd likely freeze to death before she'd make it all the way home. If the pain from the unbalanced walk didn't do her in first.

There was a bus stop ahead, should she try? No. Not really. Not without planning first. Aside from not knowing which route she'd need to get her home, she had no idea if she could stomach the ride. She wouldn't be buckled in and any little jarring could potentially fling her out of her seat. Assuming she could even sit on the bus. Many times, she'd noticed buses driving by with it's passengers standing. The horror.

What about a cab? Could she manage that? A stranger would be driving her. What if she had an issue and needed to stop? Would a taxi driver be so accommodating? Very unlikely. She scratched the thought from her mind as she rounded the corner and shuffled onto the main road.

Resigned there were no other options, she tightened up her

jacket, shifted her bag, and mentally tracked out the path to get her home the quickest, including a couple of stops at the corner stores to warm up. It would be a long walk.

Hot tears streaked down her cooled cheeks, but she didn't bother wiping them away. She limped along, the achiness building in her hips with each step. The magical powers of the perc were wearing off, and the other hidden pills were at her apartment—which according to Google maps—was at least an hour's walk away. It was going to be a long fucking evening.

A car honked in the distance. It wasn't uncommon to hear it in the city, but this honking was more insistent. And unrelenting as it repeated. She turned to see where it was coming from and stopped in her tracks when she recognised Nate's red car pulling into the side road where she limped along.

He pulled up alongside her and rolled down his window. "Aurora, get in the car."

She tried to ignore him, and thrust her chin out, storming away from him. It wasn't fast at all, but at least he was still behind her.

"Aurora," he said as he approached her again. "Please, get in the car. You'll freeze out here."

"I'd rather freeze than be with you right now, Nate. Besides, you shouldn't be seen with someone like me."

The growl rolled out of the car, sailed past the falling flakes and pierced her ears. "I don't care about that right now. I care about you and making sure you're okay."

"I'm *not* okay. How can I be okay?" Her hands left the warmth of her pockets and flew. "You have completely changed our future. Without asking me. How can I be okay with that?"

"Can we please discuss this in the car? It's freezing out here, and dressed in that thin joke of a jacket, I imagine you are ridiculously cold."

She didn't want to stop moving as it *was* keeping her semi-warm, but a hot knife of pain stabbed her in her lower back and made her buckle. *Fucking sciatica.* As she re-balanced herself, she stared at him and put her hand up in the stop position. There was no way she'd make it all the way home feeling like this.

His concern for her was all over his face and he shoved the car into park, racing over to her. Instinctively, he'd reached out for her but backed up when she glared at him. "Please."

"I'm walking home." Some way, somehow.

"Let me drive you."

She ambled away from him and took a few steps. "Don't you get it? I don't want to be with you right now."

"Aurora," he said firmly, "you are my responsibility. I will drive you home."

She nearly lost her balance as she forcefully stopped. Spinning toward him, her voice laced with anger, she said, "Your responsibility? I'm not a child, Nate. Your responsibility lies with Marissa and your child. I am no longer a part of that equation." More tears fell. "How long have you known?"

He advanced on her.

"Tell me. How long?"

"Get in the car and I'll tell you about it."

Her hip ached more than it had in the last few months. Thin pants did nothing to keep her warm, nor did the feather-light socks she wore. There had been no plans to be outside for any length of time and she was kicking herself for not planning better. She glanced toward his vehicle and imagined the warmth inside. The toes on her bad foot were starting to lose feeling. Would it be so terrible to get in and warm up? If she got out of the cold, would it be considered giving in? All she wanted was to put distance between them. She needed to think.

"Fine. But you're driving me straight home." She hopped inside and revelled in the instant heat, wigging her feet under the dash.

The silence between them was deafening, but she knew better than to talk to him while he drove. She didn't need to be the reason for any distractions and potential crashes. No, if she sat there and stewed in her head, at least he'd get her home safely. After all she was his responsibility. What a fucking joke! The thought made her blood boil.

No sooner than he had pulled the car into the visitor stall, did she begin. "So… how long have you known you were going to be a father?"

A long, exasperated sigh fill the interior. "Honestly?" Knuckles whitened as he gripped the steering wheel. "I've known since Thanksgiving."

Wow.

He knew at the banquet. *That's* why Marissa had glared at her.

"What are you going to do about it?"

"The honourable thing, of course."

"You're going to marry her? Because that would be the honourable thing."

"This isn't the 1950s, Aurora." He shook his head and closed his eyes. "I'm going to provide for her, for our child. Shared custody and all that. That's the bare minimum I can do. Taking this contract is a start."

"Shared custody? How? You'll be an absent father. How is *that* providing for her? A child needs a mother and a father." Hearing it roll off her tongue, she stopped herself. What the hell was wrong with her? A child didn't need a mother *and* a father, did they? A child could be happy with any loving parent, even two mothers. Oh boy. She heard Kaitlyn's parents in her own statement and it made her feel terrible. Shit.

"A child needs a nurturing environment. Say what you want about Marissa, I know Lucas certainly has, but she's a great person and once you get to know her, you'll see it. She's loving and warm and tender."

"Stop." She didn't the mental images of a tender Marissa with her beautiful hands all over Nate. "I don't buy how she's all sunshine and roses. Lucas told me how she changed you and made you an angry person. How she affected your driving and got into your head."

"It's complicated."

"You're telling me."

He twisted in his seat after he put the car in park. "You'd make a great step-mom."

"Like hell I would. Nate, I'm twenty years old. I'm in school. I'm unstable, remember? I'm hardly fit to be a step-mother. Besides, that would require us being married."

He cocked an eyebrow, hope spreading across his face. "Something to consider."

"Thirty minutes ago, you agreed with me that marriage was too fast and now you want me to think about it?" She opened the car door and stepped back out into the nippy air. "Marriage is compromise and working through things together. In one swift move, you've determined our future without any input from me." Her voice pitched. "You've created a child with another woman. You assumed I'd say yes to a weak marriage proposal, if that's what you asked. And right now, I'm about as far from ever saying yes as I ever could be. Goodbye Nate."

With a shove harder than she expected, the car door slammed shut, making her freeze for a heartbeat. Unable to turn around, she marched herself into the lobby of her building, fighting to keep herself together until she was in the safety of her home. Once the door clicked lock behind her, she threw herself on her bed and sobbed.

Morning greeted her with a giant middle finger. Her eyes hurt to open. They were swollen and tender to touch. Not only were her eyes sore, her body ached too. And not the normal aches and pains associated with her leg and hip. No, these were new. Her arms tingled and her head throbbed. She feared her rib cage was bruising on the inside from her heart pounding on it, trying to free itself. Anger coursed through her veins, and she couldn't understand where it came from.

What the fuck did that pill do to me?

That was a helluva pill she took last night. It was new, and it sounded good. Like a stronger Xanax. This was the total opposite. When the Xanax wore off, she'd never felt like this. She'd gone from total peace to a rageaholic in a matter of a few hours.

Feeling beyond hurt last night, she needed a mental escape which would've been impossible without something chemical.

Her phone had chimed with an incoming text from Nate. *Don't do anything crazy. There's a Xanax taped to the bottom of the blue mixing bowl.* But she needed something stronger than Xanax's proposed offer and remembered the Ks she'd hidden. It worked, and it took her out of her mind, but if this is what waking up from it felt like, she wasn't going to take them again. She felt like hammered shit. Angry hammered shit.

Retrieving the four remaining pills from their hiding spot in the living room, she walked over to the sink and rinsed them down.

Maybe Nate was right. Maybe she did need constant monitoring. However, she wished he'd asked her to move in because he loved her or something more romantic, not because of the obvious reasons. Would've been nice if the so-called proposal happened some place charming and elegant, not in his car as an afterthought.

An annoying buzz alerted her to someone trying to get into the building.

"I'm not here so leave a message," she said to the air as she walked down the hall and climbed back into bed.

The buzzer sounded again, but she refused to answer it. Too tired to get out of bed and no desire to see anyone right now. The appeal of falling back to sleep was greater than the appeal for a visit. From anyone.

As if fate had other plans for her, her phone rang beside her.

Lucas.

"Hey," she said, her words biting as they spilled out.

"Are you okay?"

"No."

"Are you home?"

"Yeah."

"Were you still sleeping?"

"I'd hoped to."

"It's eleven."

"So."

"Let me in."

"Not today, Lucas."

"Let me in please." The buzzer at her door sounded again. "I'll keep buzzing until you give in, and I know first hand it won't take much."

During the summer, she refused to let him up. It was early morning, and she was flat out exhausted. He warned her he'd keep pressing the buzzer, and she ignored it. However, after thirty seconds of pushing, she buzzed him up. Apparently, he was game for another round.

Growling as she hobbled out of bed, she dragged herself down the hall. Matted hair hung in her face, and she pushed it to the side. The buzzer depressed under her fingers and she leaned against the wall, waiting for Lucas's arrival.

He knocked once before he twisted the handle and entered. "Morning." He smelled sweeter than usual. A hint of the familiar Old Spice teased her nose.

It didn't matter though, she was still raging. "What do you want, Lucas?"

"You look like shit."

"Thanks. I feel about the same." She headed back to her room. With significant effort, she sat on the bed and pulled up her foot. *Geezus it's heavy. And swollen too?* A side effect from that nasty pill. God, was she thankful she tossed them. She didn't like feeling like this. Next time she'd stick to what she knew.

He walked in jacket-less and stared at her, narrowing his eyes. "You're acting funny." Remembrance flashed in his eyes. "What did you take?"

"Why is that the first thing everyone asks me?"

"I don't know, why is that? What would make us think that?" He gave a simple shrug and crossed his arms over his chest.

"I really wish I knew." Hostility poured out of her.

"Because old habits die hard?"

"Yeah, and maybe you don't know everything."

"So, enlighten me." A few feet away from her he stood, his

blue-grey gaze piercing her soul.

"I took a couple of Xanax, shoot me."

He didn't buy it. He gave her that look—one she hated seeing during their training sessions—the one telling her the shit oozed from her. "How many did you buy?"

"Seriously, what the hell is up with everyone tracking my pill usage? It's like being in fucking jail." Her fists slammed into the softness of the mattress.

"I doubt that very much." He smoothed out the blankets before he sat on the bed and touched her hand. "There's something I should probably tell you about us Johnsons because I don't think you've figured it out yet. We're a fiercely stubborn, if not loyal bunch. When we love, we love with all our heart and soul. Even if that love is not reciprocated."

Her focus shifted from their hands to his eyes on the last statement.

"Like it's in our genes to never give up on someone."

"But–"

"Shh, I'm not finished." The bed bounced a little as he positioned himself closer to her. "Nate's got that gene something fierce and I know what he's feeling."

Instinctively she retracted her hand a little but didn't let go. The longer he touched her, the calmer she became. It tingled up her arm and settled over her heart.

He shook his head. "Because I'm sensitive to people's emotions, Aurora."

She nodded with subtlety but suspected more. There was a time, not so long ago where she highly suspected he had feelings for her. It scared her, only because she fought those same feelings within herself. If she wasn't trying to win Nate back… Nah. The whole thing reeked of weirdness.

Lucas carried on. "It's borderline scary how bad he has it for you. Sad thing is, you don't even realise that."

"It's kind of hard when you learn he's going to be a father and it's not *my child*–"

"Yeah, what a huge surprise."

The heaviness in her leg started aching, and she scooted back further on the bed to prop a pillow under it. "Did you know?"

"Found out when you did, remember?" Lucas readjusted the mound under her swollen foot and sat beside her.

She placed her head on his shoulder. "How could he father a child with her? It's not fair." Her voice threatened to crack, but she held it together. For now.

"No, it isn't."

"I'm really mad at him for this."

"I'm pretty sure he knows."

"I'm hurt and confused. It took so much for us to get back together only to be on the edge of losing it all over again. It's like the universe is conspiring against us."

"It just seems like it."

"You think I should go back to him?" She waited for an answer that never came. "He's leaving in a couple of months. He made *that* decision all by himself. I wasn't consulted or asked what I–"

His finger covered her lips. "And what would you have said?"

The tiny fight building in her disappeared like a fart in the wind. She slumped into him as his arm wrapped around her. "I don't know. I would've talked about it more, and discussed everything, instead of keeping it all to myself."

"Like the way you are forthcoming and share everything?"

"Oh, shut up. I needed them to get through these last couple of weeks." She curled into him and lowered her voice. "But my past hasn't become my future."

He wiggled back and forth. "Yeah it has. Your accident forever changed who you are, and what you do with your life. It's in every decision you make. Yesterday, could you have taken a cab home?"

She shook her head.

"What about the bus? Was that an option?"

"Only because I didn't know the route to take."

"Aurora."

"Fine. I crossed it off my list as soon as it entered my mind."

"See… your accident is your future. And you're working so very hard on overcoming it. But it's always there."

"So, you do think I should accept this whole baby situation? Move in with him and be an insta-family?"

"Would it be so bad? Everything you'd need would be right there."

"But I have all that here."

"You're distanced from it. There, you'd be a part of the day-to-day family stuff. Nate knows he can't be here to be with you, to help you when you need it but won't ask for it. Knows what he's giving up for a once in a lifetime opportunity because they are the very reasons he almost turned Rooker down. He's trying to find the best way to keep you–"

"Safe?"

"No. That's not it." He took a deep breath. "He's only wants to keep you close. Yeah, I get how it's beyond weird to move in with your boyfriend when he's not gonna be there, and his mother is above you."

"And his brother is down the hall."

"Actually no, I'm on the main floor." Lucas smiled. "And Chris is a few blocks away." A wink. "But that's not the reason. It's his way of keeping you close. When he comes home, he'll truly be coming home. You'll be sleeping in his bed. Your scent will be all over his things."

"My scent? What am I, a dog?"

"It's called pheromones. You should really ask Chris or Dr. Navin about it." His long legs stretched out. "Anyways, he wants a home with you, he wants his future with you. And until he's back, this was the best he could come up with. Could you fly down there and travel with him between cities?"

Her eyes grew large. "It would take so long to get between. I'm not ready for that. I understand my limitations, better than anyone else does."

"Then cut him some slack, he's under a lot of pressure."

"I know." Her fingers rubbed under her knee, pressing on the itchy, swollen skin. "Trust me, I know what it's like to be under a lot of pressure."

He patted her leg. "I know you do."

"But I'm not ready for all of this. It's not even the signing the contract. Somehow, I think we could've made that work. It's the whole baby situation." She grabbed a pillow and hugged it. "I don't want to be a step-mom. It's not like he knocked me up and we're struggling how to make a baby work in our relationship. He knocked up someone else and then got into a relationship with *me*. He'll be a part time father, if that, depending on how often he comes home. I don't want to be the girlfriend living in her absent boyfriend's bed, babysitting the child he had with someone else. I… I…"

She closed her eyes and listened to his breathes as he contemplated her rant. There was so much to consider, and none of it positive. She was young, too young to be a wife if she was reading between the lines of what Nate had said. Definitely too young to be a step-mom. She was pretty sure it would be the world's hardest romance to be with someone who wasn't living in the same country most of the time. How would they ever make it work? It would be more like a friend with benefits type of thing, and you didn't need to be a in a relationship for that. Besides, once the baby arrived, he should, if he were to do the proper thing, he should be spending as much time as he could with his son or daughter. Which pushed her further down the list. He'd be coming home to have sex with her essentially. A lingering sigh escaped her and filled the room with despair.

"I can't do it, Lucas. I can't." A tear slipped down her cheek. "I can't be his girlfriend. Not right now."

"Because?"

"The timing's wrong. His focus is elsewhere and I don't think he should be focusing solely on me, but I'm not even on his radar."

"Sure you are."

"If our relationship was so fantastic, don't you think he should've discussed the dream with me?"

Lucas sighed.

"If it was your dad having to make that decision, do you think he would've talked about it with your mom?"

"You're comparing apples to oranges."

"Yeah, it's a bad habit."

"It's different."

"Lucas, you share more with me than Nate does and we're just friends." She sought out his blue-grey eyes. "Am I right?"

He didn't answer but held her gaze as he squeezed her tight.

Her tears kept falling. Tears of sadness. Tears of self-pity. Tears from knowing her immediate future would be Nate-less.

A soothing hand caressed her head but silence filled the room.

She breathed in a gulp of air and courage. "I took a pill last night. Something called the Kays."

As he inhaled sharply, his chest stiffened beneath her.

"I bought them from someone in my OC class, along with the Xanax Nate mentioned. I needed something stronger than the Xanax."

Lucas ran his hand down her arm.

"I took one last night to help me sleep or to make me forget or not care. I was hurting; emotionally, physically, mentally. And it worked until I woke up. My leg is swollen, everything hurts and I feel terrible."

He pulled her closer, so they were hip to hip.

"But you need to know I tossed them. The remaining Kays. Watched them go down the drain." She sniffled and buried into him as she sobbed. "I can't be with Nate for everything he's done and he can't be with me for the drugs I've taken. We're no longer a perfect fit in each other's lives." Tears fell fast and furious, like a flash flood. An ache in her heart formed. "It doesn't matter how much I love him. This will always be between us. The drugs. The baby. We're two separate entities no longer able to mesh."

Lucas smeared her cheeks as he tried wiping them away with his free hand.

"Since we've been back together, I'm so lonely." She tugged down on her sleeve and wiped her nose. "Isn't that weird?"

"A little," he said. "Have you talked to Nate about it?"

"When would there have been time? He's so focused on his classes, or on this contract and likely on Marissa's baby, he's not really here. Even when he's here, he's elsewhere. I can't give him sex all the time."

"Whoa, whoa, whoa. No, no, no. I do *not* need to hear that."

"But it's the truth. That felt like the only time we were connecting."

Lucas shifted slightly and pulled away from her. "Can I give you a nickel's worth of free advice?"

"Do I have to listen to it?"

"I would say you probably should."

"Fine." Her tears would fall regardless of what he had to say. "Let's hear it."

"I suggest you talk to Nate. If you truly want to end it, lay your cards on the table and let the chips fall where they may. He needs to hear what's on your mind and if you're gonna let him go, there needs to be a clean break. Trust me, it's easier to heal from, rather than wondering about all the what-ifs."

♥Chapter Twenty-Four♥

"Aurora, aren't you coming in?" Dr. Navin stood at the entrance to the hallway leading to his office.

She sat on the hard, plastic chair in the two-chaired waiting room, the only sound echoing off the walls was the receptionist clicking on the computer. Unable to make eye contact with her shrink, she violently flipped the pages of a parenting magazine, anger filling her as pictures of happy babies smiled up at her. "You know, I don't think I can do this today."

Dr. Navin waddled his way over, the chair moaning as he sat beside her. "Because?"

"I don't feel like talking."

"So why did you call and change your appointment time for now?"

"Because I didn't want to rely on anyone getting me here later."

After a long, exhausting night, she'd barely slept. In the morning, Lucas said he needed to get to class, and she bailed on going as she'd planned on catching a few winks. With a promise she'd be fine, he'd left. But she was tired of needing him so much. This, getting to therapy, should be something she could do on her own.

"You walked here?" The brown eyes beneath the greying bushy brows grew large.

"Yeah."

"With your foot in that?" He pointed to the grey air-boot.

Her foot throbbed as she looked down at it, pretty sure it was swollen again as wiggling her toes was tough. "Yeah."

"You really do have a stubborn streak." A gentle laugh filled the small space. "Tell you what. Before you walk back home why don't you come into my office and put your foot up for a bit and rest. I'll get you a warm drink and when you're ready, you can go home. No pressure. No requirement to talk. Just a safe place to rest for a bit."

She raised an eyebrow.

"You're being billed for the time anyways, may as well take advantage of it."

"Fine." The magazine fluttered from her hands and landed on the tiny table between the chairs. Pushing herself up, she hobbled down the hall and removed her jacket when she entered his office.

"Planning on staying awhile?"

"No, but if I keep my coat on now, it won't feel as warm when I go back out. Momma told me that when I was little." She inched her way over to the couch and settled in. Lifting her sore leg, she sighed with relief as she rested it along the length of the sofa.

"I see. Does a hot chocolate work?"

"Sure, thanks."

As he ambled out of the office, her phone chirped. *Lucas.* Are you up yet?

She typed back. Yeah. At the shrink's.

Your appt was at 4. I was taking you after class.

I called and changed the time.

You walked there? In this?

Part of being crazy. I can handle it.

Aurora! When are you done?

I'll be fine. Honestly. The walk gives me time to think.

I'll pick you up in a bit.

I won't be here in a bit. I'm not staying. I can't adult today.

She sighed. She wasn't staying long enough for him to drive

over from his class. His last class ended at three seventeen, which was why he'd planned on taking her. Simply resting her foot and warming up, and she'd be on her way.

Dr. Navin returned and placed a cup of hot chocolate on the coffee table. He stood by the door. "Should I close this, or leave it open?"

She stretched out her neck and shrugged. "You can close it if you like."

The door latched behind her and he shuffled over to the other couch. "What happened to your foot? Is that why you cancelled two weeks ago?"

"Yeah. I jumped out of a swing and rolled it. But I'm out of the crutches now, so it shouldn't be long and I'll be out of this boot too." The toes peeked out and gave him a wiggly wave.

The scent of chocolate tickled her nose, and she took a cautious sip. It was warm, not hot, the perfect temperature to take a longer taste.

"How long until that happens?"

"Another four to six weeks, if I'm good. Definitely before Christmas."

"Define good."

"If I push myself but not too the breaking point, but also give it time to rest."

"That's good. Must be hard to get around though."

"Actually, it is. The height difference doesn't seem like much until you've walked a distance. It's murder on my hips. They ache a lot more now."

He nodded slowly and reached behind his desk absently. Her folder, thick as it was, was held tightly in his hand. "Do you do anything non-medicinal for pain relief?"

"Hot water bottles and muscle rub, but I'm tired of the menthol smell. It's hard to take a bath when I'm home alone and the shower, well, there's only so long I can stand on the good leg."

"Have you…"

Taken drugs for it? Every muscle in her body tensed and her hands curled into tight little wads.

"I was going to suggest chiropractic therapy, but I see I've struck a nerve." His focus dropped to her fists. "Chiropractors would really help. I can refer a couple to you if you'd like."

"Fine," she said, growling under her breath.

He grabbed his Rolodex and flipped through. Jotting down names and numbers, he ripped off the paper and passed it to her. "I think they are both very close to you, in the medical centre east of here."

"Thanks." She shoved the paper into the pocket of her leggings.

"Do you want to talk about the shift in your mood?"

"No."

"Remember, anything you say here is held in confidence. It never leaves this room."

"Yeah it does. It gets written into my file." She focused on the thick assortment of papers piled on his lap.

"Only for future reference." He pushed the folder into the middle of the table. "But today, I will leave it closed if there's anything you want to share with me. Off the record."

She stared at the folder and let her gaze travel over to the shrink's face. He was totally sincere in his comment. A low sigh rumbled out of her. "I wouldn't even know where to start."

"Let's see," he said, giving his bearded chin a rub. "How about you start after our last appointment?"

God, that seemed like so long ago, but it was only a month. How could so much have happened in so short of a time span? She chuckled.

"Something funny?"

"No, I don't think there's enough time."

"Try."

"Well, let's see." Different images floated through her mind. "Well, I went to a banquet with Nate, where he met this PR guy who offered him a contract to race with his company which requires him to travel all over the US and parts of Canada. I think. Nate keeps pushing me to get behind the wheel again and took me back to the scene of the accident and I had a mini re-lapse." She didn't miss the slight twitch as he went to reach for her folder and pulled back quick. "But it wasn't as bad as everyone feared as I got into a car in less than twenty-four hours just fine. Two weeks ago, I sprained my ankle and got a nice little hit of morphine to go with it. Nate moved in for a few days to help me. On Friday night, he surprised me with a key to his house, hoping I'd move in there. But I turned him down and walked away."

Dr. Navin rubbed his beard. "Because he asked you to move in?"

It was building, and dammit, her resolve was fading. Tears welled in her eyes, fighting to push out beyond their holds. Her heart ached and her breathing quickened. From her soul to the tips of her fingers, everything in between started to tingle. "No." The dam breached. The tears fell. "Because he knocked her up." Intense pressure caved in on her. "And I… And I… I can't deal with him being gone for so long." A loud sniff and she reached for the tissues, yanking a few out.

A subtle little shake. "Who's pregnant?"

"Marissa. His summer girlfriend." She wiped the tears streaming down her cheeks with the sleeve of her shirt.

He nodded and again his hand twitched. "When you say he's going to be gone, does this mean he accepted the contract?"

"Yep." She blew her nose into tissue after tissue, and dropped it into the garbage pail Dr. Navin set in front of her.

"And how do you feel about that? His contract."

"Horribly conflicted." More tissue balled up in her fists. "I want him to go for his dreams but at the same time, we just got back together. I don't want him to leave."

"Did you break up?"

"I walked away, but no, not yet. I needed space to think it through. But…" She listened to the clock tick. "I wasn't a part of the process. He never asked me my opinion on it, only expressed what a chance this is for him. He kept reiterating how it was only for ten months or so, and it's not a chance you say no to."

"Okay."

"No, it's not okay. I would've told him to take it regardless, all

I wanted was to be involved. He told me I was his girlfriend and yet he never shared any of it with me. I'd ask about details on the contract and he'd change the topic. I know it's a golden ticket for him, but it's such a huge decision. How's there supposed to be a future for us, if something as major as this, he can't really discuss with me? You know, he didn't even share details with Lucas. Well, not as many anyway. And if he did, Lucas kept pretty mum about it." She inhaled long and hard, trying to calm her body down to a manageable level. Doing as he would've instructed, she breathed in, held it for three and released it slowly.

"Lucas is in a hard spot."

"I know he is, and I hate that he's in it. But he's my best friend. The one I can tell anything to."

"What about Kaitlyn?"

"I love her to bits, but she's a little wrapped up in her fiancée right now. Tatiana's here and they are very consumed with each other. I don't want to be the drama queen and pull her away from her happiness. She's got a lot on her own plate right now. She doesn't need to be consumed with my problems."

"That's what friends are for."

"I know. But I also want her to bask in her happiness. She's all lit up inside and I want it to stay with her for as long as possible. It doesn't last long."

"How's that?"

"With Nate, that wrapped in butterflies feeling faded so quickly. The first time we were together, it was non-stop, and now? It's gone."

"That's because you're comfortable with each other."

"Maybe. Maybe not. He's known he's going to be a father since Thanksgiving, only two weeks after we got back together. Even Lucas didn't know until Friday."

"I'm sure Nate needed time to figure things out."

"Why are you on his side?"

"I'm not. I'm just trying to help you see Nate's side of it. Trust me, I take no sides."

She narrowed her eyes and wiggled her toes. The swelling had reduced and her toes flexed with a little more ease. Her fingertips wiped under her eyes and an unsettled feeling of doom washed over her. It was time to go. She came, she rested and said more than she expected. She was done.

"How's your foot?"

"It's better, thanks." Her hand rubbed a dull ache in her hip.

"Still sore?"

"Perpetually."

"Try the chiropractors."

"I just need another perc," she said absently. As the hard C rolled off her tongue, her eyes got wide as did Dr. Navin's.

"Care to share? Remember, it's off the record."

It wouldn't make her feel any worse to share it, so she spilled. "After the hit of morphine in the hospital, I craved that feeling again. It was so wonderful for a moment in time. To get lost in it. To not give a damn about anything at all. The ER doc gave me a handful of T3s but only enough for a couple of days, and Nate was like, super hesitant to take me to the doctor's to get a refill. Advil did fuck-all. I happened to whisper under my breath in my organic chemistry class how I needed some drugs. When I got back from a bathroom break, a piece of paper with a phone number was on my chair and the words *need chem help? Call me.* So, I texted, what the hell. I actually did need chem help so it would've been cool either way. But one thing led to another and before I knew it, I made my first purchase." God, it felt so good to confess the whole thing to someone. Someone who shouldn't judge her as he was required to be diplomatic. At least she hoped. He hadn't yet touched her folder.

He cleared his throat. "How many?"

"Enough to get me through a few days."

"And Nate never noticed?"

"Nate wasn't around."

"Ah." He studied her. "And they took the edge off the pain?"

"Yeah. Except for one type of pill. It was good at the time and did what I hoped but when it wore off, I was a rageaholic, like Hulksmash angry. I hurt more, my foot was swollen, and I felt bloated. I was a hot mess. So, I dumped those down the drain."

"That's a start."

"I'll stick to what I have now. They take away the hurt." Which she was thankful for, otherwise, there would have been no way she could've made the long walk to the office.

"Assuming of course you're getting legit pills, which you probably didn't receive based on your reaction to whatever it was you took last. But I'll leave that with you to digest." He inched closer to her and folded his hands into his lap. "Aurora, you don't need me to tell you about the dangers of addictions, as I'm sure you can get that lecture from any of your friends. However, I am concerned with you taking the pills as a way to escape, especially considering they are black market drugs." He studied her. "It's not just for your leg and hip, am I right?"

She stared blankly at him.

"That's not chronic pain needing to be addressed, it's more than that. I want to help you but you have to want to help yourself first. I firmly believe a battle brews within you, and I'm confident, together, we can win this war."

She pulled back into the softness of the sofa. "I'm beyond help."

"I don't believe that, and I'm pretty sure you don't either. Not really. You wouldn't have dragged yourself here in the freezing weather if a part of you wasn't reaching out for help."

"I want to zone out. There's nothing wrong with that."

"You're right, there isn't. But when you're using drugs to do it, we need to find other ways of managing that need."

"They help me sleep at night," she offered up for a suggestion.

"Temporarily. But what are you afraid of facing? What are you trying to hide from?"

"I'm not hiding."

He raised his bushy brow at her.

"I'm not."

"Why aren't you sleeping?"

"Nightmares."

"Consisting of?"

"Car crashes."

"Your own?"

"Nate or Lucas's."

"Why do you think they keep surfacing?"

"Hell if I know. The internet hasn't helped much either. Those dream dictionaries are a joke."

"Why? What have they said?" Elbows on his thighs, he leaned toward her.

"Seeing a loved one in a crash suggests something within me is already dead and how it's symbolic of my relationship with that person. One website suggested I'm lacking ambition and goals."

"Are you?"

"No. I have goals."

"Share them with me."

She blinked rapidly. "I'm putting out feelers for Northern Lights Racing. It's Nate's company that Lucas will be racing under. I've started up secret social media accounts following racers and teams and sponsoring companies. I'm trying to get a better handle on the non-racing component so I can be of assistance to them and help them with the business side. The politics of racing are crazy and I sense a ginormous learning curve ahead of me, but I think I'll be able to understand it better soon. Lucas says he's unable to handle much of the business component and Nate will be completely unavailable since he'll now have to sever ties. Well… I don't want them to be in the lurch, so if I can do this little thing for them..."

"But why the secrecy? Why the fake accounts?"

"Because if I say anything before I achieve the goal I've set out for them, then I'm a failure."

"You're not."

"Not yet, but if I can't secure anything for them, I will have failed."

"I can't see how trying to help them out, especially when a fear is there, can fail."

"It's like the money I gave to Lucas a few weeks ago. Do you think if he knew I was going to do that, would've helped? Not likely. Would've thought I was hiring him for a job as opposed to thanking him. It was hard enough to get him to accept the cash as it was. Same thing with this. If at the end of the day I can talk shop with them, and we're all on the same page, it would be great for business. I wouldn't need a translator to help me understand."

"I'm proud of you for taking those steps."

"You are?"

"Yeah. When you first came here, you couldn't ride in a vehicle, and here you are trying to drum up business for a racing company, and learn about the career Nate loves so much."

Those words warmed her heart.

"But I think you need to stop hiding behind the secrets. *Any* secrets. I take it no one knows about the drug purchases?"

"Yeah, they do now. Nate knew, but he thought it was only Xanax. And he told Lucas."

"I see. Were you mad at Nate for telling?"

She slumped in her seat. "Actually, not really. I was shocked, but not mad."

"Why do you think that is?"

"I don't know."

"And what was Lucas's reaction?"

"Shock as well. But he was finding out a lot of info in a small amount of time. I wasn't sure if he really heard the drug thing after the whole baby surprise. Regardless though, the next day he came over to talk to me about Nate, and I spilled the beans on the bad pills I'd flushed."

"Does he know about the other drugs?"

She shook her head.

He glanced up to the wall. "Damn, I wish we had more time. The hour's almost up."

"What? I just got here." She craned her neck toward the clock. "Wow. That went by fast."

"Considering this new development, I think we should increase our appointments to weekly. Do you agree?"

She hesitated before answering. "Yeah."

"Good. I'm also going to strongly suggest you join a Narcotics Anonymous program. You're on the right path getting rid of the contraband, and I want to help you succeed in your efforts."

She swallowed. "I don't know if I'm ready for that yet."

He sighed. "While you contemplate it, I want you to complete a homework assignment for me."

"Are you serious?" The last homework assignment was to make a list of 50 things that made her happy. It took her weeks to finish. "What kind of list do I need to complete this time?"

He laughed. "No list, not today. I want you to stop with the secrets. If you're trying to hide something, then you'll know what you're doing is wrong. And if it's wrong, ask yourself why you're doing it, and see if there's another solution."

"Sounds tougher than making a list."

"Good. I know you like a challenge."

"Ha-ha."

"The little moments where you feel like you need to hide away, write them down as it helps with accountability."

She pushed herself to a standing position.

"I expect to hear of a couple of moments by next week." He scratched his pen across a sticky note. "Here."

Don't hide the secrets, you only give them power. Expose them and you shall be set free.

She re-read the passage multiple times. "You're asking a lot."

"I only push my patients if I feel I will be pushed back. I have a feeling you're going to push me, and that's a good thing."

"Thanks Doctor, for today."

"Thanks for coming and for taking charge of your health."

Taking charge of my health. Hmm.

She grabbed her coat and shuffled into it, hobbling down the hall. As she rounded the corner to the waiting room, she spotted him.

Long jean-covered legs stretched out, and his strawberry-blond head bent over whatever was holding his interest on his phone.

"What are you doing here, Lucas?"

"Cutting class." He rose and gave a half-hearted wave to Dr. Navin. "You're not walking home in this." The underlying tone was caution.

"I'll be fine, I made it here, didn't I?"

"And it's cold. You are many things, but you're not foolish. I'll drive you home. Besides, we need to talk."

♥Chapter Twenty-Five♥

The blowing snow and rapidly dropping temperatures had descended upon the city in the hour she'd poured her thoughts out to Dr. Navin. She shook off the accumulating snowflakes on her head as she stomped into the main entrance of her apartment building.

"Thanks for getting me home, Lucas." She dusted off the sleeves of her jacket. How could she get so covered in snow walking from the parking lot into the building? There was going to be a blanket of white on the ground when Kaitlyn picked her up to go dress shopping later. She shuddered at the thought.

"I said we were gonna talk, and we're not doing it here. Let's go up."

A hesitation in her step. The book with the hidden contraband sat on her coffee table. She couldn't remember if it was closed or open? Until she either remembered or checked personally, there was no way he was coming into the apartment.

"Not right now."

"Why?" His eyes narrowed a touch, and he bridged the distance between them.

"Because…" *Think, Aurora.* "Because… it's messy and–"

He laughed. "I've seen it messy several times before."

"Yeah? Well it's really bad today."

"Whatever." He pushed the up button for the elevator. "I'm not there to check on your housekeeping skills. I want to talk to you."

Sigh.

The elevator chimed, and they stepped inside.

"Honestly," Lucas said, "how messy could you have made it in—" he checked his watch "—a few hours. It wasn't that bad when I left at seven thirty this morning."

He was right. It wasn't bad when he left. He needed to leave earlier than normal to run home and change his clothes. When he'd come to check on her last night, there'd been no plan on staying.

"It's just…" She watched the numbers light up, each one getting her closer and closer to her home. "It's just… I'm all talked out today. After talking all day yesterday, and this morning, I'm emotionally wrung out."

"I understand." He held open the doors for her when they stopped on her floor. "Even more reason for me to talk to you. You'll interrupt me less and hear what I want to tell you."

She cocked an eyebrow at him and led him down the hall. Tossing her purse onto her shoes, she flung her jacket over the back of a chair and hobbled over to the couch. The contraband hiding book was closed. Relief settled over her like a wave.

"What's on your mind, Lucas?" She flopped down on the couch and fiddled with the air-boot, the Velcro ripping as she separated her foot from its confines.

"I want to talk about your future."

"We've been through this."

"Nate's coming here in a bit."

"He's what?"

"You two need to talk through this. You running away–"

"I hardly ran, and besides he caught up to me."

"My point is you need to face this. Face him and talk."

"Why?"

"What do you mean why?"

"Why is it so god-damn important we discuss this? It's over." She smacked the couch cushions for effect. "No matter what happens, Marissa will always be involved in his life. Forever. There is nothing, I repeat, nothing to change that."

"I know that."

"She's going to be a part of *your* family. You're the one who needs to face it, not me."

"I'm not here to discuss Marissa's involvement in our family, because quite frankly it disgusts me. If he was to have kids with anyone, it should be with you."

She snorted. "Yeah, well that's never going to happen."

"It still could."

"No."

"Just because you've broken up…"

"Just because I have no uterus."

His face dissolved from softening anger into total confusion, and he dropped onto the sofa beside her. "What?"

"The accident made sure I would never reproduce." Disgusted, she twisted away from him and stared at the picture of her family. "Sorry, I thought you knew."

"I'm sorry." Air escaped from him in a loud whoosh. "That explains the anger around the pregnancy. I figured you were just jealous."

She laid her head on her arm. "I am. For that reason. I can never give him a blood descendant. She can and has."

"But there's so much more you can give him. He's a better person with you. You have so much in common."

A sad laugh breezed out of her as the buzzer rang. "We have nothing in common."

Lucas walked to the door. Leaning into the speaker, he asked, "Hello?"

"It's Nate."

"You said he was coming later."

"It is later." He pushed the door unlock button. "You need to make this a clean break. Either make up or break up. I know how you feel and I know how he feels, but neither of you knows how the other feels. And that's wrong." Silently, he leaned against the wall, waiting for his brother to arrive.

Panic settled in for a little snuggle as she glanced around. She shook out the special sock and yanked it over her tender foot, wincing as her ankle wiggled. A peek to the book. Could she sneak out a pill before Nate arrived? Not if Lucas kept staring at her. A knock on the door as it opened.

Nate stood at the entrance to her apartment. He looked a wreck, the dark circles under his eyes gave him an exhausted appearance. The five o'clock shadow from Friday had grown into a light beard, the sexiness long gone. His broad shoulders rolled inwards and his hands hung limply in the pockets of his leather coat.

"I guess I should invite you in?" She cast her gaze down as her foot slid into the cavity of the boot. With a solid yank on the last Velcro strap, she winced in pain.

"Don't take your anger with me out on your foot," Nate said with concern in his voice and crossed the floor, standing feet away from her. "It'll never heal."

She loosened the straps and re-did them, easing up on the yanking.

"I'm sorry, Aurora. I never meant for this to happen."

"Which part?" Her tone was tart as she snapped at him.

Lucas inched himself into the room, carrying a chair for Nate. He motioned for Nate to sit while he sat on the other couch.

A pained expression shadowed Nate's features. "Not discussing any of it with you."

"Are you sorry for shutting me out?"

"I think so."

"You think so? Wow." She challenged Lucas, balling her hands into tight fists. "This was a great idea. I can see we're going to clear the air and work out our differences this way."

"Now you listen here, Aurora, and hear me out." Nate's tone

had an edge to it and it caught her attention. "I needed to see all angles of this contract. Your fall–"

"Which was your brilliant idea."

"It changed everything. I had to re-evaluate the contract. I had to see if I thought you would be good on your own. I worried about it, and watching you fall under the spell of the morphine, I was concerned. And when you begged for more drugs, I became even more worried. I saw my contract go up in flames."

She huffed and looked over his shoulder, to one of Carmen's paintings hanging above the kitchen table. "Am I hearing you correctly? Are you saying I'm a liability?"

"You absolutely are." He shook his head. "I'm sorry, it's the truth and I'm not going to sugar coat it. But…"

The sting of his answer wounded her, but she held back her tears. There was no way he would get to see them fall. Not anymore. She focused on Lucas, trying to draw strength from him. It failed. He didn't make eye contact with her, or his brother.

Disgusted by Nate's honesty, she barked out. "At least I know where I stand in the scheme of things."

"That's the thing. You don't." He shifted his chair, facing her head on. "You think you rank low in my life, somewhere after my career and this baby, but the truth of the matter is you're the first thing I think about when I wake up and the last thing I think of when I fall asleep."

"Your career?" Her voice pitched unnecessarily high. "Your career? Need I remind you, you'd planned on retiring a few weeks back? Re-tire, Nate. As in give up racing all together."

"I know what retiring means."

"Then why be so focused on this new career, if seven weeks ago, it wasn't even in the cards for you?"

"Something changed."

"Clearly. What was it?"

"You." He stared at her. "And Marissa."

She gasped and looked to Lucas, who shook his head with disapproval but said nothing.

"Both of you changed me. Yes, seven weeks ago I was ready to turn my back on the sport I love, for you, until you showed up at the track, and suddenly, I had it all. I had you back, and I still had my dream. When we travelled by car, you proved it could be done without drugs. Everything seemed easy." He got a far off look on his face and he ran his hands down the length of his thighs. "Until Thanksgiving, when Marissa dropped her news on my lap. Then the contracted offer appeared. Then your fall, along with your constant need for the drugs." He rubbed his hands together. "I was afraid if I lost one of those things; you, the offer, my baby, that I'd lose out on everything."

"I'm so confused."

"That makes two of us," Lucas said, narrowing his eyes at Nate.

"I knew deep down I wanted the offer, the absolute second he told me about it. Do you know how hard I fought to not sign it right then and there?"

She shook her head. "What stopped you?"

"Because I knew about the baby. I worried about being a good father if I was gone so much? And you, I knew what accepting the offer would mean to you. I know how being apart affected your own parent's relationship, and I worried how it would affect us too. Travelling by car between locations would seriously slow me down as it would take too long to get there. There were so many things to consider. It wasn't just me I was thinking about. If I had…" He faced Lucas. "If I was your age and single, with a new girl hanging off my arm each week, I wouldn't have delayed in signing. I would've been a Rooker Racer before five minutes passed, as I'm sure you would've."

"Nah. That's the difference between me and you, Nate. I don't see racing cars as anything more than a fun hobby. My path is different."

Nate shrugged. "Anyways… The thing with Rooker is the drug-free part. Anyone connected to me needs to be clean. It's part of the deal. If they knew you were abusing drugs, I'm done."

"But I'm not." She looked between the brothers. "I'm not. Really." But she didn't believe that. It was tough to avoid even checking on her prized collection sitting out in the open, between them all.

"That's why I wanted you to move in with me."

"So I could be watched?"

"If you want me to be honest, yes."

"Thanks," she growled. "You should know better than anyone, I will always manage on my own. I can take care of myself."

Nate placed his hands in his lap, but his hands wrung together. "Yeah? And how did that work out for you? You lived on your own for two years and became a drug addict."

"Geezus, you say it like I'm a mass murderer or something. I was taking prescription drugs. Not cocaine or heroine. I wasn't stealing to support my habit." She air-quoted *habit*. "I didn't break any laws."

"The point I was getting to was… while you were under Lucas' guidance, you did better. You reduced your habit. I only suggested you moving so the security you've grown used to by having me around–"

She laughed out loud. "You around? You're hardly around, Nate."

"But you've come to rely on Chris and in a small way, my mother. She'd be a few steps away whenever you needed her." He turned slowly to Lucas, but she couldn't read the expression in his eyes. "And as much as I hate to say it, you'd be there too."

Lucas crinkled up his nose and shifted his gaze between his brother and Aurora.

Nate carried on. "Everything you need in one package. It would be a way for me to keep tabs on you, for you to feel loved and wanted, and protected."

"You'd hardly be able to protect me when you're thousands of miles away."

Nate's focus locked onto hers and hope sprung into those deep brown eyes. "So, come with me. Rooker has an apartment rented. Nothing major. A little one bedroom. We could start our lives there."

She blinked. Multiple times. Did she hear correctly? Move there with him? Fear bubbled up inside. It was too fast. Way too fast. She was too young. "Nate…" Her tone raw and unexpected. It blind-sided her.

"That's what I figured."

She focused on him. Watched as a glimmer of hope he'd held in his eyes slowly faded away. A peek at Lucas who looked shell shocked as if this was the first he was hearing of Nate's proposed plan. Back to Nate. She swallowed, a lump forming in her throat. "Oh, Nate. I love you. I really do. But I can't pack up my life and leave. There's too much for me here."

"Like what? The schooling you don't enjoy? The job you're in love with?"

There was no job holding her back. The app-testing jobs she applied for could be done anywhere. But yeah, the schooling held her back. She was seriously considering the idea of becoming a nurse… And then there was everything else.

Kaitlyn and Tatiana. She couldn't leave them behind. And her Daddy. Sure, she didn't see him every day, but things were getting better and better between them. If she were to move so far away that you'd need a plane to visit... Well what then? A quick look to Lucas. And what about her daily dose of him? Her best friend. She'd be lost. Her apartment. The place she'd made into her home, her sanctuary. It wasn't perfect, but it was hers. And she wasn't about to leave it all behind for Nate. No matter how much she loved him.

A sharp intake of air rushed into her lungs. Her gaze floated between the brothers and over to the patio door, out into the hazy grey of winter. The view fell away as she stared at her hands, twisting them on her lap.

"I can't do it, Nate. I can't pick up my life and move it four thousand kilometres away. I know my life here seems meaningless and trite, but it's *my* life. This apartment, it's my home. My safe haven. All my friends live here. Your family, and by proxy, sort of *my* family, they're all here. I have plans for my future, nothing huge and full of grandeur like yours, but they don't include moving to Charlotte and they sure as hell don't include a baby." It was hard, but she stopped her voice from cracking. Slowly shifting her gaze away from her hands, the look on Nate's face was pure disappointment, and it broke her heart.

"I never saw the baby either."

"Yeah, you did."

"Never once."

A pitch as she said, "Nate. You told me, before our first time together, you could never have sexual relations with a woman if you weren't prepared for any possible accidents. That part of you would never have allowed you to have sex with Marissa, so I think you were a little prepared for it."

"I wasn't."

"You were."

"I wasn't. Aurora, every time we had sex I was drunk."

"What?"

"I know it's not what you want to hear, but it's the truth. I drank so when I was with her, I didn't see her. I only saw you."

"Gross."

"No different than with Matthew." He raised an eyebrow and a petty smugness filled his face.

Hearing that name caused her blood to boil instantly. "It's *so* different. I did it with Matthew ONCE and I didn't get high so I would see you instead of him because I never planned on having sex with that asshole. The sex happened *because* I was high, not the other way around. You… You did it with Marissa multiple times and needed to get drunk to do it. It's so *not* the same thing." She rose and hobbled around the living room, shaking her hands as she paced, trying to rid herself of the anger racing through her. "Ugh!" she grunted, slamming her palm against the cool of the patio window. "I wish you understood how this feels for me. Imagine if I was pregnant with Matthew's baby and asked you to toss aside your plans and just accept it was his baby I was carrying, could you do it?" She spun around. Both his and Lucas' face morphed into total disgust. "You couldn't do it, right?"

"Aurora, I'd find a way to make it work. Because I love you."

"And I love you, Nate. I really do. But we need to set that aside for a moment." She felt like she was vibrating, the anger and sorrow taking her through a roller coaster of emotions. "Admit it though, it would be so hard for you to watch me carry around something that belongs to another, especially from a man you detest so much." She stared at him, anger boiling beneath the surface.

He shuddered. "Fine, you're right. It would make me physically ill to know that... But Marissa's good people. She's not like that jerk Matthew." His shoulders squared, and he tipped his head up, prepped for a battle she wouldn't give in to. Marissa would always be tied to him.

A small part of her would always be connected to Matthew because of the accident, but she had no reason to have him in her life. The same could not be said about Marissa.

"That's all I wanted... I needed you to understand how her pregnancy makes me feel. I feel *that* way about her baby. And even if someday I wanted a child with you, I'd never be able to. Ever." The tears battled against her lids to escape but she managed to keep them in, even as it momentarily blurred her vision of a crushed Nate.

Nate slumped, the confidence he held a breath ago had completely disappeared. "So, what do we do? How do we go forward?"

"I don't know." Her voice cracked. "I don't think we can. Not right now. Matthew and I were a ginormous mistake, and yet you throw it at me constantly. I can't have you doing that to me. I've apologised for it over and over, yet you still bring it up. Face it, Nate, this isn't working out."

His face crinkled.

She fought to keep control of hers, but her resolve faltered the longer she remained looking at him. "You withheld details of the contract from me, until you signed. You withheld news of your child from me. It makes me wonder what else you'd hide from me?"

"You're not so innocent."

"I know I'm not." Her voice fell.

"Aurora," he said softly as the tears rolled down his cheek.

"I know I'm a liability. My drug use is something I'll fight for the rest of my life. It's who I am, and I make no apologies for it. And I get that that's a problem for you, and I understand why." She turned away from him, away from the crushing disappointment he bore. Her forehead touched the cool glass of the patio door, and the tears she'd been holding onto, released like a tidal wave. "I'm ending it, Nate. I'm ending us."

"Aurora." Her name floated through the air.

"I can't be what you need me to be. I can't be that perfect person who accepts everything and goes with the flow. I can't pick up and move my life for you. I'm sorry."

"So just like that, it's over? You won't even try?"

She spun around. "What is it you want me to try, Nate? I won't change my life for you. I can't. I'm happy with the way things are. Or were, until all of this started unfolding."

"For what it's worth, I never stopped loving you."

"I wish that was enough, and our problems could be solved with a click. But things don't work that way." Her legs started shaking. "I'm sorry, Nate, but you need to go."

"Please… Aurora." He stood and stepped closer to her.

Tears streamed down her cheeks, and she desperately wanted to feel his arms around her. Instead she thrust up her hand, halting him. "I'm sorry, Nate. It's over."

Hearts cracked and breaths hitched the longer he stood motionless a few feet in front of her. Afraid she'd crumble if she had to look in his direction any longer, she faced the grey of winter, it's misery wrapping around her soul, turning it cold and bleak.

Eventually, Nate's footsteps retreated, and the door clicked shut.

"You okay?" Lucas' voice was soft, and just behind her.

Her body wracked with sobs and her hands covered her face.

"Come here." He wrapped his arms around her.

She rubbed her cheek against the softness of his shirt, allowing the tears to puddle in the tight space until the shirt absorbed them. One arm held tightly around her while the other gently rubbed her back.

Nate was gone. Again. Maybe in a few years, when they were each sure what they wanted—what they needed—from each other, it could work. But for now, she needed to let go. He had bigger things to deal with.

The ache from standing in one spot pulled her out of her Nate-less misery. She pushed out of Lucas' embrace and gave her hip a rub with one hand while the other smeared her mascara-stained tears across her face.

"You okay?"

"Not in the remotest sense, but my hip hurts and I need to rest it. At least that I can do something about." She limped over to the couch and lowered herself onto it.

"Gonna air out your foot?"

Nodding, she un-velcro'd the boot and pulled her foot free, giving the ankle a much-needed stretch. The sock rolled off her foot and she let it fall to the carpet.

"Time to wash that sock," Lucas said as he fanned his nose.

No smile came to her face. "I have another."

"Where?"

She'd get it herself, but the ache was building. If he went into her room and located it, it should give her enough time to retrieve a pill. Her gaze fell to the book staring up at her from the coffee table. How could she have been so foolish and left it laying out in the open? It was like a neon sign, especially since she never read any erotica. Anyone could've found it and then what? How much explaining would she have to do?

Dr. Navin's note surfaced to the front of her brain. *Don't hide the secrets, you only give them power. Expose them and you shall be set free.* Yeah, well not today buddy. Everything was starting to ache, and that was no secret.

"Aurora?" Lucas stood in front of her, his movement unseen.

"Yeah?"

"Welcome back."

"Thanks?"

"You disappeared on me for a minute there."

"Oh, sorry. I was thinking."

"About?"

"Nothing in particular and everything."

"Ah, one of those thoughts eh?" He sat down beside her. "Anything you want to share?"

She shrugged. "No, not really."

"How's the leg doing?" Warm fingers ran tenderly over the top of her foot, and he gave each toe a wiggle. "This little piggy-"

"Stop it," she said, a hint of a smile forming on the edge of her lips. He wiggled each toe, but kept the song to himself, although she had no issue singing along in her own head.

He dropped his hand and inched forward on the couch, reaching for the contraband-enclosed book. "Interesting reading material."

"No," she gasped instinctively and lunged for it. A sigh of relief washed over her once the pages were gripped in her hand.

"What? I wasn't gonna flip through it."

"Thank god." Her heart beat at cardio workout levels. He stared at her with an intensity she hadn't seen in a while.

"What's the big deal?"

"It's a reference manual."

Lucas laughed and crimson coloured his cheeks. "Oh okay. Whatever floats your boat."

Guilt consumed her, and she hated lying to him, but no matter what Dr. Navin's little note read, she wasn't ready to reveal anything yet. Today had been trying enough.

"Shouldn't you be back in class? Lunch is over."

"Nah, it'll be fine." He waved as he leaned back into the couch, spreading his arm across the top. "Just a lecture I'm missing. Nothing major. Shouldn't you be in class?"

"Yeah right. I'm so far behind, I think I'm ahead."

"What are you gonna do?"

"Transfer to another program."

"Seriously? Why?"

She shrugged. "I don't follow a lot of the material."

"Would probably help if you showed up."

"Ha-ha. I think it's because I missed the beginning. Trying it from home and going to class, I lost something along the way. Missed the foundation building. However, I've been thinking a lot, and where I couldn't handle the hard-core work of being a doctor, I do think I could handle being a nurse. Or an EMT, like Max."

"No offence, but you should re-think the EMT thing. They respond to a lot of car crashes and I don't know if you'd be able to handle that."

"Maybe it would help desensitise me?"

"I highly doubt it. And you don't want to find out the hard way that you can't handle it. I'd suggest you talk to Max if you're really considering it, attempt a ride along." A warm hand touched her foot. She didn't realise her foot was so cold.

"Maybe. But I definitely want to stay in the sciences."

"Good for you. We may even be in some of the same classes together." A flash of hope danced across his eyes and vanished. "We'll compare schedules."

She shifted and lifted her foot to the end of the couch, snuggling into Lucas. Her head rested against his chest and a low sigh leaked out of her. "What's going to happen?"

"What do you mean?"

Craning her neck, she twisted to meet his blue-grey gaze. "With you and I, and things between Nate and I?"

His hands wiped over his face and a puff of air escaped. "What do you want to happen?"

"I don't want you to be in a bad spot. If Nate and I are truly done, would you and I still be…" A sob built up within her. It was hard enough to lose Nate but to lose her best friend over Nate, the thought scared her. Fresh tears fell and Lucas blurred at the edges.

His long finger wiped across her cheek. "Hey, hey, hey. It's gonna be okay. I promise. You can't lose me that easily." He tightened his grip around her. "I'm not going anywhere. You're my best friend, Aurora. It would take more than you breaking up with my brother for me to walk away from you."

She sniffed. "You promise?"

"You have my word."

♥Chapter Twenty-Six♥

Aurora flopped onto the oversized, fuchsia sofa centered in the middle of the tiny wedding dress shop. In favour of dress shopping, Kaitlyn and Aurora skipped out on their weekly Tuesday afternoon coffee.

"Kaitlyn, I can't try on any more bridesmaid dresses. I can't." She gave her leg a rub, pushing under the top of the air-boot and trying to relieve the aching.

Her tall, blonde friend paraded out from behind a wall of silk and satin and taffeta, a rose-coloured gown held high. "Are you sure?"

"Yes. I'm sorry, but I'm exhausted. Thirteen dresses should be enough to choose from, right?" Her stomach rumbled, and she realised it was already supper time.

Kaitlyn rehung the dress and grabbed her phone, thumbing through the pictures. "It will be, but you're beautiful in all of them, it'll be a hard choice."

"Maybe we should've stopped at the first half-dozen, just to make the decision easier on you and Tatiana."

She tapped on a picture. "I love this colour on you. The deep purple is beautiful."

"She," Aurora cocked her head in the direction of the sales person, "called it orchid."

"Whatever. Purple is purple."

"And you call yourself a girl." A hard laugh escaped. "As the bride, you should know the difference between orchid, amethyst, and concord."

Kaitlyn dropped the phone onto her lap. "That may be true of those brides on tv who go ape-shit over the tiniest little detail, but I couldn't care less. Besides, I'm buying off the rack, anyway."

"If you ever decide."

"Yeah, that." Kaitlyn smoothed out her Golden Bears sweatpants. "What style is Tatiana wearing? It would make it easier for me to decide on my own dress."

As she shook her head, the sensation of falling hair tickled the back of her neck. She could barely hold herself together, and even the messy bun wasn't working. "If I knew, I couldn't share it with you. You're both supposed to be surprised at what the other is wearing."

"I get that but I don't want to end up with the same thing as my beautiful bride."

"I highly doubt that's even possible." Aurora leaned back in the sofa and stretched her right arm across the back. "How's it going to work anyways? Who will be up at the front, and who's walking down the aisle?"

"Well," Kaitlyn said as her face split in half from the smile. "If it goes how I envision, one of us will emerge from one side of the coat room area and the other from the other side." She giggled.

Due to a connection with her Language Arts professors, Kaitlyn had managed to book a conference room at the defunct museum for New Year's Eve. She'd argued the space would be more than adequate for the few people she planned on having present, none of which were her or Tatiana's parents.

A restaurant was booked for an early dinner party reservation for ten, with Nate being one of the guests. She hadn't had the heart to tell her best friend he wouldn't be in attendance. A long, black stretch limousine was also ready to chauffer the wedding party around and drop them off at Urban DC for a night of dancing.

"I. Can't. Wait," Aurora said, enthusiasm rolling off her tongue. "It'll be the perfect way to end the year."

"I know, right?" Kaitlyn drifted away as her face went all slack and dreamy. "Can I try on two more?" In a quick push from the sofa, Kaitlyn jumped up and blended into a rack of white and cream dresses. She extracted two more that caught her eye and danced into the change room.

The salesperson, visibly absent a minute ago, appeared out of thin air and followed her into the change area.

Kaitlyn asked, "Are you sure you won't tell me if any of the dresses I'm picking are the same as hers?"

"Honestly, how would I know? Tatiana and I aren't shopping together."

"But she didn't tell you anything?" Her voice echoed out the change room.

Although Kaitlyn wasn't in the open area, Aurora still shook her head and stared at the salesperson. Judging by her blank, vacant expression, you'd think this was perfectly normal talk. "You told me her dress was being shipped from home."

"But I don't know what it looks like."

Aurora laughed. Brides could be so uptight and focused on one thing. "And I would know how exactly? Maybe she's wearing her mother's dress or an aunt's? Have you seen pictures of her mother in hers?"

"Not that I remember." A grunt came from deep within the change room. "You'd think they'd make these blessed things easy to get in and out of. There should be a quick release, so when the night is over, boom, it's off. Damn, there are a lot of buttons."

"Do you want a hand?"

"Nah, I got it." Another grunt. "Oh shit, it's caught on something."

The salesperson rapped on the door. "I can help."

"I fixed it."

Aurora did not miss the eye roll.

"We really should decide on the colour today before we leave so we can get Nate a matching tie and kerchief. He has a tux, right, or a really nice suit? What did he wear to the banquet?"

Sigh. *Nate.* The throbbing and aching in her heart bloomed. If only things had been as easy as they were before the summer. Why couldn't their relationship be sunshine and roses? He was supposed to have caught her. Instead, the miss and subsequent ankle twisting, did the same to their connection. Granted things were starting to strain, but still.

It didn't take too long for a full body ache to settle into her joints. With a heavy sadness, she grabbed at her purse as she stifled a sob. There was no way she would let Kaitlyn see her hurting–this day of shopping was for her. She dug through the contents and retrieved the container with the one Xanax *and* the added perc. Figuring it was best to have a backup, she added it before leaving. She was glad she did.

The pill rolled out of the container and into her palm.

"What's that?"

She hadn't heard Kaitlyn emerge from the dressing room. Radiant in layers of satin, she resembled a Russian Princess at the turn of the century. The Twentieth century. She couldn't stop from staring. "Oh my god, Kaitlyn. You look wow. That's the dress."

"What's in your hand?"

"A perc." *Fuck.*

"As in a Percocet?"

It was too late to backtrack. "Yeah," she admitted with a grimace. With a quick flick of her wrist, the pill popped from her hand into her mouth.

"I thought you quit those?" She wore her concern better than the dress, and she wore the dress as if it were made for her.

"When I got rid of the crutches, the height difference between my feet caused a lot of pain and aches. The doctor prescribed me a few percs until the boot can come off fully."

Kaitlyn stood above her, staring down at her. Her eyes danced back and forth as she glared at her with scepticism. "Let me see the container."

"I don't have it. I added it to this container to save space. I threw it away before you picked me up. This was the last pill though." It was truth. It was the last Percocet. However, she was buying stronger drugs on her next request, but Kaitlyn didn't need to know that. She just needed her to buy the story she was selling.

Kaitlyn shifted her weight and said, "Okay. I believe you."

She released the air she didn't realise she'd held tight to.

"I'll confirm later with Nate when I drop you off."

She winced. She hadn't meant to, but it happened.

"What? Why the face?"

"Nate won't be there when you drop me off."

"Oh - kay." A hint of curiosity mingled in her voice.

"I didn't want to do this today and most definitely not here."

The salesperson stood silently to the left of Kaitlyn. Couldn't she hang out somewhere else?

"Why, what's going on?"

She sighed, harder and longer than she wanted. "We broke up."

"What? When? Why?"

Aurora pushed herself up and limped around the space, trying to avoid looking in Kaitlyn's direction. But it was hard. Multiple full-length mirrors reflected Kaitlyn's concern. "I *really* don't want to discuss this here." She grabbed her phone. "Forget it, okay? Smile and pose for me." The biggest, fakest smile jumped onto her face. Fake it 'til you make it, right? "I want to take a few pictures of you in this dress. Seriously, Kait, this is *the* dress."

After thanking the salesperson and putting *the* dress on hold, Kaitlyn pulled Aurora out into the corridor of the mall which was packed with the lively sounds of chattering people and the rustling of shopping bags. A group of teenagers sauntered by, and one stopped to give Kaitlyn a complete once over.

"I'm gay," she said to the man-child.

Beet red, he hiked up his pants as he ran and joined his buddies.

Kaitlyn dragged her a little further until they approached a comfy seating area and she dropped her bag on the floor in front of a black ottoman-type seat.

"Spill it. What happened? I thought everything was going great? You spent the weekend at a fancy hotel."

Aurora couldn't face her friend–today was supposed to be fun and all things wedding. Guilt that her problems overshadowed her friend's joy weighed on it, but not for long. Her stomach was empty when she took the perc, so it didn't take long to reach out and dull the hurt and aches, and wipe away a touch of the guilt. No matter how good it worked on the physical sensations, the emotional aches and pains would require a stronger shushing.

"Tell me."

The tears burst out of her, try as she may to fight it. "I wish I could say it was… but the truth is… I don't know how to accept…"

"Slow down, Tiger. You're not making any sense."

Her breath did a double hitch, and she folded into herself as she sat. "He signed the contract. He's leaving after Christmas."

She squeezed her hand. "I'm so sorry. I know it's not what you wanted but how do you turn down the dream?"

"It's more than that. He didn't share any of the details with me."

Kaitlyn nodded. "That was a huge source of frustration for you, but I'm sure he was in a difficult position of trying to do what was best for everyone involved."

"Well, there's more." She dug through her purse and found a napkin to wipe her nose. "He has to stay clean as does his immediate family."

"Uh-oh, I can see where this is going," she said under her breath, but loud enough to hear.

"And that's a problem, right? This twisted ankle of mine is causing a problem because I need the drugs."

"Totally understandable."

"Not when there's a history of drug abuse, it's not. Apparently, Nate said he had to do some pretty heavy convincing."

"But it worked, right? He got the contract." Kaitlyn sighed.

Aurora sagged. "He called me a liability."

"What? He didn't."

"He did, but I agree with him. So, I cut him free. Kait, I can't have him fulfil his dreams with me being the issue possibly wrecking it for him."

"But the percs are prescribed to you, right? That's why Nate was able to convince that guy you'll be okay."

"I wish it were that easy." She shrugged. "But there's something else. And it changes everything."

Kaitlyn held her breath.

"She's pregnant."

"Who?"

"Marissa."

Kaitlyn's eyes widened, making her irises small in comparison to the amount of white. "The ex-girlfriend, Marissa?"

Aurora nodded.

"Oh, dear God." Kaitlyn's high-pitched voice carried out into the open space.

"Yeah." As Aurora closed her eyes to the passersby, tears streaked down her cheeks. "Clearly it's not the best time for us to be together. If it's not one thing, it's another. He's jealous of Lucas and my's friendship, but I don't really understand why. He constantly throws Matthew back in my face, we don't spend a lot of time together anymore and now this on top of it all. I needed to walk away from him." She buried her face in her hands.

"Give it time. Maybe you just need to think this through?"

"Maybe, but I doubt it. This hurt, the hurt I feel here–" she placed a hand over her heart, "–doesn't feel like a we'll get back together in a year when the season's done, and we've each had time to reassess. This hurt feels like a forever. It's worse than when we broke up before the summer."

"Aw, honey. It only feels that way. When he's back, things will be different."

"Yeah. He'll be a father. He could have another year with this group. Maybe he'll be signed with another company. Anything could happen." Hot tears burned as they fell. "But it won't include me. I don't know how to make it all work. I can't figure out how to wrap my head around the fact he'll be a dad, with a dream career in his hands. I don't know how to fit into his lifestyle, even if I am thrilled he gets a shot at his dream. I can barely fit into it now and he's still here."

"Shit. I'm really sorry. I had high hopes you'd catch my bouquet and be the next one married."

"It'll have to be someone else."

Kaitlyn leaned in and gave her a hug. In the distance, a mariachi band played *Joy to the World.*

"Christmas music already?"

"The mall always starts early." Kaitlyn rolled her eyes.

"Here I'm struggling to make it through the week and the mall already has decorations strung up." As she glanced around, a huge decorated Christmas tree sat in the centre of the corridor, with giant snowflakes strung from the glass roof.

"What about Lucas?"

"He said it'll be fine and it won't change things between us."

"And you believe him?"

"Yeah, I do. He was pretty good at keeping me a secret from Nate over the summer, and he never shared much unless I begged, and even then. Besides, Nate won't be around, so I believe him when he says it won't change. I do worry, though, about what it may do to their relationship."

"I suppose it would depend on what you do with *your* relationship with Lucas."

"Not this again, Kait."

"Yes, this again. You need to tread very carefully in these waters. You're very emotional and unsteady, and Lucas–"

"And what? Lucas is my friend. My best friend. I know him well enough to know he would never sweep in and take advantage of me."

"That's not what I was going to say."

"Then what?"

"Lucas is in a pickle, right? Loyal to his brother, comforting shoulder for you. All I'm saying is to watch out."

"I plan on it." She stood up and started walking away.

Her friend caught up to her, not like it was hard to do. "Hey, all I'm saying is to not go into the rebound right away."

"I certainly hadn't planned anything of the sort. We just broke up. At least give me to the end of the year before you start thinking I'll rebound on someone."

"You could bring a fresh date to the wedding. With you going solo, and me having already booked a spot for Nate, there's a plus one."

"I think I'd rather go solo right now. I can focus on being the best bridesmaid ever. Having a boyfriend around will only spoil that."

"Bring Lucas."

She laughed. "A minute ago, you're accusing me of rebounding onto him, which I haven't done, and now you want me to invite him to the wedding?"

"He already has plans, huh?" Kaitlyn could always see right through her.

"Yeah. A big track thing. Apparently, this little community of racers are pretty tight and they have a helluva party out at one of the racers farms. He has a big shop he converts and makes it into a mini disco. People crash there overnight so there's no worry about driving. It actually sounds like a sweet set up."

"Indeed." Kaitlyn linked arms with her. "Regardless, there's a spot reserved for your plus one. Whoever he may be."

"Save it for your mom or dad. Who knows, maybe after Friday night, they'll decide to come. You're their only daughter. They won't hate you forever."

Friday night Kaitlyn planned on introducing her parents to Tatiana. The plan was to have her parents settled at a table and have Tatiana come join them. The actual unveiling plans changed from day to day, she figured it could be something else entirely by Friday night.

"Do you want me to come? Like a mediator?"

"Nah. Father can't get too loud in a restaurant, can he?"

"I doubt it."

Kaitlyn's brow crinkled.

"I'm sure it'll be fine."

"Can we come over afterwards?"

"Of course, as I'll want all the details."

"Come on, we'll go for supper and then I'll drive you home."

♥Chapter Twenty-Seven♥

Aurora paced in her apartment, relishing in the sensations of a naked foot squishing into the carpet. It was amazing what trivial things you take for granted when it's taken away. Today she allowed the toes on her bad foot to dig into the plush ground. It felt good to walk evenly, at least as evenly as she could. There would always be a limp from the accident, but it wasn't nearly as severe as walking with that ever-loving boot on.

"You're really enjoying that, aren't you?" Lucas asked from the kitchen table as she walked by him for the twentieth time.

"You have no idea."

Focused still on the textbook, he didn't make eye contact. "Don't push it."

She laughed. "Right. Because you know, pushing myself hard never resulted in anything good."

He faced her, a wide smile stretching across his face. "Exactly."

"It feels good though."

"I can see how it does. It's been a while since you've sported a grin."

"I know, and I'm sorry. I'm not pleasant company right now."

"You're fine, I'm giving you a hard time."

"You can dish it out as much as you want. I'll take it." She sat beside him at the table. "Can I ask you something?"

"Of course. You should know that."

"It's just..." She stopped and stared into his eyes. Maybe it was too hard to ask. Maybe she should wait until another day. Maybe she shouldn't be such a coward.

"What are you thinking? You got this serious look on your face."

She folded her arms on the table and rested her head on them. "I've been thinking lately and I can't wrap my head around it."

"Around what?"

A sigh. "Well, you, mainly."

"Uh-oh. What did I do?"

"Nothing. I just keep wondering why you tried so hard to keep Nate and I together. Did you know about the drug contingency?"

"I had an inkling, but didn't think too much about it. You were clean as far as I knew. It wasn't until you mentioned those other pills you bought and trashed that made me worry."

"About?"

"The path you were headed down. It's one thing to be a prescription drug abuser because at least those are prescribed to you. It's entirely different to be buying drugs from someone not in a pharmacy."

So, I'm back to being a bad person. Damnit.

She cast her gaze to the edge of the textbook. "But why try so hard to keep us together."

"You wouldn't understand if I tried explaining it."

"Because it's horribly complicated, like mechanics?"

"No because I don't really understand it, myself. All I know is I need you in my life. You're my best friend, and I was worried if you and Nate broke up, it would be awkward."

"Right... because having your shrink sister, and her EMT boyfriend who brought me out of a fainting spell, and your mother who thinks I'm a tad bat-shit crazy doesn't make things weird."

Lucas laughed, and it put her at ease. "When you put it like that..."

"You and the rest of the Johnsons are my family. For better. And worse. For the first time in a long time, I have a mother-figure in my life, even if she thinks I'm not all there, but it comforts me in an odd way. I have a sister- and brother-in-law, and I have you and Nate. Although, I guess time will tell what will happen between Nate and me. If we could ever be friends again."

"Would you want that?"

She didn't not want him in her life. He'd been there for her major turning points, and she couldn't imagine a future without him in it. But would it be weird? Especially since they'd been intimate with each other. Could they ever really go back to being friends?

"See, that face there…" His finger circled her head. "You're not sure it would work out, you just being friends."

"Well it would be awkward at first. But after his season in the US, maybe things will be different."

"Would you ever get back together with him?"

A peek to his eyes before dashing them away to stare into the darkened living room. She rose and slowly made her way over to the couch where she sat and lifted her leg to rest.

"Aurora? You didn't answer my question."

"That's a really tough thing to answer. There are so many reasons to stay apart."

"And how many reasons to stay together?"

"One."

"Isn't that enough?" He walked over and joined her on the couch.

"No. Love isn't enough. You heard him. I'm a liability. I'm the reason his whole contract could go up in flames. By breaking up with him, I'm doing him a favour. I'm eliminating the doubt, the smidgen of fear ruining his dream. Besides, I'm just not ready to pack up my life here." The silence descended over them until the chirping of her phone punctured it. "Hey, Daddy," Aurora said as she answered.

"I'm passing through and thought I would stop in and say hello."

"Are you coming up?"

"Shortly. I'm almost there. Can we go for dinner?"

"Umm. Sure? Lucas is over."

There was silence on the other side of the line for a few breaths.

"Sorry, traffic," he said, "I'll be there in fifteen minutes."

She tossed her phone on the coffee table. "Well, a surprise visit from my dad. He'll be here shortly."

"Should I go?"

"Never. Go work on your homework." She rose and started tidying up, taking the dishes to the kitchen and putting them into the dishwasher.

Lucas fluffed the pillows and resumed his seat at the table.

Cole entered the apartment a few short minutes later. "Hey Princess. Hey Lucas." He nodded and shook hands with the young man.

"Thought you weren't coming until next weekend, Daddy?"

"Well, I have a meeting in Calgary tomorrow morning, and hadn't planned on interrupting you. But I was getting hungry as I approached and thought I could take you out for dinner. Besides, there's something I'd like to discuss with you, and I'm tired of keeping it from you."

"Um, sure?"

"Don't sound so excited to have dinner with your old man."

"It's not that. I can't be late. Kaitlyn and Tatiana are coming over after eight."

"No prob." He glanced at his watch. "I'll have you back before seven." He turned to Lucas who had walked into the kitchen and leaned against the fridge. "Do you want to join us? My treat."

"No thanks, Cole. I have a huge assignment due on Monday I'd better tackle."

"You're welcome to stay here while we're gone." She smiled at her best friend. "It's practically your place anyways."

"What does that mean?" Cole's eyes widened at the statement.

"It's just, well, Lucas spends a lot of time here. As you'll recall, he lived on the couch in the summer."

Cole's gaze flipped between his daughter and her best friend. "And now?"

"Well, lately he's been sleeping in the spare room."

"And Nate's okay with that?"

The bottom of the chair rose and greeted her as she fell into it.

Five days. Five long days since she ended things. Five days of dealing with the ache of knowing she wasn't his one. Five days of endless questioning to Lucas about how Nate was doing—about as well as she was. She could never be everything he needed and she was the liability to his dream. But it all still hurt.

"What's going on?"

Lucas sat down beside her.

"We broke up." No emotion, no feeling, just a statement.

"Again? Jesus Christ, Aurora. What did you do this time?" He stood over her.

She gave him a point-form list of what went down and with each point, his expression darkened.

"You're afraid to be happy, aren't you?"

"What? No, I'm not."

"You sure as hell are. You could make the pregnancy work. It's not like you'd be a full-time mother anyways. You'd get all the benefits in the few hours you'd have to deal with it. All the snuggles, the wonderful baby smell. You'd miss the bad shit. The middle of the night wake ups, the stretch marks, the labour, the leaking from every orifice. Your mother said that was the worst."

"But I don't want any part of it. That's the point."

"Do you love him?"

"I did."

"And what, you stopped the second you found out he'd knocked up Melinda?"

"Marissa. And no. It's complicated."

"Doesn't sound like it. Sounds like you were looking for excuses to get out of the relationship."

"Was not."

"Princess. I know better. You were happy here." He tapped her forehead. "But you weren't happy here." He pointed toward her chest. "Not in your heart. And you wanted to, gawd, I know you did, but those two couldn't connect. Because you're afraid."

She stared at her hands as they twisted together on top of the table. "I'm not afraid."

"You are. You're afraid to let him see you at your worst, you're afraid he'll run away from you. You're afraid of moving on. And when you start thinking that, well… something's missing. Did you ever really let Nate in? Did he see you at your worst?"

"He saw me in the hospital when I twisted my ankle."

"Yeah, but did you really let him in?"

She watched as Lucas picked up a pen and aimlessly doodled on the back of an envelope. No surprise, it was the quick outline of a race car.

"I don't know, Princess, but it sounds like you're trying to go back in time. You're not seventeen anymore. Everyone's either moved on or in the process of, and you're still…" He waved his hand up and down. "I love you, and you know that, but sometimes you just need to grow up." He took a deep breath. "Anyways," Cole said after a minute had passed and clapped his daughter on the shoulder. "I'm not here to give you grief about your love life or dating situation. I wanted to share with you about mine."

She snapped her head up and studied her father. "You're dating?"

"Is it weird?" A long finger scratched at his greying temple.

"Umm... no… not really, I don't think so." Her head was spinning with so many questions and thoughts. Who is she? How did they meet? What is she like? Is he in love? She swallowed. "Tell me about her."

"Do you remember who James Tarker is."

She shook her head.

"He's a foreman at one of the sites I work at. Anyways, he suggested we go to this Speed Dating thing."

She burst into laughter. "You went speed dating?"

Lucas was sporting a smile too. At least she wasn't the only one who thought it strange for a man in his fifties to go to such a thing.

Cole pulled out a chair. "Oh my god, it was so terrible and trying to impress these complete strangers in a two-minute conversation, it was beyond weird." His hand rubbed across his forehead. "All of them were either in their thirties or forties. Too young for my blood."

Relief settled over her and she released her breath.

"But this one, this Judy, she's about my age and well… she and I clicked. She's a widow too. We exchanged numbers, but she never responded to my texts. Finally, she calls me back explaining she was helping her daughter get married in Vegas, and never expected I'd actually call." He shook his head. "Anyways, we chatted for over an hour and met for dinner the next day. We've only gone out a few times, but she's really nice."

"Daddy, that's wonderful." It was nice listening to him talk about something other than work or her schooling or her life. She was happy he seemed… well, happy. It was different to see him excited like he was.

"Yeah, Cole, that's really great."

"Her son lives in Lacombe and her daughter lives here, so she'll be here for Christmas."

"Wow."

"And, well, if things continue to go as they are, I'd really like for us all to get together, so everyone has a chance to meet."

She swallowed. The possibility of meeting this woman and her two grown children excited her as much as it terrified her.

Cole disrupted her thoughts before she could get a hold on them. "Want to hear something funny?"

Aurora raised her eyebrows, ideas still circling in her mind. "Sure."

"She's RCMP."

"She's what? Oh. Well… that's umm… interesting."

"Like daughter, like father." Lucas said as he refocused.

Aurora playfully nudged him. "What do you mean?"

"You, with your vehicular PTSD, fell for a race car driver of all things, and now your father—what does Kaitlyn call him, a recreational pharmacist?—is dating an RCMP officer. You two certainly fall for your complete polar opposites."

"I haven't fallen for her," Cole said to Lucas, but there was no hostility in his voice. A touch of fear perhaps, but it wasn't directed at Lucas.

"So, what are you going to do about that?"

Cole shrugged. "Keep everything on the down low for now. If things become serious, I may need to stop, um, dispensing if you will and step back."

"Can you give it up?"

"Depends on how things go with her I guess. But if I need to scale back, I may need to reconsider how much allowance, if you will, I can send you."

Aurora held her breath. "When?" She'd need to start putting aside more savings if she would be on her own, financially.

Cole's fingers ran the length of his jaw. "Relax. Nothing major to get worked up about right now. We'll cross that bridge if—and when—we get to it. Let's see how this thing with Judy goes first."

"Okay," she said, a sigh of relief floating out of her.

"Good, now let's grab a bite." He patted Lucas on the shoulder. "Sure you won't come along?"

"Positive, sir."

"Hey," Aurora said, returning to the apartment after supper, dangling a doggie bag in one hand and a cup in the other. "I brought you dessert. How goes the assignment?"

"Brutal, but I'm getting through it." He set his pen down and pinched the bridge of his nose. "How was dinner with your dad?"

"Good. I think he's a little more serious about this Judy than he let on."

"Cool. You okay with him dating?"

She closed the fridge and leaned against it. "I think I am."

"You don't sound sure."

"I just want him to be happy. It's been two and half years, and whatever length of time it was prior to…" She swallowed. *The accident.*

"Can I share something with you?" Lucas thumbed the edges of his notebook, but refused to make eye contact.

Aurora sat in the chair across from him. "What's on your mind?"

"It's okay if you're not, you know? I sure as hell wasn't when Mom started dating. To me it was way too soon."

"How long after?"

"Less than a year. Of course, it wasn't serious. I don't even remember his name. My therapist suggested it was because she was content in her marriage and that's why she was seeking out a boyfriend. Not to replace Dad, but more for the companionship she missed. Still." He shrugged. "And now? She's quite comfortable and serious about Bill."

"They *are* cute together."

"You think so?"

"I do. I watched them at the banquet. She gave off the impression she was happy. Mind you I have nothing to compare it to. I don't know what things were like with your parents."

"I hope she's happy." He drummed his fingers on the table. "She's certainly been less of a bitch around him."

"Lucas!" Surprise fell out of her mouth.

"What? Maybe it's because she's dating Bill, or because she's starting to accept the idea she's gonna be a grandmother…"

Aurora's thoughts blocked out the rest of Lucas' ramblings. Brenda being a grandmother. Nate being a father. Chris and Lucas would be aunt and uncle. The big picture was getting bigger. Just thinking of her sweet, dimpled Nate holding a newborn caused her heart to ache. She wondered if he would be happy with the baby, and whether he'd–

"I don't care," she whispered to herself, however she seemed to have responded to a comment she hadn't heard completely.

"Of course, you don't." He winked. "You're not over him. Not yet."

"I don't know if I ever will be."

"Hopefully some day you will be. And you'll be able to move on with someone better. Someone who understands you, knows what you like and don't like, and knows everything about you; good and bad."

She said nothing. Does a person ever truly know another? Surely her parents had kept things from each other and they were married for many years. "Nate fit all that."

"Not all of it. But yeah, he was close. And I tried."

"What do you mean?"

"I tried my best to keep you together, but sometimes…"

"Sometimes it's not enough." Her phone vibrated deep in her pocket, breaking the hold her eyes had on him. "I'll buzz you up."

"Kaitlyn?"

"Yeah, and she's crying." She pushed the door button allowing Kaitlyn and Tatiana up. Water splashed into the bottom of the kettle she filled while waiting for the ladies to reach her apartment. She clicked the kettle on, and the water started boiling.

A soft knock sounded on the door.

"Hey," Kaitlyn said, her voice weak and thin, as she pushed it open and stepped inside.

"Allo," Tatiana said as she breezed into the apartment.

She leaned against the wall of the kitchen. "How did it go?"

"About as well as we expected." Kaitlyn's eyes were rimmed in red.

"Oh, Kait, I'm so sorry."

Lucas tidied up the table and made space for the ladies to sit.

Kaitlyn wrapped her coat around the back of the chair as did Tatiana. Kaitlyn fell into her seat like she was unable to tolerate standing on her legs anymore. "He was so mad he said I was out of the will, not that I cared anyway. But it meant it was over. He disowned me." Kaitlyn buried her head into the crook of her arm. "He called us sinners. Said it was against God's plan and will. How can true love between two people be evil?"

"It bad. He yell so loud."

"What about your mom?" Aurora pulled out a chair and slipped in beside Kaitlyn.

"She didn't speak at all, except to pray a bunch. Mostly hung her head. She could hardly look at me."

"I tank she cry." Tatiana added, her face solemn.

"She did?" Kaitlyn looked at her fiancée, despair washing over her.

"Yak. Little bit." Tatiana placed her hand on Kaitlyn's back and rubbed.

Aurora's voice fell. "That sucks, Kait. It really does."

"Doesn't matter. We're getting married regardless of whether or not they give me their blessing. Screw them." She gave her eyes a wipe. "We don't need them anyways."

"No," Tatiana added and squeezed Kaitlyn's hand.

"We'll do it our way. If that's how they are going to be, their loss."

"That's right."

Kaitlyn turned to Tatiana. "Let's elope. Tomorrow."

"Ee-lope?"

Quickly, in her native Russian, she spoke, and probably explained as Tatiana shook her head. "No. We wait. Like plan."

"But I can't wait. My life as a Kariyev is over." Kaitlyn held Tatiana's hand and interlocked her fingers with her fiancée's.

Lucas set down mugs full of tea and a plate of cookies. "Are you taking Tatiana's last name?"

"I don't know. We never really discussed it."

"What's your last name, Tatiana?" Aurora asked.

"Timoshenko."

"It has a nice ring to it," Lucas said, as the name rolled off his tongue. He grabbed a cookie and joined the ladies.

"Well, you have time to decide."

"Ya. Six weeks a go."

Kaitlyn rested her head against Tatiana. "Yeah. Six more weeks."

"There's a lot to do still," Aurora said. "We need to plan a bachelorette party and make the decorations, and all the important things that go along with a wedding."

Kaitlyn sighed. "I suppose I should finish up this term first. Finals aren't too far away."

"No, they're not." Lucas said. "I can't wait."

"Looking forward to switching?" Kaitlyn asked.

"Just as much as you are to be getting married."

Kaitlyn laughed. "That bad, eh?"

♥Chapter Twenty-Eight♥

She tiptoed down the hall following the faint glow coming from the living room, making sure to walk as slowly as she felt she could manage. What she really wanted to do was match the speed of her racing heart and bolt, but she knew she'd only get caught. And she wasn't ready to explain herself. First, she needed to prove to herself it was a dream. After that, she'd tell others.

Lugging her newly re-balanced body into the living room, she spotted Lucas passed out cold on the couch, the light creating shadows across his eyes. She preferred him sleeping in the spare bedroom where it was more comfortable, and he normally complied. Tonight, a textbook on the floor in disarray told her he fell asleep while reading it. Good, that meant he was out.

She stood behind the chair his coat wrapped around. A pat to the pockets and she found the bulge she sought. Her hand thrust into it and the cool metal of the keys touched her fingers. Slipping them around, she held the keys tight and pulled out. Another glance to Lucas, who hadn't moved a muscle.

Sneaking her own jacket from the back of another kitchen chair, she folded it over her arm and against the pounding in her chest, calmly walked over to the door. Fingers trembled on the chain as she slid it back and placed it against the doorframe.

Another peek on Lucas. Still sleeping.

Hand on the door knob, she squeezed it tightly and twisted it until she was sure it was free from the catch. She opened the door a crack and light from the hall flooded into the entrance of the door. Damn! Looks like the Super finally changed the dead bulb lighting up her doorway like a neon sign.

Angling her body, she slithered through the smallest opening she could, birthing herself into the hallway. With the door quietly pulled shut, she wiped the sweat from her forehead and fanned her armpits.

Her swallowed breath caught in the back of her throat until she reached the elevator and stepped inside.

"Oh my god, that was so close," she said into the empty elevator car, tightening her grip as the keys dug into her palm.

You can change your mind.

But it wasn't going to happen. Not tonight. Sick and tired of the nightmares invading her mind and her soul, repeating over and over in one form or another, what a coward she was. They laughed at her, those dreams. They showed her a future where she was crippled and frozen, her life never being hers, always belonging to the PTSD. Not anymore.

The strides she'd made over the last few weeks had been quieter than the pushing she did over the summer. Oh, how she'd pushed herself to the breaking point back then, but never over. She'd come close, but she'd always survived. But it was time for a solid push, or at least a solid attempt. Hopefully, if she was successful, when the morning light touched her, she vowed it would burn away the last remnants of her PTSD. And hope is a strong motivator, but not as strong as fear. It was the fear coursing through her veins pushing her out of the elevator and through the main doors.

The crisp December night air blasted against her warm skin, chilling her to the bone in a heartbeat. Trudging through the snow, she shivered underneath her coat, questioning why she needed to prove this to herself now. Couldn't it wait until it was warmer?

Extracting the keys from her grip, she flipped through until she found the car key. She activated the door unlock button on the remote and the familiar thump-whump sound of the door unlocking rang against her ears, the blowing snow doing nothing to mute their sound. Lifting the handle, she inhaled a gust of frozen air and pulled it open.

The driver's seat stretched out before her. The seat further back than the passenger side, and the arm rest she'd come to rely on was on the wrong side. Could she really do this? Nate had total faith that she could.

The blood rushed through her ears, drowning out the screaming from her brain. She glanced around the people-free parking lot. No one milled about. The blanket of snow around her didn't have tire tracks, but it did have the telltale markings of a bunny hop. A gust of wind and ice-cold snow pushed her against the side of the car, and she braced herself against it as the keys dropped from her hands. She dug through the snow and retrieved them, giving them a wipe on the bottom of her visible sweatshirt.

"I can do this."

Steeling herself, she took a deep breath and closed her eyes. Slumping into the arctic-frozen seat, she huddled further into her coat.

It feels the same as my side.

The pounding of her heart was enough to give her a headache, and she didn't need one right now. She was doing this under her own power and didn't want to cover it up with anything chemical. She wanted—and needed—the rawness of the moment, headache or not. No matter how hard she pushed against herself right now, she knew she'd survive. Unless of course her heart raced so hard it sent her into cardiac arrest.

A roving check of her symptoms. She wasn't near that stage. This was fear. Untamed and wild. But conquerable.

Her stomach rolled as her mind reminded her what seat she sat in. The cool of the fabric leaking through the thin pants she wore out in the dead of night, chilled her more than she believed possible. The overhead lamp dissolved, and the orange light from the street lamps cast a darkened, but not dark glow in the interior.

She dropped Lucas' keyring into her lap, the clanking and

clustering sounds bouncing around the interior, amplifying the noise. A large breath of crisp air filled her lungs.

Do it. Do it.

Her mind taunted her.

Coward.

"Fuck that," she said to the wintery air and thrust her hands from the edges of her sleeves until her fingertips touched the steering wheel. Her breath came in short, muffled sounds, her fingers reached around the leather-covered wheel until they touched her palms.

"Holy shit."

She opened her eyes and stared. It was real. Her hands were on a real steering wheel, in a real car, with a blanket of snow covering the windshield, hiding it all from the real world.

"I'm doing it. Nate! Lucas!" she yelled, her voice cracking as she yanked her hands back into the confines of the jacket sleeve. "I actually did it." Only quick puffs of warmed, exhaled air hung around her. For applause, for now, this would have to do.

Can we push it a bit more?

Her fingers felt for the keyring in her lap and she held up the keys, searching for the key. Singling it out, she held it up to gaze at and study it. All she needed to do was put it in the ignition and twist. But she couldn't remember if she needed to step on the brake first or not?

Okay, okay. We're not there. We're not breaking his car to prove something. We've done enough already.

Pride radiated out of her, and in the midst, the inside of the vehicle brightened, making it less scary than it had when she'd come down. She had set out to prove she could sit in the car. In the driver's seat. And survive. It was a giant step. And Nate had been right. Maybe driving—solo—wouldn't be so bad. But no passengers. Never. At least if another accident happened, it would only be her.

Nodding, she opened the door and gripped the keys in her palm, the remote dangling free. She stood and glanced around. The howling wind moved around her, and through her, plummeting her body temperature. She shivered and closed the door, pressing the lock button.

Two amazingly loud beeps echoed throughout the parking lot.

Pulling her coat across her body, she shielded her eyes against the blowing snow and pushed herself up onto the sidewalk, following the fresh prints into the main building. Back in the warmth the main entrance provided, she shook off the accumulated snow and stopped dead. It dawned on her. She hadn't yet given Lucas a key to the apartment and had no way to get back into the building.

Fuck!

She had two choices. Wait until someone else arrived and follow them in, which could be hours at this time of night, or buzz her own place until Lucas woke up and answered. She didn't know what time it was, but it was three-thirty ish when she left her bedroom, but how long had she been gone? An hour? More? Less? She let her head bang against the glass doors.

Hoping against hope, she gave the door a yank back. Nope, it was locked. Of course, it was. Was she really so stupid to have planned her return so poorly?

With a trembling finger, she pushed her buzzer number. Counting to ten, enough time to have it start to rouse Lucas, she pushed it again. No answer, she waited a breath or two and re-pushed.

"Hello?" a voice crackled through.

"Lucas, it's Aurora. Buzz me in please."

"Aurora? What are you doing down there?"

"You wouldn't believe me if I told you. Please let me in."

The door buzzed, and she pulled it open.

"Thank you."

The walk to the elevator and the ride up was long. The middle of the night adventure was supposed to be a secret. Had it been successful, she could've done it alone until she perfected it.

Don't hide the secrets, you only give them power. Expose them and you shall be set free.

"Damn you, Dr. Navin. This isn't even a bad secret," she muttered as the elevator stopped on her floor. She shuffled out toward her apartment.

Lucas leaned against the opened door, curiosity mixed with the sleepiness on his face.

She approached, her heart hammering as hard as when she snuck out.

"I suppose you have a good reason for being outside? It's freezing."

"You're telling me."

The door clicked shut, and the chain slid across. She kicked off her shoes, removed her jacket and shivering, walked into the living room. The lamp on the side table lit up the area like daytime for the middle of the night.

"Oh, these are yours."

Lucas' jaw dropped as she dangled his car keys in front of him. "You took… my car?" The keys fell into his opened palm and he tossed them on the table. "That's impossible."

"Yeah, no." She dropped into the couch, which was still warm from where he'd been sleeping. Her hands ran under the blankets savouring the heat. "I wanted to try something."

He shuffled across the floor, hiking up his pants. "And?"

"I did better than I thought I would. I would've pushed myself harder but I couldn't figure out a part."

His blue-greys narrowed at her and he ran his hands over his face. "I thought I was following you but now I'm lost."

"I sat in the driver's seat." Her gaze connected with his. "I would've started up the car, but I couldn't remember if I needed to step on the brake or not first. Figured I'd watch you the next time."

"Wow, Aurora. I'm in shock."

"Couldn't be that much. You thought I took your car."

"I didn't know what else to think when you produced my keys." He sat beside her,

moving his pillow off to the side. "I'm impressed?"

"Why the question?"

"Honestly, I didn't think you'd ever get to that point. I thought you were happy with simply being a passenger."

"I was. I mean I am. I just wanted… Oh hell. I want to be done with this. I'm so tired of everything being connected to the PTSD. I'm tired of it controlling my life. If I can sit in a car without too much difficulty these days, I can sure as hell try sitting behind the wheel."

"I don't know what to say except wow!"

"I'll take wow."

"Where did all this come from?"

"I had a bad dream."

"Again?"

"Yeah. I can't explain it really well now, but it was like being physically chained to a monster and the monster was fighting off all attackers."

He chuckled. "You're saying the monster is the PTSD?"

"Sounds silly, right?"

"Weird maybe, but not silly." He scratched at his chin. "It's very metaphorical though and I'm kind of intrigued by it. And this all came from the nightmare?"

She took a deep breath and sighed. "Mostly."

"But…"

"It's hard to explain. I can't. I don't know how. Maybe it was something Kaitlyn said about doing the wedding her way regardless of her parent's involvement, or lack of I should say. She's always done things her own way, and it's chained to a set direction. Same with Nate. He has a dream, to race with the big guys, and he's going to be out there making it happen." She faced him. "And you. Look at you. You're switching into a faculty you really want, not one you feel forced to do."

"Are you feeling left out?"

"Maybe."

"But you're doing things in your own way too. You're going to switch faculties–"

"Again."

"You're still going for something *you* want to do. You've made huge leaps and strides with getting into a car, and now you're wanting to sit in the driver's seat. You're growing up."

"Ah shit, I didn't want to do that." She winked.

"Well I'm proud of you. I love your determination to kick this. What will you do now?"

"Like tonight? I'm too jacked up to sleep, so I have no idea."

His hands ran over his puffy, sleep-lacking eyes. "I meant in general, but sure, okay, we can focus on tonight." A yawn fought its way through and he covered his mouth. "Sorry."

"You know what, you go back to sleep. I'm going to grab my laptop and watch a movie in the bedroom."

"What are you gonna watch?"

"*While You Were Sleeping.*"

"Okay, then wait. I'll be asleep soon." He yawned again and gave his arms a rub.

"No silly, it's the name of the movie. It's a Sandra Bullock film, and it's really cute."

His mouth opened wide, and he covered his yawn. "Chick's movie?"

"Yeah."

"Fine." He stumbled down the hall.

"Where are you going?" She jumped up and walked over to him.

"You said you were watching in the bedroom."

"I didn't think you'd want to watch."

"I do, but I really need to stretch out."

She watched him saunter into her bedroom. Stunned, she followed. Inside he'd already climbed onto the bed—on top of the covers—and laid down. She retrieved the blanket from the couch and when she returned to her bedroom, he was already lightly snoring. Covering him up, she fired up her laptop and started the movie.

♥Chapter Twenty-Nine♥

Lucas

"What the?" He blinked rapidly and looked around.

It was dark in the room, but a glimmer of light edged the blackout drapes, and he was stretched out on a bed, a heavy fleece blanket covering him. Water running from a shower ran in the background, but other than that, it was quiet. He inched himself over to glance at the clock, it wasn't eight a.m. yet. Allowing his head to fall onto the pillow, he immediately was surrounded by a citrus scent.

Aurora's smell.

He inhaled deeply, relief it wasn't some random girl's place, but someone he knew, and knew well. Concern washed over him.

What am I doing in her bed? Right. She mentioned a movie. Did I watch a movie? There's no tv in here.

He rubbed his eyes and stretched out his ears. She was in the shower, humming, and the mere thought of her naked aroused him. If they were in a relationship, a wild and romantic one, he'd surprise her and join in on the action. But that wasn't his reality. No matter what she said, he knew she was still in love with his brother and he'd have to try harder to hide his feelings and get over her. They would never happen. It didn't matter if Nate was leaving in less than a month, she was still attached to him. And it was against bro code to lust after the brother's ex-girlfriend.

Although it was anything but lust. In conversations with his driving buddy Michael, he said it was love. And he hated himself for having those feelings toward Aurora, but it was so hard to not love her. Unlike any woman he's ever met, she captured his heart with her unique and albeit different outlook on life. He loved who she was and how much she'd changed for the better since the first day he met her. There was no other Aurora to be found. She was an original. And he wished she loved him the way he loved her.

Groaning, he rolled over and threw the blanket off. After a giant yawn and bigger stretch, he padded down to the kitchen and started a pot of coffee, setting out two cups. He filled hers with two spoonful's of sugar and set it aside as he made his own. While the coffee dripped and the aroma of it circled around him, he grabbed his phone from the coffee table. He stumbled and banged into the edge of the table. The jolt caused Aurora's 'reference book' to fall, and it rattled as it bounced on the floor. Bending down with his head cocked, he picked up the book and a sticker-less orange pill container fell out, along with two baggies.

No! No! No! Please say these aren't what I think they are.

He examined the inside of the book.

Jesus, Aurora.

Closing the book, he placed it back on the coffee table, but the container and baggies he kept in his hand.

Do I bring this up? Wait for her to tell me? Leave them out some place visible? Wait for her to go hunting for them and not find them? But then she may go back to her dealer and get more. What the hell do I do?

He needed more time to think, and in haste, he raced over to his jacket and shoved them into a pocket. A keyring glittered on the table and it all started to come back. Aurora had taken his keys and sat in the driver's seat. Having discovered the pills, he couldn't help but wonder if she was high when she attempted it.

"Good morning," she called out from behind him.

He jumped, unaware she had left the bedroom.

"Nervous?" Her laugh, normally music to his ears, irked him.

Was she high now?

And he hated how he second-guessed himself. Maybe he wasn't as good a therapist-in-training if he hadn't realised she was sneaking pills. He could read her and read her so well. Was it all a lie?

"You okay?"

He shook his head and ran his fingers through his hair. "Just tired."

"I wonder how the coffee is?" She laughed as she patted him on the shoulder and walked into the kitchen.

"Strong, I hope. Sorry I crashed in your bed."

"Meh. It didn't bother me much, but you did snore a lot."

"What? I don't snore."

"Oh yes, you do. But it's cute."

"You think I'm cute?" He bit his lip.

She smiled. "I said your snoring is cute."

Well, there goes that. "Oh. I see."

"I'd like to rectify your lack of keys to my place. Next time we're out, I'll get you your own set."

He joined her in the kitchen when the machine beeped. "Yeah, the buzzer going off at three fifty-two was a complete surprise." Slowly, he filled her mug and passed it to her.

"Thanks."

"What are your thoughts on it all today?"

Tentatively, she took a sip and dropped her gaze. "I think I'd like to try it again."

He nearly spit out his coffee. "Today?"

"Not sure. Maybe. I was plenty jacked up when I got back in, and didn't sleep much, so I don't know if it's wise to try today."

He sat at the table, despair filling him. *She said she was too jacked up. Had she taken something?* The more he stewed about it, the worse he felt.

She sat beside him, her eyebrows knit together in concern. "Are you sure you're okay?"

"Yeah." He took a sip and swallowed down the foul-tasting

coffee. Way too strong. Hers was better. "Anything you want to tell me?"

Her shoulders rolled inward, and she hunched over her cup. "I'm sorry for taking your keys without asking but I wanted to see if I could do it on my own, without outside pressure."

She was being cute by apologising for taking his keys, but it wasn't what he wanted to hear. "Yeah, well… I'd be mad at you if I wasn't so damn proud." He gave her arm a squeeze. "But why so jacked up?"

"Wouldn't you be? I did what I thought I could never do. The adrenaline rush was something else. How do you sleep after that?" Her delicate hands rubbed her face, splashes of colour surfacing when she stopped. Her cheeks a lovely rosy shade.

She had a point. "Yes, I get it. I'm just tired and I think my dreams are mixing with reality."

"Why?"

"I had a dream you were high." He studied her, searching for any telltale signs she was about to hide.

"I wish." She locked her gaze on his. "It would take away a lot of the hurt."

The sadness clouded her face, revealing the truth. As much as she wanted the drugs, she hadn't taken any. At least not before she got in the car.

"Because of?"

"Everything, but mostly Nate."

"I'm really sorry things didn't go as planned."

"Yeah, me too." Her breath caught, and she twisted away from him.

"If it were only the contract, would you still stay with him?"

She fiddled with her long, dark hair, working it quickly into a loose braid. "Lucas, we can't go back in time and erase the fact he's going to be a father before his next birthday."

"But if we could?"

She slumped further. "I don't know. The contract is a big deal.

He didn't let me in."

"He didn't tell me much about it either."

Her warm hand wrapped over his. "He really closed up to both of us, didn't he? Shut us both out."

"That he did."

"Do you ever dream of going big?"

"Hell no."

His response must've surprised her as she bolted upright. "Really?"

"It's a fun hobby, but no. I enjoy racing and being a part of the spectacle on the weekends, but I'm not a fan of travelling all over. I'm totally content to stay here and be surrounded by people I love."

"Yeah, but your fans would follow you everywhere."

My fans may, but would you? "Wouldn't even be close to the same thing." He swallowed another gulp of coffee unable to make eye contact. "I'm more than happy to race under the new banner and drive a super stock but that's about it. If I do well in a new class, I'll be a content man."

"Well, Mr. Content, I'm going to make you breakfast and then I have work to do."

"What work is that?"

She rose, the light pink sweater that had to have been Carmen's as it was too big for her, slipped off her right shoulder. A quick adjustment and she covered it back up. "I should probably do some school work, but you know I'll avoid it like the plague. I'll hang out on social media all day and waste my time there instead."

"How is that work?"

"Because I'll have emails to send and hopefully reply to, and it may take up a large part of my day."

"Have fun."

"Well, it's not like we'll be going anywhere today. There has to be at least a foot of snow on the ground."

He walked over to the patio door and pulled back the curtain. Indeed, the city was blanketed in white. It was beautiful, and large fluffy flakes added to the delight. "There goes any notion of going for a drive."

"We can still sit in the car though, right?"

He turned around to see her. A curious smile played on her full lips and her blue eyes lit up with hope. Her hands tucked into the pocket of her sweater. "Of course, I'd like to watch that."

"Great. Maybe after lunch." She danced away from him, her tight little ass in her yoga pants driving him wild.

He'd sat at the kitchen table for the better part of the day working on his assignment. Every time she walked into the living room, he lifted his eyes from his paper long enough to watch what she was doing, and never once did she attempt to open her 'reference book' as she called it.

She only took a break from her endless baking when he insisted, and that was to drive her to the grocery store for more supplies and get a key cut for him. She'd vehemently refused to try sitting in the driver's seat, preferring to wait until she was feeling stronger, and to do so alone. At least for the next couple of attempts.

The ride was quieter than usual, the sound of her breathing bothered him. She was clearly bothered by something and refused to make eye contact with him. It bugged him that he couldn't put his finger on her behaviour change. Where she'd been fun and flirty in the morning, by noon, she'd become sullen and closed-off.

After whipping up batch after batch of sweet baked goodies, she dedicated the remainder of the afternoon to clean up and forced him to sample the pastries and cookies and muffins. Who was he kidding? Forcing? Only because it was adorable to listen to her beg him to try a bite of whatever she offered inches from his lips. After a sizeable tasting of each, he declared the strawberry-chocolate muffins his favourite.

No matter what she did though, she certainly wasn't reaching for any drugs, but he'd only found *one* book. Were there others?

Still, he watched her. Waited to see if a smile would pop up, or if she'd look in his direction. Nothing. So deep in herself, she didn't look up when his phone chirped with a message. *Up for a little Saturday night fun?*

Always the same, and most of the time, he said yes. It was his way to deal with things. Go to a party on campus and forget about the world, or if he were being honest, forget about her. A month had passed since he'd gone, and he itched to go and dance and drink and have a fun time. Not that he didn't have fun with Aurora, it was just a more intimate fun. They hung out in her apartment, studying, playing cards or having video game battles. But they hadn't gone out-out. Not in a long while anyways.

Aurora likes dancing. I wonder if she'd come if I asked? It would be good for both of us.

He searched for his best friend in the living room. She wasn't there. Right, she'd gone down the hall. Was she napping? It was awfully quiet. He tiptoed down the hall to check on her.

Debris scattered around her and in the middle, she was folded up, sitting on the floor, knees to chest, her arms wrapped tightly around them, the corner of a picture frame peeking out. Tears streamed down her face.

He dropped to the floor in front of her, pushing aside a small pile of men's clothing. "Aurora?"

Her eyes remained firmly shut.

Using a delicate motion, he swept her bangs off her face. "What's going on?" His heart ached seeing her so upset. Tenderly, he wiped away a tear. It wasn't the time for pushing and asking questions although he was so curious about her thoughts. Instead, he wiggled up beside her.

"I… I… miss him." A low sob ebbed out of her. "We were happy… once. But he… secured his future… with Marissa." Her breath hitched.

"Breathe, Aurora." He wrapped his arms around her. She was falling apart, and he was going to make sure he held her together.

"But I was thinking as I baked, how it wasn't his fault. Not really. I didn't let him in. I didn't want him to see me at my worst, at my most insecure and raw. I was afraid he'd run away. The accident was sort of a saving grace, really. The drugs gave me a chance to hide my insecurity, but it's not a good thing for a relationship, is it?"

He shook his head.

"It was all on me."

"I wouldn't say it's all on you. Nate put up his own walls too."

"Yeah." She wiped her eyes and inhaled sharply. "What am I going to do?"

"What is it you hoped to do?" He surveyed the mess. Not a tidy person by nature, her room was a bona fide disaster.

"I figured packing up his things and clearing that away would ease it a bit. But it hurts more."

"Because you're not ready to say goodbye."

She opened her blue eyes and stared through him. The whites had turned pink with sadness, and a puffiness surrounded them. It hurt him to see her so distraught.

A quick image of the bags of drugs he'd hidden. Would she need them now? Would the breakup wreck her completely and send her spiralling backwards, or does she just need a lot of support to get her through this patch so she can come out stronger on the other side? He wished he knew. One thing was certain, he wasn't going anywhere. He'd sit beside her, holding her until she said otherwise. She didn't need the drugs to get through this. She needed physical comfort, and he was good at that.

He ran his thumb down her cheek, hoping each stroke soothed her. It seemed to work as her breathing calmed down. Her head rested against his shoulder, the weight of it growing with each deep breath she shuddered out.

"You doing okay?"

"Eventually."

♥Chapter Thirty♥

Aurora could've stayed in his arms for the better part of the day, however, her good hip gave her a bit of grief and she needed to move. Sitting up, she moved away from Lucas and gave her eyes a wipe with the sleeve of Carmen's sweater.

Lucas gave her arm a rub.

"I'm sorry."

"For what? Having feelings?" He shook each of his legs as he balanced on them. A gentle hand extended in her direction and he pulled her onto her feet. "You're allowed to be human."

She shrugged. "I need something to drink. Want a tea?"

"I'd prefer a hot chocolate."

"Okay."

With heavy feet, she padded down the hall and fought to find a spot for the kettle. It seemed like every space in her kitchen was filled with baked goods in some form or another. She walked into the living room, wanting to grab the containers she'd picked up earlier to package up the baking. Walking past her special book, she chanced a glance behind her. The light leaked out from under the bottom of the bathroom door.

She didn't need a pill right then, but just wanted to see them. To have them reassure her one way or another she'd be okay, and that she'd get through this mess in her life. Pulling open the book, her heart crashed to the ground. The inside of the book was empty.

Two baggies and one orange container were missing. Without a trace. She spun around, searching under the coffee table, her eyes running over every conceivable surface hoping to see something that was out of place.

Clapping her hand to her forehead, she paced the living room. She was so sure the last time she used any pills from there, she'd put them right back. But when was that? A week ago? That morning, before Lucas had come to check on her, she'd dumped the remaining Kays down the drain, but she was sure she'd left the others in the book. She was so sure. So why weren't they there? *Son of a bitch!*

Her heart raced as her mind circulated through all the *possible* hiding places. They could be anywhere, but they *should* be in the book. She was many things, but she wasn't someone who misplaced things. Not these things, anyway.

Fuck!

She paced some more, and a new form of anxiety built within her. Not so much anxiety but fear. Pure, unadulterated fear. The fear of being caught.

"Water's boiling."

She jumped, clutching the book to her chest. "Geezus, you scared me."

"Clearly." His eyes roved up and down, settling on her reference manual. "Gonna do some reading?"

"Huh?" She looked down, forcing down a swallow of panic. "No. I was just looking for something."

"What? Maybe I can help?" He stepped closer to her.

Needing to keep distance between them, she retreated to the kitchen. "No, it's okay." She tucked the worthless book into the cupboard and pulled out two mugs, dropping a tea bag in one and a few spoonful's of cocoa in another.

"You seem really flustered." He leaned against the wall and took his cup when she offered to him.

"I'm not. I think I lost something." She covered her eyes with a hand. *Think. Where did you last use them?* It had been a week ago, but the book hadn't moved. It had sat out in the open where anyone could find it. Anyone. She looked over at Lucas. Had he discovered them? If so, what had he done with them? There was well over a hundred dollars worth of drugs hidden.

He seemed generally concerned as he stared at her. "What did you lose?"

"Something I'd saved up for." That should be enough to satisfy him. She slumped into a kitchen chair that faced into the living room, scouring the area thoroughly.

Lucas blocked her view. "What was that?"

With a sigh, she dropped her head onto her arm. "I–"

Lucas' phone rang. "Hey, what's up?... Of course, I can. I'm on my way. Give me fifteen at least." He jumped up and grabbed his coat.

"What's going on?" Her head popped up with the rise and pitch in Lucas' voice.

"Justin needs my help. He's stuck in a snow rut not far from here."

"Want some company?"

"No. Stay here where it's warm. Besides, we just got you healed. Let's not do anything to make it worse."

It stung a little to not be wanted, but she stayed in her seat. She had no plans on re-injuring her ankle trying to push someone out of the snow.

He fed his arms into the jacket and reached for the door. His face morphed into concern. "You'll be okay while I'm gone?"

She looked around her apartment. How much trouble could she get into, especially when her pills were playing hide and seek? "Yeah. I'll be fine."

His eyes held something back, and she cursed herself for not being able to read him as well as he always read her. "I'll be back soon." Slowly, with a hint of hesitation, he exited the apartment, the door latching behind him.

With him gone, she had a chance to search the apartment properly. If they weren't here, then she'd be asking Lucas some damn important questions. But first, into the living room she went.

"I was here. On the couch," she said to herself. That night after finding out about Nate accepting the contract *and* Marissa's baby, she had taken a Kay. She'd sat on the couch and fumbled with them, debating whether she needed one or two. Deciding that one would be best, she tucked them back into the baggie, and put the baggie in the book. She was sure of it. But the night had fogged over fairly quick. Had she really put them away?

Yes! Because the next day, she grabbed the pills *from* the book and flushed them down the sink. They had been in there, she was positive. At no point during the week had she attempted to grab anymore, always confident that they were there should she need them. But… Lucas had been over all week. He could've grabbed them anytime. So could've Nate. Maybe when her back was turned?

Both were aware she'd purchased drugs, whereas Nate thought it just Xanax and Percocet, Lucas knew there had been something else. But how would they have known where she hid them? There was no way. She simply put them elsewhere, and in her heart broken week, her memory failed her.

She walked over to the bookshelf. There, staring at her, was the first book she attempted to make a hiding place out of. A self-help book she'd purchased from the discount bin at the grocery store. Retrieving it from the shelf, she opened it. Nothing. The cut pages only deep enough to hold a stick of gum, not a container of contraband.

Stepping over to next row of shelves, she started flinging books onto the floor. As her desperation grew, and her heart pounded harder than ever before, she opened each book and tossed it aside, the search time on each shortening with each new book.

The shelves were empty, but she'd located nothing aside from a five-dollar bill she'd used as a bookmark. Frantic, she rummaged through the living room, papers flying, pillows becoming airborne as she thrust her hands between the couch cushions in a feeble attempt to happen upon what she already knew in her heart wasn't there.

Her hands checked behind the gaming consoles and shifted the games onto the carpet as she continued to ransack her own apartment.

Running into the kitchen, she opened and shut drawers, hoping that in her moment of panic, she'd spot them. The cutlery rattled as she gave one a particularly hard slam. "Dammit." However, the more she hunted for the pills she knew were gone, the more the rage boiled inside.

Lucas really hadn't found them, had he?

She stormed out of the kitchen and over to the bathroom. Towels dropped, and bottles hit the floor with a thud. The only bathroom drawer was freed from it's confines. As it fell to the floor, a baggie taped to the bottom caught her eye. She collapsed beside it and pulled the drawer onto her lap. Her fingernail picked at the tape and pulled the baggie loose. Inside was a single Xanax. *Nate.*

Her heart shattered, and the rage blew out of her. Tears washed down her cheeks as she closed her eyes, the baggie clenched in her palm.

"What the hell, Aurora?" Lucas' sharp voice cut through her sorrow.

She blinked through the fuzzy version of him glaring down at her. "I found one he left behind." Her palm opened, blood rushing into it from releasing her death grip on the baggie. "He hid Xanax for me around the apartment."

"And you felt you needed one?" The baggie fell into Lucas' outstretched hand.

"No."

"Talk to me, tell me what's on your mind. You were flustered before I left, and now, not even an hour later, your apartment looks like a bomb went off it in."

The mess surrounded her and she couldn't help but feel shame over it all. "I swear to God I wasn't going to take them, but I wanted to see them. To reassure myself that no matter how much my heart hurt, something would be there to comfort me."

Lucas acted as if he'd been sucker-punched. "You destroyed your place for a…" He studied the single pill. "For a Xanax?"

She avoided eye contact and stared at the cascade of towels.

"It doesn't matter to you that *I'm* here for you, and that *I'll* comfort you because the drugs are more important to you, right?"

"That's not what I'm saying." Her voice pitched. "I wasn't going to take them. It's like money in the bank. You still check it's there even if you don't touch it." She pushed the toiletries to the side with a resounding thud and got to her feet.

"That's bullshit and you know it." He lifted himself from his crouch. "Admit it, you've been abusing drugs."

"I am not." She stomped her foot onto the floor, her fists clenched at her sides.

"So those pills you took last week were harmless?"

Her eyes grew wide and her lips tightened into a sneer. "I told you, I threw them down the sink." She growled recalling that moment.

"And how do I believe that?"

"Because I did." She went to step around him, but he thrust up his arm blocking her exit. Her tone lowered, and she pleaded with him. "You have to believe me, Lucas. I only bought those, the percs and extra Xanax. And I sent the bad ones down the drain."

"What about the percs and the Xanax?" His blue-greys narrowed at her.

Her voice hit the floor. "I can't find them." A wave of despair, combined with currents of sadness and shame fell out of her. "I'd hidden the drugs in a book but when I went to check on them they were gone." She braced herself against the bathroom sink and closed her eyes, visualising what exactly she was missing. "I had two baggies of percs. I think there were five in one, and three in another. There was also an orange container which contained extra Xanax." She thought about how many should be left in there. It had been a while since she used any of the extra stash. "I think there are three in there. Maybe four."

Lucas lowered his hand and thrust it into his pocket. He dropped the two baggies and the container on the counter. "You were close. There were four Xanax, and all the percs you said there were."

"What? You? You knew?" Too many emotions surfaced in her

brain. Anger. Gratitude. Fear. Shame. She wanted to be angry mad and wanted to hit him for keeping it hidden from her and making her panic. And yet, she was grateful that it was him that found them, not someone else. For some strange reason, she wanted to thank him, but she wasn't sure *why* she wanted to thank him. "When?" she spat out, the anger surfacing.

"This morning, before breakfast."

"Before breakfast," she repeated. "Can I have them back?" She wasn't going to make a move toward them until he said so.

His eyes remained locked on hers. "Why?"

"I want to throw them away."

He nodded. "So, go ahead."

Hesitantly, she wrapped her hand around them, wondering if the rush from them would still be there. There was nothing anymore. All she felt was anger toward them and the power they had held over her. Walking with authority, she marched into the kitchen and turned on the faucet, dropping her pills on the counter. The first baggie ripped open, she released each one unceremoniously into the running water. Splunk, splunk, splunk. Each swirled around the sink and dropped into the darkness. She reached for the unopened bag and tore it apart. One, two, three, four, five. The remaining percs washed down the drain, forever out of her hands.

She released her breath.

"You okay?" Lucas said from beside her, and his hand rested on the small of her back.

The combination of his presence and his touch calmed her. "Better than I thought I'd be. I know there are better ways of dealing with heartache than the drugs."

"Yes, there are."

"But I'm scared."

"Of?"

She inhaled sharply. "Of truly letting the pain in."

He rubbed nice fluid motions from shoulder to the small of her back. "But that's how you heal. If you keep avoiding them, they build up until they break you. Let the emotions in, and we'll deal with them together. I won't let them break you. I promise." He brushed her hair from her shoulder. "But you have to let me in too."

Nodding, she reached for the container, and her hand trembled as she tried to twist the lid open. With a hard push, the lid released, and she tumbled the four last Xanax into the palm of her hand. Cupping her hand over the sink, her hand shook violently, but it wouldn't twist and dump the contents. A sour buildup in her stomach burned the longer her hand stayed over the running water.

Lucas reached around her and twisted the tap, stopping the water. He picked up the container and pushed it into her upturned hand, capturing all four Xanax.

"Yeah, we're not there yet," he said, securing the lid and setting it down. "You actually need those."

Frozen in the spot, she didn't move. Her hand still dangled above the sink.

Lucas' warm hand closed it up and pinned it to her chest. With her arms folded into her chest, he hugged her. "I'm proud of what you did. No more percs?"

She shook her head.

"Good. You don't need them anyways." He kissed her forehead. "No more secrets."

"No more."

He held her tight until her heart resumed its normal beat and her breathing calmed down.

"All better?"

It was like a weight lifted from her and she wasn't tied down to her demons anymore. "But the Xanax."

"We'll keep it around because you really do suffer with anxiety. Hopefully as time passes it will get better, but maybe it won't. But we'll keep an eye on it together and see how it goes."

Together? Her heart strummed the word repeatedly over in her head. *Together.*

♥Chapter Thirty-One♥

Together.

We'll keep an eye on it, together.

The words circled around her. Every day she read more into those words than she should've. And every day she dismissed the words as something a friend would say; a best friend. Something to comfort someone in distress.

Because they were just friends. That was all.

So what if he drove her to university every day? If he waited for her just outside her last class? She did the same for him. Well, not the driving part but still. They hung out all the time, and most of the time, they didn't even talk. They'd just worked on assignments and prepared for finals.

He even gave up his *flavour of the week* for gaming night with her on Saturdays.

It had been three weeks. Three weeks since she'd pitched the percs. Three weeks since she'd looked at or held a Xanax. She didn't need it. There had been no need. If anything, she needed an upper more. Something to spark her. Something to make her crave life.

"You know, maybe it's the post-final blues."

"What was that?" She lifted her head off the pillow on the couch, the glow from the tv doctors lighting up the living room.

"I mean, it's been a few weeks since you washed the drugs away, and I know you've not touched any." He tipped his head to the orange container that sat in clear sight on top of the kitchen table. "But you're very melancholy."

She sighed, incapable of much else.

"I think we need to get out."

"I'm comfortable here."

"You're too comfortable." He pulled himself off the floor. "Exams are done. We should be celebrating."

"You go right ahead."

He crouched down in front of her. "I want to celebrate. With you." He leaned closer to her. "Now get up." His soft hand reached for hers and he dragged her to a standing position. "We're going shopping."

"Why? I hate shopping."

"You're a terrible liar." He pushed her down the hall to her bedroom. "You have ten minutes to make yourself presentable."

"Do jammies count?"

"Hell no." His arms crossed across his chest. "Jeans and tee. Anything over and above that is a bonus." A long finger tapped against his watch. "Nine minutes."

Nine minutes? There was barely time to dabble on some concealer to reduce the dark splotches under her eyes in nine minutes, let alone get dressed and be presentable. Sheesh.

But she traded her pajamas for a clean pair of black, skinny jeans and a dark grey and black striped sweater. She used her fingers to quickly half-ass braid her hair, and open the door to the hallway.

"You're lucky," he said. "I was just about to come in." His smile taunted her. She wanted to return it, but didn't have the heart. "You look nice."

"Thanks. So do you." Had he changed? She hadn't noticed what he was wearing, but she didn't think he'd been in a navy-blue shirt and tan pants. Her eyes roved up and down quickly. Had he been in that? She really needed to pull herself together. How did she not remember?

He laughed and pulled her toward the door, tossing her a jacket.

"Come on. You're gonna to help me find a present for mom. I have no idea what to get her."

"World's Number One Mom?" she deadpanned, and her lips stretched out. Not enough to be considered a smile, but more than the lacklustre look she'd been sporting.

"Not this year." He waited as she pulled the door closed and twisted her keys out of the lock before he reached for her hand.

She stared at the linking. "Do you think I'm going to run away?"

"I know you better than that."

He didn't really answer her question, and she didn't push it. It was oddly comforting to hold it, even if it meant nothing.

They stopped on the driver's side and Lucas opened the door.

"Really? Not this time. My heart's not in it."

"Your heart's never in it, and yet you do it anyways." The silver keys dangled before her eyes.

She debated staring him down, seeing how long it would take before he got frustrated with her and took the keys back, but she knew she'd never win. She'd tried it twice. The longest she got was ten minutes, and that was only because she was getting cold. Had she been better dressed…

The keys snapped out of his hand. "That's my girl."

Twice a day he pulled this stunt—refusing to drive her anywhere until she sat in the driver's seat. A quick sit, both legs in, hands on the wheel, time to get out. A minute or less. She cursed herself daily for not having been prepared that night with a way back into the apartment. Then she'd perform this task on her own, at her own pace.

She slumped into the seat, her feet still ankle deep in the snow. The only time her heart got a workout was pulling her feet up and tucking them under the steering column. With a huge intake of air, she had her whole body inside the car. Slamming her eyes shut, she listened to the rhythmic pounding in her chest as it rushed the blood through her ears. Hand extended, she wrapped her fingers around the cool wheel, while the other inserted the key into the ignition and counted to ten.

"Excellent," Lucas said, his smile growing as he admired her.

"Now can we go?" She jumped out.

"Anywhere you want."

"Great." She walked over to her side.

"Whew, thought you were gonna head back up."

"Since I'm dressed, I may as well go out."

"That's the spirit."

Minutes later they were parked, and putzing around one of several arms of the mall, that branched of the main corridor. Christmas lights twinkled, and had there been music, it would've probably matched the frantic pace the shoppers marched. Everyone in a hurry, their bags dangled from their arms.

"What do you think your mom would like?"

"I haven't the foggiest. What do you think?"

She shrugged. "She's your mom, but I'm sure we'll find something here." They walked past a comedy bar, the kind that had giant neon arrows pointing to its entrance and loud, thumping music seeping out from behind the grey metal doors. "Get her tickets to a show."

"I'm not sure she'd go."

"Sure she would, who doesn't like to laugh and enjoy a night out?"

He stopped and stared at her. "You don't."

"Just lately." She pointed to Christmas package pricing. "She could take Bill. And it's fairly affordable for two."

Lucas gave her an odd look.

"It'd be kind of awkward to go on her own."

"Yeah, but it's weird, getting him a gift." Lucas stared at the list, shrugging and turning his back to it.

"Having a hard time with this, aren't you?"

"I never know what to buy mom."

"I meant with her and Bill."

Lucas hung his head.

She scooped lower and looked up into his face. "Why does it bug you so much?"

"Why doesn't it bother you about your dad and Judy?"

"Because all I want for him is to be happy. He deserves it and if she treats him right, then that's all I can ask for." She stared into his eyes. "Doesn't your mom deserve to be happy?"

"No," he said, but the tone in his voice said he wasn't serious. "But why Bill?"

"Because he…" she thought for a phrase that would make him giggle. "Jump starts her heart. Maybe more."

"Eww." But he was smiling. "I don't need to know anymore." He pointed to a night out for two. "What do you think about this package?"

She nodded, and looked to the back when the door opened and the music volume increased. "Yeah, that looks good."

Lucas rapped on the box office window. "Two for the Holiday Ha-ha."

The worker, who was a day older than Lucas, if that, spoke into the microphone, "All I have available for tonight is seats at the back. Row 12 C and D."

"Whatever, we'll take it."

Aurora yanked on his arm. "What? Lucas, no. We're supposed to be shopping for your mom."

He smirked. "We'll test drive it. If it works on you, I'll get it for her." He winked at her, and a shimmer of hope flashed in his eyes. "Admit it, you could use the mental break." Lucas refocused on the attendant and passed him a credit card.

"Through those doors," the microphone said as the tickets slid out.

"Well, let's go have some holiday ha-ha." Lucas held open the door.

"Okay," Lucas said, wiping tears away as the last comic left the stage and the house lights turned on. "We're getting that for mom."

Aurora gripped her stomach. "I hurt from laughing so hard. Oh my god, when he referenced pet owners, I thought I'd die."

"Yeah, I noticed that. Your nose still burning?"

In a fit of laughter, her diet coke had travelled up and out her nose. "Not so much, but I can still smell it."

"God that last guy was hilarious."

She gave her face a good rub with a clean napkin. The laughter reddened her complexion and with it, a band of sweat appeared across her forehead.

Servers bustled around gathering payment, and theirs stopped at their table.

"I got this," Aurora said, grabbing the bill. Without looking at it, she produced her credit card.

"Enjoy your night," the server said as she gave back the card and a copy of the receipt.

"Ready to go?" Lucas asked.

"I suppose, although all the stores will be closed now."

"So, we'll window shop. I still need ideas for Chris and I'll buy it online. That's why that was invented." He slipped out of the two-person booth and waited expectantly. His jaw slack, and his shoulders back, he was happy and relaxed.

"Pretty sure that's *not* why it was invented." A smirk played on the edge of her mouth as she stared up at Lucas. "What? What's with that look?"

"It's nice to see you smiling again. To hear you laugh."

"You're a good friend, Lucas, better than you need to be." She scooted out of her seat, and they joined the mass exodus of people from the theatre.

Once out in the mall, they walked to the main corridor where she stopped at the fountains. Colourful lights lit up the water, and the streams danced to the Christmas music playing in the overhead speakers. It wasn't very loud, and was probably drowned out during the hustle and bustle of frantic shoppers during the day, but it was the perfect volume to hear Mariah Carey's *All I Want For Christmas*.

She sat on one of the seats and watched, entranced by the movement of the water.

"Soothing, eh?" Lucas sat on the seat beside hers.

"It really is." Her eyes followed the purple lights as they morphed into blues and greens and back again.

Lucas cleared his throat. "If I wanted to be more, would you go for it?"

Her vision jumped from the watery lights to his eyes. She swallowed, sure she'd misheard him. "Umm…" Blood raced in her veins, and a shot of adrenaline coursed through her. For once in her life, her mind was a blank canvas.

His gaze fell to his knees where his hands twisted in his lap. "I can't deny it anymore, and if you say it can't happen, then I'll find a way to live with that, because I'd rather be your best friend than nothing at all. But I need to know…" His eyes locked with hers. "I feel something with you, from you, so I know I'm not putting myself out there completely blind. Do you…" A trembling hand wrapped around hers, and his rough thumb rubbed across her knuckles. "Do you ever think about me the way I think about you?"

"I… don't know." Unable to look away, she was drawn into the depths of his soul.

His head tipped to the side and his eyes narrowed slightly. "What are you thinking?"

"I don't know…" Other words failed to form as the world around her faded. The music drowned out by the pulsating and pounding of her heart. The only thing she saw was his face as he waited for her to say or do anything. The warmth of his hand kept her on the ground although she was pretty sure she'd float away if he let go.

He leaned closer, and his hand travelled to her face where his thumb quivered and caressed his cheek.

Her breath caught in her throat, but she didn't fight it. Rather, she tipped her own head and fluttered her eyes as she leaned closer.

A heartbeat passed and…

Lips softer and cooler than she expected grazed across hers. Pushing for more, her hands pulled him closer, and she parted her lips in anticipation. Breathing him in, the heat from his tongue as it probed between her lips, raised her body temperature a million degrees.

As her lips kissed with wanton desire, her hand found his chest and pushed him away. "I can't…" An invisible elephant rendered her breathless as it sat on her chest, making it difficult to breathe.

"Don't you want…"

She rolled the bottom of her lip between her teeth. "I don't know what I want." Shakes and trembles rippled through her.

"What are you afraid of?" His voice as soft as his lips had been, gentle and serene.

"You," she breathed out.

"You're hilarious. As if I'd hurt you."

"Let me try to explain." She quivered as she breathed. "I'm terrified of falling for you and having it go south, that I'm afraid to make that leap. If we end up breaking up, there'd be no more friendship. And I love our friendship too much to test its strength. I *need* our friendship."

"And I promise to catch you if you fall. Our friendship, it's strong. We've been through a lot together." He broke eye contact with her.

With a still racing heart, she whispered to her hands, wringing and twisting together. "I'd rather have you as my best friend for the rest of my life, than to have two minutes of utter happiness, knowing I'd lose it all after."

"You won't lose it."

"There's no guarantee." By turning him down, their friendship stood at a fork in the road, but there was no going back now. After that kiss, the feelings inside her brewed. She had always loved him, but was it more? She'd thought it once, but she'd believed it was because she'd missed Nate so much. And now? Even if what she felt was the real deal, he was her ex's brother. It was so confusing.

"Aurora?"

"I love you, Lucas, I really do but what about Nate?" It hurt to look at him, so she tried to focus on the music or the dancing streams. But his voice was the only thing she heard, and his face, twisted with his own confusion, the only thing she saw.

"He screwed up. Besides, he's moving away and starting his own life." He tipped her chin up. "I love you, Aurora. I'm so in love with you."

She studied him, seeing the truth of his words in his eyes. So much honesty and boldness, something she truly envied. But she needed time to process. To think it all through. Away from distractions. To make sure a decision made with her heart matched the one her brain screamed at her to wait on.

"Lucas, I need to go home."

♥Chapter Thirty-Two♥

Suitcase in hand, Aurora stood in the entrance way to her building, Lucas silent beside her. She watched her ride, pull up and stop beyond the glass doors.

Lucas squeezed her hand. "You ready?"

She searched his eyes, a sadness within her heart as she took him in. He looked as physically wrecked as she was. It had been a quick decision to get away, but one that was needed. To figure out what she wanted, truly wanted, from her life. If it was him or the idea of him. There was no way she'd risk the friendship if she wasn't sure. But it was more than that. It was Nate. She needed to make sure he was out of her system before she moved on. Before she dared to move on with his brother. His declaration through her into a tailspin.

"I'm ready." She tightened her grip on his hand, glad that he hadn't pulled back when she said she needed time. He seemed to understand.

Cole opened the first set of doors, a blast of cool air wrapping around the trio. "Hey Princess."

"Daddy," she said, her voice vacant.

"Lucas." He nodded in his direction and reached for Aurora's suitcase. "You're sure you want to do this?"

"If you don't mind."

"As long as I live, I'll never mind you coming home." He looked between Aurora and Lucas. "I'll put this in the car and give you two a couple of minutes. Come out when you're ready."

She nodded softly and watched as he walked out into the cold. Turning to face Lucas, she wrapped her arms around him. "Thank you."

"For what? I didn't do anything."

"For being you." Tears built rapidly.

"I wish there was more I could do."

"There are some things I just need to figure out on my own. This is the only way I can do that. I need to be able to distance myself and see things objectively."

He squeezed her. "I understand."

"I know you do. That's why I love you."

A fleck of happiness flashed in his eyes.

"Please stay in the apartment. You have your own key now." She forced a smile.

"Text me when you get there? Or on the way, if you'd like."

"I'm hoping to sleep most of the way." Indeed, it was after one in the morning. When she called her daddy, he was finishing up a meeting in Calgary. A brief discussion ensued, and both agreed it would be easier if Aurora slept on the way. Graciously Cole drove from his meeting to pick her up and drive the five hours north. "But I'll call you if there are any issues."

A long blink from him, followed by a yawn. "Promise?"

"You have my word." She gave him a reassuring squeeze and yawned herself.

"Time to go. Your dad's waiting."

Her lip quivered, and she leaned into him.

"Take all the time you need."

"I'm just going for a few days. I'll be back before Christmas and Kaitlyn's wedding." She led them out into the chill of the night.

"Nice car, Cole." Lucas gave the white vehicle a solid scan.

"Much better than the giant, especially for all these long-distance trips."

Lucas helped Aurora into the front passenger seat, his hand holding hers longer than was necessary. Not that she minded.

Cole nodded at him. “She’ll call you soon, and I promise to drive safely.”

“That’s all I ask, sir.” Lifting Aurora’s hand, he planted a kiss on top. “Soon.”

She covered her mouth with a yawn. “Soon.”

Cole climbed inside and put the car in drive. “It’s been a long while since you’ve been home.”

“Yes, it has.”

“Too long, if you ask me.” Cole gave her arm a pat. “You holler if there’s anything I need to do.”

“I’m hoping to sleep. That should help immensely.” She waved to Lucas who stood frozen on the spot.

“Lucas is a good kid,” Cole said, eyes focused on the road.

“He’s in love with me.”

“Any fool can see that. I’ve known it for some time.”

“What?”

“Princess, a daddy knows things. The thing is, how do you feel about that?”

“Lost. That’s why I need the break.” She looked out the window, the passing lights zooming by. Unable to watch, she closed her eyes and thought about Lucas, and Kaitlyn, and Nate. Thoughts swirled into her head until she was unable to fight the urge to stay awake.

“Hey, Princess, we’re home.”

She opened her eyes and stared out. Cole had driven up the long driveway, parking in the garage that nested itself behind her childhood home. She exited the vehicle, the cold early morning air nipping at her severely as it froze her lungs. “It’s freezing here.”

“Minus twenty-seven.” He slammed the door and after retrieving her suitcase, led her into the back of the house. “Make yourself at home.” His boots went flying as he kicked them off, and he hung up his coat on the hook. “You’ll find that things look a little different, but… Well, you'll see." He walked up the five stairs into the back of the kitchen.

Aurora followed him and stood beside the fridge as Cole turned on the range hood light, throwing a beam out across the hardwood floors. "You changed them?"

"Yeah. Seems as though salsa left on lino stains them, so it needed to be ripped out. The hardwood goes through the whole main floor." He yawned. "I don't mean to be a party pooper, but I've been up for thirty-six hours straight. I need a nap. Eat something, make a coffee or whatever. I'll get up at noon and we can go shopping. Sound good?"

She nodded. "Get some sleep."

He walked over to her and gave her a bear hug. "It's so nice having you home. Even if it's only for a few days." He disappeared down the hall.

Aurora sent a text to Lucas. *Made it fine. Slept most of the way.*

Lucas texted back. *Glad to hear it.*

Did you sleep much?

Not really.

Sorry.

Stop it.

Get some sleep. I'm going to explore my old house. Text me after you've slept.

I will.

I love you. <3

I love you.

The solid wall that used to separate the living room from the kitchen had been cut in half. A beam on either side of the four-foot-high wall had shutters closed between them, blocking out the view. She unlatched them and slid them open, marvelling at the change before her.

The living room once a bright shade of sunshine—a colour she and Carmen helped select—was a muted shade of mushroom. However, it matched well with the hardwood floors. Gone were the small but plentiful pictures her momma hung all around, a weird assortment of flowers and leaves, replaced with a giant New York City skyline on canvas. It dominated the wall with it's night time view.

She paced the length of the room, surprised at how much it had changed. The floral furniture, a relic from her grandparents, replaced by dark leather couches and ottomans and oversized pillows. It was relaxing to look at and inviting to snuggle into. Where was this décor when she was recovering from her pelvic injuries? Surely it would've been more soothing to stare at these walls all day. Maybe. Maybe not. There hadn't been much to sooth her rattled nerves back then.

Hesitantly, she descended the stairs at the front, tiptoeing down into the basement to where her room had been. The second stair from the bottom since creaked when touched and she shook her head.

At least that didn't change.

Since the accident, she'd spent a week total in her bedroom. Forced to stay on a floor that served all her needs, she had to abandon her privacy for the floor above. A floor with a kitchen and a bathroom.

Everything seemed the same. The laundry area still smelled of dryer sheets and Tide, and as she peeked around the wall, baskets of clean clothes still sat in the corner. Those had been there when she was there last and were likely covered in dust and cobwebs. A frilly pink swatch of fabric caught her eye, an old sweater of momma's. She sighed and inched her way to her bedroom in the furthest corner.

She stopped at Carmen's old room, and quietly pushed open Carmen's door, expecting to see posters of NF6, her favourite rock band, still on the wall. Instead, the room was barren, save for a white dresser, two mattresses on a bed frame, and a coat of powder blue paint which contrasted against the brown shag carpeting. Gone was the floral wallpaper Carmen tried to hide with pictures of muscled men and rock stars. Aurora sat down on the edge of the bed. For all she knew, this room was no longer familiar. There was nothing in there to remind her of Carmen. Her heart shuddered at the thought of Daddy having completely cleared it out.

With trepidation in her footsteps, she carried herself to her old room. Inhaling the light taste of must, her fingers wrapped around the knob and she creaked the door open. Another empty room. However, in the corner were a few boxes with her name on them. More than a little surprised as there wouldn't have been much that she left behind, she'd taken most of it when she moved to the big city. Still it shocked her to see the room empty. No white bedspread with the pink frilly edging, and the abundance of pillow shams. No swimming trophies lining her bookshelves. Those must be in one of the boxes. No pictures of her former friends, the ones where they'd all linked arms, laughing and have the time of their lives. She'd hoped he had the good sense to toss those. She didn't need those reminders of what was, of what could've been. Of friends who'd abandoned her when she needed them most.

Her thoughts fluttered to Lucas. No matter what she went through, he'd never left.

Her heart was heavy. The house was no longer her childhood home and had become a barren wasteland. There wasn't much familiar anymore. She supposed over the course of the past thirty months that Cole had done some *cleaning* of his own. He may have had plans to move out that fateful weekend, but someone above had other plans. Instead, he got an empty house filled with constant reminders of what he had had. A wife who had admitted to no longer feeling the same about their marriage. A daughter whose life had taken her five hours away as she carved out her own mark on the world. And another daughter who desperately clung to everything that happened before May 24th and refused to let go.

She headed back upstairs to where her suitcase was. After lunch, she'd figure out where she'd be sleeping for the next few days. Until then, she'd nap on the couch.

Cole stumbled into the kitchen, the light in his eyes a little brighter. "Hey, Princess."

"Coffee's ready, and I'm just flipping the last pancake now."

The table was set for two, and she was happy to see the same plates and cutlery in the cupboard. Pouring herself a mug of coffee, she joined her daddy at the table.

"Eat up," she encouraged and pushed a stack his way.

"Sorry there wasn't much to choose from. I'm not home much, so I don't keep much in the fridge. We'll go shopping after I clean up."

She picked at her pancakes and sipped her hot drink. "Everything looks so different."

He surveyed the area. "Yeah, I guess a few things changed."

"The living room doesn't even look the same."

"I got a pretty sweet deal on the couches. When I was painting, I lost my balance on the ladder which held the paint. Needless to say, it soaked Grandma's couch."

Aurora pictured the mess that would've made.

"But luckily, the floors hadn't gone in yet."

"Yeah, that would've been a pricey slip." She wrapped her hands around her mug, a chill in the air reminding her how cool the house always felt in the dead of winter. "What about the basement?"

Cole's face brightened. "Oh yes. Your room. Sorry I should've warned you."

"What happened?"

"Time to clean it out."

"It's our dressers and mattresses."

"I use those rooms for some of my workers. Until they get on their feet, they have a place to stay. They can spend as long as they need, but most of the time, it's a couple of weeks."

She looked at her daddy with wonder. "You rent them out?" No wonder they were devoid of posters and personal effects. Pretty sure rig workers weren't overjoyed about staying in a room where half-naked guys hung about.

"Not really rent them. In return for the room, they pitch in and help around the house. Like the floors." Cole devoured his stack and stabbed at another. "You should see the backyard. Brand new deck. Just cost me the wood."

It was a pretty sweet deal when she thought it through, and rather genius.

"But I haven't had anyone here for a bit, with the downfall in the economy. House has been pretty silent."

"Well I don't know what I can help with."

"You're not helping with anything. You came up here to take a break and figure things out, and that's what you're going to do." He chugged back his coffee and made a face, shaking it off. "Anything you want to talk about?"

"I don't even know where to begin."

"How's Kaitlyn?"

"Great." She beamed. "Wedding is coming quickly. You know I have a plus one, why don't you come to her wedding? I'm sure Kaitlyn would be thrilled to have you there." She pictured Kaitlyn lovingly patting Cole on the shoulders and flirting with him before walking down the isle. Maybe Cole could even give her away since her own father had cut her off.

"Already sent back my reply." The wrinkles deepened as the smile pushed into his eyes. "Which reminds me, can I give you some cash to purchase them something really nice? You know better than I what they'd like."

She nodded. "Of course."

"Why isn't Lucas going to be your date?"

"The Johnsons always go to this big party on New Year's Eve. And he'd already RSVP'd he was going before the wedding date was officially selected. And I had planned to go with Nate." A pluck to her heartstrings.

"Wow. Got to admire the boy, chasing after his dream and all."

"You think?"

"Absolutely. Takes a lot of guts to pack up and start over in a brand-new city. That boy is growing up. I'm sorry to see him leaving, and to see you hurting so much over it, but I think you'll both come out better on the other side. He'll have his life and you'll have yours."

She sighed and took a sip of the foul coffee. Next time, she'd add less grounds. "I miss him so much, Daddy."

"Aw, Princess, I know you do." He retrieved a box of tissues from the top of the fridge. "He's not your one though. If he was, he really would've been more forthcoming about everything, like Lucas does."

"Did you share everything with momma?"

"If I thought it had any impact on our future or you kids, yes. We had our issues for sure, and disagreed about many things, but we discussed it."

"That's what I thought." She wiped her nose and balled up the tissue in her palm.

"I was a little harsh on you last time I saw you, and I'm sorry. I should've been more compassionate."

"No, you were right. I wasn't happy in my heart and I think I was looking for excuses. Well maybe not excuses, but a way out. And not even a way out because I love Nate. I just needed…" She buried her head in her hands. "As much as I love him, somewhere along the way, I realised I wasn't in love with him. And I wanted to be. I really did."

"So, what changed?"

"I wish I knew."

"I think you already do, you're just not willing to admit it to yourself. But you will. In time."

Her long hair framed her face and made it a curtain. Pushing it back, she eyed her daddy. "I did something bad."

Cole's chair scrapped against the floor as he inched forward.

Aurora poured her heart out about the drugs she'd purchased, the hold they'd held over her and how, in the end, she dumped them down the drain.

"Wow," he said, leaning back in his chair and giving his chin a rub. "I'm mighty proud of you."

"What? Why? I'm a bad person."

"Aurora Jasmine, I don't want to ever hear that come out of your mouth again. You are not a bad person. You've made questionable decisions, but we all have." He shook a fatherly finger in her direction. "Look at you. Look at how far you've come."

"How far I've come? Are you joking? I haven't come very far at all."

"That's not true. Before the accident, you were willfully naïve, if you will. You had big plans for med school and you wanted to make a difference in the world. Then the unfortunate happened, and for the longest time, I hadn't only lost your mom and sister, I'd lost you. You were alive, but you weren't living." She went to speak, but he put his finger up. "You were sullen and miserable, and in a very dark space. You were dependant on the drugs to get you through each day. You refused to get into vehicles. Now, after a few months with those Johnson boys, you've taken control of your life. You owned up to your drug addiction, and by flushing them, you gained control over that. You're sitting in a car again and even sat for a five-hour ride."

"I slept most of the way."

"Could you have done that a year ago? Six months ago? Hell, even a couple of months ago?"

She shook her head.

"So why aren't you proud of those accomplishments? Those are huge!" He smiled. "You wanted to make a difference to the world, but you didn't realise, you made a difference in your own life."

"But schooling and everything else…"

"Let's talk about that. What are your plans for next semester?"

"I want to go into nursing school."

"Because?" He raised an greying eyebrow.

"Because after everything I've been through, I'd like to think I can impart a little wisdom on someone else. Convince them that life is worth living."

"Is it?"

She smiled. "A year ago, I would've said no. But now… yeah. Absolutely."

"That's my girl." He smiled ever bigger. "That girl you wished to be like, that younger you, she can't even hold a candle to the woman sitting in front of me."

Breakfast, or lunch, behind them Cole stood at the back door. "Do you have a warmer coat than that?"

She eyed her navy suede jacket. "This is warm."

"Like stand outside for a while warm?"

"It'll work."

Cole rifled through a basket. "Take these." He passed her a leather hat with ear flaps, a thick plaid scarf and a sizable pair of mittens clearly designed for a man. "You'll need them."

She stepped into the cold, the first inhale of air freezing in her lungs. It got cold in the big city, but wow, it was much colder in Fort McMurray. She was grateful for the seat warming beneath her.

"I know I keep saying it, but I'm really proud of you."

"Thanks."

"I mean it."

"Where are we going?" She kept her focus out the window, noting the slight changes along the way. How the spruce tree on the corner was taller than the house. The traffic lights that dominated the drive where it used to be a free-flow into the core.

"Flower shop."

She raised her brow and a small smirk escaped. "Are you going to see Judy tonight?"

"Yes, but that's not why. She doesn't like fresh cut flowers."

"That's weird." She loved them. The way their fragrance danced around the room. Lucas had bought her flowers, ones she'd mentioned used to grow at her house.

Cole pulled into the parking lot of the flower shop and walked inside. He returned a couple minutes later baring four long-stem roses, two each in yellow and white. "Hold these."

Tenderly she laid them across her lap, the delicate smell floating up to her nose. "They're beautiful."

Quiet and focused on the road, he drove around a bend and up a small hill.

"Where are we going?"

"You'll see."

She focused on the landscape, but it didn't look familiar. However, the higher they drove up the hillside, the more impressive the view of downtown, even with the blanket of white surrounding it. She'd never really noticed before how pretty her hometown was.

The engine quieted, and she stared out the window. Beyond the confines of the warm car, a wrought-iron sign, flanked with iron roses, read *Wingrove Memorial Gardens*.

"Are we…?" She couldn't even get the words out.

He swallowed, but didn't speak. As the door opened, he extended his hand.

She gave him the roses, and slipped her hands into the mittens, her heart pounding hard in her chest. Linking her arm through his, she followed him, as they quietly stepped into the cemetery. A whisper of a breeze danced on her exposed cheeks, cooling them. Footsteps crunched on the snow as they passed headstones marking the long lives most had. Sadness filled her heart, and then she came to an abrupt stop when her eyes fell on one oversized headstone.

It bore the MacIntyre name, with her momma's birth and death date on the left, and Carmen's on the right. The surrounding snow had been recently brushed off, but the brown, dried out flowers in the cement vase still stood.

Instant tears welled up in her eyes and she collapsed onto her knees in the snow.

Cole walked carefully between the graves to the headstone and replaced the flowers with the fresh roses, tears staining his cheeks.

She focused back to the granite stone, thinking about the last time she saw their faces, laughing and singing, no idea how all their lives would change so quickly. How she'd been in the hospital, hundreds of kilometres away, when the funeral had taken place. How she'd mentioned to Nate she didn't get the chance to say goodbye. And how much that pain never dissipated. She didn't need closure, yet… she knelt at her momma and Carmen's feet.

Her daddy walked back and crouched down beside her, his voice shaky, "I asked God above to help me find a way to help you. I've asked many times what I could do to be a better father and help you through this all. He answered my prayers when you called me last night and asked to come home. I can't do much, but I can give you the chance you never had." He squeezed her shoulder. "Take all the time you need." A small blanket appeared, and he placed it at Carmen and Angelica's feet. "Sit on this though." The crunching of the snow under his feet faded away as he trudged back to the car.

She stared at the headstones, wishing she could see their faces. Instead she closed her eyes, and a vision of a plumper Carmen with perfect peaches and cream skin, dark wavy hair and brown eyes floated into view. She was joined by their mother, an older, thinner version of Carmen, but with shorter hair and eyes marked with crow's feet, and deep wrinkles from smiling often.

"Oh momma."

The vision smiled at her as she often did.

"Carmen." The images floated in front of her. Her heart cracked knowing it wasn't real. "I'm so sorry." Her voice broke, and with it, a flood of tears followed. "I'm so sorry." She shook as days, weeks, months and years of sadness poured out of her. Of all the things they didn't get to see and do.

No university grad for Carmen, no more garden tending for momma. No more weekend trips filled with shopping and pedicures and over-indulgence in rich foods. Carmen would never walk down the aisle, never have babies, never be with the man who brought her to life. The agony of all that was taken away from Carmen pressed on Aurora, and she dipped closer to the ground, hugging her chest tightly.

And her momma. She was young too, fresh into her fifties, with so much life in her. Always the entertainer, she loved having guests over and she made sure no one was ever alone. There was no way to be lonely around her, and even the shyest person felt welcomed and part of whatever Angelica had invited them to. She hoped, in heaven, there were many parties and more laughter than tears.

A warm hand wrapped through hers, and a weight pressed gently across her shoulders. A cool breeze with a hint of citrus floated past. No doubt in her mind, they were with her. She didn't want to move for fear they'd disappear, so she inhaled deeply, allowing her tears to fall, breathing in a presence she didn't know she needed so much.

A voice rang out in her head, from a training session held over the summer, when Lucas discovered a way to get her over the roughest patch in their driving. *It's not your fault. There was nothing you could've done. It was not your fault.*

"I'm so sorry," she repeated and opened her eyes, fixated on the grey headstone. But it was more than just apologising for the accident. She was overwhelmed with grief at her own life she'd let die. The weeks; the months; the years. All that time, she'd been the one who survived, but she truly had failed to live. But not anymore. Carmen wouldn't want her sitting on the sidelines being a passenger in life, and her momma had raised her to be the go-getter. Well, it was high time to switch seats, and get what she wanted.

"I'll always love you," she breathed out over them.

The weight from her shoulders evaporated and the warmth in her hand cooled, but the love in her heart blossomed. She pulled her fingers free from the mitten and drew three linking hearts over the grave. "I promise to try harder."

Nodding, she rolled off the ground, retrieving the small blanket. A look to the heavens where she blew two kisses. "Thank you." A weak smile touched the edge of her lips.

She made her way back to the car where her daddy stood, leaning against it, his eyes as red as his rosy cheeks. Without a word, she wrapped her arms around him, the cool touch of his jacket rubbing against her tear-soaked skin.

In his arms, which squeezed her close, she felt peace. The boulder she'd been carrying for too long, finally rolled off. She believed in her heart that everything important in her life would work out. She just needed to get home and share this with the one person she shared everything with. The one who stole her heart. The one who kept her going. The one who loved her best.

Cole kissed the top of her head.

"Thank you," she said, her voice gaining a bit a strength. "Time to go home."

♥Chapter Thirty-Three♥

Aurora sat in the front seat of her daddy's car, twitching and twisting. The highway was dark and long, the nearest town miles away in either direction. The last stop had been in Boyle, a lonely place with few amenities but at least it was a stop. A place to stretch out, unwind and regroup for the final leg home. She had to admit, the trips had become easier to handle. The anxiety was still there, but in healthy amounts. Her mind was packed with coping mechanisms, and her heart filled with hope.

"You okay?"

"Yeah," she said with a hint of agitation. "Just eager to get home."

"And see someone?" Her daddy winked.

In the past couple days back home, Aurora concluded that everyone had moved on. Most of her high school friends had scattered to the wind, her former friend Jessica told her when she stumbled across the cashier at the supermarket. All out there living their grown-up lives. When Jessica asked why she was still living at home, it hit a raw nerve. She grabbed the groceries and stormed away.

She wasn't living at home with her daddy. Instead she had a man waiting for her at *her* home. Someone she loved with her whole heart. Someone who never judged her when maybe he should've, several times over. And she couldn't get home fast enough to tell him that yes, she was in love with him too.

"How much farther?"

"An hour until we hit city limits, and another thirty after that."

"Ugh."

Cole patted her arm, which was tightly clenched, ending in a fist. The other hand squeezed the arm rest on the door. "We'll get there."

"I know, but I want to tell him."

"And you will."

"I miss him so much."

"Yes, you do. And I'm glad you figured that out."

It had taken a toll on her to put her feelings aside for Nate. He had done so much for her. He'd planted the seeds and got her to touch a car, furthering her growth by encouraging her to sit in one. He'd brought her out of her shell and shown her that there was more to life than what she'd been living. And for the rest of her life, she'll never forget that. He had loved her when she'd been unlovable.

But Lucas was more. It was him she turned to when she really needed to push herself and learn how to deal with riding in vehicles. He had been the one to discover why she'd blacked out at a specific point every time and encouraged new steps to conquer that. To admit it wasn't her fault, and she wanted to do right by him.

With Nate, he had accepted her drug abuse as part of who she was. He didn't like it, but accepted it nonetheless. Lucas never had, and she willingly admitted defeat to him about it. Her darkest and deepest secrets were exposed to him. His presence was a drug unlike any other, and with him around, she never truly needed the others.

Nate would always be her first love, but her true love, the one her heart belonged to was Lucas. The part that confused her was she didn't know when it happened.

"City limits," her daddy said.

She straightened up and gazed out the window, thrilled to being so much closer to home. The anxiety building wasn't caused from the long road trip. It was the eagerness to see his handsome face; those blue-grey eyes; his chapped lips which were so soft the last time… To hold his rough hands, calloused from manual labour. To breathe in his delicate scent of freshly washed linen. Her heart beat in pounding rhythms, and for the first time in a long while, she wanted to go faster.

"Almost there," he said. "You're getting antsy."

"A part of me wants you to drive faster, but I'm really okay with the speed you're going."

"You're doing so well."

"I'll have a lot to discuss with Dr. Navin after the holidays."

Cole laughed. "I can imagine. It's been an eventful few days and I'm sorry you won't be home for Christmas."

"You won't be there either." Cole was off to the job site for six days, which unfortunately had him gone over Christmas. However, he'd be down for New Year's and then they'd celebrate the holidays and Kaitlyn's wedding and anything else they'd come up with in those few days.

"I'm so glad you came home."

"Me too." She felt lighter and happier and more at peace with things. Had she known all she needed was a trip back home, she would've done it sooner. Then again, maybe the timing wouldn't have been right. Who knows?

As they pulled into the parking lot, she spotted his car. He was home.

He stopped outside her building and retrieved her suitcase. "Let me know how it goes."

"I will," she said, glancing up the outside. Her hands shook with excitement.

"Go."

She opened the door and spun around, running back to him. Wrapping her arms around him, she said, "Thank you for everything."

"Anything for you, Princess." He kissed her forehead. "Now go."

Her palms sweated as she rode the elevator, giving them a wipe on her scarf as she stepped off. She couldn't remember in recent history where she'd walked as fast as she did from the elevator to her door. Trying to be hastily sneaky, she slowly inserted the key into the lock and twisted.

The foyer was dark and stepping inside, no lights beckoned.

Yes, she was coming home a day earlier than she said, but she wanted to surprise him. Seems the surprise was on her. He wasn't here.

She flipped on the kitchen light. Someone had been busy in her absence as all the shiny surfaces reflected the overhead lights. A small hint of cleaner mixed with citrus tickled at her nose.

Damn him. Why did he need to clean? And why wasn't he at home? She dropped her suitcase off in her bedroom, which thankfully, hadn't changed. The bed unmade and a pile of clothes still sat crumpled in the corner.

She picked up her phone, and trying to be casual, typed *Hey, are you at home?*

A few frantic paces down the hall and back again, he typed back. *No, I'm at UBs. Needed some fresh air and karaoke. Do you want to me to leave and call you?*

Yes, but no. She wanted him home to tell him all that she'd been holding back but at the same time, if she told him to come home, it might give it away. And it was supposed to be a surprise.

Nah. I'll talk to you soon.

You sure?

Totally.

She needed to think. How to surprise him? She paced in the kitchen and came to a full stop when she spied his keys sitting on the table. Could she do it? Could she really drive to UBs? It wasn't far. Less than a couple minutes of drive time. Probably closer to ten minutes if *she* drove. Just imagining the shocked look on his face, caused a sly grin to bubble out of her. Could she really do it?

She inhaled sharply, and with his car keys firmly gripped in her hands, stood at the driver's door. The adrenaline pumped hard and fast, making her pretty sure if she could run, she'd get there before the car even got into gear. She glanced around the empty parking lot. There wasn't a lot of activity and no one paid her any attention, although she fully expected someone to jump out from somewhere and yell stop.

Opening the car door with a trembling hand, she slipped into Lucas' seat. Her heart rapidly pounded, but no more than when she usually sat in his place. The buzzing in her head was consistent with previous attempts, and her breathing was fast. But not out of the ordinary.

I can do this. I will do this.

She jabbed the key into the ignition and twisted, surprise overwhelming her as the vehicle rumbled beneath her.

Holy shit!

Her hands rubbed together in front of her face as she blew warm air over them. The steering wheel was freezing. If she did nothing else, she was amazed. It was happening. Breathing short, wispy breaths, she tipped her head back and focused on the roof. *One. Two. Three.* She counted it out twice. Three times. No way would she'd be able to drive jacked up as she was. It was dangerous. Not only to her, but to everyone on the roads. Scary dangerous.

The driving route was planned out in her mind; a route she'd been a passenger on, and one she'd walked several times, still it was daunting. She needed to reverse the vehicle and put in to gear. Drive slowly out and turn right. Drive slowly again and full stop at the stop sign. Left turn–if it was safe. Slowly work her way a few blocks and turn right into the parking lot. Park the car and shut her down. Simple enough. Sure. Right. Yeah there was no way she could do it. No way.

Taking another deep breath, she put her left hand on the wheel and her right on the shifter. Even with so many steps to remember, somehow it happened, and Lucas' car backed up, inching closer to the main entrance.

Turning the wheel, she managed to get it decently straight before she shook her head and put it into drive.

OH MY GOD.

She eased it slowly to the end of her parking lot, riding the brake and lurching every few feet. A debate warred—whether to park it right there and explain later, or to see it through.

No, it's better to see this through.

Her hand trembled, so she gripped the wheel even harder, the knuckles turning white and threatening to break skin. She checked both ways and checked again. No one was on the road, so she slowly lifted her foot off the brake and turned right.

HOLY SHIT.

The vehicle crawled along, eventually making its way to the secondary road. Could she do it? She'd need to go faster than idle, but she wasn't sure if she'd manage putting her foot on the gas pedal. The brake was her friend right now and as it was, it was pressed right to floor while she sat at the stop sign.

She needed to warn the other drivers what an idiot she was and put on the special blinkers. The ones Lucas referred to as idiot lights. That should help. Then if she wanted to only keep the car in gear for the duration of the drive, it should be fine. These were residential roads anyways, and only morons zipped down them.

Triple checking that the road was free of oncoming traffic, she released the brake–her foot hovering millimetres above it. She turned left, the blinkers the only sound as it echoed around her. Easing the car into the right lane, her heart pounded and her vision darkened.

NO!

She blinked several times and inched the car to the side of the road where she parked.

You can and you ARE doing this. Do NOT wimp out.

She screamed at the top of her lungs, put the car back into gear, and after checking again, moved back onto the road. Thankfully it was quiet, and the driveway into UBs parking lot appeared.

OH MY GOD!

Hands gripping the wheel, she turned right and the vehicle followed. But a hill she'd need to ascend rolled before her. Not a big one, but one that would require a bit of gas to climb up and leaving it in gear wouldn't work.

FUCK!

She transferred her foot to the gas and lightly pressed. It didn't move the car which settled at the base of the small hill. Pushing a little more, the engine roared, and the vehicle climbed up and evened out on the pavement. Chancing a quick swipe, she let go of the wheel with one hand and brushed it over her sweaty forehead. She drove straight and pulled into the first available parking spot, one she didn't need to manoeuvre the car to fit into.

She twisted the ignition off and jumped out, screaming, "Holy shit! I really fucking did it!"

A couple stopped and stared at her, whispering to one another.

She danced in her spot. "I did it. I did it." With a press of the button, she locked the vehicle and pocketed the keys. Breathing in the night time air, things felt different, and looked different. Like anything was possible.

Feeling brave, she snuck into the sports pub and stood transfixed at the entrance. High pitched squeals of singing from a group of middle aged drunk ladies bounced off the terrible 1970s décor. The sound absorption was terrible, but the singing was worse. She covered her ears and looked around the pub.

Lucas sat on a bar stool, chatting with two guys she recognised from the track. Her heart pounded, and she wondered if she were truly capable of declaring her feelings with his friends around. Which was harder? Driving the car or admitting what was in her heart? A tough debate because when she originally thought it through, the plan was that he be alone. And she hadn't needed to drive anywhere. And they were both at home where things could progress naturally.

She ducked behind a wall, and a waitress sauntered on by.

"Can I help you?"

"Yeah, I think you can." She explained what she wanted to do, and the waitress nodded along.

"Let me see if we have that. I'll be right back, honey." The fringe across her shoulders bounced from side to side as she hopped around the wall.

Aurora leaned back, shaking her head, questioning her sanity.

Why did everything end up being such a public declaration? She'd done it to stop Nate's retirement and now here she was ready to admit how she felt about Lucas, surrounded by drunk patrons.

The waitress returned. "I selected that one for you. You'll be up after the set of four guys beside the stage. Then I'll distract your guy."

"Thank you," she said, her voice suddenly dry.

The waitress handed her a glass of water. "For what it's worth, I think it's romantic."

She chugged back the warm liquid, wishing there'd been ice in it. With the ladies finished, the guys took to the mock stage. Arms extended high, their voices hit the high notes, and she cringed. Pretty sure the Four Season's hadn't meant for drunk guys to wail out 'Walk Like A Man'. They took a final bow, and one nearly fell off the stage. So much for being able to sneak up on stage.

She rolled her eyes and watched as the waitress nodded at her. As the waitress made her way over to Lucas' table, Aurora hugged the wall and took the stage. The lights were minimal with only one focused on the stage, so she could still stand up there and not be the focus of attention, just some random girl singing poorly. Perfect. It also helped that from her viewpoint, the entire pub was sprawled out before her and the waitress stood at Lucas' table.

The music started playing. There was no need to follow along, she knew the words by heart. As the first lyrics belted out of her, Lucas twisted in his seat; his face aglow. Maybe because it was her, or because of the Taylor Swift song she'd selected—the one they always seemed to dance to—or both.

As the song ended, he slipped off his bar stool and walked to the stage. Standing a couple of feet from her, he whispered, "I suddenly have a brand-new appreciation for Taylor now." His smirk was a mile wide, and a sparkle danced in his eyes. "You're terrible, but the crowd loves you."

She inched closer to him, her heart beating its own melody. "It's our song."

"Our song? I didn't think we had a song."

"Of course we do." She winked at him and searched his eyes. "Can I be your love story?"

"Is that what you really want?" A smile broke out over his face. He already knew the answer.

"If you say yes."

He stared down at her, his lips parting slightly. "Yes."

"I love you, Lucas. I'm sorry it took me so long to figure that out."

"You're worth waiting for."

"What? No, I love you back?"

"I love you back." He leaned closer, his breath ticking her lips. "But never forget who said it first."

"Just shut up and kiss me already."

He bent his head down toward hers, and his hands clasped gently around her cheeks. Lips like velvet grazed across hers, and her eyes fluttered close. As his hands fell away and wrapped around the small of her back, she threaded her fingers in his hair, pulling him closer. In all her life, there had never been a kiss so full of love, so full of tenderness and so full of perfection. And it had been there all this time.

♥Epilogue♥

Three and a half years later

"Are you ready?" Cole asked, as he straightened out his black suit and smoothed down the lapels.

"No, but this is as ready as I'll get." She stepped out from behind the screen, her wedding dress swooshing with each movement. The pristine white, scoop neck, lace overlaying a sweetheart neckline gave her the appearance of a bust, and the chiffon floor-length gown skimmed the tips of her heels as she waltzed into view.

Cole blinked. "Princess, you look like, well, you look like the princess you are." He walked closer to her, slipping around the desk. "You are breathtaking."

She twirled on the spot, her dress billowing out, and her cathedral length veil twisting around her. They stood in the small office building in the centre of the pit which for today, served as a makeshift change area for Aurora. A private place she could prepare herself for her big day.

"Thanks, Daddy." A gentle heat warmed up her cheeks.

A knock came from the door.

"Can I come in yet?" *Kaitlyn.*

"Of course you can." Cole open the door. "No one else is with you?"

"Nope. Coast is clear." Kaitlyn waddled in, making sure to give

Cole a tender arm pat. "Hey, Tiger."

She'd let Kaitlyn choose whatever dress she wanted to wear, given her expanding midsection, and Kaitlyn did not disappoint. Stunning as always, she wore a knee length sun dress in a magnificent hue of orchid, something the ladies had a giggle over when trying on said dress.

"Where's Anna?" she asked.

Anna, not quite two, was the flower-girl. She was Tatiana's biological child, with the help of donor sperm. Kaitlyn was seven months pregnant with Anna's half-brother, Mikhail. The married ladies had wasted no time in getting a family started.

"She's with Tatiana, and Baba." It had taken some time, but Kaitlyn's mother had come around and accepted Kaitlyn's choice of life partner. She was even a surprise guest at their New Year's Eve wedding. Kaitlyn's dad on the other hand, still refused to acknowledge his daughter, her new wife or his grandchildren.

"How're you feeling?"

"Not so bad. My ankles are swollen and I'm making more trips to the johnny on the spot than is legally allowed, but it's all good." Kaitlyn's laugh filled the small space with its delightful sound. "A curl fell out. Got a bobby pin so I can fix it?"

"In the case there."

Kaitlyn manoeuvred her way over and with the skill of a stylist, quickly popped Aurora's wayward strand into a new holding position. "Beautiful." She placed a quick peck on her cheek.

"May I?" she asked before placing a hand on Kaitlyn's expanding belly.

Kaitlyn nodded.

Her hands rested against the sides of Kaitlyn's stomach. "He's quiet today."

Kaitlyn gave a maternal rub across the top of her belly. "Should be, after the party he had in there last night." She waddled around. "Are you ready?"

"Not sure what else I need to do."

Cole addressed Kaitlyn. "Is everyone ready out there?"

"Yeah, the fans are in the stands, but the important people are seated, waiting for the big moment."

She inhaled sharply. "I'm ready."

"Ah, Kaitlyn, can you give me a couple minutes first?" Cole asked, his face turning serious.

"Sure thing. Knock when you're ready to walk." She exited the small building.

Cole beamed at his daughter. "You really look beautiful. Your momma would be so proud."

She wasn't going to cry. Not today and not this way. Instead she looked into her daddy's eyes and swallowed down a morsel of grief. "I know she would be."

"Here," he said as he pulled something out of his left pocket. "She'd want you to have this."

"What…" She stopped when she spied a little blue box.

"It was hers. Since we were separating that weekend, she'd already pulled it off and put it in her jewellery box. I'd saved it for today."

How she never noticed the absence of a wedding ring on her momma, she'd never know. Hands shaking, she stretched out her hand to her daddy.

He removed the ring and placed it on a finger on her right hand. "Now you have something old."

"I get to keep it?"

"It's yours."

Unable to speak, she stared at the simple, yet elegant ring. "Thank you," she breathed out. She placed a kiss on her father's cheek.

"Now you'll know she's here with you."

"There was never any doubt before." Her eyes welled up. "This means a lot."

He reached into his right pocket and pulled out another package. A frayed blue piece of fabric, which he dabbed under her eyes. "Something blue. It was part of Carmen's blankie. Don't cry." He passed her the six by six sized square of satin. "Now Carmen's with you too."

"Thank you." She checked the small, portable mirror to see how much mascara had ran. Thankfully, none.

"That's your something old, and something blue."

"Dad, you know I'm not a traditionalist in the slightest. We're getting married at a race track for crying out loud."

"Yeah, yeah, but Judy says it's good luck. Now what am I missing? Ah, yes, the something borrowed." He retrieved another box. "They're clip-ons."

With a trembling hand, she opened the lid. Inside were a pair of diamond earrings.

"Oh, Daddy."

"She assures me they're not real, but they sure look it. She'd love it if you *borrowed* them." He winked. "I'm supposed to stress that."

Being careful, she attached each earring to her lobe. "It's snug, but they'll stay on."

"And the something new." From an inside pocket, he retrieved a long black box.

Her mouth fell open when the sparkling tennis bracelet glittered up at her.

"You have no jewellery, and a Princess should be enveloped in it."

"Oh wow." The weight of it pulled on her wrist as it circled and closed. The tears fell.

"You're not supposed to cry, remember?" He gave her a hug.

"Thank you so much, Daddy."

"One other thing, and then we'll get the schmaltz show over with." He produced a sixpence. "This is from London. Judy got a friend to mail it over. It's your wedding year and you're supposed to wear it in your left shoe for prosperity and luck." He kissed the top of her head. "Now stop crying. Today is supposed to be a new leaf remember?"

How could she forget? Six years ago, her life was put on hold and forever changed. The accident took away half her family and left her mangled and scarred. Two years after, her heart started healing as a new family filled in that void. It was only fitting to choose May 24th as her wedding day. A fresh start. A new name. And more family than she'd ever imagined.

Cole and July had married two years back, and with it, she got an older step sister with a husband and kids, plus an older step brother with his wife and kids. Then there was Kaitlyn and Tatiana, and their expanding family. Finally, the family she was marrying into. The one who had stolen her heart. And the youngest member of that family who waited for her at the finish line.

She inhaled a sharp breath and proclaimed, "Let's do this. My groom awaits." Opening the door an inch, she spied Kaitlyn. "I'm ready."

"She's ready," Kaitlyn yelled.

Beyond the door, the beats and rhythms from a favourite song played over the grandstand speakers.

She opened the door and waltzed out into the perfect May afternoon–slightly overcast, and the perfect temperature. Kaitlyn ahead of them holding Anna's sweet little hand, they walked the makeshift aisle, across the rows in the pit where the racers parked.

At the entrance to the paved track, she stopped. Beyond the finish line, sat a newly painted, sparkling race car—Lucas'. She giggled when she saw tin cans on strings attached to the bumper and a sign reading *finally married.* For all the times they've mentioned being anything but traditional, there sure were a lot of traditional wedding themes at play.

She scanned the guests, family mostly, who filled the white chairs. The back rows contained the racing families, the great groups of drivers and crew she saw each weekend, who had become an extension of her already expanded family.

A few rows up, she spied her step siblings. Her brother and sister, their spouses and all five of her step nieces and nephews were there, the youngest sitting on Grandma Judy's lap. Judy smiled and wiped a tear.

Tatiana and Anna stood in the front row on the left. Baba,

Kaitlyn's mom, had come as well to help with the active toddler.

A few faces over, the few Johnsons who were not directly involved in the wedding sat. Chris and Max, with Nate's three-year-old son Blair between them, tried to keep him quiet. Having moved east with lucrative job prospects nineteen months ago, they'd flown in for the weekend. It thrilled Brenda, who sat in the front row with Bill, to have all her kids, and lone grandchild, back in one place. They'd set up another trailer in the back lot so her family could all have pancakes in the morning. With the nine of them all together, it was going to be a big breakfast.

She recognised the blonde sitting beside Bill, but only because she'd seen her on the telecasts after Nate's races, jumping up and down, and manhandling him. Emily, a South Carolina native, used to be Nate's *pit bunny* when he was in the minor leagues. But after Nate's first race as an XFINITY racer, he proposed to her. That was back in January. Until this weekend, no one in the Johnson family had actually met Emily yet. Since Nate hadn't arrived until this morning, she hadn't yet had the pleasure either. She glanced over to Nate, who raised an eyebrow and smiled at her. Not enough to see the dimple, but a genuine smile all the same.

She smiled back but her full attention went to her main man, looking as dapper as ever in his tuxedo. Already a decent height, the way the suit fit him, it made him appear taller, and his shoulders broader. His gorgeous strawberry blond hair pushed off his face, and his blue-greys covered by his shades.

Arm in arm with her daddy, she paced the length of guests and arrived in front of Lucas. Daddy took her right hand and lovingly placed it in Lucas' left, clapping him on the back as he stepped back.

"What's with the shades?" she whispered, although every word was broadcast to the guests.

"I wanted you to be the first to see my tears of happiness." He removed the sunglasses and pocketed them. Indeed, his eyes were glassy, making them more blueish than grey, but they were only looking at her. "I've never been happier."

"Never?" She winked.

"You're stunning."

"You're quite handsome yourself."

He rubbed her hand paying special attention to the gift from her daddy. "New ring?"

"Mom's."

He pointed to his lapel. On it was the Scottish Johnson family crest. "Dad's." He glanced up into the sky. "They're all here today."

"Yes, they are." She leaned against him as they stepped closer to the Justice of the Peace.

"Don't cross the finish," he said, laughing and pulling her away from the yellow line. "We're not married yet."

"Dearly beloved, we are gathered here today…" The JP began her opening speech, to which Aurora zoned out. She was unable to take her eyes off Lucas, and was so focused on him, that Lucas nudged her.

"And now for the vows," the JP said.

She passed her bouquet to Kaitlyn.

Lucas smirked. "I get to go first." He cleared his throat as the crowd giggled. "Aurora, from the moment I met you, you were someone I needed in my life. I wasn't exactly sure how to make that work until you asked for my help on a little project. When we started hanging out every day for hours on end, I couldn't help falling in love with you. With your tenacity. With your open heart. With your determination. With your sassy little spirit. I found myself excited to be in your presence, even if we were doing nothing more than homework. Since we officially got together, my life has never been the same; it's been enhanced in ways I can't fully comprehend. You make me want to be a better person. You make me want to heal the world. I love how you trust me with your deepest thoughts and your wildest fantasies. In sickness and health, you can count on me to be by your side. For richer or poorer, we'll work through it all. You are my first thought in the morning, and the last when I fall asleep. I'm looking forward to spending the rest of eternity with you." He gave her hand a squeeze as he slipped on her wedding ring. "Now you go." He smiled.

"Lucas, there is so much I want to say to you, but I've been given a time limit." She nodded toward the JP. "You are my best friend, the one who sees through me, and who I don't have to hide from. I know my secrets are safe with you. I don't know when it happened, but falling in love with you changed everything for the better, and even when I was raw and exposed, you rode out the storm with me. Whatever life throws at us, I know in the depths of my heart we'll be able to weather it together. For the rest of my life, I promise to always be true to you, to always be transparent, to lean on you when times are rough and to be your biggest cheerleader. I promise to hold your heart with the tenderest of hands and to cherish all that you've given me. In here." She pointed to her chest. "Without it, I'd be lost." She kissed his hand and slipped the ring onto his finger.

Lucas leaned closer, his smile as wide as the Grand Canyon. "That was good. And I agree with it all as the same could be said about you."

"Without anything further," the JP said, nodding to the couple.

He swept her legs out from under her and carried her over the finish line.

"I now pronounce you husband and wife. You may now kiss."

Gently, he set her on the track, on the other side of the finish and leaned down planting the softest, sweetest kiss on her lips. Minty and fresh, with a hint of cherry, she kissed him back, wrapping her arms around his neck.

"We're finished with our old lives, and ready to start anew. My wife."

"My husband."

They broke apart to the thunderous applause.

"Congratulations," the JP said, as she stepped back away from the newlyweds.

"Congratulations," Nate said, leaning in for a hug.

She wrapped her arms around him. "Thanks for coming up. We really appreciate it."

"Of course. Nothing was going to prevent me from being here."

He broke the embrace first and patted Lucas on the back. "Are you ready?"

Lucas looked to his new bride. "Are you?"

"Yes, let's do our victory lap."

"Lead the way," Nate said, gesturing for Lucas to walk ahead.

Aurora scanned the area. People still sat in the chairs chatting away. "What about…"

"Mom will take care of it."

And as she walked toward Lucas' car, firmly holding his hand, Brenda motioned for everyone to stand and fold their chairs.

Aurora stopped beside the race car as her heart did a double beat. For this special event, Lucas had removed the rear window, and placed a white mat across the length of the hood.

"Ready?"

"Ready."

Lucas lifted her effortlessly, sitting her on the trunk of his car. She pushed her legs through the open window, linking them on a foam-covered railing, installed for this moment. Lucas climbed up beside her, and helped her adjust her dress, before slipping his own legs into the window.

Nate stood on the driver's side. "I'm going to go really slow, but if it's too fast, just bang on the roof." He climbed into the driver's seat and the vehicle rumbled to life.

"Wait," Kaitlyn said, on the way over. "Let me fix your veil so it's floating in the breeze for pictures." A gentle tug freed it from under her where she'd sat on it. "Your bouquet."

"All good?" Nate asked.

"Give 'em hell, Tiger." She winked and rubbed her belly.

"Let's drive."

Nate slipped the car into gear, and with one hand gripping an inside roll bar, she waved with her floral-gripping hand to the audience who stood clapping and waving. The fans in the stand also stood, and whistles and cheers greeted her ears. The clanging of the tin cans behind her made her giggle.

Nate drove slower than she did on the side roads, and the sun peeked out from behind the clouds, making the veil billow and shimmer in the sunlight.

She yelled and cheered as Lucas laughed beside her, his laughter one of her favourite sounds.

For a while, everything was perfect in her world. Surrounded by family and friends, married to the man of her dreams, she had conquered her PTSD and had solid control over her addiction. Of course, it flared up from time to time but they made it through, a little more worn around the edges, but their love had never faltered. Each incident only reaffirmed their soul connection, making their love even stronger.

Dear Reader

I hope you enjoyed *If You Say Yes* as much as I enjoyed writing finishing up Aurora's story. I really love all the main characters, and I'm especially happy that Aurora is with the one she truly needs. For now their story is complete, but that never rules out a rogue chapter or two, or maybe a short story that could possibly surface. Watch my blog (www.hmshander.blogspot.com) for sneak peeks and extra content.

As an author, it makes my day when someone shares their thoughts, and gives me feedback on the characters you've invested your time with. It's because of early feedback on *Duly Noted* that *That Summer* came to be, and *If You Say Yes* needed to be told. Share with me what you liked, what you loved, or even what you hated. I'd love to hear from you. Are you #TeamNate or #TeamLucas?

Contact me via email or via my website.

Finally, I need to ask you a favour. If you are so inclined, I'd love a review or a rating of *If You Say Yes*. Loved it or hated it, I will enjoy your comments.

As I'm sure you can tell from my books, reviews are tough to come by. As a reader, you have the power to make or break a book. If you have the time, I'd love it if you posted a review on Goodreads, or even on Amazon. All posted reviews on the retailer site, or on Goodreads, will give you early access to the next novel. Something to keep in mind.

I try my very best to reward my readers, since it's because of you, I continue to write.

Thank you so much for spending time with me.

Yours,

H.M. Shander

Other Books by H.M. Shander

Run Away Charlotte

Charlotte trusts only three people in her life - those who loved her through her darkest points.
When she meets Andrew, she slowly starts opening up to him as he courts her. Together, they learn about love and fall into it together.
However, a summer apart tests their relationship.
Upon his return home, Charlotte questions everything she's put her heart into, challenging what her heart needs verses what her mind says she deserves.

Ask Me Again

Thirteen years in an unhappy marriage cause Charlotte to feel alone and unloved.
When her first true love comes back into her life via a freak accident, she finds herself fighting against the feelings he brings out in her.
He represents safety and passion. Around him, she can be herself.
When her life falls apart, she has a choice to make once again.
And this time, her life depends on it.

Duly Noted

PTSD rules Aurora's life, keeping her from being anything more than a broken, damaged, lonely nineteen-year-old.
Until she meets charming, dashing Nate.
He wants to help and wants her to be part of his world. As he guides her away from her fears, he starts healing her heart.
However, PTSD isn't finished with Aurora yet. In order to overcome her greatest fear, she'll need to face it head on.

That Summer

Aurora has nine weeks to get her shit together and win back the love of her life so she enlists in Lucas' help.
He has big plans to help her cope with her PTSD.
What they didn't plan for were the intense emotions that come from pushing yourself to the breaking point, and learning you are you and what you want.

Acknowledgements

Thank you firstly (as always) to my family – to Hubs, Bear and Buddy, and my parents. Your unending support means the world to me. You are my biggest cheerleaders, and for that I will be eternally grateful. I may get a raised eyebrow or two when you've read what I've written, but I know you'll love it regardless.

To my Critique Partner, Anya – I have no words, and thank you never seems adequate enough. Your constant support and unfailing dedication to pulling the best version of the story is a godsend. I trust your judgment and love the way you get so emotionally invested in what I've written. I couldn't stand where I am without you, so *thank you.*

To my beta readers – thank you for your thoughts and suggestions on what was missing to bring the story to completion. I cherish your advice, your wisdom and your comments.

To my cover designer Ashley – Great job! We didn't end with what we started, but I can't imagine a more perfect cover. It really caps it all off.

To my editor Irina – Thank you for your quick edits, your numerous comments and your replies to my endless questions. It's only moderately painful to clean up my mess. Hah.

If I missed you, it certainly wasn't intentional. I know I couldn't be where I am without the help of so many others. Thank you! And thank you for reading and making it all the way to the end. You all rock.

About the Author

H.M. Shander knows four languages—English, French, Sarcasm and ASL—and speaks two of them exceptionally well. Any guesses which two? She lives in the most beautiful city in Canada– Edmonton, AB, a big city with a small-town feel, where all her family live within a twenty-minute drive. As much as she'd love the beach under a blanket of stars, this is her home.

A big-time coffee addict, she prefers to start her day with a mug before attending to anything pressing. When she gave it up for Lent, totally felt Aurora's dependency and struggle through withdrawal, albeit on a much smaller scale. The Sunday morning coffees were a Godsend. She is a self-proclaimed nerd (and friends/family will back this up), reveling in all things science, however likes to be creative when there's time. Right brain, left brain? Both.

Did you know she once wanted to be a "Happy Clown" as she enjoys making people smile, but she's beyond terrified of scary clowns. How ever many different jobs she's worked, her favourite has been working as a birth doula and librarian, in addition to being an author and writing romances. Because, let's be honest, who doesn't love falling in love?

Five things she loves, in no particular order; The Colour Blue, The Smell of Coconut & Shea Butter, Star Wars, The Ocean, and Chocolate

You can follow her on Facebook, Twitter and Goodreads. She also has a blog (hmshander.blogspot.ca) she writes on from time to time.

Thanks for reading– all the way to the very end.

81097761R00195

Made in the USA
Columbia, SC
25 November 2017